"Aprilynne Pike's gift is that each book she writes is **utterly inventive.** *Glitter* is no exception. As always, her characters are interesting, vivid, and dynamic, and they play out their nail-biting scenes against a richly imagined, lush backdrop. Her books are skillfully woven and **a royal delight!**"
—Colleen Houck, *New York Times* bestselling author of the Tiger's Curse series and *Reawakened*

"The ending was **CRAZY and INTENSE!** . . . I CANNOT wait to see what happens in book two!"
—*Pandora's Books* (blog)

"The world and history Pike has created is **truly stunning.** . . . Containing a mix of sci-fi, fantasy, and historical fiction, *Glitter* is truly an **exceptional** novel and perfect for readers looking for something that's really different from your average sci-fi or fantasy novel." —*Teen Reads* (blog)

Books by Aprilynne Pike

GLITTER

SHATTER

GLITTER

APRILYNNE PIKE

EMBER

Text copyright © 2016 by Aprilynne Pike
Cover art copyright © 2016 by Emi Haze
Powder art copyright © 2016 by Shutterstock/artjazz
Map adapted from Jacques François Blondel's *Architecture Française,* vol. 4 (1756)

All rights reserved. Published in the United States by Ember,
an imprint of Random House Children's Books, a division of
Penguin Random House LLC, New York. Originally published in hardcover
in the United States by Random House Children's Books, New York, in 2016.

Ember and the E colophon are registered trademarks of Penguin Random House LLC.

Visit us on the Web! GetUnderlined.com

Educators and librarians, for a variety of teaching tools,
visit us at RHTeachersLibrarians.com

The Library of Congress has cataloged the hardcover edition of this work as follows:
Names: Pike, Aprilynne, author.
Title: Glitter / Aprilynne Pike.
Description: New York : Random House, [2016] | Series: Glitter |
Summary: "A teenager living in an alternate-history futuristic Versailles must escape
its walls by selling a happy-inducing makeup called Glitter"—Provided by publisher.
Identifiers: LCCN 2015039116 | ISBN 978-1-101-93370-1 (hardback) |
ISBN 978-1-101-93373-2 (ebook)
Subjects: | CYAC: Courts and courtiers—Fiction. | Drug dealers—Fiction. | Versailles
(France)—18th century—Fiction. | Adventure and adventurers—Fiction. | Science fiction. |
BISAC: JUVENILE FICTION / Girls & Women. | JUVENILE FICTION / Royalty. |
JUVENILE FICTION / Action & Adventure / General.
Classification: LCC PZ7.P6257 Gli 2016 | DDC [Fic]—dc23

ISBN 978-1-101-93372-5 (pbk.)

Printed in the United States of America
10 9 8 7 6 5 4 3 2 1
First Ember Edition 2018

Random House Children's Books supports the First Amendment
and celebrates the right to read.

TO KENNY,
FOR HOURS OF WORK
AND LOADS OF PATIENCE

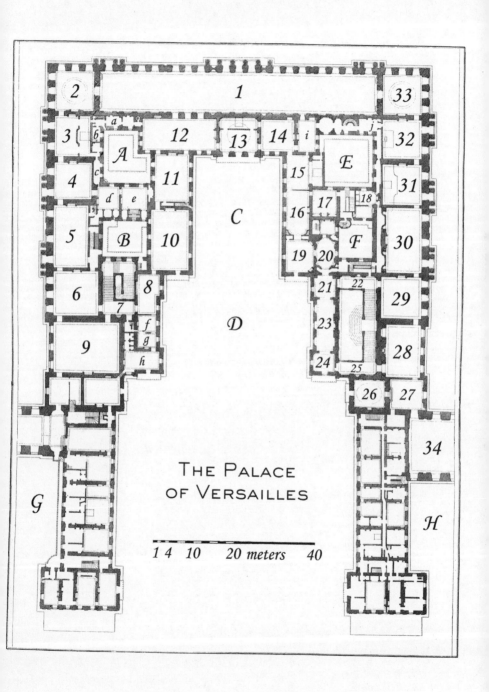

THE PALACE
OF VERSAILLES

1 4 10   20 meters   40

GLITTER

PROLOGUE

I RUSH THROUGH the catacombs, my face shrouded beneath the brim of a cap, skimming by the empty eyes of ancient skulls. I'm fast and sleek in my borrowed jeans but feel scantily clad without the heavy silk and brocade skirts to which I'm accustomed. I retained my corset: not out of an affinity for this particular one, but because my innards feel like jelly without stays, and tonight I have need of a strong spine.

I pause in the halo of a light to look at the half-crumpled bit of paper Lord Aaron passed me this afternoon. Once more I scan the hastily scrawled words and peer at the landmarks around me; as far as I can tell, I'm in the right place.

Just one more thing to do. With a dull thud my bag hits the dusty ground, and I take three brisk steps forward. I shiver—from the chill, from nerves, from exhaustion—and stand with my legs slightly apart, arms raised. Almost immediately—though I'd have sworn I was alone—there are hands searching my body, and I close my eyes against the humiliation. They pat my arms, my legs, my inner thighs, the hollow between my breasts. Mercifully, the ordeal is brief.

But a set of hands stops at the boning of my stays.

"What have we here?" My brain can't wrap around the man's words until I realize they're French. All the lords and ladies of our court study the language—speak it with passable fluency at least weekly—but this raw, native accent is something else entirely. Of course it is. I've fled from a court that's practically another world. But the reminder is jarring. I mentally fumble for a suitable response, praying my faux accent won't render it unintelligible.

"It's only a—stop!" But a shadowed form has already yanked the hem of my shirt up to my shoulder blades, and I feel a gentle tug at the laces. The binding fabric falls away, and my entire abdomen sets to quaking as the heavy undergarment drops to the ground. Two dozen cleanly sliced satin ribbons reveal that the person standing behind me has a very sharp knife. I pull my shirt back down—lest they try to cut that off too—but probing fingers merely frisk my soft belly and leave me be.

"*Intéressante,*" comes a voice from the dark, his throaty *R* so classically French. This is no Sonoman nobleman, French only in memorial and mockery of a bygone age. He says something else, too fast for me to follow, but unmistakably a command, and nimble feet patter all around me. I can see some of the people in the dim underground light, but with the shadows cast across their faces, I couldn't identify a single one.

"Do you have it?" the rumbling voice asks.

"Have what, *monsieur*?" I reply, trying to sound strong.

A bark of a laugh as he steps more fully into the light. "Runaways always think I'm stupid. They're putting their very lives in my hands, but they think I'm stupid." He's at least as old as my father and wears a scraggly half-beard that somehow doesn't strike me as casual or shoddy. A leather coat drapes his shoulders, looking almost like a cloak. His eyes are dark, and there's a black word tattooed on his neck—but the light isn't bright enough to read it. "The *money,* girl. Do you have the money?"

"I don't think you're stupid," I say first, feeling an irrational need to defend myself. "The . . . person who arranged this meeting didn't know your current price. But I brought—"

Something cold presses against my neck, stopping me even as I step toward my bag: the unmistakable feel of a gun barrel.

"I haven't gotten to where we're standing right now by getting myself dead," the man says, his voice silky. "What's in the bag?"

"Some money. Jewelry. It's all I could get my hands on." *Shut up! Don't babble!* I bite the inside of my lip and force myself to stand straight, my arms curled into a perfect ballet pose—at my sides, but not quite touching my body. Posture speaks louder than words, my dance instructor often said.

"I'm a fair man," the dark figure says as the gunman tosses my backpack to him, chilly gun barrel never breaking contact with my skin. "My rate is five hundred thousand, and I'll only take from your bag what's needed to cover that. We can fence the rest if you want; wherever you're going, I'm sure you'll need the change."

What I've stolen will surely be enough.

"I don't ask why and you don't ask me how. For five hundred we'll remove your tracer, scramble your profile, and work up a new identity, complete with a passport." As he speaks, he unzips the backpack by feel. "Have one of those faces? Another hundred thousand and I'll put you under the knife."

I suspect he's not just offering a nose job like the one my mother foisted on me before my *début*.

"That . . . might be necessary," I say at last. One week ago I was nobody—today I have one of the most recognizable faces in the world.

"I'll be the judge," the man says, much too casually, holding up a cluster of glittering sapphires on a golden chain.

The largest piece. Maybe he'll take that and be satisfied.

Lord Aaron and I . . . *liberated* this particular set of jewels from a friend. Her family. Their most treasured possession. Guilt has hollowed my insides, but if this man really can sell me my freedom, it will have been worth it.

The Frenchman is studying the sapphires and, I assume, estimating their worth—when surprise dawns in his eyes an instant before flaring into anger. "Where did you get these?" he demands, thrusting out the necklace with a sharp jangle. "How did you break into the Palace of Versailles?"

Something about his tone assures me that if I don't answer honestly and immediately, he'll have no qualms about ordering his henchman to shoot me. "I didn't break in. I broke out."

"Out? You're *from* the palace?" He stomps toward me without warning, and before I can so much as blink, he flips the cap off my head and grabs my chin with rough fingers. He twists my face from side to side, scanning my features in the dim light as I let out a stifled mew of pain. His mouth sets into a grim line before he glances down at my discarded corset and kicks it savagely. "Your pretend past getting boring? Ready to join the twenty-second

4

century? Tired of living in your stolen palace? Of wearing your stolen jewels?"

"They're not stolen," I lie. "They belong to my family!" My heart pounds so hard the sound fills my ears.

"They belong to *France!*" the man snaps, his grip tightening. My face will be bruised tomorrow—assuming I live that long. "Just like our palace, our land, and everything else you god-forsaken Louies have taken from us."

Lord Aaron and I didn't expect a smuggler with standards. And we *certainly* didn't anticipate patriotism. "I'll take them back," I say. I'm begging, falling to pieces, but I don't care. I can't care. "I'll find something else; I just need a little time." I can't imagine what I could possibly bring him that would be worth half a million euros, but there must be something. . . .

The man throws my bag to the ground at my feet and lays the necklace of blue stones gently, almost reverently, atop it.

"*Bonne nuit, mademoiselle,*" he says, touching the rim of his hat in mock salute as he backs into the darkness of the catacombs. "I can't say it's been a pleasure."

"Wait!" My voice cracks, the desperation bleeding through. "Please. Let me bring you something else. Something you'll accept. You said five hundred thousand. Maybe I—"

"That was before I saw your face," the man says, and I can tell he's turned away from me, though I can no longer see him in the blackness.

"I'm not like them." My voice is weak. Until last week I never considered whether those words were true.

He gives a derisive snort. "The fact that you're a Louie isn't what concerns me. I don't like you people. I hate it when my contacts send you to me. But if you were a different one, I might take the job for no other reason than to thumb my nose at that ridiculous boy-King of yours. But not *you*, Mademoiselle Grayson. Not you."

I can't stifle a gasp at the sound of my name; I'm still unused to my own renown. He steps back into the light, and I wish he'd stayed in the shadows as his eyes rake over me with a glint that's equal parts loathing and lust.

"You thought I wouldn't know who you are? Do you have some crazed illusion that any reasonably well-informed citizen of Earth wouldn't recognize your face in a second? With more cameras in the world than human eyes, it's hard enough to make a nobody disappear. But you? Not even remotely worth the risk."

"I can get the cash; I'm sure I—"

"Impossible," he says, and though he cuts me off, he sounds more like he's talking to himself. "Not even for a million euros. Not for *two* million. The surgery alone would be . . ."

I've heard businessmen talk like this before. No matter how much he might hate me, he loves money more. Money—and the challenge. I almost dare to hope.

"Five million. In euros," he emphasizes, and my hope shatters into pieces—five million pieces. "None of those credits your people throw around as though they were worth something." He rolls his eyes and adds, almost to himself, "Absurd currency system."

"If I bring you five million euros," I manage between clenched teeth, "you'll take the job?" There's no way I can get it—even in the months I have. But I have to ask.

He studies me, and it takes every ounce of my willpower to meet his eyes without squirming. "I'm good enough. Even for you. If you *truly* think your pathetic life is worth five million euros, then, yes, I'll take the job." He shrugs. "But it's an easy promise to make, seeing as how there's no way anyone at Sonoma would let a citizen—even your lofty self—get their hands on so much real money."

"How can I contact you?"

He laughs heartily at that. Then the smile drops from his face and he points a long, thin finger at the ceiling above me. I raise my eyes to look, but the pop of a bursting lightbulb hits my ears an instant after the tunnels are plunged into utter darkness. Fine bits of glass rain down on me, and I duck to the ground, hands over my head.

"Go back to Versailles, Your Majesty." The man's voice echoes in the darkness, coming from every direction at once. "You'll find no help in Paris tonight."

PART ONE

THE PRICE OF FREEDOM

ONE

"DANICA!" EVEN WITH her hushed whisper, Molli's giggles give her away before her high *pompadour* can claim the honor. Rather a feat—thank goodness she's not sporting feathers in her hair tonight. After a quick glance down the hallway, I join her in a small nook behind a set of heavy damask curtains. Lord Aaron and Lady Mei are with her, leaning out a picture window, sharing a cigarette. Someone has hacked M.A.R.I.E.—Lord Aaron, no doubt.

"Be careful," I say, the finicky words escaping my mouth before I can clamp down on them. "The smell seeps," I continue in an embarrassed mutter. Though it's been only two months, I feel as if I've aged ten years since my failed escape attempt, and it's starting to show. Seventeen going on thirty, I suppose.

"Oh, lord have mercy on us if we damage His Royal Highness' precious *frescoes*," Lord Aaron mocks. His eyes aren't as playful as his tone, and he meets my gaze briefly before blinking away all trace of our shared secrets.

"Lean way out," Lady Mei says, passing me the hand-rolled cigarette and shifting her skirts aside so I can bend as far through the window as my stiff bodice and wide skirts will allow.

I take a long drag, and it does soothe me—but I wonder if the night air alone would have done just as well. It tastes of freedom, that rarest of delicacies.

"Give it here," Molli says, nudging me over and carefully grasping the cigarette dangling from my fingertips. "There's only a pull or two left."

"Give it here, *Your Grace*," Lady Mei corrects. "Mustn't forget whose presence we're in."

I force a smile at her rousing, though in truth I wish I could forget. Not something I'd confide to Lady Mei; as much as I enjoy her company, she's a hopeless gossip. Lord Aaron and I were lucky to be able to replace her family's priceless jewels the day after we stole them, or the only people she *wouldn't* be talking to about it would be us.

I back away from the window and right into Lord Aaron's chest.

"Steady," he whispers in my ear, his hands encircling my upper arms protectively.

"I don't suppose it'll catch anything on fire down there, will it?" Molli asks, peering at the grounds below the window.

"If it does, M.A.R.I.E. will handle it," Lady Mei says, breathing out a long stream of smoke before pulling her head back inside. M.A.R.I.E.—the Mainframe for Autonomous Robotic Intelligence Enhancement—is the central nervous system of the Palace of Versailles. She handles the drudgework, monitors the entire complex, and controls every bot, from the ones that trim the grass to the ones that help me dress. Presumably, she would also put out little fires.

"Hurry," Mei says. "The system's going to override His Lordship's hack any second."

Sure enough, scant seconds later the window sash slides shut with a defiant click. A blue light at the lock blinks indignantly, as though scolding us, but soon the anachronism fades and our little cabal bursts into laughter.

"I don't know why you can't simply smoke outside before you dress," I say, dabbing laugh-tears from the corners of my eyes as we emerge through the curtains, back into the hallway.

"Because dressing takes an hour, at least," Lady Mei says. She flips a jet-black curl off her shoulder and puts two hands under her barely-there cleavage, pushing it up ineffectually. "Some of us take a little more work than others," she adds with a sidelong glance at the more-than-ample shadow between my breasts. She's not wrong; the gowns of the Baroque era don't really suit her figure. But the fashions in Sonoman-Versailles must be pulled from actual history books and are, thus, as unyielding as the boned corsets we all sport.

She makes the most of it, though. In her natural state Lady Mei might accurately be described as *plain,* but she's a genius with cosmetics and couturiery, and no one seeing her in full evening dress would know her with a washed face and plain nightgown. She gives her skills far too little credit; her deft cosmetics enhance her delicate Chinese features to the hilt. Plus, she's the daughter of a wealthy marquis—she'll never want for favor or adoration. Or suitors, when the time comes for such arrangements.

The same cannot be said for Molli Percy, who has neither title nor inheritance coming her way. But she's delightful and incredibly fetching, with honey-blond hair and a soft, round figure, and everyone falls in love with her despite themselves. That might be enough to make her a good marriage one day. Nothing could make her a better friend now.

"Will I do, Lord Aaron?" Molli asks, turning a circle in front of him when she finishes straightening her skirts.

"Almost." Lord Aaron adjusts a fold of her shoulder cape, straightens a strand of faux pearls in her *coiffure,* and takes a step back. "There, you look superb."

"Thank you," Molli says, flicking her fan open and fluttering it just under her nose.

"And me?" Lord Aaron asks, spinning a similar circle before them and making the velvet tails fly on his silver-and-crème jacket that sets off his gorgeous carob skin and long black curls.

"As if you need my help," Molli quips. Lord Aaron is always impeccably turned out. "Shall we?"

"Must we?" Lord Aaron and I say in tandem, and then turn to each other in surprise. Molli and Lady Mei burst into another round of giggles as Lord Aaron and I paint smiles across our faces. We were jesting—of course we were jesting.

"Go ahead," I urge them. "You know His Highness prefers that I enter alone. Besides," I say, patting Lord Aaron on the shoulder, "you've only two arms. I would be sadly neglected."

"Alas," Lord Aaron says with a twinkle in his eyes, "though I've petitioned both the Good Lord and the medical research division for more, it's true that I'm still possessed of but these two arms. And two hands," he adds, swatting Lady Mei across the backside.

Lady Mei shrieks but takes his proffered arm.

"You'll be in soon?" Molli asks over her shoulder.

"In a few minutes." I watch my friends cross the Hercules Drawing Room, making their way into the *soirée* ahead of me.

I consider returning to my quarters—not attending the party at all, instead spending the evening in my room with a book. But my mother would think nothing of finding me and dragging me back, my ear clenched hard between her fingers like a misbehaving child's. Which is precisely how she sees me.

After nearly a quarter of an hour, I can stall no longer. So I check my satin gown and posture in the many mirrors lining the hall, then present myself at the doorway of the Drawing Room of Plenty.

Plenty indeed.

There are three couples in front of me. One at a time, they hand the crier a card bearing their name and title; he glances down, then bawls the names out.

My turn. I need no card. I simply stand there, framed by red velvet drapes, waiting for the man to draw aside the curtain and present me to the crowd.

"Her Grace, Betrothed of the King, Danica Grayson."

The herald declares my cringe-worthy title at the top of his lungs, which always feels ridiculous; anyone who might have been dwelling so far under a rock that they don't know who I am can simply make eye contact, access the local web feed via their network Lens, and view my public profile. One never has to worry about remembering names at court when one is hooked into the network—one of M.A.R.I.E.'s more useful tricks. More useful than her propensity for locking windows or extinguishing tiny recreational fires, anyway.

On the other hand, the herald's verbal warning does allow for the fashionables of the court to pivot away and avoid eye contact with people they don't care to acknowledge. Also useful.

Sadly, I'm rarely in that shunned category. An underage, unknown young lady, all too quickly betrothed to the King, and jumped up well beyond her rank in court with no explanation whatsoever: scandal, perversion, and mystery all in one satin-wrapped package. Murmurs of "Your Grace" can be heard as curtsies and bows make a well-coiffed ripple across the room, as though it were the surface of a placid pond and I an offending pebble.

I am not, however, a duchess. Upon my betrothal to the King, the citizens of Sonoman-Versailles eventually afforded me that address—Your Grace—to hide the fact that I am, by birth, nobody. At least in the eyes of the fashionables at court, where wealth and title mean everything. To have neither and yet be betrothed to the King? The false address seems to make them feel better about that. It makes me feel worse.

The *soirée* is in full swing, with bots—dressed in the traditional red-and-gold livery of the seventeenth century—whirring about with trays of champagne and *canapés* among gowns of silk and satin, and the frenzied click of hundreds of jeweled heels. Delectable scents of both food and perfume waft like clouds, filling even the spaces where bodies don't fit. Orchestral tunes are piped softly through hidden speakers, and the sparkle of candlelight can't help but dazzle. For the two years since my official *début*, this crowded, frenetic atmosphere was heaven on earth to me, and even now, the elegance tempts me to rejoin my peers and drink and dance away what has become of my life.

The *salons* swarm and buzz like a hive, though unlike insects, the drones here congregate around their king rather than a queen. The constant churn of people around my *fiancé*, the King, is actually terribly helpful; it takes only a glance to know which end of the *salons* to avoid. But even as I spot the hub of the milling crowd, His Majesty catches my eye and makes it very clear he wishes to speak to me.

I grab a flute of champagne from a serving-bot's gyro-balanced tray, then hurry in the opposite direction.

Not that I make much headway. The crush of the throng is downright suffocating, and I make my way through it at a speed of approximately one meter per minute. Perhaps less.

He was waiting for me.

If he were a sensible, reasonable person, he'd simply have had M.A.R.I.E. schedule a meeting for the two of us in his private offices. But no, of course he'd rather ambush me in public. Cursed man. I'm not certain why I continue to expect some level of normal human decency from him.

I squelch panic when I sense a presence at my left side. *Don't look.*

"I was beginning to think you weren't coming," says Molli, and twines one arm with mine.

Thank all deities in the known universe—and the unknown, for good measure. I grip Molli close to my side, already feeling better, but continue my dogged trek forward.

"His Majesty certainly has eyes only for you this evening."

"I'd rather he had eyes for anyone else, and you know it," I say without dropping the affected half-smile I use to deflect unwanted attention.

"I do, yes, but try explaining that to Lady Cynthea," Molli says, inclining her head subtly toward a tall, elegant young lady in a gold brocade gown that sparkles with dots of what are no doubt very real jewels.

I stifle a smile at the mention of His Majesty's mistress— perhaps *mistress* is the wrong word. Even *girlfriend* sounds wrong when half the twosome is engaged. I suppose technically she's simply my *fiancé*'s bit of skirt.

"You'd think she was Queen, the way she holds court," Molli says, her voice dripping with distain. The court is essentially split into two camps: those who support the Queen the King has chosen—me—and those who still think Lady Cyn, with her pristine bloodlines, is more worthy of the throne.

And, indeed, with a dozen members of the high nobility arranged in a semicircle before her, Lady Cyn does look like the true Queen holding court. As though hearing our whispered conversation, Lady Cyn turns her long, elegant nose toward us. Then she whispers behind her fan to a girl standing next to her and turns halfway, giving us her back. Not quite the cut direct— she doesn't dare give me such a social dismissal—but a clear insult nonetheless.

I simply don't care.

I used to. At my coming out, when my mother made it all too obvious that she intended to parade me in front of the King like a tasty slab of meat, Lady Cyn was quick to inform me that I was unwelcome in *her* territory. Only weeks apart in age, and owing to a friendship between their mothers, Lady Cyn and the King were considered by the court to be—informally and unofficially, of course—intended.

I can still feel the sting of her satin glove smacking my face when she cornered me over a year ago, flanked by a half-circle of well-born bullies in silken gowns. It should have been merely an insult—an ancient and almost meaningless gesture. Except that Lady Cyn had taken it upon herself to put several heavy rings inside the glove.

"You're a devious climber, and you'll stop if you know what's best for you," she hissed close to my ear as I cradled my throbbing cheek.

I wished I could tell her I wasn't after her precious boyfriend. Of course, every starry-eyed *débutante* within a decade of the King's age probably entertained *some* shallow hope of a royal wedding. And I can't say I was any different—but I hardly nurtured a *tendresse* for the always-arrogant young monarch.

What drew Lady Cyn's anger wasn't *my* determination but my mother's. Through her scheming and bribes, I more often than not found myself seated beside the King at dinner, sharing his box in the palace's theater, his name programmed into my dance card.

Consequently, I also found myself avoiding empty corridors whenever humanly possible.

When my betrothal was very publicly announced two months ago, the hatred Lady Cyn already felt toward me, combined with the grievous insult, practically took on a life of its own.

I turn from my future husband's not-so-secret girlfriend and continue my trek forward. "Where are Lady Mei and Lord Aaron?" I ask. Molli is seldom by herself at these gatherings. Not enough social status to gain notice alone. We used to band together—a pair of nobodies. Now I'm happy to bring her along on my unwanted rise in prestige.

Molli flips open her fan and flutters it in front of her face. M.A.R.I.E. keeps the palace's climate at a perfect, comfortable temperature, but the motion both is decorative and conceals Molli's words from eavesdroppers with a lip-reading program on their Lens. Which, because such apps are strictly banned, is everyone. "Lady Mei and her sister have been compelled to join their parents for a family moment."

"I imagine she's thrilled," I say, half amused. The marquis and Lady Zhào are rather fond of parading their two daughters about for the marriageable nobility to see. It'll be another five years at least before either is ready for marriage, but luck favors the prepared, and betrothals can be quite lengthy.

"Lord Aaron slipped out a few minutes ago," Molli continues. "He's remarkably out of spirits this evening. He tries to hide it, but I've known the boy since he was still wetting his britches."

I'd sensed his gloomy mood myself but find it difficult to gauge. I haven't known Lord Aaron as long as Molli has, having only moved into the palace four years ago, and he does tend toward melancholy anyway. I have trouble distinguishing between his passing fits of existential angst and true distress. I'm always grateful for Molli's insight in these moments.

A feathered fan—lime-green and loud as the grating laugh of

its owner—catches my eye. "I suppose *that* has something to do with it." I nod subtly in its direction, though I'm referring not to the woman in the frothy confection of a gown but to the lean, handsome young man beside her.

"It's such a shame," Molli says, peering after them over her fan. "He and Sir Spencer are so well suited they might have been created for each other."

"Can you picture it?" I whisper. "Sir Spencer's golden hair—Lord Aaron's dark skin. They'd be gloriously striking."

"I wish they wouldn't stand on such ceremony. It's hardly a love match, even on her side. Besides, everyone in the court cheats."

I don't have to voice my agreement, as it's such a naked truth.

"Her father is so old-fashioned," Molli laments.

Lady Julianna—the young woman with the unfortunately hued fan—is the heir to the Tremain dukedom; the much more elegant man at her side is the Honorable Sir Spencer Harrisford. An American by birth, Sir Spencer inherited his title and shares when his parents—both top Sonoma executives in America, a brilliant match—were killed in a high-speed rail accident. Their son was brought to Sonoman Versailles by Duke Tremain and wed to Lady Julianna a few weeks later, on the very night of his eighteenth birthday. Not in a whirlwind romance, but simply because Sir Spencer was overly biddable in his fragile emotional state and the duke had an agenda. Still does, if dark rumors are to be believed.

It's exceptionally bad luck on both their parts that Sir Spencer and Lord Aaron fell quite instantly and madly in love at the wedding *fête*. Unfortunately, with Lady Tremain's father holding tightly to the purse strings, that means no affairs. For now.

"They should consider having a tryst as a public service," Molli says.

I pause and turn to her, baffled. "How so?"

She widens her already-luminous eyes. "Their searing glances are in danger of setting the drapes afire."

Her wry humor strikes my tight nerves just right and I laugh aloud.

"She's so very vulgar, though," Molli says, the humor draining quickly from her eyes. Molli has no status save her delightful self to recommend her, but she tries harder than anyone else I know. Certainly harder than I ever did. To see someone like Lady Julianna—so *gauche* and tasteless, utterly lacking in poise or subtlety, despite her wealth and breeding—who possesses every advantage and has earned none, feels like quite a personal insult.

I'm finding the recent run of very young marriages—including my own impending one—more problematic than any individual plight. Being engaged isn't what I wanted or expected in my seventeenth year . . . and eighteen is truly not much older.

Too late I realize that in my distraction I've allowed my progress to slow. When I next feel a presence at my shoulder, I'm certain I won't be so lucky as to turn and find a friendly face a second time.

TWO

"GAD, IT'S STIFLING in here."

My hand is lifted and damp lips brush my knuckles, leaving a chilly, wet spot on my glove that I struggle not to wipe on my skirts. I don't have to look to identify the oily voice of my betrothed: lord, chairman, chief executive, murderer, the King himself.

I wish I could gouge his eyes out.

"Indeed it is. Perhaps you should get a breath of fresh air on the balcony," I suggest blandly. "Alone."

He's dressed in a brocaded silk jacket tonight, with crème-colored breeches and jeweled heels that he clicks loudly against the faux-parquet floor, like an especially pompous cicada. His chestnut hair falls down his back in silky curls any girl might envy, and he carries his signature gold walking stick in his left hand: a replica of the one King Louis XIV was evidently never seen without. Our kingdom is based on the elaborate Baroque era of the three Kings Louis, and our present King, Justin Wyndham, does his best to mimic the earliest one as often and accurately as possible—a tendency even the press has noted, and they *never* pick up on subtlety.

"You do understand that you're not actually Louis XIV,

I hope." I flip open my fan with a well-practiced flick of my wrist. Sometimes I think he dresses so elaborately to hide his age. Nineteen is surely too young to run both a kingdom and an international company.

"No less than you understand that you are not *actually* Marie-Antoinette," he counters, gesturing at my late eighteenth-century attire. Though comparing me to Versailles's least popular monarch is a cheap shot.

"If you're going to be insulting, I'll excuse myself. Your Majesty," I say, fluttering one hand and bowing exactly low enough to placate him and not a fraction of a centimeter more. "Come, Molli," I say, clutching her arm close to my side like a lifeline. Then I turn and make my escape.

Almost.

His arm snugs about my waist from behind, fingers gripping so hard I can feel them even through my ribbon-bedecked stomacher, bodice, and corset.

"You look divine," he whispers, lips close to my cheek, where Molli cannot hear.

I paste on a half-smile because half is the best I can muster. "Your Highness is too kind." I speak at full volume, highlighting the rudeness of his secret murmurings when we're in another's presence.

"Come to the balcony with me. I've not had you alone for ages."

His breath hits my neck and I shiver. Despite the vehemence with which he originally declared that he would never marry me, once he was blackmailed into it, he rather warmed to the idea.

"Molli, look, they're serving my favorite wine," I say, gesturing at a table filled with glasses at the far end of the *Salon de Vénus*. My arms are puckered in goose bumps, and I can feel my stomach rebelling at His Majesty's nearness. "So if you'll excuse—"

"Actually, I need to speak with you."

Damn.

The King glares down at Molli. Her cold fingers tremble on my arm, as they always do in the presence of our monarch.

"Mademoiselle Percy, is it not?" the King says, lifting one of her hands to bow over it. His lips don't quite touch her glove as he pulls her away from my side. Molli makes a valiant effort to keep her fingers on my arm, but soon she cannot maintain contact without being unforgivably rude.

Which, like so many other things in life, is something my Molli cannot afford.

As soon as the two of us are separated, His Majesty's solicitous *façade* disappears and he reclaims his hand, carelessly dropping hers. "You have *something* to do, I have no doubt," he says, one eyebrow raised as he straightens the waterfall of lace on his cuff. "Be off with you." And he slides to step between us.

I see the horror in Molli's eyes as the King moves, and panic flares in my chest. She's about to receive the cut direct from the King of Sonoman-Versailles—and for someone in her position, that could amount to social execution. Everything Molli has worked to achieve, swept away like a pup tent in a tornado.

Spoiled, selfish, inconsiderate brat!

"My lord," I burst out, catching the arm of a fine silk jacket passing by, barely registering the face and body attached to it. My outburst stops His Royal Highness before his back is fully turned on Molli, and I reach blindly for her hand, pulling her toward me and smiling up at the man I've near assaulted.

Bonne chance! It's the Compte de Duarte. He's at least seventy and hardly a fashionable escort—but he's wealthy, titled, and reasonably pliant, which will satisfy my present aims.

"Lord Duarte, I fear royal business has called me away from my dearest friend, Mademoiselle Percy. If you would be so kind as to complete my task and escort this fine lady to the"—I hesitate, ever so briefly—"the Guard Room, where I believe they have set up a particularly lovely display of gourmet *petits fours.*"

In truth I have no idea what's happening in the Guard Room, but this nobleman would never consider returning to correct his future Queen. Now Molli—a young lady of little social standing—will be paraded through no fewer than five *salons,* plus the length of the Hall of Mirrors, on the arm of high nobility. Excellent. The *compte* bows to me with a smile and offers his arm to Molli.

Perhaps His Highness will think twice before trying to give a friend of mine the cut direct again, I think victoriously, watching a pleasantly flushed Molli depart with the Compte de Duarte— who looks only too pleased to have an excuse to escort such a pretty young thing, with no threat of harping from his shrewish wife.

But His Majesty seems not to have noticed the incident at all. So typical of him—nearly destroys a young woman's social standing and he remains abominably unaware. Instead, he offers his own arm to me. I see little choice but to take it.

We head toward the very balcony I suggested and—maddeningly—the crowd parts for His Highness as the Red Sea is said to have parted for Moses.

A row of delicate Jacobean *chaises* lines the perimeter of the small balcony, and when His Royal Repugnance gestures, I sit right in the middle of one, letting my *panniers* do their work. The word comes from a French name for baskets slung on either side of a pack animal, and though the comparison is hardly complimentary, it's apt. Baskets under my skirts extend the curve of my hips up to half a meter on either side of me, making the satin pouf out just enough that he can't sit beside me without crushing the fabric. Not something a gentleman of breeding would ever do.

Strangle a woman half his size during their amorous tryst? Yes. Crush her dress in public? Never.

Not that anyone else knows that. The cover-up was quite thorough. "An aneurysm," the physician—bribed by my mother—proclaimed as the cause of Sierra Jamison's death. "A terrible tragedy." But I know the truth. Justin Wyndham, fourth King of Sonoman-Versailles—raised to demand everything his little stone heart desired—handled his plaything too roughly and broke her.

And now he's moved on to me. I lower my eyelids so he can see the shimmering plum powder one of M.A.R.I.E.'s bots spread across them tonight, along with the sooty black liner and dusting of gold on my eyelashes. Lavish cosmetics are one of my favorite relics of our faux-Baroque society. Petty, perhaps, but one thing I have learned about Justin Wyndham during our short relationship is that he prefers his women striking, sensual, and subservient. For a few seconds, I look like everything I know he wants.

And he cannot have me. Not yet.

There are a handful of other nobles on the balcony, but a pointed glare and the noisy clearing of His Highness' throat has them quickly scurrying away. Curse them. My heart speeds with each person's exit until the King and I are very much alone.

I peer up at his profile as he continues to glare the nobles out of his space. His glossy brown hair always seems to fall in annoying perfection. I remember seeing him when I first moved to the castle, during one of the rare times I was allowed in the public rooms before my official *début*. He was fifteen at the time, tall already and just starting to broaden, and I and every other tween girl fancied ourselves half in love. Even now the unbiased part of my mind can't deny how attractive he is. He makes me feel false— all the grace and aesthetic appeal my mother purchased for me are his by right of excellent genetics.

That thought makes the silence feel awkward, and I force myself to speak. "What do you want, Justin?" I say, determined to claim the first point.

He stiffens. "I've told you, you may use my given name when you are my wife, or my lover." He grins and I feel like prey. "Whichever comes first."

I look away and say nothing. It seems pointless to address him so formally when we're both teens, and engaged besides. But the King is so touchy about the strangest things, and I enjoy perturbing him.

"It's time you moved into the Queen's Bedchamber," the King says.

Even with my covertly trained poise and control, I can't hide a cringe. "It most certainly is *not*," I snap, before reclaiming my composure. "We're not yet married, my lord."

"Marriage is hardly necessary for you to move to someone else's bed," he drawls.

It takes everything I have not to react to his blatant insult. Not to rise and strike him—slap his face, spit on his lapels, strangle him with the cravat tied so perfectly around his neck.

But he continues in a nasal, lofty voice. "We've deemed your parents unfit to be your guardians and require that you take up residence in the Queen's Rooms immediately."

I despise it when he slips into the royal *We*. "That's impossible." Certainly it feels that way. It must be. Move into quarters specifically designed to accommodate nightly visits from the King?

"I'm not to lay a finger on you," His Highness continues as though I hadn't spoken. "Your mother was quite insistent."

"You've spoken to my mother about this?" I shouldn't continue to feel a pang of heartbreak every time I hear of yet another layer of my mother's betrayal, but I suppose a child's hope never completely dies.

"I have to speak to your mother about *everything* these days, don't I?"

I feel a bit light-headed and struggle to keep my face impassive. At least she set some limits. A small favor, I suppose. "Why such a drastic change?"

"Where is your father?"

And it's not a question; it's the answer. My father has passed much of the last few weeks languishing in a stupor. A drunken stupor, I'm certain, except no one can figure out where he's getting

29

his liquor. Still, he spends nearly all of his days in his chambers, staring absently into space and occasionally giggling to himself. Which is most disconcerting from a man in his midfifties. My mother stopped sharing his rooms a month ago. Now she shares with *me*, which is, of course, delightful. . . .

"Fine. Why *now*?" I press.

His Majesty rolls his eyes, then lowers himself onto the *chaise* beside mine. Even so, he's a good meter away, and he looks silly leaning forward trying to whisper to me. "We have a bit of a PR problem. Rumors are cropping up. More from the outside than the inside."

The outside. In other words, the rest of the world. "Rumors? Truths, you mean?" I say, batting my eyelashes.

"Besides which," he says, ignoring my words, "you don't actually have a choice."

I chafe at his arrogance, but he's right. He's the King. As long as I remain a citizen of Sonoman-Versailles, his word is law. And as long as all I have is a company passport, there's nowhere in the world I can run where he and my mother can't find me and drag me back. Especially as a minor. Thus the catacombs two months ago.

"When I make the announcement, you must appear to be utterly delighted," he whispers, sensing my defeat. "There's a great deal riding on this."

"For you."

He takes his time, pulling his gloves off, then running a fingertip up my arm to the stripe of skin between my own glove and sleeve. The touch of his skin against mine makes me feel ill.

"You're as tangled up in this as anyone," he whispers. "Conspiracy, aiding and abetting, tampering with evidence."

That sets me shaking with fury, and though I grasp for control, it slides through my fingertips like oiled ribbons. "I didn't do anything."

"You're right," His Majesty says, and he tips his face to look me squarely in the eye. "You didn't *do* anything."

Instantly, the anger is gone, frozen out by despair. Grief. Guilt. I hate that he's right. That I let my shock overwhelm my conscience, my sense of decency. That I let the death of a girl barely older than me go utterly unpunished.

I wanted justice. Of course I wanted justice! But my mother brooked no argument. "The truth won't bring her back," she said. "It only makes sense to gain what we can from this misfortune." *Misfortune.* It's a funny way to say *murder.*

My initial refusal to marry Wyndham fell on deaf ears. By the time I realized I needed to do something else, there was nothing else to be done. We were already mere flies in my mother's web. I hate that I let myself be cajoled and pulled along by the current that night. If an opportunity ever comes to right that wrong, I swear I will.

The King takes advantage of my inattention to run his finger down my neck and across my shoulder, half bare in my formal gown.

"Don't—"

But he cuts me off, bending to place a kiss at the nape of my neck. "I was told to make this betrothal look realistic. One of us has to do our part."

I imagine his fingers wrapped tight around my neck, covering the spot his lips just brushed, squeezing the life from me. I shudder and start to pull away.

"Careful," His Majesty whispers. "She's watching us."

I turn, like a compass needle spinning to point north; I can't help myself. My eyes meet my mother's where she's stationed herself just inside the open doorway to the ballroom, preventing anyone from invading our privacy. Her gaze flits away. Pretending she wasn't actually spying.

"You'll excuse me," I say, rising and stepping away from His Majesty. From his touch. "With this turn of events, it appears I have much to do tonight." I offer a deep, mocking bow, my skirts a perfect circle around my feet.

"I've already instructed M.A.R.I.E. to fetch your belongings," he says, pushing his brocade jacket back to slip his hands into his pockets, a portrait of nonchalance. "Wouldn't want you to have to *do* anything, would we?" And he stares down at me, his blue eyes so predatory that my knees weaken. When I turn and leave the balcony, we both know I'm fleeing.

I don't so much as glance at my mother as I pass.

THREE

IT FEELS LIKE hours before I manage to extricate myself from the event. I deflect conversation from dozens of lords and ladies hoping to worm out a bit of gossip—the second-most-common currency at court. When I reach the empty staircase to the north wing, it's all I can do not to run.

I almost do—no one's looking. But I've preserved my sanity, not to mention my dignity, on the assumption that when you're in the Palace of Versailles, someone could always be watching. Something I forgot when I climbed out my window two months ago.

Out of sheer morbid curiosity, I blink twice. "Danica Grayson," I mutter under my breath, and my court profile flashes in my periphery, illuminating the monofilament display of my Lens. From the local feed it pulls my picture, rank—or lack thereof—and residence.

Queen's Bedchamber, Palace of Versailles.

Damnation! I slap my hand against the wall, but as it happens to be a marble panel, I succeed only in hurting myself. When was the change made? Before the assembly? Could I have been better prepared for this? Of course I had no reason to examine my own profile—no one does. Still, I curse myself for letting the Royal Asshole surprise me.

I almost blink to dim the Lens, then pause. "Angela Grayson. Location."

Angela Grayson, Salon de Diane, my Lens reports, illustrating the information with a glowing red dot on a tiny isometric projection of the palace.

Diana, Goddess of the Hunt. Fitting. My mother is nothing if not mercenary. She didn't follow me from the balcony, then. I blink the image away and turn down the long hallway that will lead me to the apartment that is apparently no longer my home.

After my father inherited his place at court and we moved into the palace almost four years ago, my mother started treating me more like a tool for her raging social ambition than a daughter.

But two months ago she truly became my enemy.

There was nothing outwardly special about that night, no sign that my world was about to explode. I was sneaking food after a *soirée,* for myself and Molli, who was sleeping over. It's a bit difficult to truly indulge when laced into a tight corset, so Molli and I made a frequent habit of filching leftovers from the larder.

Breaking into the kitchens is a rudimentary hack. In addition, I'd discovered a ten-meter stretch of hallway near the kitchens that M.A.R.I.E.'s camera-eyes simply don't see. It was a juicy tidbit that made me wish I had something truly naughty to get up to in that blackout spot.

As I approached the unmonitored stretch following my kitchen raid—my hands holding a delicate china plate heavy with decadent leftovers—I heard an odd shuffling. I double-blinked, checking the map on my Lens.

It told me there was no one there.

Odd. Even though the cameras have missed this little spot, the building's security grid should have picked up active identifiers. Suppressing your identifiers is a complex bit of hacking I hadn't yet managed. Lord Aaron claimed he could do it, sometimes, and had promised to teach me.

I padded closer to the corner in my satin slippers, and stifled a sigh of exasperation when I heard a low, telling moan accompanied by a rather . . . rhythmic scuffling. Lovely. I'd stumbled upon some sort of secret hookup between not one but two coders better than myself.

Awkward.

I looked down at my plate, trying to decide which would be more efficient: hacking back into the kitchen and returning the way I had come—and chancing that I'd be spotted by security—or waiting for these two to finish and then continuing on my way.

I hadn't yet made my decision when the loud sounds I'd already been trying to ignore changed in a way that made the back of my neck prickle. I felt abruptly cold and slid to the edge of the wall for a peek around the corner.

The King!

In my shock, I almost let loose a curse. No wonder the security field was blank; for his own safety, the King can't be tracked by anyone except perhaps his bodyguards. I found myself frozen in place by an avalanche of half-formed questions and competing impulses—the unwilling *voyeur* of an amorous tryst in a darkened hallway. And the sound . . .

More than anything else, it was that sound that glued my feet to the floor, forbidding me to flee. It was a gagging sound, I think, but the most desperate and distorted gagging I'd ever heard. And then I realized that, amid the flurry of limbs, the stereotypical shoving aside of clothing in the usual places, the King's hands—both of them—were around the woman's neck. Squeezing. Tight. Even as he . . . as they . . . oh lord. I'd heard of this sort of thing, but seeing it was entirely—

A crash assaulted my ears, and only when the King's arms jerked and his head turned toward me did I realize that the noise was my plate shattering on the marble tile, food spattering my hem.

We stood there, eyes locked, for what felt like a very long time.

Then the King came rather suddenly to himself and released the woman, hustling to yank his breeches back into place as her slight frame slumped to the ground.

She wasn't making that horrible sound anymore.

My brain screamed at me to run—this was the *King*—but that girl. I had to help. I couldn't leave her after that sound. My feet moved forward of their own accord, crunching on the broken china. One piece jabbed through my slipper, stinging my instep, but I hardly registered the sensation.

I approached the fallen figure, staring, detached, as though she were . . . not a woman at all. Something else: an elaborate *tableau* one of the artists at court might stage for our amusement, perhaps. She was lying on her back in a shimmering satin nightgown with a wide *décolletage* that had slid to the side, leaving one shoulder tantalizingly bare. She wasn't staff, as I'd expected from such a lurid encounter, but a lady of the court, though I didn't recognize her. Her curly red hair must have been coiffed to perfection for the ball, but now it tangled like tentacles around her face. Her arms were splayed—one rested by her side, the other arched up near her head.

"Is she dead?" I whispered before reaching out to touch her. But I drew my hand back before making contact.

The rustle of buttons and ties ceased and I sensed the King approaching behind my shoulder. "I didn't mean to" was all he said, peering down at his handiwork.

I stared at her chest, willing it to rise. But nothing happened. I suddenly realized where I was: standing in an unmonitored hallway with a dead woman and the person who'd killed her. Panic started to cast its net over me, and I began backing away from him, lifting my nightgown's hem so I could run.

"Danica!" My name sounded in a whisper, but it cut through the fog in my brain. Not from the King, but from the other end of the hallway.

My mother. I hurried to her and yanked on her hand, trying to pull her along with me. "He killed her," I hissed, desperate to explain.

"Shhh," she said, pulling me close and taking my face in her hands. "I will handle this. Do you understand?" I caught a telltale glint in her eye.

The cobweb-thin platinum ring encircling the edge of a network Lens was enough to alert me to its existence. I'd taken mine out in preparation for bed, and would be willing to wager the King wasn't wearing his. The ice in my stomach melted a little as I realized there would be a record of whatever happened next.

My mother turned to the King and raised herself to her full height. No one who saw her at that moment would have guessed she'd been raised working-class and had only gained entrance to the nobility by marrying my father. She looked almost as much a queen as the portraits that lined the palace walls—even in a white nightdress and shawl, with her long hair wound into a thick braid, face washed free of cosmetics. When she spoke, somehow she managed to sound aghast, motherly, and poisonous all at once. "Justin, what have you done?"

As I arrive at the Grayson suites, I shake off the memories of that awful night two months ago. That was the last moment when I truly believed everything would be all right. That justice would be served. That my mother was on my side. I know better now— Angela Grayson is always on Angela Grayson's side.

After closing the entrance doors behind me, I don't bother checking on my father—considering his behavior helped to set this latest catastrophe in motion, he can rot in his study for all I care. I go straight to my room, where an unfamiliar pair of bots are busying themselves with my wardrobe. Most of the bots look exactly the same: powdered wigs, blank-faced masks, and red velvet livery with gold trim. But these bots are a touch more formal. More gold braid. Royal bots.

"Send them out, M.A.R.I.E.," I command, knowing she's listening. She's *always* listening.

The bots leave my room immediately; I wasn't certain they would. I could imagine His Majesty revoking my credentials, or requiring M.A.R.I.E. to get his direct approval before following my commands.

I flop to my stomach on the lightly carpeted floor and pry a wooden box from where I've wedged it under the side rails of my bed. My fingernails work the delicate catch, and after turning my body to shield the box's contents from the ceiling-mounted dome that serves as M.A.R.I.E.'s ever-watchful eye, I peer inside.

The twine-bound stacks of euros I dig out are both comforting and depressing. I didn't give up. I've spent several weeks selling every piece of jewelry I could get my hands on, though after the Frenchman's reaction in the catacombs I'm a great deal more discerning. No antiques, no large pieces that have been worn to highly publicized events. Just the smaller bits I've been given over the years. Or my mother's jewelry, when I could get away with it. Occasionally, a piece acquired via some amateur sleight of hand. Unfortunately, all of these put together are worth far less than the better jewels. By last week I was out of pieces to hawk—and not quite three hundred thousand euros richer.

Which would have been an incredible sum if I hadn't been trying to raise five *million*. A measly six percent of the money I need, two months of my engagement already gone. Tears sting my eyes as I run my finger along what would, for many, be a glee-inducing stack of money. I'm wallowing in self-pity, and I know it, but—

My fingertips touch a loose piece of thin string. Still blocking the box from M.A.R.I.E.'s view, I peer into the space without opening the lid any farther; the empty loop of string is knotted into a circle just the right size to secure a small brick of paper bills.

I gasp and flip the top fully open, snatching up the offending string between my thumb and forefinger. A small enough amount to miss in a cursory glance, but large enough to devastate my efforts. *Who? When? Why?* The questions rage, a hurricane in my head, but one answer rises to the top, and as soon as it does, I know it's the only possibility.

Father.

Rage burns away reason and I stand, clap the lid shut, and storm from the room, the box tucked under my arm.

He would know. The box was a gift *from him.* I kept it on my dressing table in plain sight until my mother invaded my rooms. If someone knew what they were looking for, how long would it take to find a box this size in a bedroom with little space for concealment? Less time than an afternoon tea party, I'd wager, if my mother and I were both in attendance.

His study doors are closed, locked, but I know the override. I tap out the sequence on the doorframe's decorative inlay—a simple numeric keypad, really, but of course it's not allowed to look like what it is, not in Versailles—and hold still just long enough for a face scan. Without knocking, I push my way through the heavy oak doors.

A scuffle of shoes. The thud of something hitting the ground. He's not alone.

"No!" My father's voice is gravelly but strong. "I've paid you!"

That brings me up short. I watch a man in a dark cloak bend

to sweep up a stack of scattered bills, the glint of a knife at his hip. I should move. I should run. Alert security. *Something.*

But I freeze. There's something bad, something dark and secret happening here. And I am fear's slave.

My father, for once, is the active one. "Please," he begs again. "You've been paid."

I feel the cloaked man look at me, even though I can't see his eyes under the shadow of his hood. They don't waver from my face as he spins a small envelope through the air to my father. He starts to back away, and finally I find my nerve.

"Stop!" My voice bursts out so much smaller than it sounded in my head. I try again, but already he's running down the short hallway to my father's bedchamber—with a stack of money that belongs to *me.* Dropping my box onto the desk, I follow the cloaked figure, but the weight of my skirts and the width of my *panniers* hamper my progress. I round the corner as the criminal—what else could he be?—disappears through a small panel at the back wall.

I run to the wall and fall to my knees, pulling open the door and reaching into the blackness of . . . the clothes chute. Of course. A criminal just escaped my father's chambers through the damned laundry chute.

FOUR

MY FATHER WASN'T meant to be a nobleman. Not really. He was born into the gentry. We were happy and well supported by his middle-management position at Sonoma Inc., which his mother held before him. Then his stepbrother died, young and unexpectedly, and willed Father his voting shares and place at court. By accident. The document was a prenuptial formality—a relic of their parents' marriage. My step-uncle would have gotten around to updating it eventually, but no one expects to die in their twenties.

After that, everything changed. My father instantly moved his family from the city of Versailles into the palace. Into the kingdom. I was caught up in the excitement too. I'm sorry to say I took after my mother in that way—hungry for the glitz and glamour of the palace. By the time I made my *début,* I was so anxious to be a part of the scintillating court of Sonoman-Versailles that nothing could have held me back.

Anger bubbles over as I link to my father everything that's happened to us in the last few months—even though much of it truly isn't his fault. I need *someone* to blame, somewhere to vent my fury, and the obvious person just escaped.

"You've ruined *everything*!" Sobs are trying to force their way into my throat, but I'll be damned if I'll let my father see me cry. It doesn't matter that I was never going to save enough money anyway—with someone stealing from me, it really is impossible.

I feel so young, suddenly. The last few months have forced me to grow up quickly. But now, slumped on the floor and watching my father stare at his parcel, I feel very much like the teenager everyone seems to have forgotten I am. I'm too young for this game with its life-and-death stakes.

He's staring at the envelope, cradled in his hands as though it were a newborn child, utterly unaware of the daughter whose dreams he's shattered. "What is that, Father?" I say levelly.

He looks up and blinks. The confusion in his eyes makes it all too clear that he didn't notice me entering the room at all. At all. Not when I startled the criminal, not when I slammed the laundry chute closed, only now, when I shout directly at him.

"What. Is. That?"

"Dani . . . Dani, I—" He tries to conceal the envelope behind his back, of all places. But I'm surging with adrenaline and far more nimble than he, gown and all. I expect him to fight, but when I wrench the envelope away he crumples to the floor and begins to cry.

The anger drains from me, replaced by something so much worse. Pity. Disillusionment.

"Father, don't," I say gently. But I keep hold of the envelope. I study it, baffled. It's sealed and there's nothing written on it, but the lack of a pressed wax circle on the back suggests that it's from outside Sonoman-Versailles—which would explain why he had to pay for it with euros. The packet is lumpy and bulging. With a quick glance at my father, I slip a finger beneath the flap and tear it open. I tip the envelope and pour a stack of about fifteen beige squares onto my hand. The sound of weeping fades from my awareness as I try to figure out just what I'm looking at.

"What is it, Father?" Though I'm not snapping anymore, I do hold the squares in my fingertips high above him, waving them out of reach.

"Forgive me. I needed it," he says, stretching his long arms upward, woefully shy of their mark while he kneels on the floor in front of me.

"Needed *what*, Father?"

"I needed it."

I grit my teeth and curse my grasping, devious mother for driving him to this, curse the King for stealing what was left of my childhood, and even curse my father's pox-ridden stepbrother for dying and putting us all in this unbearable situation in the first place. "Tell me *exactly* what this is or I swear to you I will toss it down the chute after that criminal who gave it to you."

"No, no!" he says, splaying himself on the floor. "You can't."

"Then tell me!"

He's no longer weeping in earnest, but tears continue to leak down his once-dignified face, wetting the craggy beard I remember stroking as a child. Back then it was a carefully trimmed goatee that he pomaded to a jaunty point at the end of his chin. "You must not tell. You mustn't. It's such a secret. I promised him no one would ever know."

He looks up. I'd almost forgotten how vibrant his eyes can be. Mine are brown. Mother's, too. But his are green. Once, they

44

were striking against his deep olive skin—a reminder of his Israeli descent. Now the color only makes his pallor look more sallow.

"They make me forget. But if . . . if I don't have them, I can't—please." He stretches his hands out for the patches, and he makes such a pathetic picture, I can't do anything but hand them over.

It doesn't matter; it's already too late. The money is gone and the criminal with it. May as well let Father have whatever that stuff is—lord knows I can't do anything with it. My skirts pouf around me as I join him on the cold stone floor, feeling thoroughly defeated and wishing I could curl up on his lap the way I did as a little girl.

I turn to my father, and he freezes in terror. One of the patches is in his hand and he's peeled off half the backing. I squint at the square, and even in the dim light I see something sparkle on the adhesive side. His eyes leap from my face to the patch and back again. Then, some sort of decision made, he pushes up the unbuttoned cuffs of his linen shirt and pulls another patch away from his skin. My stomach churns—the surface of his arm is crisscrossed with blackened lines where residue from the adhesive clings. He finds a clean(ish) spot and rubs the new patch on. Only then does he release his breath in a long, luxurious sigh.

"It makes me happy," he says, his voice sparkling with bliss.

Then it dawns on me. "It's . . . it's a drug, isn't it?"

After a moment, he gives me a barely perceptible nod.

I slump against the wall. Despite the sloth, self-indulgence, and gluttony that are not only accepted but *expected* in the palace, illicit substances are absolutely forbidden. Thus far the courts have upheld Sonoma's dearly bought corporate sovereignty, but

INTERPOL is always lurking and looking for an excuse to burst through our protective veil and find a way to help the UN seize it back. There isn't much that can pierce the legal web of power and immunity that Sonoman-Versailles enjoys, but the international narcotics trade is one, and there are ridiculously crushing penalties for those who would dabble.

"How much did you pay for it?" I whisper.

"Six hundred euros."

My eyes snap to the envelope. Fifteen. The numbers tumble through my head. Forty euros *apiece*. I narrow my eyes. "How many times?"

I wouldn't have thought it possible, but his eyes become even emptier. Guilt or confusion? I can't tell.

"How often do you buy this much?" I clarify, pointing at the envelope. *How much have you stolen from me?*

"He comes once a week," my father whispers.

Six hundred euros a week?

I look up and around the perimeter of the darkened room, lit only by one set of flickering LED candles in an elaborate sconce on the wall. "How have you not been caught?" The Sonoman government does not, of course, work on the honor system. There are scanners in several areas of the palace that can detect all manner of drugs better than any trained dog.

"I never leave this room," he says simply.

But there's M.A.R.I.E. The balance between privacy and technology is a concern going back nearly a hundred years to our founding in the twenty-first century, but the convenience

M.A.R.I.E. affords us is made possible through constant audio-visual surveillance. Everything that happens in the palace is at least *potentially* recorded.

"I'm a voting member," he says, as though that were an answer.

"I don't understand."

"Voters' offices aren't monitored. It's a conflict of . . . of . . ."

"Conflict of interest," I finish for him. With the King also being the CEO, early administrators would have demanded a place to discuss business matters off the record. So all high nobility have one unmonitored office. Most are in the corporate wing of the palace. I hadn't considered the fact that my father's is in our home. *Their* home.

He waves a hand. "Your mother made the arrangements."

Of course she did.

His eyes roll over to mine. "I failed you."

The good daughter in me wants to protest—to comfort him—but it would be an untruth. He failed me in *so many* ways. Especially the night Sierra Jamison was killed. My mother plotted, schemed, informed both of us what our roles were to be. He never demanded justice, nor came to my defense. Looking back now, I understand that she couldn't have come up with such a tight plan in that moment. I've finally realized that she must have spent months looking for an opportunity to trap the King.

Justin, what have you done? she said that night. It sounded so off-the-cuff. I wonder now how long she'd been waiting to say it. What kind of disaster she might have otherwise pushed him—pushed both of us—into to make it happen. My mind jumps back to that night.

"I—I—" the King stammered in the face of my mother's question. "It was an accident."

"It wasn't!" I burst out from just behind my mother. "I saw you. You had your hands around her neck while you—you—" My face was hot and red and I could hardly comprehend, much less explain, what I'd seen.

My mother raised both eyebrows, her expression full of judgment.

He seemed to cower beneath her gaze for a moment, and I was reminded sharply that he was less than two years older than me. Young enough to be my mother's son. Youngest King in Sonoman-Versailles's admittedly brief history. But with visible effort he reclaimed his composure and set about dismissively straightening the cuffs of his light linen shirt, even though the front hung completely open, revealing his bare chest.

"Please," he scoffed. "We're both consenting and of age, and tonight was hardly the first time." He raised one eyebrow. "Haven't you ever sampled this variety of bedsport? You ought to, might loosen you up a bit."

My mother made a startled sound in her throat, but the King spoke over her before she could form actual words.

"If this situation is anyone's fault, it's hers," he added, pointing a finger right at my face. "She dropped that godforsaken plate and made me jerk and squeeze too hard. That's the moment it all went wrong."

Rage boiled off my fear and set me quivering. I wanted to speak up; I wanted to tell my mother about that awful sound. But my tongue was dry and I couldn't move past my fiery indignation at having been accused of being responsible for the dead woman at our feet.

"Do you truly think anyone will believe that when it's your fingerprints bruised into her skin?" my mother asked, and I saw a smile hover at the corner of her mouth when the King's face went pale. "Extenuating circumstances notwithstanding, you've done something unforgivable here, Justin. You have to make this right."

"Of course," he said, with all the meekness of a mouse trapped beneath a lion's paw.

"You'll marry Danica."

"What?" Our voices burst forth in perfect unison.

"I will not," His Highness said, sounding insultingly horrified.

"You will," my mother said calmly. "Or you'll lose your kingdom."

At that the King stood back, scoffing openly, hands on his hips, a wide expanse of sleek skin showing above his perilously slouching breeches. I remember how my eyes fastened onto that skin and I couldn't tear them away. We see so little bare skin at court, and this was the most desired boy in the kingdom. And a murderer. It was incredibly jarring. "You think the accidental death of a strumpet who forgot to use her safe word could take my kingdom from me?"

"No, no, I don't," my mother said, still in that deadly calm voice. "But we both know the Board of Nobles are on the verge of doing just that, murder notwithstanding."

His Majesty opened his mouth as though to argue, then had the good sense to swallow his words.

"Since we're discussing marriage, here's a proposal. Four

years ago my husband inherited his stepbrother's place in your palace and a surprisingly significant number of voting shares." She paused, looking him square in the eye. "We have enough votes to preserve your position as CEO and King. I've run the numbers, as I'm certain you have. As of the next regular meeting, without my cooperation, the nobles will succeed in their planned *coup*. We both know it."

He didn't counter her words—they must have been true. Horror lanced through me, despite everything else. Could Justin Wyndham's rule truly be so precarious?

She circled him then, treading silently on bare feet, the lace edge of her dressing gown trailing behind her. "If this scandal comes to light, I guarantee you'll lose your great-grandfather's kingdom, Justin."

He flinched at her use of his given name this time.

"You'll be nothing but a potentially brilliant nineteen-year-old forced-out CEO, with all your inherited wealth and no power to do anything with it." She paused before delivering the killing blow. "Besides, the next regular meeting isn't your only problem. At this rate even my husband's shares can't keep you in place for long."

"You're talking about the Queen's shares." The King sounded wary, and I felt a prickle of unease at the Q word.

"Just so. Those votes were mooted at your mother's death and will only become active again when you wed. You need a cooperative bride even more than you need my husband's support."

That was when I realized how calculated this move was.

How calculated her placement of me in the King's path had always been.

"You want our silence and cooperation? Not to mention access to those final crucial shares?" she asked. "Marriage to Danica is the nonnegotiable price."

With those words I was reduced to a pawn in a corporate power struggle. The total worth of my entire life was thenceforth measurable as a tiny percentage of ownership in Sonoma Inc. I became a *price tag*.

"Besides," my mother continued, in a tone so businesslike it made my skin crawl with hatred, "without the backing of the King I won't have the influence or resources to do what needs to be done to clean up this unfortunate situation." She glanced over to where the poor woman's small body lay: soft features nestled amid a sea of satin and lace. "Who is she?"

The King sighed as though this had all become, at worst, a tiresome inconvenience. "Sierra. Sir Jared Jamison's daughter."

"A nobody, then," my mother said, and my jaw dropped. Not only because it was so cold and unfeeling, but also because before my father's promotion, this dead girl would have been my social superior in every conceivable measure. Even now, it's only my potential to inherit votes from my father that raises me above her. And only just.

The titles and social status embraced by the court never mattered much to me. Perhaps because I had neither. But to dismiss a person entirely because of that lack? The sentiment struck at my belly like a bare-knuckled punch.

"That'll make things easier. A coroner will need to be bribed, false scans produced . . . of an aneurysm, I think. And any sign of bruising covered thoroughly enough that the entire world will be able to scrutinize high-resolution footage from her open-casket funeral without finding any sign of misdeed."

"We can't have an open casket," the King piped up impulsively. Foolish man. You don't argue with Angela Grayson.

"A closed casket for a nobleman's daughter—even a minor one? You may as well release a public statement that you've something to hide."

"Mother—"

"I don't need you," His Majesty spat, anger overriding his pathetic act of contrition. "I can fix this myself."

"Can you?" She paced slowly before him, her eyes never leaving his. "How will you find a coroner? How will you justify his bribe to your accountants? Do you intend to mask those bruises on her neck yourself? And those are just the easy parts. The sad truth is that a boy stupid enough to accidentally kill his own lover is far too stupid to cover it up."

My fingers rose to my mouth at my mother's boldness.

"Or," the King said, sounding bored, "I could simply make you and your lovely daughter disappear. Tomorrow."

Shards of fear ribboned down my spine.

"Can you?"

My mother and the King stood toe to toe. It looked like a perfect stalemate—until she raised her head so the Lens in her right eye caught the dim light.

"You're recording this!" the King accused. And in the most

foolish action I'd ever seen him take, he grabbed a lace-edged handkerchief from the dead woman's *décolletage* and used it to cover his face.

"I think the European Parliament would be fascinated to see the footage of the last few minutes, don't you?" my mother said with a razor-sharp edge of danger in her voice.

The King swallowed visibly. My mother had made sure to capture everything in her recording. And the lack of sound made no difference with our lip-reading technology. Creating an accurate transcript would be child's play. Possibly not admissible in a court of law, but since when was the legal system required to utterly ruin a man?

"You may feel powerful, Justin; you may be the King and CEO of one of the most prosperous companies on Earth, but if you don't cooperate, you're going to remember the hard way that this is not the seventeenth century, no matter how your employees live and dress. You are not God, and you are not even the Sun King. Can you imagine, I wonder, the lengths to which France might go to see you dethroned? This kingdom disbanded?"

"This—this is blackmail!"

"And *this* is murder," my mother said, flinging one arm toward the body on the floor. "Take your pick."

"She's a child!" he snapped, flinging an arm in my direction. "An *enfant*!"

"Danica is hardly younger than your illustrious self, my liege," she said acerbically. "You're nineteen; she'll be eighteen in six months. You marry within a week of her birthday or this deal goes away."

That snapped his mouth closed. He stared at her. And though the seconds rolled past slowly—drawn out in that way terrible situations have of bending time—I was certain that a full minute ticked by before something changed in the King's eyes and I saw surrender.

For both of us.

And I said . . . nothing.

FIVE

"HOW CAN WE bear such secrets?" my father asks, as though sharing in my silent rememberings. He sounds oddly lucid as the drug takes hold of him. "You had such a bright future ahead. With your computer programming and math skills, you'd have been a brilliant researcher, or engineer. But a Queen hasn't got time for such things ... all that potential, squandered," he whispers, his eyes closing in an expression of bliss that makes bile rise in my throat.

Typical. Even after recognizing his responsibility, he does nothing. I sit back on my heels and try to think clearly. He's grinning to himself, and though his eyes are closed, he's conscious. He does look happy, and the drug obviously works quickly. Temptation licks at my conscience, and I pick up one of the patches and hold it up to the light. Six hundred euros a week. Six hundred. A prickle traverses my spine. I know a *lot* of people who would pay well for such euphoria.

I shake my head against the thought, but math *has* always been a strength of mine, and the sums are stacking up and multiplying in my brain without provocation. I stand and pace. There are several thousand people living and working in the palace.

Could I get one hundred buyers? More? Numbers add themselves in my head until I reach a quite satisfying total. It puts me into the realm of possibility in a way that selling jewelry never did.

But drugs?

I glance up at the ceiling. A room M.A.R.I.E. doesn't monitor? Here in my home? I stare around the familiar study; it's a typical Versailles room, with paintings on every wall and gilded trim along a plaster ceiling, painted with a faux-rococo fresco. It's not just a bit of hallway, like that stretch downstairs—now haunted in memory if not in actual fact. A truly *private* room. The possibilities sprawl out before me, as though I were gazing into a pair of mirrors angled to reflect each other into infinity. Terrible, unthinkable possibilities.

If you truly think your pathetic life is worth five million euros.

Is my life worth doing what it would take to get my hands on five million euros?

A thunderous pounding puts an end to my number-crunching. My mother wouldn't knock, and none of my friends would pound that hard. The King, then.

I sent the bots away without my belongings. It appears I defied the King.

I want to weep from the bone-deep weariness I'm already feeling, only to have to face my *fiancé* again. I rise from the floor, grab my box from the desk, and turn to my father. "Do not come out," I order, pointing a finger down at him as though he were a naughty child. Not far from the truth tonight.

As I approach the atrium the pounding grows louder, but over the noise, His Majesty growls, "I will override your security in ten seconds." It's possibly an empty threat; personally forcing his way into the private rooms of nobility, even untitled nobility like my father, would almost certainly cost the King more influence than he's willing to lose.

But the angrier he gets, the less I can count on him to act in his own best interest. I spend a few precious seconds pushing back my fear and revulsion, then fling the front door wide, and my liege nearly clocks me in the face.

"Ah, Justin. It's you." I rest a hand on the doorframe and strike a pose, cocking my head to one side, my hip to the other. "I was retrieving a few personals from my father's safe and must not have heard your knock."

He rolls his eyes, and I vow I can hear his teeth grind. "You sent my bots back." When I say nothing, he adds, "Empty-handed."

"Is that where they went?" My face is utterly impassive. "I didn't realize. I simply told them to go while I packed some"—I clear my throat and arch one dark eyebrow—"delicates, and when I finished they were gone. Personally, I'm not very impressed by M.A.R.I.E.'s inability to detect obvious intention. Perhaps she's in need of an update."

I see his jaw working furiously; he wants to accuse me of *something*, but my story is too simple for holes. The best lies always are. "What's in that box?"

My lashes don't so much as flicker. "You wouldn't ask a girl to spill *all* her secrets, would you?"

He glares at me with eyes darkened by anger that spark like obsidian. "We are now your guardian as well as your intended; We would like to know what is being brought into Our wing of the palace." The *We* again. Though this time it's rather satisfying to have driven him to it.

"If you must know, it's photographs. I'm leaving hearth and home tonight; it seems only fitting to bring a few mementos of my life before you hijacked my freedom."

He hesitates, his eyes narrowed, the spots of rouge on his cheeks looking nearly—but not quite—gaudy. "I want to see them," he says, more like a two-year-old than the ruler of a wealthy principality, teenager or not. He's always been fascinating to watch in that way. A spoiled childhood has left him an emotional infant.

I don't break eye contact as I raise the top of the box.

The top compartment holds just what I said it did, and the false bottom is well crafted—though if he were to take the box from me he'd be bound to notice its unusual heft. His hands move forward, reaching for the box as though he heard my private thoughts. His gloved fingertips are centimeters away when I snap the lid closed with a clack that echoes through the chamber.

"Not yours," I say simply, enjoying the ability to deny him something. Anything.

Without being dismissed, I turn—my heavy skirts whispering against the faux-weathered-wood floor.

"Did you bring the bots back with you, Justin?" I ask over my shoulder. "I wasn't finished with them." Sometimes I think his boiling rage is the only thing left in the world that can still warm my heart.

Under the King's watchful eye, I play the perfect mistress, directing M.A.R.I.E. as the bots pack my things, from gowns and cloaks to chemises and stockings—even my rather extensive collection of silk and satin underclothes. I refuse to allow him to see how uncomfortable *that* makes me. Instead, I stand perfectly straight—so straight I can barely feel my corset—and point languidly, with long, graceful motions, making full use of the poise my mother drove me to acquire.

I see now that I shouldn't have worried about hiding the box of euros from the bots to begin with; halfway through the process, I proffer the box to a faceless bot that places it in a gilt-and-lacquer chest, where it's soon covered by a Venetian lace shawl. Curiosity isn't in M.A.R.I.E.'s programming.

I wish I'd invited Molli to spend the night instead of tearing out of the ballroom. With Molli here, I wouldn't have checked my box, I wouldn't have gone to confront my father, and I wouldn't have discovered his drug habit. Or the temptation I'm fighting. It's odd to think that my entire world would be far brighter right now if I'd only stopped to grab my best friend.

"I don't know why you're bringing all of this," His Royal Highness says, fluttering his hands—almost hidden by lace cuffs—at the heaps of satin and damask. "Half of this clothing is utterly unsuitable for a consort to the King."

"Perhaps if you had given me more notice," I say, refusing to cringe at the word *consort* and all it implies, "I could have culled my wardrobe properly. As it is, I'll have to organize later."

He mutters something unintelligible, and I return to my bored pose as the bots finish their work.

"Dani?" the King says as the final chest closes.

"Danica," I correct, for perhaps the millionth time. My family is permitted to call me Dani, not because I approve but because there's really no way to keep the people who changed your nappies from calling you whatever they wish. I suppose I was trying to make that very point when I started calling him Justin, but as usual, His Royal Obtuseness didn't catch on.

He rolls his eyes and grips my upper arm. Instantly I'm transported to the past: those hands squeezing Sierra Jamison's neck in the same sort of punishing grip. It's the first time the King has attempted to physically bully me into anything. But I'm not small. I'm only perhaps six centimeters shorter than him, and I'm solid rather than willowy. I'm simply too big to drag about thoughtlessly. With my heels planted against the floor, I force myself to resist his strength despite the pain in my arm.

His fingers slip away and he peers down at his empty hand in a moment of surprise before looking up at me. My blood feels like ice, but this is one battle I must win. Or I'll never win again.

"I am not your whore," I say very quietly.

The fury flashes again, but he says nothing, only gives me a curt nod and proffers me a more gentlemanly elbow. Resigned, I slip my fingers onto the embroidered sleeve as lightly as I can. With both of us in our finery and my arm on his, we appear to be a blissful couple headed off to a night of feverish revels—not a jailer escorting his prisoner to her cell in the first blush of sunrise.

SIX

WE BEGIN TO climb the ornate *Escalier de la Reine*, the grand staircase that leads to a set of double doors covered with gold-plated curlicues. They are perhaps the most fanciful prison bars I've ever seen.

As His Majesty approaches, the vestibule doors of the *Appartement du Roi* swing open automatically. The tremors begin in my spine, and I clench every muscle in my body to keep them from traveling down my arm, to my fingers, where His Highness might notice. For all his lofty titles, His Oh-So-Royal Highness is like any common predator—the secret is never to show fear.

We follow a plush red carpet down the middle of the rooms—the Guard Room, the Antechamber, the *Salon des Nobles*, their doors flung wide—and all too soon we're standing before the only set of closed doors.

The Queen's Bedchamber.

"At your word," the King says.

There's a surprise; he's instructed M.A.R.I.E. to open the doors only to my voice. Not his. Though I can't imagine it'll remain so for long, I'm shocked he granted me even this temporary courtesy.

But then, he does have everything to lose. I, meanwhile, have already lost everything.

"Thank you, M.A.R.I.E.," I say, stepping forward. The doors open as though pushed by invisible hands. My legs are wobbly, but somehow I stride into the world-renowned *Appartement de la Reine.*

It looks . . . like it always does.

The enormous canopied bed, golden curlicued wallpaper, feathered wall hangings, candled chandeliers. All behind a golden railing that gives the illusion of keeping dangerous things out.

The bots are already busily unpacking my clothing and putting it into the wardrobe—not a walk-in closet so much as an entire adjoining room. Every piece of my clothing will fill but a fraction of it. I remember looking at my now-former bedroom in wonder when we first relocated from our modest house in Versailles City, at the edges of the court, to the finery of our rooms in the palace. It felt like such an increase! This new step up is easily as significant. The luxury that surrounds me defies imagination, and sometimes I wonder how the Sun King of so many centuries ago *did* imagine it without the aid of digital technology.

Though the floor is convincingly wooden in front of the golden railing that divides the room, behind it lies a carpet so thick and soft it's like walking across a marshy lawn. The walls are alive with intricate silken coverings, painstakingly restored when Sonoma bought the Palace of Versailles, and the gilding on every surface glows so bright it reflects dully on my face.

The candled chandeliers are lit, and a fire is burning in the enormous golden fireplace, but even so, I shiver.

I peer back at His Highness, but he seems to have lost interest in me, instead muttering into the panel near the door that constitutes M.A.R.I.E.'s presence in this room. I should be curious as to what limitations and rules he's enacting in whispers, but it's not as though I can do anything about that right now, and exhaustion is setting in. So I open the low golden gate and step to the enormous canopied bed and wonder if it's the same bedding Justin's mother slept in before she died. Cheery thought, that.

I never wanted this. I intended to make my own place at court—maybe start in the software division. I'd been working on Sonoman algorithms long enough to qualify for an internship. I could inherit my family's shares eventually and be a Lady in my own right. Marry when and if it suited *me*. I just wanted to be a coder; they decided to make me Queen.

"I'll leave you here, then," the King says at full volume. Now that we're alone in the royal rooms, the public formality is gone from his tone. "But you know where to find me if you have a nightmare." His voice is cheeky, humorous, and you could almost believe we were friends making jabs.

"My chamber door will be locked, I hope," I say in a voice of thin glass.

"If you wish it so," he replies calmly, and sweeps me a low bow. He seems to sense he shouldn't push me any further tonight. I have no doubt he'll resume being intolerable tomorrow.

The click of my door closing echoes. I drop my *façade* and slump against the confines of my stays as I stare around at my gilded cage—the place where I'll reside for the foreseeable future.

I will never call it home.

"May I undress you?" The familiarity of the synthesized voice is the only thing that prevents me from leaping out of my skin.

"Of course," I mumble, realizing the sun is already starting to brighten the windows.

I cross the room to the dressing stool that came with my new quarters. I'll have to order a new one that isn't raised so high off the floor. By the time I finally stopped growing, I was 177 centimeters tall—five foot ten inches—and half a head taller than most full-grown women. I'd simply stand on the floor to be undressed, but the sensors in the stool orient the bots. So I tower over them the way I tower over most of the ladies at Versailles. I've grown used to it.

His Highness' mother must have been quite diminutive. She and the former King Wyndham both died when His Highness was fifteen. It's strange to think that two people can be so wealthy, so powerful, that they literally own their own kingdom . . . and accidents still happen. An electrical storm downed their jet over the ocean somewhere between Australia and India. The wreckage was found months later, but the bodies never were. There were murmurs, of course. Deluded conspiracy theorists who spun tales of deaths faked, assassinations carried out, tech tampered with. But I think the truth is simple: they died. And no one meant for it to happen.

I hold my arms out and the bots carefully remove each delicate piece of my gown. A bot plucks at my hairpins until the entire dark brown mass tumbles down from its high *pompadour*. I sigh in relief and massage my scalp, rubbing my fingertips in tiny circles.

With a few theatrical exceptions—and the artistic exterior of the bots—we've escaped the signature powdered wigs of the Baroque era, thanks in part to a convincing argument that hygiene, rather than fashion, was their impetus. But elaborate updos are still a fixture. Some of the ladies of the court use wire forms beneath their hair to achieve greater height—certainly Molli and Lady Mei do—but I've been both blessed and cursed with thick, semi-wavy hair, so I merely get dozens of hairpins.

While rubbing my scalp, I almost miss one of the bots reaching for the ties on my corset. "No!" I say, too harshly, then add an apologetic "Thank you," as if it had feelings. "I generally sleep in my stays." I try not to feel too annoyed by the mistake; M.A.R.I.E. knows my preferences, or should, but if my profile didn't transfer properly to this new room, I can hardly blame her. His Highness may have told her to start afresh. That would be just like him—to try to make his soon-to-be Queen up from scratch.

"Of course, Your Majesty," the bot replies—technically the proper title for the occupant of this room. It would have said the same thing if I'd claimed to sleep sopping wet and could she please dump a barrel of water over my head.

Tasks completed, the mask-faced bots make synchronized bows and wheel back toward their concealed cubbies, executing their standard shutdown sequence. They'll awaken again at the slightest command, but until then, I'm alone.

I stare at myself in the full-length mirror. My white silk shift strains across my breasts, still pushed up by the corset. Below my stays the shift protrudes in a light, semisheer cascade of skirt that reaches to precisely three fingers' width from the ground. My hands go to—and nearly circle—my overly cinched waist, and I try to take a deep breath, which is, of course, not possible. But it hurts, a familiar, comforting hurt that tends to settle not around my stomach, but in the form of a persistent jab at the bottom of my ribs.

It's so different from when I first started wearing corsets. I was excited to be laced into my first set of stays. It's a sign of emerging womanhood, and in her heart of hearts, I think every girl wishes she could fast-forward the arduous process of *becoming* into actually *being* a woman.

When I put on most of my height, it became apparent I wouldn't be one of those frail, willowy nymphs. I was tall, and I was solid. With another ten kilos I might even have been called stout. But while Mother's plans would never have allowed that, the fact remained that I was not and would never again be *small*. So instead Mother ordered that my corsets be maintained at the same measurements even as I continued to grow. When my body changed so rapidly that I felt almost a stranger in it, I found an inexplicable satisfaction in exploring the limits of my laces.

At the end of the day, though, I was grateful to put them away.

Until I witnessed the King killing that girl. When the time came that night to unlace my stays . . . I simply declined. Every week or two, when it stops hurting, I set the bots to pull my laces a bit tighter. Now I have nearly the smallest waist in court, despite my height. The other ladies think it's because I'm vain.

In truth, it oddly anchors me. Maybe it's the pain in my ribs that reminds me I'm alive.

SEVEN

I STAND BEFORE the door of what was my home only twelve hours ago and knock. How odd that feels. I've never knocked on this door. The realization gives me a confusing ache in my chest. After a full minute, I enter my code on the camouflaged pad and let myself in. Once alone in the foyer, I pull out a handkerchief, wipe my sweaty palms, and try to get hold of myself. This is my *father,* for crying out loud.

But he might have the answer.

Even when I was selling every piece of jewelry I could put my sometimes-sticky fingers on, the possibility of escape felt so remote as to be fantastical. But now? Maybe. Just maybe.

I tuck the handkerchief away and key open the interior door that leads to my father's rooms. While my eyes adjust from the brightness of the foyer, I peer into the shadows of his study. The space on the ground where he was huddled last night is empty. After pulling the study door closed, I head down the hall to his bedroom, and there I find him fully dressed and sprawled face-down on top of the damask bedspread.

It's a step up from the floor.

"Father." My voice doesn't rouse him, but it was worth a

five-second try. In the bathroom I find a washcloth and wet it. Then I lift my heavy skirts to sit on the bed beside him and press the chilly cloth against his cheeks and forehead until he begins to stir—with plenty of groans of protest.

His eyes are bloodshot when he opens them. "Dani?" His breath is so foul I have to hold mine.

I briefly explain my new living arrangements, more to pass the time while he gathers his wits than because I think he's going to remember. Or care very much.

But I'm wrong. "That bastard! He can't have you!" he shouts, and I put out both hands to quiet his ravings.

"He won't," I promise, sardonically amused at the tardiness of his protests. "But I need your help."

He looks at me with a touch of clarity, but before he can speak I hold up a finger for his attention. His eyes follow my hand as I dig into my pocket and remove a small contact case. I pop out my Lens and put it in the opaque container. Offline times are easier to explain than damning details. "Tell me about these patches," I say once the canister of saline is closed.

He looks stricken with shock. And guilt. "I'm sorry," he whispers.

"No," I say, cutting him off before he can get emotional. "What's done is done. How did you come to obtain them?"

His jaw flexes; he must think this is some kind of trap. "Tell me," I demand, and even to my own ears I sound more like my mother than myself, and I hate it.

He sits in stunned silence until I want to shake him, but I force myself to remain motionless and continue glaring instead.

"Two weeks after . . . after the incident." He stops, grits his teeth, and says in a shaky voice, "After your mother sold you." I can't help but be pleased that at least he understands how unforgivable it is. "I was in Versailles. The city, not the country."

It is, unfortunately, a distinction we often have to make. The name of the historic French city surrounding the palace complex is also . . . Versailles. Though Sonoma lobbied France to change the name to avoid confusion, France predictably refused. But being so close to Sonoman-Versailles—the country—the culture of our court has leaked into Versailles—the city—and it's an odd mishmash of modern and faux-Baroque culture. It's where we lived before my father inherited his palace apartment in Sonoman-Versailles—the country.

"A tavern in Versailles," my father amends, pulling my attention back. At least he's being forthright. "I was very, very drunk and a man approached me and we . . . we talked."

"About what?"

"You, mostly."

Ah, the joys of life in the public eye.

"He had no love for our King. But I did not spill your secrets."

My secrets indeed.

"We groused about His Highness and his power-hungry ways, and I confessed that I had failed to protect you. How much . . . how often I now found myself soused to drown my guilt. He told me there was something better. He told me about the patches, gave me a few."

My eyes widen. "At forty euros apiece, that's a generous gift."

But his only response is a dismissive shrug. "I tried one that night and I—" He can't hide a smile. "I'd never felt better."

"And after that?"

"I returned to the tavern. It took a few nights, but he came back. We struck a deal. Then . . ." His voice fades and he waves his hand to indicate a story that needs no telling.

My eyes dart to his arm, where—though covered by his wrinkled linen sleeve—I know his patch is affixed. "Why don't I know about this stuff?"

He snaps out of his daze. "It's *not* for *courtiers*."

I raise a questioning eyebrow, not bothering to point out the obvious fact that he is a *courtier*.

"I have to be careful. If the King finds out, I . . ."

He doesn't want to say it, but the look on his face communicates his fears well enough. At the very least, the King would put a stop to my father's illicit purchases, just as my mother and I put a stop to his drinking.

"Where's the envelope?"

Suspicion is etched deeply in his eyes, but he intuits that I'm in charge today. Besides, his pocket is hardly the most brilliant hiding place.

I rise and walk to the window, separating one patch from the others and holding it up to the light. Even through the white backing I can see the thin layer of shimmering specks that caught my eye last night. "What are you?" I whisper. Then, returning the patch to the envelope, I address him again. "You're certain the rest of the nobility doesn't know about this?"

"And you must not tell," he pleads, laying one hand beseechingly on my arm. I've never seen him so afraid; the thought of losing access to his little adhesive friends has set him to trembling.

I finger the velvet purse looped around my wrist and begin pacing. "How do you get it?"

"A man—"

"Of course," I say. "The man from last night."

"He comes to my rooms, dressed as a servant."

That throws me off a bit. Most of our servants are bots. About forty years ago the board decided that serving among the upper class creates jealousy and aspirations that could tear down our society, just as the class divide of the 1700s led to the French Revolution. So they replaced humans with bots wherever possible. Beyond the historical facts, I'd never particularly noticed nor cared.

The number of things I'm discovering I neither noticed nor cared about before is growing uncomfortably large.

Still, there are a fair number of real people on staff—it wouldn't be difficult to add another servant to the mix, not with my father's credentials. "You have a prearranged time?"

"We exchange notes."

I consider that. The obvious answer is to be present during one of these meetings, but I'm not certain I want to wait six more days.

"Could you deliver a note for me?" I ask. One note. I'll trust him with one note and then I'll never have to put my faith in him again.

"For you? But why?"

"You don't want to know, nor do I care to tell you." I sweep from the room, my skirts swishing against both sides of the doorframe as I nearly run to the desk in his study. A quick search of the top drawer yields a small supply of stationery and a ballpoint quill. I scribble a few lines, then reach into my well-hidden purse and carefully count out ten thousand euros.

It hurts to look at the stack on the desk.

Six hundred euros my father paid for one batch of patches. Six hundred. At first glance that seems hardly worth noticing—the gown I'm wearing is probably worth two or three thousand. But of course it wasn't paid for with euros. It was paid for with credits, the unimaginatively christened scrip Sonoma pays its employees and accepts at its various commercial outlets.

Credits can theoretically be exchanged for euros, or dollars, or yen, but the rate is beyond abysmal. Outside Sonoma's sphere of influence, credits might as well be the plastic chips children use when they're learning to play *piquet*. The meager contents of my cash box are already worth dramatically more than the credits in my bank account. And this stack of bills represents a not-insignificant percentage of my precious savings.

My hand shakes as I tuck the money into a fresh envelope. *A token of good faith,* reads my freshly penned missive. More like a token of desperation.

I turn to find my father standing in the doorway, studying me, confused. I'd be confused too. But I gather my composure and take small, graceful steps toward him, every centimeter the lady I pretend to be. "For your criminal man," I say sternly. "And do not take so much as a single bill from this envelope."

The packet falls into my father's palm with a faint smack. He stares at it, then me, then it.

"*If,*" I say harshly, "that note and the money inside reach its destination, I will"—I swallow hard, then force the words out—"I will take over paying for your patches." Though *take over* is misleading at best, as I've technically been paying for them all along.

The look he gives me is a confusing mixture of apology, resignation, and shame. He says nothing. After a moment, he simply nods.

"Today," I add firmly. Not only for my own designs, but it's best to remove temptation from my father's grasp as quickly as possible.

"I'd better go," I say, taking a few moments to reinsert my Lens and pull on my gloves. "Dinner plans."

"It's midafternoon," my father protests, and for the first time since I arrived—the first time in weeks—I get the impression he wants me to stay.

It's not possible, of course. "When one is dining with the devil himself," I mutter, "a vast amount of preparation is in order."

EIGHT

ON TUESDAY MORNING—before I would expect any of the fashionables to be awake—my black, self-driving car slips through the golden gates of Versailles. It's only when we've left the Sonoman-Versailles grounds that I speak my final destination to the Nav controls. Eyebrows tend to rise when one wants to go to Paris. It's no secret France hates us. And I, for one, completely understand. The founders of Sonoman-Versailles lied their way through the purchase of one of France's most beloved sites just shy of a hundred years ago.

It was a convenient storm of circumstances, really. Sonoma Inc. made its fortune and fame in 2036 by ending a worldwide famine caused by a plant disease that spread uncontrollably and killed nearly every type of grain on Earth. Sonoma's agricultural labs were the first to engineer seeds that could resist the blight. Which, of course, netted a tremendous fortune when every country in the world wanted its product.

Enter France, on the brink of economic disaster. France offered to sell the Palace of Versailles only when it came down to a choice between preserving its landmarks and feeding the French people because of said famine. And Sonoma needed something to do with all that profit. But the company hid its intentions by using a puppet corporation—the Haroldson Historical Society— to complete the purchase, luring the powers that be to grant them full sovereignty. The French government had been, unquestionably, utterly deceived.

Sonoma likes to point out that we paid full market value for the place and saved France's economy—which is technically true. But we did it through trickery and at the expense of one of France's most prized landmarks. I find the grudge entirely justifiable.

My car pulls into a quiet street on the very edge of Paris, scant kilometers from the palace, where there are several shops a bit more friendly to us Louies. A nearly identical black sedan is waiting at precisely the location I specified, at exactly the moment I requested. I have to give this criminal credit for his ability to follow directions.

My car pulls to a stop alongside the other, and I emerge just far enough for its occupants to see me. Instantly, the vehicle's rear passenger door springs open; within, I spy a set of knees clad in dark pants, but that's the only view I'm afforded of the man I paid ten thousand euros to meet.

When I slip into the confines of the sedan and look up at a masculine face, however, I feel a melting within my chest. His hair is a dark brown, and his sea-green eyes belie the obvious Asian skin and features. His brows are high and sharp, his form lithe and slender as he lounges like a great cat, one arm draped over the back of his rear-facing seat. Something in his eyes, no, his very presence, makes my spine rubbery with the strange feeling that I'm not quite safe, and a thrill of tingling excitement bursts to life in my stomach. Before I can move, before I can even speak, the door closes on its own, the man nods, and the car pulls slowly forward.

I'm not certain what to make of this person. Even sitting in the car he's tall, but then, so is the King. This person is a different kind of powerful, a kind I've rarely encountered. He's lean, but with corded muscles that even his too-large shirt and suit jacket can't hide. His hair falls across his cheekbones—unfashionably short in my world—and his eyelashes are long, longer than my own would be without their usual enhancements. But he's . . . so young. I expected an older man, and what I get is this figure who's probably younger than the King.

And I want . . . I suppose that's it, truly. I *want*. Want to slide nearer and brush that hair out of his eyes and see if his skin is as warm as it looks. Want to feel whether the power that radiates from his body is a matter of clothes making the man or something . . . deeper.

Oh.

I force down the inconvenient and ill-timed wanting; what I do here will determine my future. I meet his eyes, even if only through my semitransparent veil, and try to get hold of myself. His eyes blaze with an anger that I don't understand. He hasn't said a word, clearly waiting for me to speak first. It's a move I know well and use frequently. But I'm not in charge today. I'll be forced to begin.

Even as I make the attempt, my voice catches in my throat. I clench my stomach muscles—a motion he couldn't possibly see even if I weren't tightly laced into my stays—and lift my chin to try again. *The illusion of confidence is far more important than actually possessing the feeling.* Yet another mantra from my dance instructor. I stall for a moment and use the time to peer up at him through my veil as I compose myself. He can see my face, but I'm reasonably certain he can't make out the fear in my eyes.

"You're punctual, that's appreciated," I say in French. The words come out barely above a whisper. My heart is racing in my chest and I'm complimenting his punctuality?

He says nothing.

"I meant what I wrote in my note. I'm prepared to discuss an opportunity that I think will be immeasurably profitable for both of us."

He steeples his fingers and leans forward as though listening intently. A move calculated, I'm certain, to make me feel at ease. But it appears forced, and instinct raises the hairs on the back of my neck.

I fight the urge to lean forward myself—to close the distance between us. To feel his breath on my face and—what is it that draws me to this . . . criminal? For of course that's what he is—a dangerous criminal. I pause at that thought. Is it the danger? That sort of foolishness certainly occurs often enough in the romantic novels I've read. Is that what's happening here? But no. If I were attracted to dangerous fellows, I'd be throwing myself at the feet of the King. Is it because I have, on some level, considered becoming a criminal myself?

I study him closely, and a prickling sense of wrongness wriggles through the haze of attraction. He's young, yes, but I'm hardly one to question youth. His dress is a touch sloppy—or at the very least, not personally tailored—but what I've seen of Paris has suggested to me that this is the norm rather than the exception. Still, there's something . . .

"You're not who I asked to see," I say, forcing my voice to flow out utterly calm: a sea of glass.

A slight widening of the eyes is his only response.

"I must speak with the person in charge of this operation. That's clearly not you." I give a graceful gesture at his figure with a swirl of my wrist that takes some of the sting of the insult away. I hope. Though a large part of me is simply glad he's not who he was pretending to be: a drug lord.

"Did you expect a court dandy in fancy clothes, then?" he says. In French for certain—but not with a native accent.

I take a moment to inhale his voice, which is deeper than I'd anticipated, and with a hint of gravel. "Your clothes tell me nothing, sir; it's in your eyes."

That makes him angry. But it's true. His eyes are fire and rebellion, and the head of this sort of operation would have need of neither. Running a successful business, even an illicit one, fills men's eyes with confidence, satisfaction. This person in front of me longs for more in life.

It's a feeling I can well understand.

"Are you going to take me to your employer, or have we both wasted our time?" I ask, pinning him with my eyes.

"I have no employer."

"We're going to mince words, then?"

I note a telltale twitch at his jawline. Without breaking eye contact, he mutters, just loud enough for the Nav computer to pick it up, "Take us to him."

I'm not the least bit familiar with the streets of Paris, so I don't bother to look out the windows and try to guess where we're going. I've put my life in this man's hands, and at this moment, I feel it. Anything could happen and no one in the world would know if he slit my throat and tossed me into the Seine. My fingers tremble as I clench them in my lap, and I'm struck by how stupid it was to put my trust in people who deal in illicit wares. But soon, sooner than I'd have guessed, the car stops and the young man climbs out. A figure in black takes his place.

And my long-fractured world explodes into dust.

"Look who we have here," he says, amusement floating on his voice.

Liberté. The light is better here than it was in the catacombs, so this time I can read the word tattooed on his neck. Inside, I feel like I've been knocked over by an ocean wave and am trying to figure out which direction is up, which direction means air and light and life. For a few seconds I hold very still, looking at—though not truly seeing—the man's face.

The younger one slides back into the car from the other side, seating himself next to the man I first met in my sojourn to the catacombs. I wonder now if they were both there that night too. If the young one was one of the faces in shadow; if his were among the scurrying feet.

If he was the one who cut the satin laces on my corset.

A steady heat rises to my cheeks.

The young man gives a whispered order, and the car pulls away from the curb. Only after I've counted to twenty in my head—twice—do I trust myself to speak without shouting.

"I suppose I ought to say that it's a pleasure to see you again, *monsieur*, but I don't like to lie."

In response the blackheart laughs heartily, shamelessly, then doffs his hat, and I see his face clearly for the first time. "If you don't mind my asking," the tattooed man says once the sedan is driving along smoothly, "I told Saber not to bring you unless you specifically asked to see me—how did you know?"

Saber. Odd name. "It seemed an obvious ploy," I reply, not elaborating. Especially not in front of Saber himself. The spark of attraction makes me at least attempt to avoid offending him.

"After our encounter in the catacombs, I didn't expect ever to see you again," he says. "And I admit, I only accepted this meeting out of sheer morbid curiosity. What could the shimmering *diamant* of Sonoman-Versailles's costume-court want with a peasant such as myself?"

"I didn't know it was you, did I?"

He smirks. "No, I think you did not."

Already wearied by this man's uncouth manners, I hold up one of the patches I took from my father yesterday. The man silences himself at the sight, though he continues to smirk. Annoyingly. "Now, *Monsieur . . . ?*"

"Are you seriously asking my name?"

"You know mine."

"Everyone knows yours."

I lean forward, forcing myself to remain calm. "I did send you ten thousand euros. And you know I have every intention of conducting further business with you in the future."

"S'pose it can't hurt," he says after a long pause. "Reginald. Friends call me Reg, so you may refer to me as Reginald."

I don't react. "Tell me about the patches. What are they, exactly?"

"*Papaveris atropa.*" He reaches into his jacket and removes a very small vial filled with what looks like finely ground silver dust. "That's what the chemists call it, anyway. The newest thing in . . . street pharmaceuticals. So new most of the media hasn't even gotten a sniff of it yet."

"Really?" I ask, not hiding my skepticism.

"How do you think we got it past all the sensors in your palace?"

That would explain it—if he's telling the truth. "They don't even recognize it?"

"That's right. Totally new. But it's going to blow the others out of the water. A complex blend of opiates and gengineered belladonna, processed for transdermal delivery. Directly to the skin," he adds when I blink uncomprehendingly. "It induces bliss like heroin but leaves you conscious, and with most of your wits. Truly top of the line, for the more *cultured* consumer." He shakes the vial so the substance inside catches the sun and throws bits of light around the car. "This is ten thousand euros' worth."

"So little?" I ask, not managing to hide how breathless it makes me.

"A little goes a long way," he replies with another smirk. "But you can sell it for four to five times my bulk cost."

The numbers start ticking in my head again. "Addictive?"

"As hell."

"Hmmm." I'm not entirely happy about that, though Reginald declares it as if it were a selling point. Still, how bad can it be? I stare at the tiny vial of powder. "It must have a name. A simpler one, I mean."

He grins, showing teeth that are crooked and far from white. "On the street we just call it Glitter."

NINE

I DIDN'T EXPECT him to send me home with the vial. Yes, I'd given him the price of that surprisingly small amount of Glitter, but in my mind I'd already written off the expense as bribery. Thus my standing in the palace gardens an hour later with no idea what to do with my illicit prize. I peer into the glass canister, where the tiny silver crystals catch the light of the afternoon sun. So much potential—when it was an idea it was nerve-racking. Now that it's a physical thing, and in my possession, I'm terrified.

"Danica?"

Startled, I clench the vial so tightly I immediately fear it'll crack—which makes me emit a tiny shriek and loosen my grasp.

"My apologies," Lord Aaron says, giving me a chagrined bow.

"None of that," I say, forcing the muscles in my face to slacken as I stride over to kiss him on both cheeks, keeping my fingers out of sight until I can slip the vial down the front of my bodice. One of the oldest hiding places available to a lady—still marvelously effective. It's not that I don't trust him, but if I tell him, it feels as though I've made my decision and there'll be no going back.

"How are you?" Lord Aaron asks, his hands on my shoulders,

our cheeks nearly touching. "With the move and everything, I mean. We haven't had a chance to talk since the other night."

My instinct is to check around us for listeners, to angle away from M.A.R.I.E.'s unblinking eyes. But then, that's the reason I chose to walk in the orchard as soon as I returned from Paris: no such worries here. Robotic assistance remains just a few blinks away, but I feel safer outside the walls of the palace. An illusion, perhaps. I never noticed the omnipresence of surveillance before. Now that I'm hyperaware, it truly feels inescapable.

Lord Aaron offers me an arm and I grasp it genially. We walk in silence for a few minutes, our direction most definitely taking us farther from the palace. In half an hour I'll have to return for an "emergency" appointment with His Royal Fussiness' personal *modiste*, but for a few more minutes my time is my own.

Not that I mind sharing it with Lord Aaron—the only soul in Versailles who knows I'm trying to leave. Who's helping to make it happen, even now. Some knights appear on white steeds; mine rides bejeweled heels with satin laces. The morning of Sierra's death, I fled to Lord Aaron the instant my mother let me out of her sight, and told him everything.

Everything.

He didn't react with disbelief or even horror—only grew silent as pensive concern lined his face. "It sounds to me like you need to get out," he'd said in his soft, calm voice.

"What are the chances of that?" I replied—grumpily, I'm sure, as my tears had finally dried and I found things no better than before, with the added indignity of puffy eyes and stuffed sinuses.

"High, perhaps."

That got my attention. "How?"

The conversation that followed was unexpected, to say the least. I'd heard of the Foundation for Social Reintegration, of course, since they manage to sneak protesters into the palace a few times a year—self-righteous vandals, mostly, with a vague "social justice" ax or two to grind. They're a joke among the residents because they're always going on about breaking our chains and escaping our captors, as though courtly life at Versailles Palace were a punishment rather than a privilege. We don't even pay rent. No one is a captive in Sonoman-Versailles.

Or so I thought.

But sitting there that morning, listening to Lord Aaron, I realized that was exactly what I was: a prisoner, wearing chains forged not of steel, but of circumstance.

He spoke of the Foundation's charitable arm, explained how it primarily helps ordinary Sonoma Inc. employees when they lose their jobs and discover they have nowhere to go and little money to spend, thanks to their corporate citizenship and the unfavorable exchange rate between credits and euros. Then Lord Aaron revealed that the Foundation had even agreed to help disentangle *him* from Sonoma with his personal wealth intact—in exchange for a generous donation, *bien sûr*.

"Why would you want to leave?" I asked. Lord Aaron had always seemed enamored of palace life.

He shrugged. "I feel stifled here. Have for years. I wanted to . . . to explore what the world has to offer. To meet someone. I adore you and Molli, but . . ."

"Then go on a trip. Go to America and bring back a handsome Yankee boy and dress him up in satin and lace. Why leave forever?"

"Well, it seemed like a good idea at the time. I'm no longer so sure."

"But you were."

"Yes," he said slowly. "And the Foundation has dedicated experts working with them—they know the bureaucratic hurdles, they can handle the red tape. It was a way to completely extricate myself from Sonoman-Versailles without sacrificing my fortune. Without sacrificing the lifestyle that I, personally, would rather not do without."

I had to smile at that. As loyal and adventurous as he can be, Lord Aaron is soft. I couldn't imagine him so much as washing his own tea dishes, much less laboring for a living.

"So when I turned eighteen and received full control of my assets, I started those wheels turning."

It was almost too much to take in. Except that he was still in the palace. "What changed your mind?"

"Do you have to ask?"

"Sir Spencer?"

He shrugged and smiled sadly.

"But I don't have any assets. And I can't simply leave—I'll have to hide." Of that I felt certain: if I were to walk away from Versailles before my eighteenth birthday, Mother would find a way to claw me back. The only way out of this arranged marriage was to disappear. For that matter, as a witness to his crime, the only way for me to be safe from the King would be to disappear forever.

That, the Foundation couldn't manage—in fact, while I remained underage, they couldn't even get me out of Sonoman-Versailles. But they had referred Lord Aaron to a contact they sometimes used to perform . . . special extractions. Enter the esteemed Reginald.

"The room isn't so bad," I say with a tight smile, finally answering Lord Aaron's inquiry after my well-being. "It's only the most elegant *boudoir* in the palace. That softens the blow some."

"Are you going to last?"

"Last?"

"Until your birthday. Until you can leave."

My heart feels hollow. "Just lasting. I wish it were that simple."

"Isn't it, though? If you're ready to go on your birthday, the Foundation can finalize your paperwork and whisk you away."

"To where? To what?"

"So you're not going to leave?"

"I didn't say that." I pull a fan from my reticule and waft air toward my chest, where beads of sweat are nestling around the vial of Glitter. "Even when I reach my majority, the Foundation's help won't be sufficient. The Foundation offers rehabilitation. What I need is witness protection." I hesitate. "I need someone who can give me a new name, a new face, even, so that when I leave, *no one* will be able to find me."

"Not even me?"

A twinge in my heart. "Not even you," I say, smiling to cover it.

He clears his throat and looks away. "So you still think that man from the catacombs is the way to go?"

"I do," I whisper, realizing that in saying so, I'm halfway to committing to my insane scheme.

"But how will you pay for it?" His face splits into a grin and he chuckles wryly. "Please don't ask me to help you steal the Zhào jewels again. I'm not sure I'd survive."

I laugh. "That was quite a night, wasn't it?"

In addition to titles, pensions, and room and board at one of the world's premier architectural landmarks, the first Sonoman King—Kevin Wyndham—persuaded board members to participate in his unusual endeavor by making gifts of historic jewels that came as part and parcel of his purchase of the palace. The particular piece Lord Aaron and I purloined—a cluster of glittering sapphires on a golden chain—is rumored to have belonged to King Louis XV's mistress, the famous Madame de Pompadour. The Zhào family displays it rather garishly, right in the front atrium of their apartments. Lady Mei is always complaining of how *gauche* it is, but her comments over the years gave Lord Aaron and me just enough information—on top of our hacking skills—to steal the necklace from her family in the dead of night.

"Taking it wasn't half so bad as having to put it back three hours later," I say wryly. I remember the tingling of my fingers, the sweat rolling down my back as the horizon grew pinker and we were still crouched in front of the elaborate jewel case, trying to break through that final firewall before the household awoke.

"Indeed," Lord Aaron said, chuckling. "If I'd known you were going to be such a failure, I'd have left a few back doors open."

I ignore his faux rebuke. "You must have been furious—me bursting in on you at sunrise, demanding your assistance."

"I wasn't pleased to see you at that hour, I do confess."

"I was so stupid," I say, sobering now. "I thought I could have everything."

We stroll through the orchard, veering away from a rowdy group of young ladies who've been edging closer to us. "What's your plan now?" he asks.

"I haven't decided for sure. But I have . . . potential."

"Spill."

"It's illegal," I whisper.

"So is killing the lady you're trysting with."

"Two wrongs don't make a right."

"Sometimes I think perhaps they do," he says, stopping and looking at me gravely. "I'd do something illegal to save your life; I hope you'd do the same for me."

I let out a short, skeptical laugh. "That's the beginning and end of your standards? What if it hurts people?" I don't want to think too hard about that, so I clear my throat and continue. "Or the kingdom? What if it brings down the kingdom?"

"Then you leave, I leave—I imagine a goodly number of others leave—and to the devil with the kingdom," he adds with a little more heat. "At its heart it's only a corporation full of massively wealthy people."

But I focus on his first statement. "You leave? How will you leave?"

"The Foundation," he says. "I still fund it, you know."

I stop, my slippered feet crunching on the gravel walk. "Really?"

"Ever ready with plan B."

"Aren't you afraid you'll get caught?"

"What would they punish me for? It's not against the law."

"It's socially unacceptable. Which is practically the same thing."

He shrugs. "I'd survive such a relatively small scandal. But if the Foundation is contacted by someone less able to afford its services than I was, I want them to be able to get what they need. That's all."

"I didn't peg you as a philanthropist."

"It's possible I have ulterior motives."

"Such as?"

He swings his walking stick and raises an eyebrow at me. "If I should one day find myself wanting to leave with a terribly handsome lad in tow, who's tired of being a puppet in his father-in-law's machinations, it would be most fortuitous to have an organization such as this one indebted to me."

"*Touché,*" I say, tapping his shoulder with my fan. "I shouldn't be surprised that you have such plans."

"No, you should not," he says with a vaguely condescending smile. After several paces in silence, he remarks, "I can't believe he moved you into the Queen's Rooms. He's such a pompous ass."

"Oh, that's the least of what he is." I mean for the words to sound playful, but they don't, and a lump catches in my throat. I bend and toss a handful of pebbles into the pond. Lord Aaron stoops and grabs his own handful, though he throws his one at a time, and for a while the only sound is the gentle plop they make as they break the surface of the water.

"Are you sorry you stayed?" I ask.

"I wish I could be."

I glance over at him, an eyebrow raised in question.

"The only thing worse than not being able to *be* with the one you love is not being able to even see him."

"Do you think the time will come? After Lady Julianna's father—"

But he shakes his head vehemently. "I can't hang my hopes on that. That part is out of my control. I have to be happy—enough—with what I have. Then anything else I get is cream, and if nothing else happens, I won't spend my life feeling I've been robbed."

"An enviable philosophy," I say, and I mean it. I step closer and lay a hand on Lord Aaron's arm, itching to change the subject. "Escort me back? I have an appointment with the royal *modiste*." I say the words with a lofty lilt.

"A new gown?"

"A new wardrobe. The King took one look at my gown and insisted my current fashions are unsuitable for a King's consort."

"Consort?" Lord Aaron says in indignation. "Did he say that?"

"Indeed."

"Ass."

"Indeed," I repeat, a smile hovering at the corners of my mouth.

TEN

THE DOORS TO the *salon* just outside the *Appartement de la Reine* bang open, and it's all I can do not to fall off the dressing stool, where I've been perched for over three hours, being fitted for every sort of gown one could imagine. They've only just started on this one, so I'm standing in little more than my undergarments, corset, and stockings, but I refuse to flinch as his eyes find me and appreciation flares to life.

"Ah. Justin," I say flatly, and a wave of stifled laughter rises up from one side of the room.

His eyes go blank and a hint of color rises on his cheeks as he realizes he has an audience. I invited Molli and Lady Mei to sit in on the fitting—unfortunately, I didn't select a private enough corner when I asked them to join me, and two other ladies, Rebekah and Lady Seidra, overheard. It's a high enough social honor to be invited to attend the future Queen that they gleefully wormed themselves into the invitation as well. It's not that I don't like Rebekah or Lady Seidra, but being attended while wearing only rather flimsy undergarments is far less awkward when said attendants are one's more intimate friends.

At this moment, however, I'm grateful for the extra eyes. And reddened cheeks and embarrassed giggles.

"Dani," he says in mock deference, though I can see the tension in his jaw. "We need to talk."

I gesture wordlessly at the trappings draped over every piece of furniture in the room.

"You need a break," he snaps. "They do too."

"Omniscient as well as omnipotent, are we?" I murmur, for his ears only.

"Don't you?" he snaps at the giggling group of girls, only Molli looking white-faced and concerned.

"Indeed, Your Highness," Rebekah says, dropping into a deep curtsy.

"Most weary, Your Highness," Lady Seidra says in a matching tone, as though they hadn't been sitting on a settee being served tea and refreshments for the last hour. The King makes a shooing motion and the ladies scurry away. Molli pauses at the doorway and touches the corner of her eye, indicating that I should com her ASAP. She casts one more frustrated glare at the King's back and closes the door behind her.

The King raises an eyebrow at me, and fire smolders in my stomach. The seamstresses he ignores utterly, despite the way they rush about. He never behaves as well in front of the "help" as in front of subjects. Telling, that. "Come," he says, snapping his finger as he strides toward my bedroom.

I will not come like a dog at his snap. I remain motionless on the stool, not even looking at him. From the corner of my eye

I watch him approach the doors and turn to address me, and I see the moment of confusion when he finds me not directly behind him.

"Darling," he drawls, and gives me a half-bow. "Won't you come rest yourself and chat with me?"

There's really no point in resisting, but I wish I could. I join him beside the door, whapping his hip with the bare cage of one of my *panniers* just because. "Go ahead, M.A.R.I.E."

The doors open before us and close as soon as we pass through.

"What the hell were you doing in Paris this morning?"

I react by glancing up at the gilded bit of buttress that holds M.A.R.I.E.'s eye for this chamber.

"Forget that," His Majesty says, waving his hand in that direction. "I have several rooms programmed to cease recording as soon as I walk in. This is one of them."

Fear makes my most recent snack rise high in my throat. "How . . . reassuring."

"Isn't it?" A hint of a smile reveals his amusement.

I take a moment to retrieve a silk robe from where it lies draped over a spindle-legged armchair, and I tie it tightly around me. I wouldn't call myself dressed, but now I'm at least decent. "Who says I was in Paris?" But the indignation is false. I knew I'd get caught—there are too many safeguards on my person to prevent it. Not to mention GPS. But I left my Lens at home, so he doesn't know what actually occurred, and now I'll work it into my story.

"The Nav computer on the car you seduced out of the fleet captain."

"*Seduced* is a strong word." A flirtatious smile is as far as it went.

"You're avoiding the question."

I lower my eyelids and try to appear cowed. "I didn't want you to find out."

His Highness raises an eyebrow at that but says nothing.

"I went to visit my old dance instructor."

He spreads his hand out to both sides. "Because . . . ?"

"I haven't always been like this," I say, gesturing vaguely at my person. *Ugh! I sound like a bad cinema film!* "For example, this isn't the nose I was born with," I add wryly.

His Majesty smirks. "Truly?"

I clasp the front of my robe to my chest as though embarrassed and nod, my eyes sliding away from his. "I was only fourteen when we moved into the palace after my father's inheritance. Before, we lived in the city of Versailles: part of the Sonoman-Versailles culture, but only on the fringes of the actual court."

"So you had a Parisian dance instructor—move along."

"Patience, Justin," I say. "You know my mother, of course."

He snaps his mouth shut at that. If there's anyone who despises my mother more than I do, it's him.

"This," I say, gesturing between the two of us, "was always her dream, and as an only child I was her sole tool to get it. So imagine her dismay when I entered adolescence, grew far too quickly for my sense of balance to keep up, and sprouted a large and rather

crooked nose. And don't even get me started on my teeth," I add, almost to myself. The memory of my accelerated orthodontia still makes my mouth ache. "My mother practically hid me for almost two years while she used my father's new inheritance to mold me into bait. For you," I clarify when His Highness looks confused.

"How stupid does she think I am? I was never going to consider you," he says scornfully. "An untitled nobody? What a waste of money."

My cheeks don't even redden at his insult. The class system of the court has never meant anything to me. If I had my way, I'd still be an untitled nobody. With my old nose and gangly limbs, to be truthful. The perfect features, impeccable manners, and fey grace I'm known for at court are all as much a disguise as the costumes we wear at masquerades.

But worse, to me they represent the years of subservience I showed to my mother. Pursuing her dream through rigorous and painful methods, when all I truly wanted was to be a part of the glamorous court life, fringes or not. As on the night of Sierra's murder, I did nothing. I let life happen to me. Not anymore.

"When I was at least acceptable in my sixteenth year, I had my coming out, but I continued to train secretly in grace and poise. I needed it," I add, letting my lashes lower as though revealing a weakness, not simply baiting his rook with my pawn.

He's looking bored now, with his hands jammed in his pockets. "As fascinating and admittedly amusing as this all is, what the hell does it have to do with your trip to Paris?"

"My dance instructor. Giovanni is a renowned ballet teacher. My mother spent a small fortune for him to instill in me the grace

of a ballerina, without the ballet. I didn't learn dances; I learned how to walk without tripping." It's a simplified explanation. Hours upon hours we spent in Giovanni's mirrored dance studio, floating from pose to pose, my instructor's swift hands correcting every angle, every tilt, every curve, until I could strike any pose to utter perfection in an instant.

"I went to Paris to see if he might be amenable to taking up our lessons again. The kingdom's centennial is coming and I—I'm nervous." The lashes-lowering thing again. *Nervous, ha!* I have a half-hour practice routine personally designed by Giovanni that I do every night without fail. I haven't slid back, but I know the King won't be willing to offer me that compliment.

Sure enough, His Majesty clears his throat. "While you are, indeed, lovely—no one can deny that, least of all myself—there's always room for improvement."

Ah, pride goeth before stupidity. "I was hoping you would say so," I reply, giving him a coy smile. He narrows his eyes in suspicion, as he was hoping to provoke me. "I fear I'm slipping just a bit, right when I need to be my very best."

"You certainly do," His Highness agrees in a stern, magisterial tone that clashes ridiculously with our ages.

"Perhaps weekly lessons for the next month or two," I suggest. That gives me my excuse for Paris on my GPS. "We wouldn't want the media to detect anything amiss, would we?"

He grinds his teeth and says nothing. But after a long moment, he sighs. "Send a com, then. Fetch him here."

"Oh, that's not possible," I retort, perhaps too quickly. "I must go to him."

"I don't see why."

"His studio," I say, as though it were the most obvious thing in the world. And back when my mother was explaining it to me when I was fifteen, it seemed so, and so I parrot her words. "The floor-to-ceiling mirrors, the *barre,* the teacups and books that inevitably go crashing to the floor when I make a mistake. Besides, how will you explain his very presence?"

The King doesn't like it, I can tell. And he's trying to find something wrong with it. But he could never suspect that I have the brains—or the guts—to do what I actually intend. "I'm not paying for it," he says, evidently unable to let this go without a final jab. "Your mother will have to take it out of the Grayson household budget."

I offer a smile of gratitude, but inside my belly, rage is boiling so hot it must be melting the rest of my organs. "I'm certain she'll be happy to." Happy that I appear to be making an effort.

"Now, I believe I have a fitting to finish," I say, gesturing at the door.

His eyes are fixed on the deep V of my dressing gown, which I've forgotten to clench shut, and his mouth quirks up in a crooked smile. "Yes. I think I'll sit in on the rest of that. Just to observe, of course. I'll go fetch your friends, so they can see how very much in love we are."

I turn away before he can see the angry flush rise in my cheeks.

"ENTREZ!" I CALL distractedly when someone knocks just as a bot is putting the final touches on my hair for the *Grand Couvert*—

a fancy dinner the King holds every week for, as far as I can tell, no other reason than because Louis XIV did. It's an outrageous expense, and as the resident of the Queen's Rooms, I'm now expected to sit beside him on the golden dais: a trophy on display. This is my first one, and I'm dreading it. So I'm beyond cheered to see Molli's face burst through my door.

"I'm sorry it's so near to dinner bell," she says in both greeting and apology. "I couldn't come right when you commed. Mother needed my assistance."

I rise from the dressing table and nearly run to her to throw my arms about her shoulders. "No apologies, please. I'm glad you came at all, after the abominable way you were treated this afternoon." Despite His Royal Snootiness sitting less than a meter from the settee full of ladies, he uttered not a word to anyone, except to occasionally criticize one of the seamstresses.

Molli merely shrugs and peers around the embarrassingly ornate room.

A thought strikes me, and I kick off my heels and grab Molli's hand. "Come," I say, pulling her farther into the room, toward the enormous bed. "I want you to be numbered among the very select group of people who can say that they've jumped on Marie-Antoinette's bed." She seems reluctant in the face of the ostentatious room, so I drag her all the way through the golden gate before running a few steps to jump and flop down on the priceless brocade spread.

Molli hesitates, her eyes scanning the ceiling—looking for M.A.R.I.E.'s ubiquitous eye, I'm certain—but a smile lifts the corners of her mouth, and a few seconds later she's sprawled beside me, her gown a velvet half-circle surrounding her legs, *panniers* sticking up on either side of her hips. She looks over at me, then down at her skirts, and we both start to laugh.

I take advantage of the moment to glance down and check that the vial of Glitter is still in place. Unwilling as I was to let it leave my person, it spent half the afternoon tucked in my sweaty palm, then the other half pushed down my corset and nestled in the valley of my cleavage. Also sweaty—my nerves are getting the better of me.

The appointment with the royal *modiste* made that a particular challenge, but though the moody designer clucked her tongue in disapproval when I wouldn't let her so much as touch the laces of my unfashionably overcinched stays, she didn't press the issue, so my vial was safe.

"This room is amazing."

"It's not like you haven't been here before. It's so often open."

"But it wasn't yours," she says.

I roll my eyes. "M.A.R.I.E. hasn't changed anything. Not in five years of vacancy since the former Queen died."

"But you will, won't you? A few things, at least."

"Indeed," I say. "I think I'll tidy up my mess."

"Be serious."

My smile feels fake, but I've practiced for hours in front of a mirror and I know she won't be able to tell. Lying to Molli is harder than lying to anyone else. Harder on me. She's easy to convince—thinks all too well of me and would never suspect me of untruth. "Of course I will. In time." Not a promise I intend to keep. *In time,* I'll be gone.

"How are you coping?" Molli asks in a whisper, and it's that question that nearly breaks me, sending a searing throb into the top of my throat.

"Coping is what I do." My voice wavers, and I don't hide it. Here, when Molli and I are together, I can drop my *façade*. It feels like removing a literal weight I've been struggling to bear all day, even if the conversation solves nothing.

"It must be quite a change, though, sleeping all alone on this enormous bed . . . ?" Her voice drops away and she looks at me meaningfully.

"Yes, *alone*," I say, answering her real question. "My mother would have his manhood stuffed and mounted for display, otherwise." There's something supremely satisfying about saying that with a dazzling smile on my lips.

"There are consolations, of course," I say when Molli doesn't respond. She's likely shocked at my blunt words, even in privacy. "After all, among Versailles's blissfully wed nobility, what is the most common marital complaint?"

Molli considers this for a moment, then smirks. "They're never home," she says, angling her chin jauntily.

"Precisely. And few keep hours as long as the King himself. There's a possibility that I shall see him even less now than I used to."

"Will you be lonely?" Molli's chin is so close to my shoulder that I feel her warm breath.

While I appreciate her unfeigned concern, I can't help but bristle at the implication that I'm in need of some sort of rescue—that my problems are so shallow as to be solved by a little company. But of course the answer to her question is *yes*. Yes, I'm lonely. Even in a room full of people, I'm lonely. Trapped by the people who should keep me safe, sharing a secret with those I despise.

Of course, none of that factors into Molli's inquiry. All she knows is that I have an overbearing mother, an embarrassing father, and an unwanted political engagement to our wealthy, powerful King, which I refuse to elaborate upon. What good could possibly come of inflicting on Molli the knowledge that her sovereign lord killed not only a young member of his own court, but also a part of me? It's not a lack of trust; it's my own reluctance to destroy something as beautiful and innocent as Molli. Those often-trite parental words *for your own good* come to mind.

"Are you asking if I'll miss my parents?" I give a self-deprecating laugh at the diversion.

"Will you?" Molli asks. "You got on well with your father, at least."

"Well enough, I suppose. But I said farewell to the man my father used to be a long time ago. To tell the truth, leaving their home was a relief. The only part of this whole experience that has been."

I see her swallow hard, then nod. An electronic chime sounds, and she slips off the bed and peers into the mirror on my new dressing table to see if her hair needs repairing. "I hate this faux candlelight," she grumbles. "It flattens my complexion, which is actually one of my best features."

"Come now," I say, joining her and rearranging my skirts. "Your complexion is brilliant, always has been. It practically—" *Glitters.*

"Are you all right?" I'm not sure how long I must have been standing in silence when Molli's voice breaks through my haze.

"Molli," I say tentatively. "What if you had a cosmetic—a foundation, or maybe a liquid rouge—that had specks of something iridescent in it? Don't you think that could catch even the electric candlelight and help prevent your complexion from looking so flat?"

"I can't think the Society would approve," Molli says, invoking the name of the committee that keeps our dress and appearance in line with historical precedent.

"I can't see why not. Surely glittery substances have been used much further back in time than the Baroque. Why, mother-of-pearl must date at least to the Renaissance."

Transdermal delivery. An oil-derived base.

The second—and final—dinner chime sounds, and we both look up, in the direction of the camouflaged speaker.

"I'd better hurry," Molli says. "My parents will be waiting for me."

Before she can get away, I stop her, grasping both her hands in mine. "Thank you for coming. You've made everything so much better."

The door clicks closed behind Molli, and I nearly sprint to the small office tucked behind the *boudoir*. I wish I could send a com, but it's far too risky. Instead I pull out a half-sheet of parchment and my fountain pen and glance at the clock. Three minutes. I'll have to write fast.

Dear Reginald,
I have an idea.

ELEVEN

MY DREAMS HAVE grown strange since I moved into Marie-Antoinette's rooms. The only way women quit these apartments is through death, and I can't help but wonder how long my own occupancy will last. Nightmares are nothing new, not since that night in the servants' corridor. But lately it's not the King whose face I flee too slowly—sometimes, inexplicably, it's my own. And last night I saw Saber's face too, his eyes as piercing and unfriendly as they were when we met. These dreams are uncomfortable at best, so when consciousness begins to tug me from my nocturnal wanderings, I welcome it.

As I float between wakefulness and slumber, something seems *different*, but I can't figure out what. A breeze plays over my skin, tickling my leg where I've kicked my covers away; my thigh is bare nearly to the garter-loops of my corset. Bleary-eyed, I squint at the enormous expanse of bed surrounding me and pat about, searching for the edge of the sheet.

At my movement a ripple of hushed murmurs meets my ears, and my hand freezes.

The breeze. That's it. There's never a breeze. Not unless I specifically ask M.A.R.I.E. to generate one. The buzz around me takes on new significance as clarity pierces my sleep-addled brain.

It's *Wednesday.*

Wednesdays have been a part of my life ever since I moved into the palace at fourteen. But my duties are now very different, and as I peer out beneath my lashes, I curse His Royal Highness for not specifically mentioning that, even though I'm not yet the Queen, I'm apparently expected to take over all the responsibilities of sleeping in this room.

Including the public display of the *Lever du Roi,* the Rising of the King—of which the Queen's awakening has, since its inception, been the more interesting part.

They're here in my room, probably a hundred tourists sardined into the fifty-person space on the other side of the golden rail that, thankfully, separates me from the masses. And they're practically foaming at the mouth over their chance to gawk, to watch an underage young woman dress—a full half of the *voyeurs* are here for that, I've no doubt.

My fingers itch with rage and embarrassment as I try to figure out how to gracefully pull down a shift that's only centimeters from exposing my *derrière* to the room. To the world, likely, since these days every tourist has a recording device that streams directly onto their personal but all-too-public profile.

Roll to the left, I finally decide. That'll require me to cross the foot of the bed with no camouflaging robe at hand but will keep my shift from rising higher. The lesser of the two evils, maybe.

But first—more important than anything else—I slide my hand under my pillow and grip the tiny tube of Glitter in my fist.

Contraband secured, I count to three before rolling to the edge of the bed and, somewhere in the rising volume of delighted whispers, detect a groan or two of disappointment when the white silk drops to cover my legs again. As much as diaphanous silk ever does, that is, which isn't completely.

I pretend I don't see them—that I'm unaware of the flash photography they were all forbidden to use when they first entered the palace—as I stride around the foot of my bed, across the thick carpeting. My guests, at least those standing in the first few rows, can probably make out my nipples where my breasts press against the confines of my shift. If it were possible for tabloid editors to feel gratitude, I'd expect thank-you coms to arrive over breakfast.

I tunnel-vision on the wall panel that conceals my personal washroom, hoping that my backside isn't showing too plainly through the thin silk of my inadequate clothing. Much as they might wish to, not even the perverts who've been watching me sleep can deny me a trip to the carefully concealed water closet—a concession to modernity about which even the French government doesn't complain.

After closing the panel behind me, I release a loud breath, halfway to a sob. It's the only hint of a breakdown I can allow myself, or I won't be able to stop. I hate that I didn't think of this. I saw a *lever* once on the Internet, with the former Queen. Her ladies were waiting beside her bed when she awoke, ready to hand her a modest satin robe. Her hair was carefully plaited from the previous night, and thinking back, I realize she must have slept in light cosmetics in order to be presentable for the mass of tourists she knew would be waiting. She looked stunning. Beyond glamorous to a twelve-year-old girl.

Seems less glamorous now.

"We don't have to suffer the paparazzi," Lady Mei told me one day after I'd been complaining about our Wednesday obligations. "Not the kind that jump out of bushes and peep in your windows, at least. Ours come each Wednesday and must stay behind the ropes. It's not a terrible deal, in the end. At least we can be ready."

Except that I'm *not* ready.

"M.A.R.I.E.!"

But she's not here on Wednesdays. Not in the *Appartement de la Reine*. Or, to be fair, *du Roi;* this is a burden the Queen and King bear together. The Baroque *façade* we put on display for the world once a week must not be tainted by modern trappings. No bots, no screens, no M.A.R.I.E.

I rush to my *toilette* table and open a large glass bowl of scented talc, an essential piece of kit for the sensitive skin beneath my corset. Deep into the chalky powder goes the vial of Glitter. Turn the tap, water, a quick wash, and then I reach for my Lens.

Who can I call? Who might have any idea what needs to be done?

I want to call Molli—especially after last night—but if she even knows the routine, she's not an early riser. She'd have to get herself presentable before she could come and help do the same for me, and even then it might be the proverbial blind leading the blind. Lord Aaron would be perfect, but in keeping with the Baroque, the *lever* maintains historic gender divides. And Lady Mei? Assuming her elaborate *toilette* was complete enough for her to dare to be seen in public, she would instantly, and gleefully, spread my shame around the court, our friendship notwithstanding.

Damn, damn, damn!

I try to think of ladies older than me, who might have participated in the *lever* with the old Queen. Lady Camille Medeiros! She's always been friendly to me at assemblies, but she's older than she appears. And a countess in her own right. I'm certain she must've been invited to attend the Queen at least occasionally. I blink, activating my Lens, and hurry to the mirror so my own reflection can act as my screen for a video call.

"Call Lady Camille Medeiros," I command. "Mark it urgent." Even if she's still abed, surely even a countess will answer an urgent call from the future Queen.

One, two, three, four, five, six, sev—

"Your Grace?" Lady Medeiros's large, dark eyes appear in a tiny square in my peripheral vision.

"Lady Medeiros, I need assistance," I say in a rush, letting my Lens focus on my reflection in the bathroom mirror. It's a quick fix for certain, but it allows Lady Medeiros to see me in all my disheveled glory. "There are so many people here for—" I hesitate. I'm babbling, and I cannot afford to show such weakness in front of powerful nobility. Not now. "I need a *lever*," I say calmly.

"By the looks of you, you've missed most of it already, Your Grace," she says, her tone gently scolding.

"I confess, I was ill prepared." It's the only concession I'll make. To say that I received no warning that I'd be taking up some of the Queen's duties along with her rooms would reveal that I'm out of favor with the King; to confess that I *needed* such warning would imply either clumsiness or distraction on my part. I can afford to have the nobility saying none of these things about me, especially not right now.

But I have to give her something, because I need her. The ghost-image of Lady Medeiros being projected into my right eye is fully dressed, and if her hair isn't as formal as might be preferred for a royal assignment, it's at least coiffed. It's enough. "I'm certain with your reputation at court that you waited on the Queen. You were the first lady I thought of," I add, making a play to her pride.

"You'll need more than me."

"I trust your resourcefulness."

She hesitates.

I give a bit more. "Please?" I whisper.

Lady Medeiros's lips part and she licks her bottom lip, and I know I've won her over—at least for now. "Gabriella will be awake," she finally says. "Lady Anaya, too. But I might need as much as ten minutes."

"I can begin my own *toilette*," I say. "I'll be exceptionally slow. They won't know the difference."

"Don't underestimate them simply because they aren't wearing gowns," Lady Medeiros says seriously. "Our lady Queen never did."

She might as well have slapped me, and my cheeks burn hot. "Hurry," I say, and end the call before she can see the sheen of moisture in my eyes. I shake tension from my hands and gasp for air to fight back the tears.

Five seconds. Ten. Regain control.

My long, wavy hair is tousled in what I would otherwise call sexy bed mess, but sexy is not what I'm going for today. My shift is as bad as I feared, leaving little to the imagination, but even if I were in my wardrobe instead of my washroom, where I would actually have a change of clothing, I haven't time to unlace my corset. Perhaps with the help of a bot or two—but of course, it's Wednesday.

So I don the only robe in the bathroom—a terry cloth number that looks more like a towel than a part of my morning bedroom set, but better terry cloth than another gallery for the "celebrity wardrobe malfunctions" feed.

A collective *Ooooh!* sounds from the crowd as I emerge, eyes downcast, and I have to bite back a gag at the unfairness of it all. A simple warning that this was going to happen: "With the Queen's chambers occupied, we must, per agreement with the Fifth Republic, reinstitute exhibition of the *Lever du Roi. Vive la France!*" Is that so much to ask from the man who intends to marry me? In my *pique,* I wonder if he did this on purpose. This seems like the sort of prank that would amuse him.

My dressing table has very few cosmetics on it—something I'll change before next Wednesday—but enough for me to playact some kind of routine while my last-minute staff makes its way to my rooms. I perch on the edge of the dressing room table, and the murmur of the crowd takes a tone of displeasure as I begin brushing the curled ends of my hair.

Apparently, this is wrong.

Lady Medeiros was right—I shouldn't have underestimated them. Every person in the gallery paid a premium to attend, to witness firsthand the live performance of a piece of French culture that dates back centuries, reenacted today for the first time in over five years. For all I know, there are die-hards in the crowd who spent months watching old webcasts of weekly *levers*.

I must be the biggest letdown.

Using the general buzz of the crowd as my guide, I put down the brush and reach for a small pot of face cream instead.

More negative noise.

I have to ignore it as I rub daubs of the white stuff into my face—the only other substance on the table is a perfume diffuser, and it's decorative. In other words, empty. I'm on the verge of rising and retreating to the bathroom again when I hear a door open behind me and a cascade of giggling.

I turn with a cool half-smile as three thirtysomething matrons—Lady Medeiros in the lead—enter through a back door, their arms draped with gowns, hands filled with bottles, fake smiles fixed on their faces.

This is apparently correct, because the crowd perks up.

Lady Medeiros takes control. Of the women, of the crowd, of the entire situation.

Of me.

I don't protest when she peels the thick robe from my shoulders, exposing my barely hidden chest, and though she glances skeptically at my already-donned silk corset, she doesn't comment. Gabriella picks up the brush and pulls it through my long hair as Lady Anaya takes my hand and begins rubbing a sweet-smelling lotion into my nail beds. Apparently I'm to do nothing for myself, and that's why the crowd was so disapproving when I tried.

As they work, the women fill the air with inane chattering

about the latest spat between Duke Lancel and Lady Grey—all in French, *mais bien sûr*. So naturally do they gossip that I find myself wondering why I've never heard of Duke Lancel and Lady Grey, shortly before I realize that they don't exist. Whether rehearsed or improvised I can't tell, but this is a play—a farce, truly, a show of casual, girlish fun so far from the truth it strains credulity.

Our audience behind the railing, where I doubt anyone can hear even one word in ten, is rapt.

When Lady Medeiros pulls the sleeves of my shift off my shoulders, it's all I can do not to jump and pull them back up. Not even the lowest-cut gown I've dared wear in public reveals so much. I blush fiercely enough to feel it, and the audience murmurs with delight; through the chatter of my attendants, I swear I hear a tourist remark approvingly on my "unfeigned innocence."

I want to murder them all.

In swift, efficient movements, Lady Medeiros diffuses scented rose water onto my chest and shoulders, then pats me dry with a linen cloth. It's the most humiliating luxury I've ever experienced. I'm relieved when Lady Medeiros replaces my sleeves and pulls me to my feet, grinning at me with a severity that I belatedly realize means *I* should be smiling too.

I acquiesce.

The women drape gown after gown across the bed, layering them with a few accessories, waiting for me to choose one. I try to focus, to do my best, but all I really want is to cover my near-nakedness and get these people out of my room.

Still, a Queen must dress like one, and for all I remain

seventeen, unwed, and untitled, *Queen* is the role I'm playing in Versailles these days. So I select an ensemble of colors, fabrics, and accessories that will best enhance my finest qualities.

I simply do it with great haste.

Lady Medeiros tosses the emerald-green *robe à la Piémontaise* over my head, and the smooth satin hisses down over my shift, armoring me at last against the intrusive gaze of the audience. My fingers toy with the texture of the tiny embroidered detailing all around the bodice, and I stand straight so she can fasten the closures in the back.

"It doesn't fit," Lady Medeiros hisses, close to my ear.

"It most certainly does," I argue out of the corner of my mouth. "I wore it last week."

"It's five centimeters from closing."

Of course. "You haven't tightened my corset."

"You slept like this?"

I turn and give her what I will later consider my first Queenly staredown.

Her throat convulses, but then she nods. "Turn. I can pull the laces through the open back."

As she yanks on my corset laces, squeezing my already-confined torso down to my accustomed measurements, the women across the railing titter to one another, doubtless commenting on what they see as nothing more than masochism for beauty's sake. Lady Medeiros grumbles that she has to pull the laces so hard they tear at her delicate fingers, but I feel the world click into rightness as the boning of my stays digs into my abdomen, pulling everything back together. Soon my waist is small enough to fasten the tiny hooks down the back of my gown, beneath the ornamental cape that falls from my shoulders.

"I changed my mind about the hat," I announce as soon as the final hook is set. "I'll take that one." I point at a wide-brimmed bonnet designed not for luxury or decoration but for actually shading one's face from the sun. It'll require a simpler hairstyle— hardly more than a loose, over-the-shoulder braid—cutting the duration of my torment by twenty minutes at least.

Lady Medeiros reads my mind and casts me a sly smile that communicates her approval.

Once my hair is bound and my hat affixed, each of the three ladies takes turn after turn adorning me with smaller accessories. Far too many: a watch pinned just above my breast, a chain of delicate white gold around my neck, a row of lace tucked carefully into my low neckline—not awkward for anyone, that move—a bracelet, thin leather gloves, teardrop pearl earrings, a brooch on my hat, two more for my silk shoes, a ring big enough to be worn on the outside of my glove, a sash about my waist. Finally, another spritz of rose water and then the three ladies—I suppose I must call them ladies, girlish as they are, since each has more than ten years on me—adopt a posture of attention, brimming with anticipation.

Of what?

"Kiss their fingers," Lady Medeiros hisses at me.

This I remember. A Queenly tradition for more than just the *lever*. I step forward and offer each lady my hands, palms up. They place their fingertips in mine and I raise their fingers to my lips and kiss them quickly, and as I release them, each woman drops into a deep curtsy, her skirts a perfect circle around her.

They stay low, their heads bowed, until I kiss Lady Medeiros's hands and she joins them in their subservient position. As soon as she does, the room bursts into applause, and it's all I can do not to flinch away from the din.

Without so much as glancing at their audience, the ladies rise and file out the back door—the very one through which the infamous Marie-Antoinette made her fabled escape, so many centuries ago. I'm not sure what exactly I'm supposed to do, but in a fit of improvisation, I follow them.

As soon as the door closes behind us, the false smiles are gone and Lady Medeiros heaves a sigh of relief, rubbing at her fingers. "We all expect double pay for that circus."

"My thanks" is all I manage in reply, but I know she hears the acquiescence in my voice. I have no idea how difficult it will be to wrangle extra credits from the King, who has given me exactly enough control over my finances to maximize his convenience and my dependence, but I'll probably manage.

Satisfied, my erstwhile attendants traipse away, down to the less-gawked-at lower level of the palace where they all, no doubt, reside.

"You were worth triple," I whisper once they've gone.

TWELVE

IT WAS ONE tiny clause that France had hoped to use to revoke the sale of the Palace of Versailles and its grounds when the true identity of the Haroldson Historical Society was revealed. I once looked up the exact wording in the archives; France's contract had included an obligation to "restore, maintain, and display the Palace of Versailles as a museum of the French Baroque." The archives included a formal letter from France insisting that the newly installed King of Sonoman-Versailles fulfill the contractual obligation or return the property.

King Kevin Wyndham, the great-grandfather of my current *fiancé*, replied that of course they would be displaying the palace. "Why," he wrote in flourish-heavy script, "would I spend billions to renovate a historical landmark if I had no intention of showing it off?"

Thus we have our Wednesdays.

One day a week, the Palace of Versailles is open to the public. Meaning that we, the palace's regular inhabitants, are also open to the public.

Not our private apartments. Well, not the typical citizens' private apartments. As I've been so rudely reminded, the suites of the King and Queen—or not-yet-the-Queen, in my case—are fair game. We're separated from the masses by velvet ropes and are welcome to ignore or indulge their attentions at will. But we must be appropriately garbed, eschew uncamouflaged electronic devices, and speak French.

France tried to argue that one day a week wasn't sufficient display, but the original King Wyndham had already tripled the number of viewable rooms and added to them period dress, with reenactments of such cultural events as the *levers*. This, he argued, far outstripped any previous restoration efforts and should absolutely count as a *display*. And his enthusiasm spoke for itself. After a complimentary day at the palace, an afternoon exploring every corner of the restored *Grand Trianon,* and a sumptuous feast and formal ball in the Hall of Mirrors, the judge ruled in Sonoma's favor. I suppose not all bribery need be subtle.

Wednesdays always infect me with an acute case of cabin fever. Except for the more famous walks through the palace gardens, most of the extensive grounds are off-limits to tourists. So for as many Wednesdays as I've lived in the palace, weather permitting, I've retreated to the outdoors as soon as possible. I'm rather a keen shot at croquet as a result.

Today, my first Wednesday as Queen, everyone apparently wants to be seen speaking to me, so each time I try to get out of doors, I'm waylaid. I pride myself on a fairly slow-burning temper, but by the time afternoon rolls around, my fuse has grown quite short. Molli has been kind enough to stay by my side, but she can hardly keep others from me. A baroness I don't dare offend has been yammering at me for almost a quarter of an hour with naught but the occasional nod to spur her on, when I sense more than see someone turning in my direction at the end of the hallway.

And nearly sputter in panic.

Saber, cloaked—wearing a feathered cap, even—strolling down the corridor as though he belongs. I can't tear my eyes from him and am certain that everyone else is the same. Likely all the tourists who buzz around us as well.

"Baroness Sunderly, I'm so sorry," I say, cutting her off and not even turning my head in a pretense of looking at her. "It appears I'm needed. By the King," I add, invoking the almighty *K* word to shut her up. I pull my arm away from Molli even as her fingers grasp at me.

I pivot on my heel, my silk skirts flaring in a circle, and walk as quickly as possible toward him. His expression is amused as I approach, and I can hardly believe he's nearly smirking over this utter catastrophe. As I draw near, my arm darts out and I grab his shoulder and turn him about to walk beside me. "What the hell are you doing here?"

But rather than answer, he twists away from my hand, stands in front of me, and executes a courtly bow, with his hand outstretched, a trifolded, sealed parchment in his fingers.

I'm so stunned by this gesture—commonplace in the palace—that for a moment I forget what to do. Tiny beads of sweat are forming on my brow, and I can hear my heartbeat in my ears, deafening me to the noise surrounding us. Instinct plays its part, and my fingers reach out of their own accord to take the parchment. For just a moment he resists, and when I tug harder he whispers, "Calm down," in a tone that somehow simultaneously both demands I do so and puts me oddly at ease. Which I certainly need; I've already said too much while wearing my Lens.

I look down at the seal. Not only do I not recognize it, but it looks . . . fake. I break it anyway and open the parchment.

Take me someplace we can talk. S.

A note from Saber. My cheeks flush hot in sheer pleasure, and the flutters in my heart are for an entirely different reason now. I call myself an idiot in my head in four different languages as I fold the parchment again. "For my father, of course," I improvise. "Right this way, *monsieur*."

I turn and collide with Molli, who must have been standing directly behind me. I haven't committed such a clumsy act in at least a year. I've got to regain control.

"I'll be right back," I mutter to Molli. "Business for my father." I expect her to be staring at Saber with the same rapt fascination I did upon our first meeting, but she scarcely acknowledges his existence, just looks at me oddly.

"Cover for me?" I whisper, though the request barely makes sense. It'll keep her here while I deal with Saber; that's all I need.

I blink rapidly, trying to locate my mother and hoping she isn't in the family quarters. Thankfully, my Lens tells me she's decided to head to the great luncheon that's laid out every Wednesday to make up for the loss of serving-bots to bring meals to individual quarters. My stomach growls at that thought—I missed breakfast, thanks to the great *lever débâcle*.

I steal glances back at Saber as we stroll down the north hall-way. He was deliciously gorgeous in his otherworld clothing, but since I was raised in Baroque culture, our style is apparently my preferred mode of dress even for non-Sonoman citizens. What was masculine and appealing is now devastating and magnetic. His breeches cling to lean thighs as he walks, and his fitted waist-coat highlights the subtle triangle from hips to shoulders. I can't make myself look higher than his neck when my cheeks still feel so flushed, but I can feel his eyes boring into my back and can quite easily imagine the light green surrounded by dark lashes.

Within minutes we enter my father's study, and I'm surprised to find my father upright and fairly alert. Saber nods politely but says nothing, and I favor my father with my best smile. "Might we borrow your study for a few moments? Alone," I add when he doesn't stir.

My father looks at Saber for a long moment but silently acqui-esces and treads down the narrow hallway to his bedroom.

"You're going to use this as your safe room?" Saber asks before I can turn fully back to him.

I hold up a hand and hurry to the bathroom to pop out my Lens. "Always better to be cautious," I say, coming back and dab-bing at my cheek with a handkerchief. "But we should hurry. I'll have no warning of my mother's return now."

Saber nods. "Reginald thinks your idea is brilliant."

"Truly?" I ask, warmth spreading through me both at the compliment and at the gentle roll of Saber's voice.

"He suggests an oil-based cake-type makeup and sends word that powder won't work."

Ignoring the odd sensation of discussing cosmetics with a man, I simply nod. "We can do a cake foundation, a rub-on rouge, and lip gloss, then."

"You're sure you want so many types?"

I nod. "Variety is important. It must seem exclusive without being boring."

He only shrugs in response. He removes a piece of paper from his pocket, and I draw near as we discuss the profit margins for the bases, the price of the Glitter, and a few branding suggestions. "This room should be perfect for blending," Saber says, looking around. "I'll bring you a mini–inversion plate that can accommodate a 250-milliliter beaker, which is all you should need, and—"

"No, stop," I interrupt. "You can't possibly intend for me to create the cosmetics here. I'm not a scientist."

But Saber's already shaking his head. "Simple mixing, I assure you. It can barely be called cooking, much less science. The bases melt easily; you add the Glitter, pour it into miniature pots, done."

"Why can't Reginald send me completed product?"

"Cut your profits in half, for starters," Sabers drawls, as though he understands how important the money is to me and despises me for it. The sting I feel at his disapproval hurts more than it ought, and I try to swallow it back. "Reginald's actually giving you a significant discount to hide what he's doing from his regular Glitter people. He doesn't want anyone else to know about this new method of distribution just yet. Also, he thinks it'd be easier to send supplies into the palace on your person; you're way less likely to be searched than a large, mysterious package."

I knit my brows and look around the room. "You're certain I can manage this?"

"Trust me," he says, reaching into his pocket and removing a tiny black canister with a dab of sparkling red paste about the size of a euro coin inside. He flips it through the air to me. It looks like a fancy sample from a high-end cosmetics company. "Reginald's had me testing all night."

I look up at him now, and only once I'm consciously looking do I see signs of weariness in his face. "I'm sorry I was the cause of your suddenly working so much overtime," I say, very much meaning it. I only got the missive off to Reginald via courier at eight o'clock last night. He and Saber must have been working ever since.

"It's what I do," Saber says, but he won't meet my eyes. Perhaps sleep-deprived grumpiness is the reason for his cold treatment of me. But then, what was his excuse before?

"This is perfect," I say, looking at the cute little pot. "It's tiny and looks quite exclusive."

"If you can come up with a name, Reginald will have labels made."

"Can't we just call it Glitter?"

"But that's what it's called on the street."

"Still, it's such an innocuous word. And in a completely different form from the patches Reginald peddles. No one would note the correlation. Besides, it would prevent me from slipping up in conversation."

Saber just shrugs. "I'll check it with Reginald. I think that's everything." He looks down at his list. "You should go so that this meeting looks as though it were between your father and me. Send word when you're ready to meet in Paris again to pick up supplies." He turns his back, fully dismissing me, and I try not to feel rejected.

Now my work truly begins.

THIRTEEN

AFTER SEVERAL HOURS' contemplation, I choose red.

Once I've determined the color, the rest follows easily: a gown from Marie-Antoinette's personal fashion book, crimson lips, ruby ribbons in my hair. I'll twine them up in the back, with cascading curls in front that bounce by my face and flirt with the bare skin above my *décolletage*—early seventeenth-century hair, a *faux pas* to pair with a dress from the other end of the Baroque (doubly so on a Wednesday), but only slightly more daring than the monochrome ensemble I have in mind. A single color for a single purpose: tonight I must strain propriety.

Assuming I can find a way to get myself dressed at all.

When I get back to the Queen's Bedchamber after a long walk to calm my nerves, it still hosts a milling crowd—if smaller than the one that greeted me upon waking.

A crowd, and no bots.

No bots to fetch a plate of *charcuterie* to make up for my missed luncheon. After my missed breakfast. No bots to remove my hat, cloak, and satin-laced shoes. No bots to assist me with my evening finery.

Even knowing exactly what I intend to wear, I spend as much

time as I can laying it out, then applying my intricate makeup, until at last I'm reduced to spending a quarter hour in graceful stillness, a statue by the post of my bed, wondering how in the world I'm to prepare myself for the formal ball. And in only an hour.

I can't even unfasten my walking dress without a second set of hands. And I can't com someone for assistance. Molli volunteers for the overtime-pay role of guide duty on Wednesday afternoons. Pretty young girls are practically Sonoma's corporate mascots these days, to the point that the bust of Demeter in the company logo has on occasion been satirically recast as Persephone. If the commentators only knew. Lady Mei spends most Wednesdays in the women's center at the *Hameau de la Reine,* presumably at her father's behest, though she might be making a permanent place for herself there. Lord Aaron, who could almost certainly arrange a dresser for me, has either left Versailles on business or, in a fit of angst, hidden himself from M.A.R.I.E.—and, therefore, everyone else. I'll go naked before begging Lady Medeiros's help twice in one day, and anyway, she's surely enmeshed in her own preparations for the ball. I could raid my parents' apartments for discreet access to some dressing-bots, but all my clothing is in the Queen's Rooms. What am I to do—carry my outfit across the palace like a washerwoman?

The brisk clacking of heels heralds a deliverance in which I can take no joy. Each footfall is heavy, awkward, exactly the way I walked before Giovanni corrected me. So unmistakable is the cadence of my mother's footfalls that I have almost half a minute to camouflage my frustration and panic before she strides through the doors.

Typical Mother: avoiding me for nearly forty-eight hours after consenting to this appalling new living arrangement. If I didn't know her better, I'd say she was afraid to face me. But I'm beginning to understand how she thinks; what she wants is for the move to be fully and irrevocably completed before she has to listen to me beg her to put it back to rights.

Too late, she will say.

Except that she won't say it, because I refuse to complain. Not to her.

The dozen or so people loitering in the Queen's Bedchamber pause to ogle the new addition to what I'm sure they must have found a dull show. Without asking permission or even dropping a curtsy—as much as to say *You're not Queen yet, and don't you forget it*—my mother pushes the golden gate open and strides over to where I'm frozen in my most languid pose.

"You're not dressed," she hisses, taking in my rumpled walking gown and the pieces of my evening finery laid out on the bed.

I'm starving and exhausted, and I hate that she's here and that I'm going to have to confess my helplessness to her. "I'm not certain how I could be," I say with a tight jaw.

"You haven't a dresser?" she says, her eyebrows climbing. Everyone in the room can tell that she's appalled and disappointed in me, after I've been doing such a good job keeping them uninterested—redirecting their focus onto the filigree about the chamber instead of me. It's worse when someone else strips your carefully crafted illusion away. My mother and the King both have that irritating habit.

"In," my mother orders, pointing at the door to the wardrobe behind me and scooping the masses of fabric off the bed. "Go! I will take care of you today. We've no time for a substitute."

Together we pass through the door beside my new bed, into the wardrobe, and I can't decide which is more debasing: having my mother reduced to a dresser, or being so personally desperate as to allow it.

Even so, when she closes the door and instructs me to turn so she can unhook me, I sigh in relief that at least this undressing isn't required to be carried out in the public arena.

"Where are the Society people?" my mother demands. "You'd think those lackwits would be more punctual, seeing as how they really only have to work one day a week as it is. It's no wonder we've mostly replaced them with M.A.R.I.E.'s bots. I've half a mind to buy another block of Amalgamated."

Amalgamated Robotics Inc. manufactures all the bots in Versailles Palace, as well as their central control system, M.A.R.I.E., who even on her ostensible day of rest tirelessly attends to the palace's orderly, if marginally less roboticized, operation. Sonoma Inc. partnered with them sometime before I was born, and whenever someone fails to do my mother's bidding, she blames human frailty and threatens to buy more shares of Amalgamated stock.

"You *did* make an appointment with the Society people, didn't you?" she asks.

I wouldn't even know how. What remains of the Haroldson Historical Society is a small cadre of experts in Baroque culture, art, and fashion. I had no idea they helped the Queen dress.

But then, I've never been Queen on a Wednesday.

My silence is all the answer Mother requires, and she sighs melodramatically. "I can't believe you're so unprepared, Danica."

I doubt there's anything in the world that could make me feel more a child than being berated by my mother as she's dressing me. "Well, *Mother*, perhaps that's because no one bothered to prepare me. I might have managed with a few days' warning, which I happen to know you had."

A blush blossoms on my mother's cheeks. She says nothing, but the fingers pulling the dress from my shoulders aren't gentle. "It wasn't my decision."

And she's correct. Someone has dropped the proverbial ball today, and I continue to suspect that the King himself allowed some of these oversights merely to torment me.

Once I'm unclothed, my mother reaches for the pile of shimmering silk and gasps. "Solid red? You can't wear this."

"I can and I shall."

"I'm not certain how, as I refuse to help you into it," she says, dropping the gown into a heap on the floor.

My temper rises like magma into a volcano, but I refuse to erupt. "Well then. When the King—and the press—ask why I'm attending the ball in a shift and corset, I'll be sure to tell them whose fault it is." I stride smoothly to the wardrobe door, open it just wide enough that the crowd in my bedchamber can't see me, and beckon with a flourish. "You're dismissed, as I'm apparently finished dressing."

My mother stomps over, wrenches the door from my grasp, and slams it shut. "You will obey me, Danica, and you will select more suitable clothing."

"I won't," I say, my shoulders shaking in fury but my voice calm. "What are you going to do—evict me? I am the resident of Sonoman-Versailles's Queen's Rooms. I'll wear what I please, and you'll help me, or the tabloids are going to have an exceptionally happy day."

She mutters something about my willfulness, accompanied by a vaguely unfavorable comparison to Lady Cynthea, but I close my ears to it and simply turn when she tosses the skirt of the satin dress over my head.

It's a gown I had made two years ago; in many ways it's rather sadly out of fashion, to the extent such a thing is possible in the retro-culture of Sonoman-Versailles. But it's striking enough—and the only one I have that's wholly red.

"You should be grateful," my mother says as she fastens hooks and ties laces.

"Grateful for what? Being kicked out of my home?"

"For all of this," she says with an encompassing flutter of her hand. "This engagement. You're going to be Queen, Danica. How can that not please you?" She gives a sharp tug on the back of my dress, and it's all I can do to stay on my feet.

"He's a monster," I hiss. "A sadistic bully who gets sexual pleasure from his lovers' pain and fear. And you sold me to him. Forgive me for failing to feel any debt of gratitude for that."

My mother isn't provoked in the least. "It's not as if we're going to tuck you into your wedding bed and put your sheets on display in the morning, as they used to in these very chambers. You needn't have anything to do with him outside of the public eye."

"Thank you for permission to do exactly as I intended."

I turn back to the full-length mirror, shifting slightly so I can't see her. "You still bound me to him. I'm as blackmailed in all of this as he is."

"But your mother holds all the cards."

"That might be a comfort if I had a mother who cared for me half as much as she cares for herself."

She doesn't reply, but when she reaches the line of hooks down my back, she pauses. "This bodice is too large. We ordered this dress at least a year ago. Longer. I remember I didn't like it then, either. What's going on?"

"Nothing," I snap, then curse myself for losing control, even for that tiny instant. She fumbles at the fastenings, and it takes me a few seconds to realize she's *un*doing them. "Mother, stop," I protest, but her fingers are nimble, and before I know it, the back of the dress is entirely unfastened. I feel her hands circle my tightly laced waist, measuring.

"You're too small. My fingers almost touch. I thought you looked strange *en déshabillé*. What are you doing to yourself?"

I turn, forcing her hands off my corset, wishing suddenly that I could change into one she hasn't touched. "Going through puberty," I say darkly, knowing it's a weak excuse at best. "Unless you'd care to forbid that, too." I hadn't realized I'd constricted my waistline quite so far. Didn't want to, if I'm honest with myself. "Look, it doesn't matter. I have a new stomacher that will match. I can wear it over the top and no one will know."

"I'll know."

"No one important will know," I amend, and don't bother to watch for her reaction. I turn to a drawer in my credenza instead, rustling through a few tissue-paper-wrapped items. "Here," I say, holding the embroidered black silk stomacher across my waist while I wait wordlessly for my mother to pull the strings tight in the back. I stand, frozen in place, for nearly a minute before I finally feel her begin to thread the satin ribbons.

I'm not convinced that even the solid black of the adorning piece will work with what I'd hoped would be a completely red canvas, but once all the pieces are put together, I scrutinize myself in the mirror and decide it does. My purpose tonight isn't to scale the heights of fashion. The gown is slim, with smaller *panniers* than usual, drawing attention not to my hips, as a fuller skirt would do, but pulling the eye upward with a triangular bodice. The deep red complements my olive skin and dark brown hair beautifully, and the shiny satin has neither pattern nor excessive trim—nothing to catch the eye.

To match the last-minute stomacher, I add a black lace panel to my low, square neckline so even my shadow of cleavage is less distracting. My makeup features a dark, smoky eye, and I've coated my eyelashes more heavily than usual. Now the crowning detail.

I reach into my satin reticule and pull out small ceramic pot of red lip paint.

With glitter in it.

Not the tiny black pot Saber flipped to me; this contains a fine but simple silver glitter I found in the bottom of my trunk. From a costume at some point, I imagine. I didn't even make too excessive a mess when I mixed it with some shiny red lip gloss an hour ago in my bathroom. Away from the prying eyes of my spectators. It's not perfect—the costume glitter isn't nearly as fine as in

Saber's mixture, so the glossy red paste is a bit gritty as I brush a red curve onto my lower lip. But once I've painted bottom and top, the sparkling effect is rather stunning.

"Perfect," I whisper at the mirror through sticky, coated lips.

"What in the world is that?" my mother asks, glaring at my audacious mouth.

"The next big thing, Mother," I reply, smudging one uneven line. "The next big thing."

FOURTEEN

"PARDONNEZ, EXCELLENCE?" THE French render-
ing of my new title sounds from outside my wardrobe. The minion
His Highness always has flitting around him at formal events is
standing just outside the golden gate that cordons off my personal
space. Matt-something-or-other. At the sight of me, he bursts
out with a high-pitched "Aaah!" and pushes his way through. He
pauses a meter from where I stand and drops into a deep bow,
then continues in French. "Your Grace, His Majesty the King re-
quests your presence."

Odd. "He mustn't worry; I'll join him in time to be announced. The ball doesn't begin for another quarter of an hour."
I wave the man away dismissively and begin buttoning my finely
embroidered gloves without waiting to see if he goes.

"My apologies, Your Grace," the man says, dropping another
subservient bow. He's easily twenty years my senior and certainly
wouldn't be putting on this syrupy display were there not a dozen
wide-eyed tourists soaking in every moment, eyes gleaming un-
naturally as their Lenses subtitle our conversation for those who
don't speak French. "His Highness needs to consult with you before the ball."

I raise an eyebrow and fix the man with my most irritated glare, and it's almost amusing how quickly he begins to quake beneath it. Sometimes an audience is helpful. I tuck that little tidbit away for use in the future.

"H-he was most insistent," the man stammers, and I wonder if my supposed *beloved* hired him because he's so easy to boss about.

This wasn't my plan, but perhaps I can turn it to my benefit. "Help me, then," I say, thrusting out my still-unbuttoned glove. "I cannot leave this room improperly dressed." He almost chokes at the inferior task I've given him, but he can hardly refuse, and soon his nimble fingers have fastened twenty tiny seed-pearl buttons on each arm.

"Lead on," I say sweetly when he drops my left hand.

Murmurs of delight surround me as I glide down the halls of the *salons* in my finery, treading a roped-off path. Wouldn't want any eager tourists to reach out grubby hands and touch my pristine satin gown as I glide by, after all. Judging by their excited whispers, I've impressed them—the Americans especially—but the King will be another matter.

The reedy assistant leads me to the King's Private Office, where His Highness conducts much of his personal business, and closes the double doors behind me. His Royal Highness is sitting at his Chippendale desk, already dressed in a formal coat, with perfectly curled hair. I'm a little shocked to see him holding a small tablet—screens are supposed to be off-limits on Wednesdays, especially in the popular royal quarters. But I remember his comment earlier about the rooms M.A.R.I.E. automatically ceases to record when he enters. Why don't I have a room like that?

"Must we both waste our time?" I ask after he sits silently for the better part of a minute, eyes fixed on the screen.

He looks up as though only now realizing that I'm here, even though I know that can't be true. "What the hell is this?" He angles the screen toward me.

I have to step forward to make out the image, but I freeze in horror. It's a video of *me,* this morning, waking up. And it's worse than I thought. My entire thigh is exposed, and as I stir and begin to wake, I pull the fabric up several centimeters higher. The camera gets a very clear shot of the rounded curve of my . . . *lower* cheek.

A flush works its way across my chest and up my neck, and I hate that His Majesty is seeing this. In a horrifying moment of clarity, I realize that having a hundred random tourists see half of my rear is infinitely preferable to this one man's getting to see it, even secondhand.

"Please tell me you didn't pull such a stunt on purpose." I almost miss the twitch at the side of his mouth. He's amused by this *débâcle!*

"As if I would." My voice sounds calm, and I feel vaguely proud of myself. I'm not sure where I dredged up the will to speak at all.

He stares at me and says nothing for a long moment. When at last he speaks, each word is slow and measured. "It's never easy to tell when something is accidental with you. I can't read you."

I say nothing.

"This is unacceptable," he continues at last, snapping the cover of his tablet closed.

"In the future I will endeavor to control my every motion while sleeping, Justin," I retort.

"Where was your staff?"

"Staff?" I feign ignorance. We may as well both lie.

"Six ladies for the *lever*. It was advertised. We sold premium-price tickets, and believe me, they were not impressed."

"You advertised my first *lever* and yet told me nothing of it?" I arch an eyebrow. What I want to do is shriek at him for his infernal stupidity. Or drive for revenge. Sometimes it's difficult to read him as well.

"Your mother didn't inform you?"

"My mother wasn't the one selling tickets, was she?"

"I thought every little girl in Sonoman-Versailles dreamed of being part of the *lever* one day."

"Considering I wasn't noble enough to reside in the palace as a little girl, I wouldn't know."

"You didn't have big dreams?" he says, his voice soft, dangerous with its vague lilt of seduction.

"Not of being in this hellish position."

He rises and pushes the lapels of his elaborate coat back, baring a similarly exquisite waistcoat, and fists his hands against his hips. There's no subtlety or nuance in his sarcasm. "It is indeed difficult to imagine a greater hardship than being Queen of the wealthiest pocket sovereignty in the entire world."

"I meant being married to you."

The only sound in the room is his heavy breathing. He leans forward, his knuckles white on his desk, and I can practically hear his mind shouting at him to lash back.

But he can't fight truth.

"Get a staff," he says very quietly. "It's a well-paid position, with a side of prestige. M.A.R.I.E. has a full training program. We'll be selling premium tickets again next week, and a full *lever* will be expected. *Sans* the peep show this time, if you would. *Now* you've been told. Are you happy?"

A bitter laugh rolls from my glittering lips. "Happy? Let's not exaggerate to absurdity."

He slams his hand down on his desk. "I expect a full *lever* next week. That's a royal command. Why the hell do you think I moved you into that room before the wedding?" He looks chagrined at his own admission and toys with the lace at his cuffs, avoiding my eyes. "Too damn many people staring at me. It's the Queen's *lever* that's always been the draw, and ever since my mom died, they've all had nothing better to do than come in and gawk at me."

Of course. This upset to my entire life—both physically and emotionally—came about simply because Justin would rather fewer people witnessed his own rising from what, under other circumstances, would be his private bed. For a moment, I want to feel sorry for him when I recall that he's been performing the King's *lever* since he was barely fifteen. Likely only days after his parents' deaths. But only a moment. "If you had mentioned anything of the sort a few days ago, I feel confident in vowing that I could have risen to the occasion." I want to continue and call him out for creating a problem for the sole purpose of berating me for it, but his odd confession stops me.

He says nothing and avoids my eyes for an uncomfortable stretch. When he speaks at last, he merely says, "Mateus."

The office doors fly open. I swear the man must have been standing with his ear pressed to the door.

"My gloves and sash."

"Yes, Your Highness." The door closes again.

And then we're alone. Truly this time. No one listening at the door. He circles me, like a predator. It's his favorite move, but he's overused it, so it doesn't make me uneasy anymore. It reminds me that he's young, like me, and thinks far more of his sexual prowess than he ought. Like every other teen male at court. In this arena, what truly is the difference between the King and other boys?

"You're a scarlet vision tonight."

I stiffen, not liking the particular connotation he attaches to the word *scarlet*. But I turn, presenting His Majesty with a private viewing of my profile, eyelashes resting against my cheeks. It's time for tonight's work of theater to begin. "You're too kind."

"I'd prefer to be far kinder," he whispers, his mouth close to my ear as he falls for it completely.

I tilt minutely to the side and let my stays dig into my ribs. *You have a job. Forget everything else.* His Majesty studies me with a look that speaks very subtly of consternation before he says, "It's your mouth, isn't it?"

"Excuse me?" I say, widening my eyes.

"Your lipstick—it . . . sparkles."

It's too easy. I reach up toward my lips as though I had forgotten, stilling my fingers just shy of touching the gloss—that would be a mess. "It is pretty, isn't it?"

The silence stretches long as he stares at my mouth, and I force myself to smile. To speak.

"Striking," I press, tilting my head.

Unconsciously he leans toward me, and I can practically hear his heartbeat speed up. It would be fun to toy with him if I weren't playing a game of life and death. "It's lovely," he says.

"It's something I think we should have at court."

"Absolutely," he growls, and draws closer still, bending at first as though inspecting my mouth, but dropping the pretense an instant later as his nose drops near my neck. "Your perfume is exquisite," he breathes.

"Your mother's," I say dryly, hoping the mention of her will cool his ardor.

No luck. He breathes in deeply, and his lips touch the skin just above my *décolletage*, making my spine feel like someone has dropped crushed ice down my back.

The door bursts open; it's His Highness' man, bearing the royal formal ornamentals. I turn away as His Majesty clears his throat and straightens. "Indeed. It's time, isn't it?" he asks, pretending to be entirely unaffected as he takes his short gloves from the silver tray balanced on Mateus's fingertips.

Mateus fusses with the angle of the sash, his hands darting around the King's arms as he pulls on his gloves. Finally His Highness grows annoyed with the fluttering man and shoves him away. Mateus staggers but manages to keep his footing, then scuttles out the door, apologizing all the while.

His final touches completed, His Highness offers me his arm. On Wednesdays I'm now required to enter the grand assembly in the Hall of Mirrors on his arm like a glowing trophy. Not the kind of trophy one wins for completing a challenge; the kind one stuffs and hangs on the wall after killing it. We're announced at the doorway of the hall, and the hundred or so nobles pause and turn, then drop into low bows for our royal sovereign.

And me, since I'm by his side; promoted from scandalous *fiancée* to shiny new almost-Queen.

As the nobles genuflect, I get an unobstructed view of the line of tourists crowded into the roped-off area that runs the entire length of the hall. Our Wednesday-night guests. I've always found it amusing to watch while many of the tourists play a game of "when in Rome," bowing to the monarch of Sonoman-Versailles before straightening and looking around sheepishly. They never seem able to decide whether they're commoners looking upon a king, or patrons viewing an actor.

The truth, of course, is that royalty is and has always been performance art. It was probably William, the second King Wyndham, who understood this best. Wednesday exhibitions of the palace were originally limited to museum-style tours, passive observation of the palace residents, and intermittent ceremonial reenactments. The second King's insight was that our public day could constitute a meaningful revenue stream with the introduction of premium packages. So for a handsome sum, select tourists can attend a *lever* or watch an evening's festivities, among other things. They're even permitted to enjoy the *hors d'oeuvres* as liveried servers walk by with heavily laden silver trays—a job that, of course, would generally be done by half the number of bots.

The hall is packed with bodies. The King manages to lead me to the center of the crowd, where two couples are so quick to make way that they crash into each other, a lady in blue velvet nearly falling on her face. His Majesty, of course, notices nothing as he turns me to face him, gripping my fingertips possessively all the while. I'm scarcely aware of the music as we dance and he spins me to the outside of the circle, as if to put me between himself and our adoring public.

Hiding behind a lady smaller than him. Typical.

It's amusing to see in the tourists' midst a few men in evening coats, women with low-cut gowns of cheap cotton borne up by lumpy, uneven *panniers* and sparse powdered wigs fashioned into *pompadours* balanced precariously atop their heads. I suppose to them the resemblance is at least passing, but no woman in all of Sonoman-Versailles would be caught wearing so much as a shift of such shoddy tailoring.

I'm forced to wonder if this is what we look like to them. Can they not tell the difference? Judging from what I've observed, both in person and online, *quality* doesn't seem to be very important in the rest of the world. I know the words for their clothing: T-shirts, jeans, shorts, polos. I'm not fascinated with the fashions of the rest of the world like some of the ladies are—but we have the Internet. We're aware that we're different. But I love our fashions, our culture. Always have. If I succeed in my task—if I can meet Reginald's price—will I ever be able to dress properly again? A small enough price to pay for my liberty and my life, I suppose, but given my limited range of experience, will my own attempts to dress like them prove as absurd as their attempts to dress like me?

The music ends, and I drop a low bow to his Royal Highness, but before I can walk away, he clamps my fingertips in a bruising grip and gestures to the musicians to play another. Two dances, three. A fourth starts, and still he doesn't let me go. I can't simply decide to leave without making a scene, but if he tries for a fifth, I may be forced to beg use of the privy to get away. I'm working hard to gain his approval tonight—I want everyone here to be aware that he desires me—but sometimes my own level of success can be frustrating. *I made this happen because it's what I wanted to happen,* I remind myself. *I'm finally doing something, and it's going to help me sell Glitter.*

Finally His Majesty leads me off the dance floor and spends too long raising my hands to his lips in front of the gathered nobles, who give a soft patter of applause at his show of gentlemanly affection. Part of it—a goodly part—is simply that: a show. But some of it's real. I flirt and toy with him, and he's too simple to do anything but fall for it. Somehow, he's convinced himself that the girl who watched him murder in cold blood could actually want him.

FIFTEEN

"I THOUGHT HE had you in his nasty clutches and was never going to let you go."

Lord Aaron's barely jesting comment rings as he and Molli swoop in from both sides, rather like birds of prey. I take his arm on one side and Molli twines our elbows into a friendly link on the other; momentarily, I savor the illusion of protection.

"You look quite lovely," Molli says lightly. "Is the gown new?"

"No," I laugh, "old. In fact my mother almost refused to fasten me into it, it's so far expired."

"What's old is new, darling," Lord Aaron says with a half-grin. "Who in the entire world should understand that better than us?"

I laugh again, a sound carefully practiced to be pleasant to the ear without truly drawing attention. It took ages to learn. "No, no," Giovanni would say when I practiced. "You're not a serving wench. You are a secretive siren." I always thought his emphasis was on *siren*. Foolish young me.

"I have grand news," I say, pulling Molli and Lord Aaron along with me as I stroll down the Hall of Mirrors, red satin train trailing on the ground behind me. "For all the tradition and protocol he's broken in the process, His Royal Highness has indeed given me the Queen's Rooms. All of them. So I've decided to have a tea party in the *Salle du Sacre*."

Even if I weren't expected to hold some kind of housewarming *fête*, I would want to so the court could stop whispering about it behind hands and fans and gossip about it openly instead. In addition, I'm going to use it to launch my new cosmetics line.

"The Coronation Room?" Lord Aaron asks, eyes big. It is a bold move, but if I'm ever going to meet Reginald's fee, I'm going to have to become accustomed to boldness.

"Indeed."

"What do you have planned for the party?" Molli asks.

It's a reasonable question—one that's about *décor* and food, not illicit-drug-laced cosmetics. "I haven't gotten that far."

"No time like the present," Lord Aaron says, always up for party planning.

"Very well, whom should I invite?" I ask with a grin.

"That depends," Lord Aaron says seriously. "What's the purpose of the tea?"

He would never believe it if I were to tell him the truth—not even him. "To make as many people jealous as possible." Technically true.

"Then put Lady Cynthea at the top of the list," Molli blurts.

"She's already there."

We snicker, our gazes sliding to Lady Cyn, who's posing for the cameras in her admittedly exquisite gown. I'm wondering if she understands the difference between sightseers and paparazzi when she catches us looking and, never one to resist even the most lamentable of challenges, lights up like an LED before excusing herself and stepping toward two of her friends for a brief *tête-à-tête*. The threesome then turn and come at us, Lady Cyn in the lead, her bronze dress making her look rather like the figurehead of a grand ship.

"Molli, Lord Aaron," she says with a smile that shows a deep dimple in one cheek. A quick hesitation. "Danica."

"Cynthea," I say, dropping a curtsy as well as the requisite *Lady*, and suppress a smile at her not-quite-concealed grimace. Lady Cynthea Lefurgey is the daughter of a royal duke—though she'll only become Your Grace if she achieves similar high office for herself. The first time she found it socially expedient to address me as Your Grace, I thought she might choke on her tongue. She can't always get away with it, but she goes out of her way to call me by only my given name as often as humanly possible—to emphasize that in spite of everything, I remain technically untitled.

"You know Lady Nuala and Lady Giselle, yes?"

"Indeed," I say, inclining my head. Daughters of high nobility, of course; nothing but the best for Lady Cyn.

I have to stare hard at them for nearly ten seconds before they exchange glances and drop into shallow curtsies. As Lady Nuala rises, she fakes catching her slipper on her dress quite dreadfully and tips her hands forward so half a glass of wine splashes onto my chest.

The liquid pools between my breasts, surely coating the cylinder of Glitter nestled there, and I can feel the drops working their way downward and sopping into my underclothes. Insult by proxy. I should have seen this coming. Lady Cyn, as my rival, can't be seen stooping so low—decidedly *bourgeoise*—but her friends are another thing entirely.

"Quick, Lord Aaron, a handkerchief. Perhaps we can hide Lady Nuala's error," I hiss, plenty loud enough for the trio to hear me.

A burgeoning smirk freezes on Lady Cyn's face.

"Thank goodness my dress is red, Nuala," I say patronizingly, dropping her title. "How humiliating for it to be known that you staggered so ungracefully. Not to mention ruining my gown. I know poise has always been a challenge for you."

I blot the handkerchief across my skin, but it's Lady Nuala's face that's flushing. There must be a clumsy moment in her past of which I am unaware.

"Allowances must be made for the stress of our Wednesdays. Besides, I do so respect your mother, the countess." I could not for my life have come up with the name of Lady Nuala's mother, but somehow my memory serves up her rank.

Lady Nuala stammers an apology, and when I turn to get Lord Aaron's confirmation that the stain isn't visible, I see her shoot an angry glare at Lady Cyn. "Come," I say, tucking Lady Nuala's arm into my elbow while gesturing for Lord Aaron to join our chain on Molli's other side, "Let's stroll for a bit, and no one will be any the wiser."

I lead off, and our walking four abreast leaves Lady Cyn and Lady Giselle no choice but to follow us like sad hangers-on.

When Lady Cyn finally speaks, she has to pipe up from behind me. "I hear your circumstances have improved of late. Much good may it do you. The bedroom of Marie-Antoinette herself. Tell me," she says, getting just close enough that I can hear her but no one outside our group can, "do you think the woman is spinning in her grave to have a commoner sleeping in her bed?"

My move to the Queen's Rooms must have been a blow, but Lady Cyn won't accept anything as permanent until the ink of our duly notarized signatures has dried on the marriage contract. So she's waging a war to push me off a throne I've yet to sit on, and to set her own backside there instead.

She's welcome to it.

I pause and turn halfway so I can look at her over my shoulder, holding her friend tightly in place at my side. "I like to think she'd be happy that her place is being filled by someone deserving," I reply. "It could so easily have gone another way."

I watch with satisfaction when two pink circles show on Lady Cyn's cheeks, though her expression remains fixed.

It's become a bit of a court-wide joke how obviously Lady Cyn is throwing herself at the King—aiming to get him to break his betrothal. But beyond their very public trysting—which she's certain must be such an embarrassment to me—she's no closer to the throne than she was the night the King and I were bound by blood.

"But since you mention it"—I continue walking and force Lady Cyn to keep up if she wants to hear—"Molli and I were just discussing my upcoming social. I'm hosting a tea party next week to warm my new quarters. Yours was the first name we thought of, of course."

"Of course," Lady Cyn echoes. Because who in the world would not want her at their party?

I can feel Molli's arm—still linked with mine—trembling as she holds back laughter.

"Send me a com with the details. I'll see if I can fit it in."

Meaning she'll clear her entire schedule if need be.

I spin and let go of the very uncomfortable Lady Nuala so I can face the group fully. "All three of you, of course." I lean forward and whisper. "Truly, I won't hold tonight's unfortunate mistake against you. I'm not that sort."

Lady Nuala dips another shallow curtsy and murmurs something I can't quite understand. Both Lady Nuala and Lady Giselle were in that group of bullies who surrounded me when Lady Cyn warned me away from the King over a year ago. I don't deny the satisfaction of revenging myself publicly for their cowardly private intimidation.

"You must tell me," Lady Cyn says, and I hear hesitation in her voice, "what this . . . thing is that you're doing here." She gestures vaguely—faking disinterest—at the sparkles on my lips.

"Isn't it glorious?" I say, preening shamelessly. "His Majesty has always been attracted to things that glitter."

"I see. Well, don't worry," she says, her smile hard. "You'll acquire real jewels soon, I'm sure. Wouldn't want our Queen to appear as though she came from nowhere, would we?"

"I don't know about that," I say, scorning her weak verbal assault. "His Majesty was so enraptured by my mouth that he . . . said so specifically."

A well-timed pause is sometimes the sharpest of weapons. Lady Cyn's jaw literally drops, and I congratulate myself on shattering her careful self-control. I bring Molli and Lord Aaron back to my sides as I turn away from their group and make as if to continue our stroll.

After two steps I pause and look back over my shoulder, my companions accommodating me brilliantly, as though we'd planned the encounter to the smallest detail. I tip my head coquettishly. "I've had the lipstick specially made, so the Society people can have no objection. I suspect it will soon be all the rage. I'll have some samples to share at my party—I'm certain you'll want to be in on the latest fashion."

"Of course," Lady Cyn says, her lips thin.

"And we all want to please our King, don't we?"

SIXTEEN

TO CALL ME homely when I was fourteen would have been a compliment. I'd grown so quickly I could scarcely put one foot in front of the other without falling to my knobby knees. Add to that my rather unsightly case of acne and a nose that already strained the word *dignified,* and I was the epitome of the woes of puberty.

I was normal.

Which would have been fine if my father hadn't just inherited his position at court. Suddenly, the possibility of not merely a good marriage, but a grand or even royal one, turned my mother into a person I'd never known. Before my coming out, she took me to several dentists, surgeons, and dermatologists in Paris. She also secretly enrolled me in private lessons with Giovanni di Parma. An instructor of prima ballerinas, he was skeptical but intrigued when my mother approached him to teach me, essentially, *Elegance: The Advanced Course.*

But it ended up being so much more than that. He taught me what my newfound beauty and grace were. And what they weren't.

"These are *your* tools," he said to me one day after I broke down and told him the whole plot. "Your mother can't use them if you do not allow her to. She can force you to appear a certain way, to acquire these graces and skills, but if the desire to entrap this King doesn't come from within, it will provoke a passing base instinct in him, no more."

And he was right. I looked the way my mother expected, carried myself with the grace and poise Giovanni had given me, but though my mother threw me in the King's path at every opportunity, I never endeavored to win him. And he hardly noticed me.

Until that night when he had no choice.

Since then, the false perfection my mother bought me, the trained grace worked into me so strenuously that it appears utterly natural, have become my armor. As the King's affianced, I've been prematurely thrust into an arena of social predators, and it's helpful that, between my height and my carefully learned poise, I do seem older. The truth is that the court of King Wyndham trades mainly in favor, esteem, and beauty. All of which I have in abundance, thanks to my sociopathic mother, who thinks I'm her lever. I hate it as much as I depend on it, and if I'm honest, I often wish I were bucktoothed and awkward again.

It's precisely ten to three when we arrive at a lovely building in the Rue de la Garenne. The words *Giovanni's School of Ballet for Fine Entertainment* are etched, in French, into a marble *façade*, and the sight brings to the surface emotions I've been stifling for months.

A security troll, surely assigned by the King to spy on me, opens the car door and extends a hand. Giovanni himself awaits at the entrance—a lean man with a typical dancer's build, three centimeters shorter than me. He flashes a smile before bowing formally and kissing my gloved fingertips.

I glance at my *chaperon*. "Knock to fetch me back at four. Not a minute sooner, or later." Without waiting for a response, I precede Giovanni into the studio.

Pretense collapses with the closing of the door.

"Darling!" Giovanni cries.

I toss back my veil as he pulls me close, and I squeeze his neck so hard I wonder if I might be hurting him—but I can't make myself let go.

"I've missed you, little faerie," Giovanni says, gripping my hands in his. Despite his having been born and raised in Italy, his English is impeccable—I doubt there's a European language he doesn't speak—but unmistakably accented. He hesitates. "A faerie *Queen* now?" he asks, peering at my face as though he could stare into me. His consideration never fails. Unlike nearly everyone else in the world, he doesn't assume congratulations are in order; he asks.

He's always been that way. He saw through my mother almost immediately. Lessons became a haven of sorts after that. I could confide my troubles, and he'd tell me tales of his days on the road with traveling dance companies. It was a whole other world, there in that little dance studio. Not that the work was easy. Giovanni's not one to slack in his responsibilities, and he demanded perfection. I often went home with aching muscles, only to wake even sorer the following day.

But when my mother asked if I was ready, Giovanni continued to tell her no, even when I was. As a fringe benefit, the extra practice carried me beyond mere proficiency, all the way to the supposedly natural elegance for which I've earned a reputation at court.

It was the least of what he gave me.

I blink furiously against sudden tears, and my Lens responds with the time.

I have five minutes.

"Giovanni, I've come to you because I trust you more than anyone else in this city. No, in the entire world." Sad how true that is.

His soft blue eyes sober. "What can I do for you? Your com was most . . . general," he says with a gentle smile.

"Pretend you're giving me further instruction in grace and poise."

"But you don't need—"

"And do not ask questions when I come to you." I press on before I can lose my nerve.

He pauses. Looks me up and down. I'm in a black *robe à la Piémontaise* today, simply cut. Subtle, if there is such a thing in Baroque fashion. Not severe enough to indicate mourning—not with my daring *décolletage* and dark green satin trim—but plain enough that Giovanni will deduce that I'm attempting to blend in. "How often will you be coming?"

"We'll have a standing weekly appointment on the day of your choosing." And though I know he'd be willing to do it for nothing, I add, "Your standard fee will be deposited, as before."

He nods. His eyes are hooded and I know he wants to press further, but his affection for me holds him back. "Should I be concerned for your safety, *chouchou*?" is all he says.

My smile is calm, but sure and steady. "That need not be your concern."

His expression darkens at my nonanswer, but he doesn't say more.

I decide he deserves something. "I'm not going to be Queen," I say. "Not if I can help it." It'll have to suffice. "Might I make use of your back door?"

He doesn't like it, but I know already that he'll help me. At two minutes of three I slip out the back door of his dance studio. No black sedan is in sight, but with a quick glance down the alley I find Saber waiting, a dark gray coat swathed around his shoulders despite the warmth in the air. He's dressed to draw absolutely no undue attention to himself, and an unembellished black hat sits low on his forehead, shadowing his features. I walk over and stand before him, one eyebrow raised expectantly. "You're taking me to Reginald?"

"Reginald doesn't want to see you."

"But—" I snap my mouth closed, refusing to argue with this man who, I must remind myself, though he's handsome enough to have invaded my dreams every night these past few days, is simply a cog in the machinery of an illegal industry I'm being forced to participate in. A grumpy cog. I don't want his friendship even if he were inclined to offer it. I don't. "He promised me supplies, and he must know I can't simply shuttle down to Paris at his bidding."

"Can't you?" Saber spares me a quick glance, and his eyes freeze me in place not only with their color, but also with their coldness. They're green, a hue I always thought of as warm, but his gaze reminds me of nothing so much as iced *crème de menthe*.

I stand straighter, making full use of my above-average height, and lift my chin so the shadow from my hat covers only my eyes.

"No, I cannot. I'm a lady of the court of Sonoman-Versailles, not to mention affianced of the King. I'm watched and questioned and badgered constantly."

"Then maybe this isn't a great idea," Saber says, his face impassive, his lips barely moving.

I deflate, struggling to cover my dismay at the way this man—a *drug dealer,* for heaven's sake—has seen right through me. I fix him with a stony glare, and he matches it.

But after only a few seconds, he backs down, looks away, and digs through a messenger bag at his hip. So it was a bluff—Reginald hasn't actually empowered Saber to terminate our arrangement. I breathe carefully, my hands shaking at what should have been a minor confrontation. He rattles me as no one else can, not even His Illustrious Majesty.

By the time he holds out a packet wrapped in brown paper, I'm back to myself—my posture erect, my face neutral. But I won't soon forget the way he stripped away my defenses with a handful of words.

"These are empty pots and makeup bases. Now, you listen for a sec," Saber says when I reach for the packet. My hands are clasped on one end and his on the other, one flinch from a tug-of-war. I have to grit my teeth to prevent myself from yanking it away and clasping it safely against my chest. "Pay close attention to dosage—these aren't cupcake sprinkles. Don't get lavish."

"You think I don't know that?" I hiss.

"I'm about to spend an uncomfortably short amount of time instructing you on the tiniest slice of what you *don't* know about Glitter. My lady," he adds when I shoot him a cutting glare.

I don't correct him. The fact that someone from the "real" world offered me a title at all is unusual.

He spends several minutes explaining how each piece works and how to prepare a batch of dosed cosmetics. I listen carefully, even though it is as he said yesterday—as simple as melt and mix. "It's the measurements that are key," he says, handing me a small bit of paper that simply has three sets of ratios on it. Found on the floor, it could refer to anything. Smart. "Prepare it wrong and you'll have all the King's horses and all the King's men on us in a day, and if that happens they *will* trace it back to you. Do you understand me?"

My chin jerks up and down because my mouth is too dry to speak.

"This is everything you'll need for one hundred containers of your cosmetic . . . stuff. I'll bring the same amount next week, and then we'll reevaluate demand."

"That seems reasonable."

He holds out a small black bit of plastic, perhaps ten centimeters square. "Digital scale. Measures in micrograms. Reginald figures you'll want no more than a hundredth part of Glitter in those cosmetics."

"So little?"

"He wasn't kidding when he told you it's strong. Higher doses are exponentially more effective. The difference between a good weekend, a bad weekend, and a funeral can be measured out on the tip of your pinky. Better too little than too much—especially since you can't control how much makeup your friends are going to smear on themselves."

My legs start to tremble at his warning, but I'm busy committing his words to memory, so I don't reply.

He pulls more from his leather bag: a tiny inverter hot plate, a few glass dishes, some glass rods called pipettes. "And this," he says, handing me two tubes of plain lip balm. "Reg says you're making some colorless?"

"For the men," I confirm. "Though some will probably also use the rouge."

He scoffs openly at that. "The men? I thought you were just going to pass it around to the executives' wives while you all sit around and drink tea."

"Oh, gentlemen will be in attendance too. The palace has more than its fair share of kept men." I lean forward, allowing my pushed-up cleavage to show a little, just to throw off his tightly held composure. "You don't think our company has run so smoothly for nearly a hundred years because men were in charge, do you?"

His eyes jump up from my breasts to my face, and it's clear he assumed exactly that.

I straighten, removing my enchantments from his view again with a jolt of satisfaction. "We may emulate the court of the Sun King, but make no mistake: Sonoma is a modern corporation, and its court isn't so backward-thinking as you clearly believe. Many of our men routinely use cosmetics, and even those who don't certainly aren't intimidated by a little sparkle now and then. Are you?"

His cheeks flush, and after clearing his throat, he continues. "Okay, so you have your little party with your friends, you drink tea, you have snacks, and then you pass around the spiked cosmetics. That's your plan?"

He makes it sound ridiculous, and the furor in his green eyes throws me irrationally off-balance. "I'll have you know I've been laying groundwork for this for two days. The court is already—"

He holds up his hands. "I really don't want to know. Just make sure you don't let anyone leave for a good hour after you bring out the cosmetics."

"As though any decent hostess would." My voice is dripping with condescension and I don't even try to hide it. He's exquisitely beautiful, brimming with power and simmering anger, but I certainly wouldn't consult him on the fine art of the luncheon.

"Decent hostess," Saber says with a deep, low laugh. "What you're essentially doing is tricking these women—these *people*—into a serious addiction. I don't think the word *decent* has any place in this conversation."

His bluntness might be refreshing, were he not using it to bludgeon me.

It's not like I have a choice. Telling them what the cosmetics truly are is out of the question. I trust the discretion of my fellow nobles about as far as I trust His Majesty the King. If any of them guess what's really in my special cosmetics, their likely refusal to make future purchases will be the least of my problems. I have to keep the dosage low enough that they don't realize they've been drugged at all—that they just feel good whenever they use the makeup I gave them, so they'll buy more.

This will also maintain a veneer of plausible deniability for me; how was I to know what was in the historically appropriate makeup my supplier sold me? I was as duped as anyone! All the court of Sonoman-Versailles needs to believe is that my secret makeup supplier is the best in the world and my product well worth the outrageous price.

And it's temporary, I remind myself. A few months. Nothing can be so bad for a few months. It's not like this can kill them—look at my father. He's been using for ages.

"Once they put it on their skin, you've got about five minutes before—"

"Euphoria will kick in, yes. I remember from watching my father," I interrupt.

Saber gives me a silent stare, and I'm just starting to think I'm going to have to say something—possibly even *apologize*—to get him going again when he resumes. "You watched your father receive a very high but carefully moderated dose of a substance he's been using for over a month. This'll be different. The reaction of first-timers can vary from a pleasant drowsiness to fits of bliss to manic energy—even at doses low enough that they're unlikely to realize they've been drugged. We almost never start newbies on doses as high as your father."

A prickle of unease travels up my spine. "Why not?"

"Reginald needed him hooked hard and fast, didn't he?"

My entire neck grows warm. There's something wrong here. "Why would—"

Saber's face flushes red, and I realize he's told me something he shouldn't have.

"My father was targeted."

Saber tries to get the conversation back to the supplies, but I'm having none of that.

"This is why my father's the only noble in the palace using Glitter, and also *happens* to be getting it from the only Parisian drug dealer, who *happens* to know that his daughter is trying to escape from Sonoman-Versailles."

When Saber's mouth snaps shut, I know I'm onto the truth. This isn't about my father. This isn't even precisely about Glitter. This is about *me*. Seemingly unimportant words from my conversation with my father sail into my thoughts. About the night he met Reginald.

We talked.

About what?

You, mostly.

Pieces like little bits of a puzzle are coming together in my mind, revealing one brilliant, devastating whole. My father was bait. Getting Glitter into the high-priced world of Sonoman-Versailles was Reginald's aim. Possibly since the moment he realized who I was in the catacombs. "This is a setup."

"I don't know what you're talking about."

"Liar!"

My accusation makes Saber's fidgeting hands still.

"He's been playing an elaborate game of chess with my life." I count off on gloved fingers. "He knew who my father was when he approached him in the tavern. He gave him free merchandise, knowing he would become a regular client, which was bound to attract my notice eventually. And he's too careful for me to put this all down to coincidence. The pieces are lined up precisely where he wants them."

Saber says nothing, which only confirms the veracity of my theory. Reginald would have denied it, but he's not here.

I'm practically speaking to myself now as I verbalize my thoughts even as they form in my head. "He wanted the Sonoman-Versailles market, but he knew I wouldn't give it to him unless I thought it was my own idea. I'm such an idiot."

"Pretty much."

I grit my teeth against a violent retort. It's strange, talking to Saber. He's a minion of some kind—I don't know exactly what his role is—but he acts like he's doing me a huge favor by deigning to even speak with me. Like I'm a rotten fruit he's been assigned to clean up. Not simply like he's better than me, but like there's something wrong with me.

To be treated like a distasteful chore doesn't sit well. Worse, I want to impress him—this silent, moody person. I want to sparkle for him and see his eyes light up when I come around. But he scarcely seems even to see me. His eyes slide away whenever they meet mine, and I know it's not because he's shy. I can tell.

"So, is this little reveal enough to make you pack up shop?" Saber asks, letting his messenger bag fall back to his hip and crossing his arms over his chest.

And I don't have an immediate answer. Is it? Is the fact that Reginald placed this opportunity in front of me a reason not to accept it? I've spent months wracking my brain for an answer, and this is the only one that has suited. Besides, I've already set the stage by parading my faux-Glitter lip gloss about the palace for the last two days, and news of my party is spreading like wildfire through the grapevines of the nobility. It feels like a high-speed rail engine—too much momentum to stop. "No." I mean to declare the word, but it comes out in a whisper.

Saber looks down, hiding his face, but I catch his expression nonetheless. He's disappointed. Which doesn't make sense either. Why does he hold me to such a high standard? Why is he repulsed that I'm enmeshing myself in *his* industry? "Your decision." He removes and unrolls an odd white contraption from his bag and drops to one knee. "If you could lift your skirts."

"Excuse me?" I nearly shriek, pulling my hem back and away from his hands.

But he only looks up at me with impatience. "Should I give you my bag instead? So you can carry your miniature drug lab into the palace on your shoulder?"

Oh. It's some kind of pouch, then, to fasten under my skirts. Still. "I'll do it," I say, holding out my hand for the fabric.

"Oh, so you'd like me to hold your skirts up waist-high so you can reach beneath them with both hands."

My face flames so hot I have trouble drawing breath. He has a point, but admitting that means I must let him . . .

"This is ridiculous," I say, turning my head away and lifting my hem perhaps halfway to my knees. "Watch yourself under there."

His only reply is a snort.

He does a decent job, his gaze decidedly vacant as he reaches under my gown, hands barely skimming my thighs, then carefully securing a Velcro strap about my hips, just below my tight bodice.

It's the work of less than half a minute, but my insides explode with butterflies at each intimate brush of his fingers, and by the time he withdraws his hands, I feel I might very well swoon.

The belt is heavy with my supplies, but they hang balanced on either side of my hips, much like my *panniers,* and so feel almost natural. I step back and forth a few times and admit, "This will be fine, I think."

Saber says nothing else, and I'm turning back toward Giovanni's when he grabs my arm, his fingers digging painfully into my flesh. "If you don't listen, you'll wish you had," he says, and the calm in his voice belies the strength of his grip. But I don't sense anger. More like desperation. He almost looks . . . scared? "You seem to think you're dealing with something that's a happy cross between alcohol and sleeping pills."

I open my mouth to protest, but can't say anything because it's actually a good articulation of precisely what I thought.

"Glitter's going to send them flying because they've never had anything like it before, and they'll be begging for more. As long as you make sure no one gets too much, you should be fine. Remember what I said—it's plenty strong; better too little than too much. If you ever suspect anyone of getting close to the truth, threaten to cut them off. Trust me, losing their fix will be the strongest threat you can make."

Like with my father. I pull at my arm again, hard enough that Saber realizes how tight he's holding on and releases me. I clear my throat and straighten my hat.

"And try to limit them to one container at a time."

"Why? Variety sells." Between lipstick, foundation, and rouge,

I'd rather hoped to sell several doses at once, in the interest of front-loading my income.

But I suppose if they were to apply multiple kinds of Glitter-infused makeup, they'd be taking an instant double or even triple dose. My heart pounds as I realize that Saber has just saved me from a simple, stupid, possibly deadly mistake. It must show on my face, because he relaxes—not entirely, but enough that I notice.

"Looks like maybe I've finally gotten it through that pretty head of yours."

I'm not sure whether to be complimented, insulted, or simply shocked.

"Better too little than too much," he repeats.

I think I nod. He spins away with hardly a sound and turns the corner so gracefully I could believe he vanished into thin air—might even convince myself he'd never been there at all.

SEVENTEEN

I SET MY hands at my tightly bound waist, drawing courage from the deep, stiff curve I find there. My new bot tightened my corset to its preset measurement this morning, and once again, it wasn't enough. We managed another full two centimeters before I felt prepared to tackle this *soirée*.

Everything's ready.

About half of my new gowns were delivered from the royal *modiste* just this morning, so I'm as decorated as the room in an oh-so-innocent pink satin gown with candy-floss feathers sprouting from my *coiffure*. My eyes are fully lined in black—the feminine equivalent of war paint. I've learned, and not only from Lady Mei and her exquisite talents, never to underestimate the power of cosmetics. And isn't that sentiment *apropos* today.

I can't help wishing Saber could see me like this, instead of in the drab getup I've worn to Paris both times. Or the hastily chosen outfit from Wednesday's *lever,* the day he snuck into the palace. I can't seem to banish him from my thoughts—to whittle him down to nothing more than a gear in Reginald's oily engine of crime. The look in his eyes, the way he grabbed my arm so desperately . . .

the more I think about it, the less I can attribute his apparent distaste for me to a simple cultural divide. In fact, I'm beginning to wonder if he simply hates his job—but if so, why continue?

A knock sounds from the doorway and I nearly jump out of my skin, but it's only Lord Aaron and Molli, arriving early at my behest. I'm grateful for the distraction. I don't need moody green eyes on my mind right now.

"Come in, come in," I say, beckoning. I close the door quickly behind them. We have only a few minutes, but I don't want anyone who might be loitering outside to see the elaborate *décor* until I'm ready for the unveiling.

The throne room is draped in white and rose silk with bunches of fresh flowers tied at every *ruche*. Tall crystal candlesticks grace every table, and I ordered the use of the palace's nicest set of tea china. Miniature spoons lean against the edges of twenty-five gold-rimmed teacups, and fine tungsten strainers balance on top.

Lord Aaron takes my hands and air-kisses my cheeks an instant before gushing his appreciation. "It's divine, Danica. You said you were going to outdo yourself, but this is incredible!"

Molli rushes to the tables to observe the tiny delicacies I've ordered, which are *décor* as much as the actual decorations. Delicate cake pops with curlicued swirls of ivory fondant and pale pink buttercream frosting, tiny *macarons* in four shades of pink, two raised platters with hundreds of white-chocolate-drizzled cream puffs in perfect *croquembouches,* a three-tiered tray of miniature cakes with frosting piped to make them look like tiny wrapped gifts in an array of pastels, a veritable mountain of iced marchpane, and a nod to the gentlemen in the form of an oak board filled with ham-heavy *petites quiches,* assorted cheeses, and *charcuterie.*

"I won't be able to eat any of this, Dani. It's too pretty!"

I glide over and lean close to her ear. "I'm assured it tastes twice as good as it looks. I was hoping you two would fill a plate before the rest of the guests arrive," I say. "That way, no one will feel awkward, being the first."

Molli has always loved sweets, and the standoffish look she's giving the confections melts away instantly. "If you insist," she says, feigning reluctance theatrically. Having Molli here makes everything feel better and worse at the same time, and dwelling on that too long only makes my stomach upset.

"I do, but just a moment," I say, taking her hand and pulling her close to Lord Aaron so we stand in a tight triangle. "I have one other favor to ask." I try to sound friendly rather than terse. But terse is how I feel—wound like a spring, ready to pop at the slightest provocation.

As though sensing my distress, Lord Aaron takes one of my hands—bare, as I haven't yet donned my elbow-length gloves—and rubs my fingers for a few seconds, then raises them to his lips and brushes a kiss across my knuckles. "Name it," he says softly.

"Wear some of my new line of cosmetics?"

Lord Aaron raises an eyebrow at that. His clothing is always fine and in exceptional taste, but even in a culture that caters to fops and the effeminate—regardless of their sexual orientation—his makeup, when he wears it at all, is tastefully understated.

"On your lips, or your cheeks. Not too much. I'm assured there's historic precedent," I add, though that's an exaggeration at best. I haven't asked anyone—I'm making assumptions. But if anyone checks up on me, I'll forget who it was who told me it was acceptable.

Fortunately, glitter as an adornment reaches back into prehistory, and brand loyalty is already a feature of the cosmetics trade around Sonoman-Versailles.

"Very well," Lord Aaron says, with a light grin.

"Here," I say, retrieving two special pots from my reticule. One is the lipstick I'll wear for the next few months—the one I wore for the ball last Wednesday. Both are made with costume glitter, not Reginald's narcotic. It wasn't a decision I made lightly. In fact, Lord Aaron is ever the indulgent sort; given the truth, he might well opt to try the real thing. But I can't give it to them, not after seeing my father. Not after Saber's warning. Hopefully, when I pass the spiked cosmetics around, my friends won't feel the need to reapply. I still don't think the small doses I'm giving everyone else could possibly be that harmful, but with these two, I don't want to chance anything.

"Glitter," Lord Aaron says, reading the sticker on the pot I've just handed him. I was pleasantly surprised that Reginald provided a subtle, elegant font for the label. I feared a *gauche*, glitter-enameled name in Comic Sans.

"Fitting, I think," I say with a smile.

A few nights ago, under the pretense of visiting my father, I set everything up in his office. It wasn't very difficult; the inverter hot plate melted the cosmetic bases in less than a minute, and the scale worked beautifully to measure out the tiny doses of Glitter.

So small were the doses that most batches of makeup required additional costume glitter to achieve the right look.

It was odd to look at the little pile of Glitter sitting on the scale. "Better too little than too much," I muttered to myself. Easier said than done. Less than in a spoonful of sugar, such as one might add to a single cup of tea, and it was literally hundreds of doses. The mathematician in me is impressed by the sheer profitability of such a substance.

The most time-consuming part was using the pipettes to carefully transfer a mere two grams of the liquid mixture into fifty empty makeup pots. It seems like such a meager amount, but Saber suggested that the ideal dose to sell is a single week's worth. If anyone would know, he would.

The guilt has set in, sharp and cutting as an actual blade. I truly did consider my endeavor as a matter of simply giving a harmless high to the lords and ladies of the court and fleecing them for the cost. And it will be for only a few months at worst. But Saber's warning, and his disdain, have been holding me back like invisible hands, and though my path is clear, I struggle to move forward.

With a forced smile, I paint Molli's lips the sparkly red that matches mine and let Lord Aaron apply just a touch of glittering rouge to his cheeks at the small mirror by the closed doors. When he tries to hand his back, I suggest, lightly, that they both keep the little pots I've given them.

"You'll be toasted as trendsetters by the end of the week," I say with a wink. "Now shoo, the both of you, and get food." With lips and cheeks ashine, they acquiesce, Molli with an adorable giggle so perfectly happy and innocent it makes my heart twinge.

About a minute after I've commanded M.A.R.I.E. to open the doors, a hovering footman announces Lady Cynthea Lefurgey. It's a delicate balance, being on time without being early, and I'm sadly unsurprised that she strikes it well.

I am surprised, however, that she chose to wear red. Not the best color against her auburn hair, but a gorgeous ensemble clearly designed to outshine my own outdated red dress from the assembly last Wednesday. As lovely as it is, she now clashes rather terribly with the pink *décor*.

"Lady Cyn," I say with my most demure smile. "So very pleased you could attend. And your sister." I drop a perfect curtsy and trust that Lady Cyn will be paying close enough attention to realize I aim my bow only at her sister. Her *younger* sister.

The flush at the top of Lady Cyn's cheeks tells me she noticed.

"Please," I say, gesturing, "give your wrap to one of the bots and help yourself to refreshments."

Lady Cyn says nothing, just turns toward the *chaises* and settees forming a large semicircle around the actual coronation throne I've had dragged forward and draped with white satin and pink bows as my own seat of honor. An eyelash's width from truly over-the-top, but I think it works. Lady Cyn's little sister, who currently outranks me, drops an unnecessary curtsy before scurrying after her horrible sibling. By the time I turn from her retreating back, there's a line of six guests waiting to be greeted.

The younger brides of various board members follow behind Lady Cyn, then a handful of nobles' daughters nearer my age.

There are three other gentlemen—including, of course, Sir Spencer, for Lord Aaron's sake. I'm unsurprised when the two of them bunch together, and I suspect they'll be inseparable for the duration of the *soirée*.

Lady Mei arrives in the middle of the crowd, and I squelch the guilt that sprouts within my chest at the sight of her. I opted against bringing her early with Lord Aaron and Molli—she's just so notoriously indiscreet. I have to draw the line somewhere.

None of this lessens the ache as she blows me a kiss over her lace-clad shoulder and turns to squeal over the miniature *macarons*.

Lady Giselle barely glances at me as she completes her greeting and goes straight to Lady Cyn's side like a magnet, but Lady Nuala pauses to grip my hand. She leans forward and whispers, "I must apologize again for my behavior at the assembly. I know you must have realized what was actually meant to happen."

I raise my eyebrows, insinuating agreement without actually saying anything.

"I considered it later, and you were absolutely right. Even if you had been more embarrassed by my . . . my actions, it would still have reflected badly on me. I should never have agreed to a scheme from which I had nothing to gain." Her face is red, and I don't dare glance at Lady Cyn to see if she's watching us.

"Indeed." I hold her stare but let a firmness slip in. "This isn't the first time you've been so used. I recall another encounter with Lady Cyn."

Lady Nuala's face drains of blood until her cosmetics look garish on her ashen skin as she plainly remembers that awful day. "I should not . . . I should not have—"

"No," I say, gently now, letting her a little off the hook. "Despite a certain lady's opinion, one cannot tell someone's potential by their current court ranking. An enemy can be quite expensive."

"I will remember, Your Grace," she says in a whisper.

"Very wise," I say softly, squeezing her fingers. "A young lady who continues to show such wisdom will always be welcome in my circles." She smiles with naked relief, and I can't help but feel I've made a sort of conquest. I catch Molli's eyes as a shaken Lady Nuala leaves me, and she returns my secret smirk.

Fifteen minutes pass before a soft chime dings through M.A.R.I.E.'s camouflaged speakers, signaling the arrival of all the guests. The doors automatically swing shut, barricading the intimate party inside. We all find our seats, and I beckon to one of the bots to bring in its silver cart, laden with delicate teapots.

"Please eat," I say, gesturing at the lovely food as I take up the hostess role of pouring and distributing the tea.

When everyone has a cup, I glance up at the clock. Half an hour of food and drink. Then I'll bring out the cosmetics. Half an hour to change my mind—to send everyone home after a relatively uneventful tea party with fabulous appetizers.

It would be enough.

I don't have to do this.

My teacup clicks against my saucer, and I tighten my grip to stop my fingers from trembling.

What if I don't? I'll be stuck fending off the perverse sexual appetites of a sadist with no one to hold him in check. My mother assures me knowledge is my best protection; that forewarned is forearmed. But is it truly? Once the vows are spoken, the nuptial contracts signed, I'll be his wife, but that won't be the end of my mother's plotting.

I'll be an adult by that time, of course—I could seek an annulment, or file for divorce, or just say no. I could use the Queen's shares and build an alliance against the King instead of for him. But the moment I refuse to cooperate, I become a loose end. When I first fled Versailles I was afraid, but I didn't yet fully appreciate the complexities of blackmailing so powerful a person. Whatever precautions my mother has put in place, I have no reason to suppose that they will work to my benefit. And once we're married? Then what? How can a murderous King possibly be good for anyone in the kingdom? No one would be safe from that kind of power.

She has a tiger by the tail, but I'm the one staring up at his fangs. This is the only way I can restore myself as mistress of my own fate.

Though I raise my warm teacup to my lips, I don't drink. My stomach is too nervous. Hopefully no one will notice. That's what the food is for—a gourmet distraction. The chatter in the room rises at exactly the time I expect it to. Tummies are full, blood sugar is elevated, and the enjoyable part of the party is beginning.

Now or never.

I tap the edge of a crystal champagne flute with a small sugar spoon and wait patiently for the roomful of guests to turn to me. Once they do, I open my mouth, then freeze, petrified by the reality of what I'm about to do. Damn Saber and his sinister warnings! But my eyes find Molli's smiling face, and somehow I remember to breathe, and like snow melting under the warmth of the sun, I can move again.

"Thank you *so* much for coming today," I say, in the same voice I use for the King. The voice that says nothing in the world could give me more pleasure than being right here, right now, doing exactly what I'm doing.

My lying voice.

"I have one more little treat for everyone. Nothing too extravagant, I'm afraid," I laugh. "But so many of you have been asking me about it that it seemed shamefully impolite to keep it to myself." Apart from Lady Cyn, in fact, no one has mentioned it at all, but perception is reality. "I found a Parisian who imports the most delightful cosmetics—better than anything I've ever used before. And they have such lovely sparkle! Fortunately, glitter goes back forever, so I can wear it whenever I like. Even on Wednesdays."

A titter of polite laughter.

"His Majesty commented the first night I wore it that it was utterly exquisite. With so many of you inquiring, I decided that all of my dearest friends should have a chance to wear it."

My guests express their polite appreciation with a smattering of applause before Lord Aaron speaks over them, formal and ingratiating. "We're unworthy of Your Grace's favor. I'm certain I speak for all here when I say that we're so looking forward to the day you officially take the crown. In this very room."

Bless Lord Aaron for mentioning that little tidbit to anyone thick enough not to understand the significance of our setting. "Thank you, Lord Aaron," I say, grinning widely, feeling more false than ever. "But I see my gift comes too late—it would appear that you've already ferreted out my supplier!"

Lord Aaron laughs and then preens dramatically, letting the light catch on the glitter adorning his cheekbones. An appreciative breath sounds from Sir Spencer, but he coughs and covers it. It's often obvious that Sir Spencer wasn't raised in the palace; he doesn't guard his expressions as we've all been scrupulously taught. In truth, it's rather refreshing.

A few of the assembled have noticed Molli's sparkles now too, and she's receiving a number of approving smiles. Amazing how easy it is to get people to think something by simply assuring them that it's something they already think.

I reach into a cleverly designed pocket at the top of my *panniers* and remove several Glittered containers of lip color, cake foundation, and rouge, including some colorless gloss for my more conservative guests. The guilt washes over me again as I hand one of those to Lord Aaron's love, but I remind myself that perhaps with a bit of loosening up, Sir Spencer would be willing to . . . dally with Aaron a bit more. As they both so desperately desire. Perhaps . . .

Focus.

I hold up the container, label forward, and say, "It is, of course, aptly named, and my supplier has given me exclusive rights to distribute this line." Another smattering of applause, and I incline my head graciously.

Lady Cyn looks at her gift with skepticism, but I lean forward as though confiding in her and say, "You truly should indulge, Lady Cynthea. It's utterly magical. His Highness is such an admirer." Her lips tighten, but she removes her glove and dips a finger before passing it to her sister. That look assuages my guilt at least on one person's behalf.

The deed done, I spend the rest of the party on tenterhooks, half expecting someone to faint into a puddle of bliss. But of course not all of them have even applied my little gift, and I made certain the dose was low. Are they laughing more loudly than usual? Is their behavior more relaxed, friendlier? Are any of them experiencing *euphoria*?

In the end, no one slumps to the floor in mindless ecstasy, or even succumbs to an uncontrollable fit of the giggles. On their way out, several do thank me for the lovely event, declaring it an unmitigated success.

Only when Lady Cyn's sister sends me a com the next morning, asking if she can order directly through me, do I tentatively agree.

PART TWO

THE PRICE OF FRIENDSHIP

PART TWO

EIGHTEEN
TWO MONTHS LATER

"LADY CHEN WOULD like to sample the rouge this week," Mademoiselle Olivier says as she brushes a dab of sparkling blush on my own cheeks.

"Certainly," I reply, tilting my head so she can reach the other side.

"She's also requested that her friend Lady Ebele Sesay receive a pot of gloss, as a gift. Paid in advance."

I let myself smile a little. New client. I don't even keep track anymore. This week I shattered my previous record, moving just shy of seven hundred units of Glitter. I can't be bothered to count individual customers. "Tamae, make a note—let's gift-wrap that one and have it delivered," I say to a different young lady, sitting just off to the side. Extra effort, but Lady Chen is one of my best customers—adding sometimes five new names in a week—so I'll do it for her.

It's my Wednesday *lever,* and I'm surrounded by six ladies chosen specifically to help me run my new business. Tamae's ballpoint quill scratches out the order on a decorative scroll of parchment I keep in my room especially for this purpose. As we discuss the cosmetics going on my face, we're also cataloging the product going out the door, all without a single tourist any the wiser.

Even though I'd run the figures in my head, I hadn't really understood how difficult it was going to be to satisfy the number of nobles necessary to make the profits I require. The first few weeks were easy enough; orders trickled in for three days after the party, until nearly every attendee had ordered something. It took three weeks to move my first hundred units of Glitter, but then word of mouth began snowballing. I'd estimated that each customer would need one pot a week, but this turned into three, four, sometimes five, not because they were overindulging, but because they were sharing.

Despite Saber's repeated warnings each and every Thursday, after the first month I had to stop trying to regulate how many units each person received. I simply let them have what they wanted and reminded them sternly how exceptionally *gauche* it would be to wear more than one type of Glitter at a time. In fact, at one of the Wednesday-night assemblies, Lady Neema Gueye approached me gleefully sporting both the lip gloss and the rouge, and I made a haughty comment about overindulgence and gave her the cut direct.

No one has done it since.

What more can I do?

Last week was an incredible milestone—I banked my first million euros. It took eight weeks to reach twenty percent of my goal, but my *clientèle* continues to grow exponentially, and if present trends continue, I expect to meet Reginald's price in six to seven weeks.

And I have nine. Nine weeks until I turn eighteen and my mother forces the marriage.

Unfortunately, last week I also had to put up my white flag of surrender and ask Reginald for help.

Visiting my father once and even twice a week to prepare the cosmetics was perfectly acceptable at first. No one noticed a thing. But once I crossed two hundred units, I had to go more frequently. I've gotten better at concealing my movements from M.A.R.I.E., so I can make unscheduled trips without the court making note, but last week I was in Father's rooms into the early hours every night and spent my days in a bleary stupor.

Unacceptable.

I expected Reginald to be angry at the note I sent him demanding help, but the following Thursday he showed up at Giovanni's—the first time I'd caught sight of him in weeks—rubbing his hands with glee as I told him what sort of assistance I needed.

"Tell your lordship husband—"

"Affianced," I corrected him instantly.

"Him, too. Tell him you'll be needing a secretary. I'll send you an assistant. You find a way for him to come and go, place to sleep, make sure you feed him, and he'll take over prepping the product and fetching deliveries."

I nearly crumpled in relief. "At what price?" I asked, raising one eyebrow. Reginald always has a price.

"Call it a company perk," he said with a grin that almost looked friendly. "You're moving more product; I'm making more money. One man won't cost me hardly anything."

"You're too kind," I said flatly, my teeth clenched together.

But a gift is a gift, and it's refreshing to know that tonight is the last night I'll have to sneak to my father's room to prepare tiny pots of Glitter, the finest makeup in Sonoman-Versailles. Just ask anyone; the occasional off-brands that enterprising imitators have attempted to hawk just don't go on as smoothly, don't wear as comfortably as the name-brand product from my secret Parisian supplier. At least, that's what my customers tell themselves—and others—when cheaper alternatives somehow fail to . . . satisfy.

The ladies finish up the motions of the *lever,* the crowd applauds, and finally we can make our exit into the dressing room behind my very public bedroom. "Thank you, ladies," I say. "Does anyone have money for me?"

This part we can't do in front of the crowd. *Pannier* pockets open and my staff begin handing me stacks of euros, which I'll count, organize, and bind later. I collect money only on Wednesdays, due to the lessened computerized surveillance, but everyone knows they can give their fee to any of these six ladies to receive their cosmetics on any day.

"Your supplier must be happy with you," Lady Nuala says as the stack in my hands grows. I have to dump it rather unceremoniously onto my dressing table lest I drop it on the floor. I took a risk deciding to hire Lady Nuala for my *lever* team less than a week after our . . . incident with the wine, but she's proved to be a very loyal traitor. Flattery goes far with her. "Has he ever said why he won't sell Glitter over the feeds? It seems to me that courier delivery could triple his business overnight."

"Oh, everything has to be an art project with Parisians these days," I say, holding my voice steady. "Give them *avant-garde* or give them death. I think his angle is 'makeup so fine, you have to buy it from a Queen.' Although," I say heavily, lifting a gloved hand to my forehead, "it's becoming most fatiguing. I suspect I'll have to bow out soon."

"Surely once you're wed," chimes in Lady Cardozo, the one married woman I brought onto my team. "You'll have other things to do."

"Indeed," I say, drawing my fan up to my face as though covering a pleased blush.

"Then your supplier will have to sell directly." The hope in Lady Cardozo's voice is cringe-worthy.

"Likely," I demur, grasping about for a new subject. "Oh! For you all."

Though it rather pinches to do so, I buy both the services and the secrecy of my ladies—on top of the wage M.A.R.I.E. pays them—with one free pot of Glitter each Wednesday. It's hard to see three thousand euros' worth of product walk away from me in pastel silks every week, but I know the ladies are generous with it, and I'm certain they attract more customers than I sacrifice in profits. Surely.

Regardless, I need them. And one must pay one's employees.

As they leave, the adrenaline that always comes with the *lever*, as well as the rush of doing business, drains from me and loneliness envelops me. Not for the first time I wish Molli were on my staff. And I know Molli wishes she were as well. It's a position with both a high wage and high prestige—two things Molli stands in need of. I didn't ask her; I couldn't, once I realized it was the best way to conduct my business under the King's nose. And I want Molli to have nothing to do with this whole affair. But it's driven a wedge into our friendship. Not a big wedge—neither of us would allow that to happen. But it's a small wedge, and like a tiny splinter, it agitates, stinging a bit more each time it's jostled.

I stroll down the hallways of the palace toward my family's dwelling, not acknowledging the tourists but keeping my pace leisurely so that they can take their damned pictures and intone softly about my gown. A brief consultation with my Lens confirms that my mother isn't inside—she almost never is—and I let myself in, ignoring the disappointed mumbles of the crowd as I close the thick door behind me.

I quickly rid myself of my Lens and head to my father's study. I don't bother to knock or call out to my father. He's accustomed to my walking in, and I'm accustomed to finding him blissed out on the floor.

Today, however, he nearly bowls me over in his haste to get down the hallway.

"Gracious, Father, I am breakable," I mutter, righting myself even as I put both hands to his shoulders to hold him steady.

"Do you have it?"

"Have it?"

He doesn't speak, but his eyes widen meaningfully. A growl builds in my throat, but I censor it—even here, in the sanctity of a room in which M.A.R.I.E. is blind and deaf to its occupants. "Father," I say, my tone brusque as I turn away from him to place my reticule on his desk, "it's not Thursday."

"What?"

"I'll have your patches tomorrow. It's Wednesday, and I've not seen your criminal man." I continue to call Reginald—I suppose it might have been Saber, technically—that silly name and act as though I have nothing to do with him. If my father were to discover that the makeup I'm preparing in his office has his beloved Glitter in it . . . well, that would be most unfortunate.

I was here at four this morning finishing up an enormous batch of scarlet lip gloss, and the tiny pots are arranged in a perfect ten-by-twenty grid across a sideboard that runs the length of the wall. They're set now and look perfect, their shiny surfaces smooth but dotted with the faint sparkle of additives both narcotic and benign.

"But I'm out," my father protests as I begin screwing lids onto the round pots, then immediately flipping them over to hide the little stickers declaring them to be Glitter.

"Then you've miscounted your patches. Or perhaps," I add in an undertone, "you've been miscounting the hours in the day."

"I only need one more. That'll spell me."

Frustration edges out the guilt. "You speak as though I have any," I snap. "I don't. I acquire them on my trip to Paris every Thursday, and I give every single one to you." I open up the pockets on each side of my dress and begin filling one side with the new pots of gloss. The other I'll stock with rouge I made two nights ago, currently locked in a desk drawer.

I'm rather proud of my little innovation. The hip satchels Saber provided me with are supremely useful for bringing supplies in from Paris each week. But for distribution around the palace, I needed something that wouldn't require me to flash my legs to the court in order to access it.

Small *pannier* pockets are common in court—a simple ribbon-tied closure or cleverly concealed zipper at the top of one's skirts gives access to a drop pocket that descends into the empty cage of each *pannier*. A handy place to carry cosmetics, or a Lens case, or even to stash a small tablet on Wednesdays. But I've taken it a step further. With the assistance of a seamstress I happened to know would soon be leaving Sonoma's employ, I rigged up a satin lining on all of my *panniers* that allows the entire circular cavern to be utilized. A few snips to the bottom of my existing *pannier* pockets and I can fill the entire cage, on both hips, with product. Or with money.

Though I do have to be careful with my glide. If I allow my hips to swing, I . . . clatter. And the *panniers* are heavy when filled; after I had bruising the first week, I added padding on both of my hips. It's awkward and took a fair bit of getting used to, but I think I carry it off admirably.

Perhaps my new assistant will be able to bear some of the literal weight.

"Dani, please." A childlike tug on my sleeve pulls my attention back to the addict at hand.

"Father," I say, feeling grumpy and sleep-deprived. "I don't have any. I don't know what you expect of me."

He gulps air like he's on the verge of suffocating, but at least he doesn't cry. There's been more than one bout of tears the last few weeks, and it's embarrassing for both of us. He's more like a child than a parent, and shame eats at my insides when I think too hard about the fact that I'm enabling his addiction.

Not that I've been left with any other choice. The fact is, he's one of the people responsible for my circumstances. Natural consequences?

"It's Wednesday?" I know he's asking me, but he looks down

at his hands, wringing them savagely, and it appears more that he's speaking to himself.

"Indeed," I reply, trying not to sound either interested or concerned as I move lip gloss into my *panniers*. Wednesdays are the best day for distribution. I'll likely pass out more than half of the entire week's orders by the end of the assembly tonight. How I used to loathe Wednesdays. Now they're my salvation.

"One more. I could make it on one more. Maybe I have one . . ." His voice trails off as he begins patting his pockets and opening the front of his waistcoat as though a spare forty-euro patch might just, oh, fall out. I hold my anger at bay until he turns to the drawers of his massive desk and begins yanking on the handles of the drawers.

"Father, stop!" My own voice surprises me. I'm so thoroughly trained never to raise my voice. Even the night I watched the King strangle Sierra, I never yelled. Not once.

But this desk is mine now. It's full of product and supplies. It's locked, of course; I confiscated the key ages ago. But my father's been using this desk years longer than I have; who knows if there are tricks for getting around the locks, or to what lengths he'll go in his crazed state?

Damnation. I'll have to do something.

"Father," I say, gently now. "Come with me. I'll help you." I lead him down the hallway toward his bedroom.

"But . . . but—"

"I can help you. Just don't ask," I add, knowing that sometimes no answer is the best answer. I lead him to his bathroom and carefully remove his waistcoat and shirt and run warm water into the sink. He needs a full shower, but that is certainly not my job. Still, I apply foamy soap to a washcloth and help him wash his face and chest.

I wish I had completely altruistic motives, but what I really need is for him to don a new shirt, and I simply can't bear to place one on such a filthy frame. His thin arms are covered with adhesive black marks. The lack of such a thing is a prime benefit of my method of Glitter distribution. Still, I'll have to ask Saber how to get them off. Surely he'll know. Assuming he doesn't fall into a snit and refuse to tell me. He's touchy, that one.

Doesn't stop my heart from racing every time I see him. But touchy.

When my father smells half-human again, I retrieve a fresh linen shirt and loose waistcoat from his armoire and sit him on the edge of his bed. Once he's seated, I look him in the eye. "I'll make you feel better. Do you understand?"

He looks confused but nods.

"You should rest after this. Lie down. I'll return tomorrow, but in the meanwhile you'll fare better if you remain calm."

"Calm," he echoes, and I'm not sure he truly comprehends. But he's docile enough. And I only need twenty-four hours.

Lifting my heavy skirts—made even weightier with over two hundred tiny pots of Glitter—I kneel on the bed behind him, and once I'm completely out of his sight, I reach into my *panniers* and remove a pot of colorless gloss. I start by rubbing his back and am pleased to discover that that does part of my job for me. My father groans as I find masses of knotted muscles in his neck and shoulders, and once my hands are tired and my self-disgust tamped down, I reach for his shirt with one hand and the gloss with the other.

Once the shirt is tossed over his head, I dip a gloved fingertip into the pot, hoping it won't bleed through to my own skin. It'll ruin the glove, but my budget for gloves is exceptionally generous. I absolutely can't risk touching the Glitter. Down that road lie madness and financial devastation.

Saber said my father has been on a particularly high dose. The better to get him addicted quickly and reel in the fish Reginald was actually after: me. I consider whether I could slowly wean him off the Glitter . . . but that would mean coming here every day instead of giving him the patches. And risking him figuring out about the makeup. Not to mention that I don't know what exact dose he's on now and Reginald certainly isn't going to share that information, so I might just mess everything up. *High* is all Saber said, so I'm liberal with the gloss I spread at the back of his neck, where there's no way he can see it.

The glimmer would give it away. He'd know, and then I'd get no peace. Not a moment. Tamping down a sense of horror at what I've just done, I button his shirt so it covers the sticky spot, then gather his long hair into a queue, tied with a black satin ribbon.

"There," I say, slipping off my soiled glove. "You look much better now, and I've no doubt you'll soon feel better as well. Lie down," I add before he can argue. I need him to hold as still as possible so the Glitter can get into his system before he unknowingly wipes it away.

My father looks unconvinced but obeys. I fuss with his blanket and pillows and start a film on the wallscreen that looks like a painting of a tide-bound Mont Saint-Michel until I fiddle with the controls concealed in its frame. Once he's distracted, I grab a clean set of very plain clothing for my new assistant. I don't expect Reginald to be astute enough to consider such details—or perhaps what I expect is for him to be malicious and "accidentally" forget them.

Only when a glassy expression steals into my father's eyes do I feel safe sneaking away, the lump of iron in my heart heavier by far than the product in my skirts.

NINETEEN

"*MON DIEU!*" GIOVANNI exclaims when I reveal this week's stack of euros to be stored in his safe. "*Chouchou*, I must—"

"Please don't ask," I beg. Truly, he's been a paragon of patience. This is only the second time he's tried to query me in the nine weeks since I arrived in his studio after almost a two-year absence. I smile and lay a hand on his shoulder. "I've already lied to one person today—please don't make me do it again."

Molli caught me on the way to the car this morning. I almost told the truth when I said I was going to see Giovanni. She knows about the lessons I used to have with him.

"Can I come?" she asked. "My day is free, and I'm so curious about what you do there."

"It's embarrassing," I said after a long pause.

"But it's just me," she said quietly. And there was an answer to far more than the day's schedule in those words.

I've been keeping her at arm's length the last two months, and she knows it. How could she not know it? My heart wept as I fobbed her off and drove away. She watched my car all the way out the golden gates.

"I'm a liar!" I shouted at the Nav computer when it asked where I wanted to go. "I'm a lying liar who lies."

"I'm sorry," the computer replied. "I didn't get that. Please repeat your destination."

And here's Giovanni, asking me to lie again. I can't. But there's a reason I chose him as my secret-keeper of sorts. He's utterly trustworthy and loyal. In the end, after a long, heavy silence, he gathers me into his arms and whispers in my ear, "You know you can always ask for my help, yes?"

I pull back, smiling, though inside I want to cry. "I do. But at the moment, *this* is the assistance I need."

"Then it's the assistance you'll receive."

"Thank you," I say, though words feel grossly inadequate. When he agreed to let me make use of his business safe, I thought the large, heavy rectangle would be more than enough space. I had no idea the footage a million in euros actually takes up, and as soon as next week I'll have to flow over onto the floor. Odd, that thought: euros stacked on a closet floor because there's no room in the safe.

With my father's pilfered clothing tucked under my arm, I slip out Giovanni's back door to find both Saber and Reginald waiting for me. I peer around them but see no one else.

"You made me a promise," I say sternly to Reginald. I hold a thick envelope—this week's payment for his Glitter—where he can see, but I don't proffer it.

"Are you blind?" Reginald asks, and knocks Saber with his shoulder.

Only then do I realize that Saber's dressed not in his usual black jeans and the sacklike gray garment the world calls a hoodie but in the same Baroque costume he was wearing the last time he came to me at the palace.

"No," I say before I even realize I'm about to speak. "Not him."

"I'd like one good reason why not," Reginald says, sounding most affronted.

But what to say? That I don't think I can concentrate when Saber is around because the sound of my own heartbeat fills my ears? That his green eyes are so hypnotizing I feel as though I'm taking drugs rather than selling them? Or maybe simply that I'm already fighting my conscience so hard that I don't think I can tolerate this person who treats me like a particularly putrid bit of mud on his boot?

I had considered this possibility but dismissed it instantly. "He's your second-in-command," I argue. "You can't think to send him to live in the palace for two months."

I don't expect Reginald to laugh. I certainly don't expect him to bend over and howl. Saber avoids my eyes and color stains his cheeks and somehow, I'm not in on the joke.

"Don't worry," Reginald says, dabbing at his eyes once he's recovered. "Saber's no one. I can do without him."

I don't dare even glance at Saber to see how he bears that insult. "He's conspicuous." Lord knows *I* can focus on nothing else when he's around.

"I dressed him up." Reginald sounds petulant, like a child wanting praise for his abysmal art project.

"It's not his appearance. Or rather, it's more than his appearance. It's his very presence. He draws the eye." An almost-honest answer.

"Then why haven't you noticed him before?" Reginald says, a strange smile on his face.

"Pardonnez?"

"Why. Haven't. You. Noticed. Him. Before?" Reginald repeats slowly, mockingly, as though I were a lackwit.

Wordlessly, I give him my best look of regal displeasure.

"He's in your palace often. Used to bring your father his patches—scouted the place for me when you first started. In case you weren't up to snuff and I had to take matters into my own hands," Reginald adds, because he can't let pass an opportunity to slight me.

"But—" I'm trying to avoid looking at Saber, even though I can feel his eyes boring into me as he stands, determinedly saying nothing, even as we speak of him. I remember how Molli's eyes slid by him in the hallway. Is it truly just me?

"He blends in quite nicely, I think," Reginald says. "He's been working with you for months, he knows the palace, he knows the product. Maybe the problem, Your Highness, is that *your* eye is drawn to him."

I suck in a breath in a hiss of indignation, but though my mind whirls, I can't think of a single thing to say in response. If Reginald wanted to sabotage any degree of friendship Saber and I have been able to cobble together the last several weeks, he's just pulled it off magnificently. With a sigh of faux resignation, I attempt to mend my tattered dignity. "I suppose I won't need my father's clothes, then. I confess myself surprised to find you so prepared."

"Pleasantly, *bien sûr*," Reginald says with a grin.

I only shoot him a glare.

"Saber has better ways to communicate with me than you do. So any messages can go through him. I can also get the raw Glitter to him more often, so you won't have to worry about these meetings."

I raise an eyebrow. "I have my own reasons for coming to Giovanni," I say, letting a trace of false innuendo slip into my tone.

"Of course you do," Reginald says, his drawl fairly sopping with sarcasm.

There *is* a real reason: I keep my money at Giovanni's.

I'm feeling somewhat more in control until Saber lets a snort of laughter escape and I've a sudden wish to expire where I stand.

Instead, I glance over at him skeptically. "Any particular instructions, beyond feed it and dress it?"

That makes Saber shut his mouth. And clench his jaw.

And makes me feel awful. I suspect his opinion wasn't solicited on this assignment either. I swallow the urge to apologize—at least in front of Reginald.

"He's got an extra set of clothes and—"

"They won't do. I'll have him fully outfitted."

"He's always been fine there before."

"He wasn't the future Queen's personal secretary before. He'll need full livery."

Reginald raises both eyebrows at this. "I'm not paying for fancy-pants Louie duds."

"Of course not," I snap. "His Majesty will provide."

A grin splits Reginald's face. "Ah, very poetic."

I incline my head ever so slightly in agreement and let a smile touch my lips. Our eyes meet in shared amusement, and somehow we're back on course. "Saber does seem a good choice," I admit. "The fact that we don't get on needn't hinder us. After all, you and I don't think much of each other either, do we?"

"We certainly don't," Reginald replies, with far too much humor for my taste.

"I suppose he'll do, then," I say. Saber looks as disgruntled as ever. What is it about him that turns me into such a *trou d'balle*? It's worse than my mother! "Come along, then."

I turn and simply expect Saber to follow. He begins to, but Reginald stops him and mutters several sentences into his ear in such low and fast French that I can barely hear, much less comprehend, what he's saying. But Saber only gives a vague grunt of agreement before hefting his messenger bag higher onto his shoulder and following me into Giovanni's studio.

"You've picked up a friend," Giovanni says, eyeing Saber appreciatively.

So much for the not-so-effective ruse that I was visiting Giovanni for romantic reasons.

"Employee," I correct, oddly not wanting him to get the wrong idea. "I doubt you'll see him again, though."

"Shame." Giovanni kisses me on both cheeks and walks me to the front door.

We enter the car silently, and I murmur instructions to the Nav computer. As we pull away, I stare at Saber's scuffed but definitely heeled shoes and try to think what else to say, lest we travel the entire journey in silence. It's a short distance, but not that short. "So, Saber," I say brightly, cringing at my own tone. "Is there a surname?"

"Not anymore."

Odd. "Were you raised in France?"

"No."

"Family? Parents? Any—"

"Must we?" Saber says, cutting me off, sounding weary.

"I simply thought that if we're to spend the next months working so closely together, we ought to know—"

"I already know everything about you that I have any desire to know."

"You've no right to judge me," I snap.

"I have *every* right to judge you!" He leans forward with his words, our noses only centimeters apart, and I tremble, frozen, staring into the fountains of raw anger in his eyes.

But it lasts only a moment before the shutters descend and his eyes are unreadable once more. He moves slowly away, as though I might claw him if he were to startle me. Once he's leaning back against the seat again, staring out the tinted windows at the streets of Versailles, he says softly, "What do I call you?"

"Your Grace," I say weakly.

He only nods.

"*En français* on Wednesdays, of course," I add lamely. "*Excellence.*"

Another nod.

"I truly am pleased to have you," I offer after a long moment of tense silence.

"You mean you're pleased to have *someone*," he corrects.

I say nothing more the entire drive and focus instead on trying to slow the beating of my heart.

The car pulls through the golden gates, around to the back of the palace, and into the underground garage. Since we're trying to keep my visits to the dance studio in Paris a secret—His Highness for false reasons, me for real ones—it would hardly do to parade through the front. As the car descends into the darkness, I'm pleased to see a flicker of surprise on Saber's face. He wasn't aware of the garage's existence at all. Considering the lack of motorized vehicles in the seventeenth century, I can hardly blame him. Most people from outside Sonoman-Versailles are unaware of the new complex beneath the palace's formidable expanse. A far more modern facility, this area houses not only the motor pool, but also M.A.R.I.E.'s server farm, the vaults, some more modern office spaces, and even a dormitory for nonpalace staff.

At least, that's what I know of from sneaking visits down here when we first moved in and everything about the palace was new and exciting. The court rarely bothers to descend belowstairs at all.

"This way, please," I say to Saber, trying my best to be polite as a member of the motorcade staff holds open my door and we head toward the lift.

The lift doors open as we approach, and I curse inwardly as they reveal Saber's first hurdle. My constant hurdle. His Majesty. Why couldn't it have been Lord Aaron or Molli, or Lady Nuala? Even Lady Cyn would be more welcome.

"Good, I caught you," His Highness says. I don't even pause as I enter the lift, as though I'd been fully expecting to find the Loathsome Lord within.

"Take the next one," the King grumbles, turning his back to block Saber's entrance.

"He's with me, Justin," I say with no inflection while putting out a jeweled slipper to stop the door from closing.

The King gives him a slow once-over, apparently finding him lacking. "You're certain?"

"My new secretary."

He pauses, looking between the two of us several times. "Your what?"

"Secretary. It was approved by the finance committee last week." A lie. "You must have been absent." A truth.

"What the bloody hell do you need a secretary for?"

"You have Mateus; what precisely do you use him for?"

"I have a company to run!"

"And I have preparations to make if I'm to fulfill my own rather key role in that company."

He gives me an appraising look, then drops his arm and allows Saber into the lift. "He's a bit shabby," the King says.

"I'm taking him to be liveried now," I say, a bristle of defensiveness in my voice against the very insult I bestowed upon Saber not an hour ago. "Allowances must be made for one's first day."

"Yes, you do know something about that, don't you, sweet cheeks?"

The back of my neck prickles. My weekly *lever* has gone

flawlessly for months, but the King never misses an opportunity to mention that first one. "Would you press *L* for me, please, Your *Gracious* Majesty? I'm taking him right to the staff tailor."

The lift starts up with scarcely a bump and I turn to my *fiancé*. "What is it you were so anxious to speak to me about?" I ask, knowing that whatever it was, he won't breathe a word with Saber standing at my shoulder.

Sure enough, he flicks his lace-bedecked hand airily and says, "We can discuss it later."

"Perhaps you should make an appointment," I say as the doors open to the lower level of the palace—almost in sight of the hallway where His Majesty once strangled a woman. "Saber can help you with that."

The King shoots an angry look at my new employee, but Saber—rising rather beautifully to the occasion, if I do say so myself—stretches out one foot and, with a swirl of his cloak, bows low over it and murmurs, "Your Royal Highness," before following me out of the lift.

TWENTY

SABER ENTERS THE livery office with the expression of a man mounting the gallows—an attitude that doesn't improve when the tailor begins to poke and prod him with devices that must, judging from his usual mode of dress, be utterly unfamiliar. A lifetime of fittings has inured me to the beeps and clicks of laser calipers and nanostitchers, but through Saber's eyes I can see how the uninitiated might confuse such mundane objects with surgical devices—or instruments of torture.

I get the impression that Saber might prefer instruments of torture.

As his shirt comes off to make way for the red-and-gold livery, butterflies trouble my tightly bound stomach. His skin is a bronze—no, a deep sienna that complements his dark brown hair, sharp cheekbones, and angular eyes that speak of origins in the East, though I'm not sure exactly where. Several centimeters above the inside of his left wrist I notice a black tattoo—a disjointed symbol that looks like the mutant offspring of Mandarin hanzi and a quick-response bar code. My Lens makes no attempt to subtitle it, however, suggesting that it's neither of those things. Perhaps a religious symbol?

The tailor proves as unaccustomed to fitting surly Parisian criminals as Saber is to being fitted, and the two come nearly to blows when Saber steadfastly refuses to remove the pair of shorts that apparently serve as his undergarments. I intervene again when the tailor brings in a pair of heeled slippers and Saber looks as though he might actually bolt.

"No, no," I say. "A pair of riding boots would be more suitable."

"Thank you for that," Saber breathes when the tailor scurries off after the requested footwear, grumbling about mismatched outfits and the besmirching of his reputation with the Historical Society.

I intend to speak as I meet Saber's eyes—to say something snarky about being a gracious taskmistress—but the genuine gratitude in his expression drives the words from my head and I avert my eyes with a blush.

It's going to be a long two months.

"M.A.R.I.E. keeps track of us in three ways," I explain as I lead him toward the Queen's Rooms, several changes of fresh-fabbed livery in his arms. "Biometrics, radio tags, and audiovisual addressing. Anyone who isn't broadcasting an authorized key to the local feed is automatically treated as a visitor, meaning they get extra attention from the audiovisual addressing. It's easy to misdirect if you know how to DOS it with your Lens, but . . ." I notice that I'm getting a penetrating look from Saber. "What?"

"You're smart," Saber says, continuing to regard me with furrowed brow.

Unsure quite how to respond, I roll my eyes. "I didn't dream of being a Queen when I was taking all my advanced programming classes."

"I figured . . . whatever. You have state-of-the-art technology, blah, blah. Continue."

His rudeness is jarring at best, but I soldier on. "The point is, you're going to need this," I say, handing him a Lens case. "The Lens is your best friend and your worst enemy. It can tell you where most anyone is, but it also keeps track of where *you* are—"

"I know how Lenses work," Saber snaps, with sudden heat. "I'm from Paris, not the Stone Age." Although Sonoma prides itself on keeping the occupants of the palace on the very cutting edge of technology, I do need to remember that the rest of the world is only a very small step behind. "Just tell me what I need to do and make sure I don't get caught doing it. That's all I need from you."

I snap my spine straight at his sudden anger and push back an urge to tear up. Everything Saber says feels so personal, and for some reason the emotional shield that works quite well against people like my mother and the King has no power to protect me from his words. I nod as we pass students, pensioners, and kept spouses lounging in the rooms leading up to my bedchamber. One woman approaches to ask if she can procure a pot of rouge. I don't remember her name but pretend we're the most intimate of acquaintances. "At the assembly tonight," I say softly. "I'll have everything."

She titters and runs off, and I swear I can feel Saber's glare searing into my *pompadour*. I catch sight of Molli sitting in a chair across the vestibule, reading on her tablet. She doesn't raise her head, but something in her posture tells me she knows I'm there and is trying to avoid eye contact. I'd ignore me too, after this morning. Still, in all our years of friendship, it's so rarely been Molli who's been the avoider, and it's a sharper sting than I would have predicted. I owe her an apology. But what kind of apology can I give that isn't packed with more lies?

Saber and I are both silent until we're safely ensconced in my bedchamber.

"Alone at last," Saber says, and anyone would think it was an attempt at humor if they couldn't see the flash of bitterness in his eyes.

"Oh, we're *never* alone," I say, and before he can utter any potentially damning response, I add, "M.A.R.I.E., fire," to illustrate my point.

His eyes dart over to the fireplace as flames burst to life within. "Then why are we here? There are . . . quieter places."

"Indeed," I say, grateful the message was received. "And we shall visit them soon. But I thought you'd like to see your lodgings first. Put away your clothing."

His eyebrows rise a fraction as his gaze sweeps to the enormous bed.

My cheeks flush when I realize the question he's silently asking.

"Not with me!" I say quickly. Too quickly, and now we're both blushing. It's not as though I didn't try to think up something different. But I can hardly risk assigning a ghost employee to the dormitories, I'm not foolish enough to ask him to share an apartment with my mother, and I'm far too embarrassed to even suggest he share quarters with my pathetic father.

The public rooms of the Queen's wing are quite large and, as one would imagine . . . public. However, behind the Queen's Bedchamber is a spiral of small rooms that are not only *not* open to the public, but have mostly been repurposed. One of the largest rooms, formerly the library, was turned into the bathroom. The *Cabinet de la Méridienne* is my dressing room, the library annex became the room in which my very large gowns are stored, and so forth. There's a small room that was once called the Duchesse de Bourgogne's Cabinet—the history of which, I confess, I don't know—that's now a small guest chamber.

It seemed like a better idea before my new assistant turned out to be Saber.

I lead Saber through the concealed door beside my bed and down a short hallway to a small, fanciful—and very feminine—chamber. White detailing covers the walls and molding, and soft lace curtains cover the single window, which overlooks a private courtyard reserved for the use of the Queen and her intimates. I push back a hysterical giggle as Saber stares at the light blue daybed with silken drapes scalloped along the top and hanging down on either end. It barely looks large enough to fit him at all, and though it's likely more expensive and elegant than any bed he's ever slept in, it seems most unsuitable.

But it keeps him near me and gives him access to all of the concealed passages associated with the Queen's Rooms. As long as

I avoid drawing attention to our unorthodox arrangement, I doubt anyone will question it. Everyone will assume he goes somewhere at night, like the rest of the servants.

Saber doesn't seem to be nearly as pleased. He's dropped his parcels to the floor and is regarding the bed with resigned disbelief.

"M.A.R.I.E., tidy up," I say, so automatically I don't even consider Saber's reaction. A bot rolls in from the hallway leading from my bedchamber and immediately begins picking up the parcels and unwrapping them.

"Hey!" Saber begins, moving as if to stop the bot, and I grasp his arm with both hands, holding him back. I'm not sure how I'd explain it if my new employee were to actually break a top-of-the-line Amalgamated service bot.

He hesitates and looks down at me—something many men are physically incapable of doing. Particularly when I'm sporting heels. Though the look he's giving me says *let go,* almost of their own accord my fingers tighten on his arm, feeling the ripple of muscle there. It's strange to want to say so many things and feel the words stick in my throat.

He despises me. He'd likely despise me even more if he knew the reactions I have when he's near.

"It's better if you let them," I say, struggling to regain my poise. "Even if you unpacked on your own, they'd rearrange everything once you were gone. It's their way. M.A.R.I.E.'s way."

"So this is how it's going to be?" he asks softly. Venomously. "I sleep in here like your pet, follow you around and take orders, do your bidding in my cute little uniform? Did you actually need help, or were you just trying to lure me to the palace?"

"I didn't know it would be you," I explode.

"You had to have suspected."

"I thought—" I thought he was too important. But I don't want to remind him of the insult Reginald gave him in Paris. That he's nobody. Indignant tears sting my eyes, and I blink them back. "I'll have you know I've been running on fewer than four hours of sleep at a time for a fortnight. I can't keep up on my own, and I can't risk sending the work out. This," I say, gesturing at the dainty room, "is the safest place for you to be in the entire palace. And not just for my sake; what do you think His . . . *he* would do if he discovered the truth about you?"

More emotions race across Saber's face than I could possibly attempt to decipher, but finally his shoulders slump. "I'm sorry. Look, I don't want to be here. But it's not fair to take it out on you."

"I'm sorry too," it's my turn to say. And I mean it; I sense Saber's not one to apologize easily. "Come, let's leave the bots to their duties—I'll show you the back corridor."

"You know," Saber says, following me, "you don't have to talk so formally when we're alone."

"Pardon?" I ask, pausing with my hand on the door handle.

"This formal speech," he says, waving his hand vaguely through the air. "When it's just the two of us, you don't have to . . . ." His voice trails off. "Damn. You have no idea what I'm talking about. It's not an act, is it?"

I simply stare, still uncomprehending.

"You talk all . . . hoity," he says, not meeting my eyes again.

"Do I?"

"A bit. Okay, a lot. I guess I thought you relaxed a little when you weren't on show."

"On show?" I find myself feeling slighted, though I can't put my finger on precisely why.

"Around normal people."

"Oh." I pause, then say, "No, this is actually how I speak—my apologies if that disappoints you. Though now that you bring it up, I think the problem is going to be the opposite. It's your vernacular that isn't quite the thing here in the palace. It's a bit . . . vulgar."

He just grins, apparently not feeling slighted in the least.

I look away from his smile. "You'll give yourself away in three words. I think it best that you not speak to anyone we encounter at all."

"Oh, goody," he grumbles.

"That sort of response is precisely what I mean."

"So was yours."

"I suppose it was." I peer up at him, trying to think. "Most of the board members who have secretaries are endlessly whispering back and forth. Hissing like snakes, in point of fact. That may be the most logical course for us as well. When in doubt, you can simply speak French."

Saber sighs. "You're the boss."

Then why does it feel the other way around?

TWENTY-ONE

SABER IS SUITABLY impressed by the organization in my father's study, and even more so by the lack of M.A.R.I.E. waiting to accommodate our every need.

"It's my safe place," I say, then chastise myself for revealing something so personal.

"Where's your father?" Saber asks when I clear my throat and turn my face away.

"Down the hall in his room," I say, pointing. "Asleep. I checked on him before I unlocked the desk. He can never know."

"Certainly not," Saber agrees grimly.

"He's no danger, though. Beyond being an addict. Easily mollified and mostly harmless. It's my mother you have to watch out for."

"And she lives here?"

"Not in my father's chambers. She sleeps in my old room." I run my fingers along the edge of the desk. "I keep everything in here." I unlock each drawer and explain how I've been running things and which duties I'll need him to take over.

"It's a pretty slick operation," he says, and I'm about to thank him for the compliment when he continues. "I doubt that drugging people against their will has ever been so profitable."

The warm flush of shame—which I've grown very good at ignoring—kindles in my chest, hotter and more painful than usual. Though I'd always hoped the business would grow fast, it's exceeded all my expectations. Which means I have to face the fact that the drug is stronger, more addictive, than I assumed at the outset. That Saber's warnings were as dire as he said. But it's too late to change anything, and all I can do is try to fight the guilt and soldier on. I'm halfway into the proverbial woods, and continuing forward seems like the only reasonable choice.

"I don't understand you," he says after a long spell of silence. "I was there that night, you know."

My mind goes instantly to the night the King killed Sierra. *He was there? How?*

"In the catacombs."

Oh. *That* night.

"That very first time. You were . . ." He pauses, and I'm not certain I want to know what his impression of me was, that awful night. "Desperate," he finally says. "And you seemed so small, but real. So real. Then, two months ago, you got into the car with me in Paris and you were a different person. Bold and controlling but ultimately—" He cuts himself off and is silent for several seconds. "What happened to her?"

"To who?" I ask, fear a cold block of ice in my throat as I wonder for a moment if he's referring to Sierra.

"The girl in the catacombs," he says as he picks up a pot of Glitter rouge and peers at the smooth circle within. "She's gone."

"I—"

"I liked her," Saber finishes, tossing the pot onto the desk with a clatter.

AT HIS INSISTENCE that he isn't tired, I leave Saber in my father's study to put away our newest batch of supplies and make himself familiar with the microlab. He wanted to start blending the makeup as well, but it's too risky during the day. My mother might walk in at any moment. At night she's nearer, but with my light feet and her long history with sleep aids, I actually feel more confident in my ability to avoid detection. Saber rolls his eyes but promises to only organize things, and I hurry out of my parents' apartments.

I have amends to make.

Blinking rapidly, I come around a corner and look up to see the very person I was just queuing up my Lens to locate. We both slow as we approach, the air thick between us, though Molli manages a wan smile.

"I was looking for you," I say before she can speak.

"I found you on my Lens," Molli says. After everything, she decided to come find me.

"I'm so sorry," I say. I don't have a story, or an excuse. Not one I can tell her. But the sentiment is real. I am sorry. For more than I can ever confess.

"No," Molli says, staring at the ground. "I was oversensitive."

"You weren't. I should have let you come." That one is a lie, but I do wish I were in a position to have allowed her to come.

I suddenly wish she'd met Giovanni when I first started going to him, and I picture lessons where we laugh when I mess up, and she claps when I master a pose. It would have been fun. "It's this new dance," I say, tucking her arm into mine as though it could erase the gaping falsehood I'm about to spin. "I just couldn't get the steps. I needed help. I should have trusted you wouldn't mock me."

The Historical Society's Master of Ceremonies wants to *début* a traditional dance number at a ball a few weeks hence. As a newly made high noblewoman, I'm expected to participate. As an untitled lady labeled of little value to the haughty court, my Molli is expected to sit out. Six months ago we'd have sat out together and neither of us would have cared. Now the imaginary distance between us chafes at us both.

But that doesn't mean I can't teach her the steps. Besides, I've been looking for opportunities to spend time with her. The last two weeks, I've hardly seen her at all as Glitter manufacturing has been draining such a large amount of my leisure time. Today is likely the best opportunity I'll have for a while.

We gather in the Hall of Mirrors with Lady Mei and Molli and a few other court ladies our age. Lady Mei and her cousin Lady Kata are playing word games on their tablets, and Lady Nuala is reading an actual paper tabloid someone snuck in from Paris.

Molli and I go through the steps, side by side. I actually like this particular dance—it's slow and graceful, making use of long lines and languid arms. Despite what I told Molli, I picked it up very quickly.

"It feels awkward," Molli complains with a giggle. "It's so slow."

"Watch me," I say, using a remote to set the music back to the beginning of the practice track, then striking the first pose. "It should be alluring. Sensual, even." This is truly where Giovanni's lessons shine through—steps that require an awareness of one's entire body, from fingertips to toes. I'm so caught up in the steps, I don't notice the ladies around me growing silent until I see Molli's wide eyes staring not at me but just over my shoulder.

Somehow sensing what I'm about to find, I pull my limbs into a stiff, upright position—shoulders back, neck straight—and turn my head to see His Majesty watching me. His eyes are dark and intense, and before he can shutter them, I see that same look he gave Sierra Jamison in that shadowed hallway.

Animal wanting.

I'm used to His Highness' lascivious looks—actions, even. But this is something more. A legitimate spark of desire beyond his simple propensity for agitation. It's something *real*. A dark foreboding tells me that this is the first moment His Highness has realized I could be not only his unwanted affianced, but a compelling plaything.

He steps forward slowly, and an entirely different breed of terror squeezes my spine and dries my tongue. Not for my physical self—for something deeper.

"That was lovely," he says.

I force myself to smile even as I struggle to make my legs hold me. His Highness places a finger under my chin, and though every cell of my body cries out against it, he bends his head and places a kiss on my lips. Not a hard, savage thing—but one that could almost pass as a caress from a gentleman truly in love.

Which is even more frightening, more invasive. The moment his mouth leaves mine, I duck my chin and slant my head to the side, hoping the flush on my cheeks looks like pleasure rather than rage.

I don't know why I raise my eyelids; perhaps it's that hint of premonition when one is being watched. Regardless, I meet Lady Cyn's eyes and wish I'd stayed in my chambers today.

She's frozen in the very act of stepping forward, her body balanced awkwardly. She must have seen exactly what I saw—that whatever the King was feeling today, there was no pretense, no act. The King wants me. Wants me desperately. I think Lady Cyn understands, now, that she's lost.

But she also saw *my* eyes. She knows I'm utterly false. She's lost her hopes, her dreams, her ambitions; all to a pretender who's just as bad as she is.

A light smattering of applause accompanies His Highness' little act of *amour,* and the sound breaks the connection between me and Lady Cyn. His Highness preens at the attention, and with one last murderous look, Lady Cyn spins on her heel and clicks away.

The King never sees her.

TWENTY-TWO

"ISN'T *HE* DELICIOUS," Lord Aaron says, leaning in close to my ear at the assembly that night.

"He's not for you," I say, arching an eyebrow.

"Doesn't mean I can't observe," Lord Aaron retorts, glancing over his shoulder to where Saber is treading two steps behind my ruffled train. I hadn't intended to bring Saber out so soon, but His Highness himself sent me a com asking how my new toy was coming along. Considering the events of this afternoon, I had little choice but to bring him out of spite. "Much to my eternal disappointment, I'm not actually in a committed relationship and therefore have no reason to feel guilty for a roving eye."

"He's a servant," I press, appealing to Lord Aaron's streak of snobbery instead.

"All the better. Not going to expect me to marry him, is he?"

"You're all talk," I say, whapping his shoulder lightly with my fan. "You wouldn't step out on Sir Spencer for anything in the world and you know it."

"Yes, I do," Lord Aaron says, smiling at the crowd with sadness in his eyes. "Unfortunately, you know it too; what fun is that? Speaking of," he adds, taking my gloved hand and placing it on his arm while simultaneously tucking a rather considerable wad of folded bills into my palm, "Spence would like a bit more of the colorless."

"Spence?" I question, palming the money.

"He likes to put it around his eyes. They have that gray touch to them, and the glimmering bits really heighten it."

"Spence?" I repeat, tilting my head in his direction to invite a confidence I'm hoping he'll share.

"Damnation, Your Grace, can't a man speak intimately of his friends?" But he looks nervous, and Lord Aaron is never nervous.

"You haven't before. Nor have you ever fetched his order from me."

He looks so stiff and straight as he strides along wordlessly that I let nigh a minute pass in silence.

"There's been a development?" I ask, squeezing his arm as I make a guess.

"I can't say," Lord Aaron says stiffly.

"Aaron—"

"Danica, *I can't say.*" He turns to face me. "You know how this works. You, of all people."

He's right, of course. "Then I'll be happy for you, inferentially."

Finally a smile lifts one corner of Lord Aaron's mouth. "You've always been quite good at inferring, Your Grace."

The thought of Lord Aaron and his love getting even stolen moments together lifts my spirits considerably, even if it is accompanied by a twinge of sadness lightly cloaked in jealousy. I don't even feel too awful as I extract a pot of colorless Glitter gloss from the tiny reticule hanging on my wrist.

"I'm off to the ladies' retiring room, my lord, to dabble in a spot of that most vulgar sport: trade," I say with a smile—a joke about the society we mirror. One in which, despite its having been built on exorbitant wealth, it was rated uncouth for a woman to even know where money came from, much less how to generate it. Thankfully, such attitudes died with the dawning of the twentieth century, but we still don't flaunt our sales in front of the court. It's an attitude that works in my favor by helping to keep my operation low-key.

"And I'm off to feast with my eyes upon delicacies I would far rather sample with my mouth."

"Naughty," I whisper, but send him on his way. "An arm, Saber," I say, lifting my hand without looking back.

"I'm sorry, what?" he asks as he steps beside me.

He's like a puppy that needs training. "Your arm," I repeat in a whisper. "Escort me?"

Luckily, he's not a complete stranger in the palace and recovers quickly. With my fingers tight on his sleeve and my arm held carefully rigid, I manage to steer him about while looking as though I'm being led.

"When we reach the doorway, release me and bow, and then stand and wait. People will hand you money—act as though you know who they are," I instruct in a whisper.

We reach the doorway, and I make a half-turn with a flourish of my skirts. Saber bows low and murmurs, "Your Grace," before standing tall and even looking, if I dare to use the word, a touch regal.

"And for God's sake remember to incline your head to anyone

who approaches you," I add in a hiss, needing to find something to criticize him about before gliding through the doors that open automatically as I approach.

The instant the doors close behind me, the ladies crowded into the room descend in a flurry of twittering. My *lever* staff is here, ready to be given a dozen pots each to distribute, and I empty half of both *panniers* in less than five minutes.

It's quite clever, if I do say so myself. Owing to their intimate nature, M.A.R.I.E. has no eyes in the retiring rooms, and her ears will hear nothing but a discussion about cosmetics. It's astounding how many relatively surveillance-light places I've found since embarking upon my illegal activities.

"Your Grace?"

I turn when I hear the low, nearly unmistakable voice of Duchess Ryka Darzi. She's the crowning jewel of my *clientèle*. Her husband's great-grandfather was given the very first dukedom by the founding King Wyndham, and the Darzis have maintained that coveted spot on the board ever since. Prior to marriage, the Duchess Darzi was a countess in her own right and has been Sonoma Inc.'s chief media officer for the last five years. She'll be the second-ranking lady to me if I ever actually become Queen, and even then her influence at court will continue to outstrip mine.

My heart nearly stopped when I first gave her a complimentary pot of rouge a few weeks ago. My *clientèle* nearly tripled the week she requested her second.

I face her with my practiced smile and incline my head in a respectful bow, but inside I quake like gelatin. If she's displeased, every woman in this room will run to spread the word, and rather than grow, my sales will drop.

Perhaps. I suppose at that point I'd discover which is stronger: addiction, or gossip.

"Are you certain you can't accept account credits for your Glitter? It'd be so much more convenient," the duchess says.

Not yet good or bad, but I don't have the answer she wants. "I do wish I could, Your Grace. Certainly it would be easier for me as well. But you know how the French are. They'll have nothing to do with our"—I look about, then lean forward in a show of secrecy, though I don't lower my voice at all—"dirty money."

"Indeed," the duchess says, rolling her eyes. "I'm simply having trouble getting my hands on the cash. It's not the funds, of course—Sonoma Inc. has had a banner year and bonuses this quarter were healthy. But I was lunching with His Grace, Duke Florentine—the CFO, you understand—and he commented that the palace bank has been exchanging euros for palace residents at a far higher rate than usual. He's concerned that if it keeps up, they'll have to raise the exchange rate. Certainly I wouldn't want to be part of *that* problem."

My mouth is as dry as a desert and an ocean of blood roars in my ears. Without knowing of the scope of my business, the duchess can't have put the pieces together—despite mentioning them in the same sentence—but my siphoning of over a million euros from the economy of Sonoman-Versailles has been noticed. It's not enough to truly disrupt it—but even that notice makes my fingers tremble.

I need to pull out an additional four million in the next month, and I've already attracted the CFO's attention. This couldn't even have happened if the exchange rate of credits hadn't already been so damnably inflated, but that's another problem entirely. In my mind I see my profits draining away, like ink splashed by water, trickling down the page. I cannot let this happen.

But the duchess hasn't finished. "Perhaps . . . perhaps you can think of a way to solve this little dilemma. Merely until the market stabilizes, of course." There's an edge of desperation in her voice, a pleading in her eyes, and I realize exactly why she's asking me.

She's hooked.

The chill that engulfed me a moment ago ignites into a wave of heat so quickly I fear I might faint dead away.

But the answer emerges with startling clarity as I remember my first attempt to raise money. I laugh casually, and before I've spoken at all, the mood around me lightens. It seems Duchess Darzi isn't the only one paranoid about her ability to get her fix. "It's ever so simple," I say. "I used to do this as a child in Versailles, and I can't imagine it would be any more difficult here. You've a secretary, no? Or a trusted maid?"

"I do," the duchess says, the hope shining in her eyes making a sickening sludge of shame well up in my belly.

"Send her or him on an errand to Paris. And then give them a piece of jewelry you no longer want. There're all sorts of shops in Paris that will buy used jewels. A decent diamond necklace would set you up for weeks, wouldn't it? Surely the exchange rate will have settled by then." I reach out to grasp her gloved hands and pull her a little closer. "Neither His Grace Duke Florentine nor

His Grace your husband need ever know. And on top of that," I add with a devious smile, "you can claim to have lost the piece and get your husband to buy you a new one, more suited to your tastes. Economic stimulation."

The duchess looks at me with wide eyes, and for a moment, I think she's appalled. I freeze, holding very still as I will her to accept this rather underhanded method. Then she breaks into a grin and waggles her finger at me. "Shameless," she says. "I absolutely adore it."

"And, of course," I say, reaching into my *pannier* pocket, "I fully trust in your ability to carry out such an endeavor, so you may have double today, and pay me next week."

"*Bien sûr!*" she says, seriously now. "I'm always timely with my accounts."

"I would never think otherwise," I say with a smile, my heart easing back toward its regular cadence. "That reminds me, I suppose you should all hear this," I say, stepping back to allow all of the ladies present to join our *tête-à-tête*. "At any time, you may settle your account with my new man of affairs, Saber."

"Is that the luscious thing who's been trailing you all evening?" I nearly blanch at Lady Cabral, who has stepped forward and looks rather . . . hungry.

"Unless there's a second man I'm unaware of," I say stiffly.

She doesn't seem to notice. "What sort of staff is he?" she asks, plumping up her cleavage in the mirror.

I've never liked Lady Cabral much, but I now find that I'm holding myself back to keep from flying at her, fingernails first. "He's my secretary."

"That's not what I mean." She turns and gives me a suggestive grin. "Is one allowed to partake?"

What? "No! No, indeed not," I snap. "You're married," I add softly, as though that were the substance of my dismay.

"As though that matters. So you're partaking exclusively?"

"No. I—of course not."

"Don't be embarrassed, Your Grace. We all do it. What good is having a handsome young man at your beck and call if you can't have first dibs?" She straightens and twitches her skirts back into place. "Don't let His Highness find out," she says, plucking a pot of rouge from my hand and sweeping toward the door. "I think I'll go settle up now." About half of the inhabitants of the retiring room exit in a rush of whispers.

Trying to salvage some scrap of my dignity, I edge closer to Duchess Darzi. "Clearly I'm new to all of this, but does everyone truly dally with their secretaries?"

"Not everyone, of course, but it's a centuries-old tradition, my dear. Surely even you can't be surprised." She turns to me. "I assumed you were trying to make a statement to His Highness. Were you not?"

At my alarmed face, she lets out a low chuckle. Perhaps I should have realized, but I avoid thinking of Saber and the King in the same sphere whatsoever.

"You've got some PR work to do, don't you?"

"Oh, goody," I say under my breath as the duchess leaves the room and I have no choice but to follow.

"I hope you've enjoyed making a fool out of me."

I nearly jump and crash into Saber when His Majesty

ambushes me the moment I step from the retiring room. "Good lord, Justin, but I shall have to put a bell around your neck," I say, trying not to look affected.

"I'd like to put something else around yours." I'm not sure how he maneuvered me up against the wall, but his body is nearly flush with mine and his hand spans my collarbones in a near-embrace sure to look romantic to passersby—and there are a good few of them. His lips brush the side of my neck and I turn my face away instinctively, only to find my eyes locking with Saber's.

My body stills and humiliation fills me from the toes up, but I can't look away from his damning gaze. I'm too terrified to move, but everything within me wants to scream, to protest to Saber that I don't want this. Don't want him. That my life is a sham and what I really want is—

I force my eyes shut. I can't even let myself think it. Not with His Highness' steaming breath on my skin and the heat from his body seeping through my clothes. Then, blessedly, the hand is gone and His Highness has pulled me from the wall and placed my hand in the crook of his elbow and is sweeping me into the Hall of Mirrors. "I don't give a damn if it's true or not, but you'd better convince all of *them* that it's not."

"What?"

"Your piece of eye candy back there. You want to keep him? I expect you to prove to everyone that you haven't brought him in for the sole purpose of cuckolding me, which is precisely how it appears at the moment."

"I didn't know," I protest when he hands me a flute of champagne. "I had no idea there were rules and . . . and claims."

"I'll fire him and toss him from the palace myself if the rumors don't stop, and now."

"How in the world am I—"

But he answers by pulling his arms tight around me, pressing his mouth hard on mine; I taste the brandy he's been drinking and understand. If I'm to keep Saber, I'll have to play the lovesick fool—the pretty bit of finery delighted to hang on the King's arm. I wonder how much this fit of pique has to do with our encounter this afternoon. Whether he's truly jealous.

His face separates from mine and he raises his glass and shouts, "Her Grace!" The crowds around me raise their own glasses and return the toast. I smile until my cheeks hurt.

I don't dare look at Saber—can't even glance in his direction. His Highness sweeps me off to the dance floor, and my feet pay for the audacity of bringing in such a handsome young secretary. I'm forced to dance for nearly an hour without pause before being unceremoniously escorted to a wall and left there, alone.

I'm grateful for the moment, though—I need to compose myself and rid my skin of the crawling sensation of being near my *fiancé*.

"Sorry to be so very tardy," Molli says, sidling up beside me a few minutes later and linking her elbow with mine. "I'm afraid Mother isn't feeling well tonight and I wanted to see her settled before I began getting ready. And you know how long that takes. So," she says, hardly drawing a breath, "what have I missed?"

TWENTY-THREE

IT TAKES A few days to satisfy my sleep deficit, but Saber turns out to be well accustomed to working into the small hours of the morning. Moreover, for all his grumbling, he seems to navigate the palace—and life within its walls—without serious incident.

"Saber?" I call softly, knocking at the small door to his quarters.

"Come in; I'm almost ready."

I clear my throat politely when the door opens to Saber tucking his shirt into his unbuttoned breeches, but he neither pauses nor hurries. Every motion is mechanically precise, like a clock ticking along, one task after the next. Artless, but efficient almost to the point of choreography. It's the same when he's mixing product; perhaps I shouldn't be surprised that he dresses in such a manner as well.

Still, it's not until his waistcoat is buttoned and his jacket pulled snugly over the whole ensemble that I find myself drawing regular breaths.

"Can you help me with this thing or do I need to call one of those bots in here?" He holds up a crisply pressed cravat. "I can tie a full Windsor in ten seconds, but this? This is impossible."

Windsor? I have no idea what he's talking about. Sadly, I also have no idea how to tie a cravat, never having been sufficiently intimate with a man to necessitate such a skill. Nor do I have time to search for a tutorial on my Lens. But I'll be damned if I'm going to toss away the opportunity to lay my hands on Saber's neck.

"I think perhaps like this?" I say, working out something resembling a bow, with the ends puffed out to look like the loops, before loosening the knot and trying again. I fiddle with it for several minutes before tilting my head to the side and deciding I've done a worthy enough job. "What do you think?" I ask, gesturing to a small vanity mirror affixed to the wall. The knot is perhaps not traditional, but it's simple and has a nice symmetry, if I do say so myself. "I can call the bots to redo it," I offer when he scrutinizes the white linen for longer than seems strictly necessary.

"No, no, I think this is fine." He straightens and meets my eyes for a moment, then looks away, seeming to dislike—or perhaps disapprove of—what he finds there. "Honestly, having your bots do it creeps me out. Ironing clothes is one thing, dressing me is something else. I haven't needed help dressing since I was a child, and certainly not from a machine."

That provokes a laugh. "You, sir, are clearly accustomed to clothing that's even *possible* to don without help. I've had to have bots dressing me since I began wearing full gowns. I find bots far more comfortable than humans, having now experienced both."

"I guess," Saber says, slicking his hair back with a comb and a bit of water and attempting, once again, to pull it back with a ribbon.

I appreciate the effort, but he's going to need another few centimeters before that becomes even remotely feasible.

"Will I do?"

I seize the opportunity to scrutinize him from head to toe. He does look quite fine, but more importantly, he looks like he belongs. "Stunning," I say, allowing myself a moment of honesty.

But he apparently takes my praise for sarcasm and shoots me an exasperated look.

"I mean it." I consider laying a hand on his arm but lose my nerve. "You've done a commendable job blending in. Everyone has accepted you as my secretary without so much as a second glance."

"Except your beloved *fiancé*, who thinks I'm your lover."

I'm certain I fail to keep the annoyance from my eyes. "He thinks nothing of the sort. Not truly. He merely likes to torture me."

"Torture you?" He laughs. "Is that what that was?"

My cheeks are hot and surely bright red as I try to shove away the memory of Saber standing there, just watching the King paw at me. "What would you call it? I'm doing this, all of this, to get away from him."

"So I gather. I don't know why you agreed to marry him in the first place—even breaking up with a King has to be easier than all this."

"If only that were true," I say softly, before clearing my throat.

"I don't . . . I don't understand this thing you guys do," Saber says, waving his hand vaguely. "I mean, I get why you live here. Free rent! And even why the first group of you lived like this. I mean, that Kevin Wyndham guy? Apparently he was crazy."

"*Eccentric* is a more appropriate word," I retort, a bit offended. "He loved the culture he created. Adored it."

"Whatever. But after he died, why not go back to normal?"

"Normal is in the eye of the beholder, to borrow the phrase." I fight the urge to put my hands on my hips and lecture him. "No matter how a child is raised, they think theirs is the normal life. The fact that I was brought up in silk and satin skirts, had a miniature pony cart to get about, and lived in the shadow of one of the greatest castles in all of Europe meant nothing to me."

"You have to know you're different, though."

I chuckle. "It isn't that we don't know the rest of the world exists—with Paris not fifteen kilometers distant, we could hardly have simply not noticed—it's just that as a whole we aren't very interested in the rest of the world. Sonoman-Versailles is home. Our customs are home."

"It's just so . . . engrained. Everyone here seems to really think it's great to live here. Like this. Doesn't it feel fake?"

"It's not fake," I say with a wry smile now. "It's *art*. We live our art." I swallow hard and look up at the gilded walls. "You may doubt my words, but I'll miss it dreadfully."

"Not me," Saber says, though his tone isn't quite so scornful.

Nonetheless, a change of topic is in order before I make myself maudlin. "Tonight is the *Grand Couvert,* a big dinner, essentially. I've arranged for you to sit with a friend of mine, Lord Aaron. I imagine you'll get along famously. Mostly you'll be collecting money from those in attendance who're due. Watch for some of the older ladies—they're liable to tuck bills right into your breeches."

Saber opens his mouth, and then claps it shut. I don't give him time to recover before I sweep from the room, knowing he'll follow in my wake.

His Highness insists on perpetuating the farce that he and I are lovesick fools, and I can hardly contend the point in front of an audience. So I paste on a grin as he pops small bits of cheese and fruit into my mouth, and simper again as he feeds me spoonfuls of dessert. I hesitate when he tips his glass of champagne toward me, then decide that getting as much alcohol into my system as I can might make the night go faster.

We're on the third tray of desserts—after about nine courses of everything else; even eating lightly, I feel uncomfortably full within my corset—when His Majesty rises from his seat and taps his crystal champagne flute with his solid-gold spoon.

Chairs clatter and clothing rustles as everyone in the line of open *salons* endeavors to rise with their sovereign. I'm beyond grateful that the small handful of us at the high table on the dais aren't required to observe this particular nicety. Instead I sit very still and stare at the bubbles in my glass.

"A toast!" the King pronounces jubilantly. "And an announcement. You're all aware that our great nation will soon celebrate the centennial of its founding."

He pauses as a wave of polite applause rolls through the rooms.

"The event will be attended by everyone in residence at the palace, of course, but also by Sonoma Inc. administrators from around the world, representatives from our corporate partners, ambassadors, dignitaries, and yes, even our beloved press." He pauses for the crowd's predictably wry laughter.

"It's a very special time for me," the King continues soberly, and a hush falls over the crowd. So quiet the King hardly needs the speakers M.A.R.I.E. engaged as soon as he opened his address. "But also a solemn one, as I always expected to celebrate our hundredth anniversary with my parents. Their untimely passing came as a great shock to me, as I'm sure it did to each of you, but I can think of no better way to honor their memory than to make this the most glorious celebration in the history of Sonoman-Versailles. So in their name, and in pursuit of our own joy and happiness, my beloved affianced and I have chosen to crown the centennial with the solemnization of our marriage."

The crowd bursts into applause, and I can't keep my head from swiveling to peer up at him, trying to figure out what he's playing at. The centennial is in *three weeks,* more than a month before my eighteenth birthday. It completely destroys the timeline set by my mother—the timeline by which I've been setting my own financial expectations.

The King reaches out and grasps the tips of my fingers, and I'm grateful I'm wearing gloves. "I'd like you all to raise your glasses with me in a special toast to my bride of choice, Her Grace and your future Queen: Danica Grayson." He lifts his glass high. "To the future Queen!"

The ocean itself could not have tumbled me more wildly than the wave of sound that rolls forth from the assembled court as they spew back the King's echoed words. He's tugging on my hand, and I realize I have to rise. My knees barely support me, but somehow I manage, and His Highness draws me close beside him.

"This wasn't the deal," I hiss through clenched teeth.

"Smile, bitch."

And I do. Because there's no other choice. Our glasses are re-filled by circling bots, and His Majesty continues to raise his in all directions, punctuating his gestures with sips of champagne. Lift and sip, lift and sip. I try to do the same, but my stomach roils and burns, a volcano in a sea of alcohol. I have to simply wet my lips and pretend to swallow while sucking deep breaths in an effort to hold nausea at bay.

I thought I had time to spare. Instead, I have none at all, and I can almost hear each moment passing, an insistent digital beep counting down the seconds before my life explodes.

At last the King sets down his glass and makes a great show of kissing my hands before leading me off the dais and out of the *salons*. I try to pull away the instant we're through the doorway, but though he drops my hand, the King's fingers immediately find my arm. He pulls—really drags—me, and my last sight before I stagger into the King's private office is Saber's eyes, watching.

Then the door slams.

"Would you like to tell me just what the hell that was, *Justin*?" I demand, recovering myself as quickly as possible.

He doesn't even look ruffled, never mind having just bodily dragged me into this room. He bends, looking into a mirror and fixing an errant strand of hair. "That was me foiling a secret ouster. Someone in court has private plans. Plans I have to stop."

"By wedding a minor," I say cynically.

"By having the Queen's shares active and in my corner," he says, straightening. "The marriage was always going to be a scandal anyway, and the headache of guardianship paperwork is easily delegated to an overpaid attorney. Meanwhile, my opponents are going to call an emergency meeting the day after the centennial celebration, while the relevant players are all in Sonoman-Versailles. Ordinarily, such a secret meeting of the nobility would be impossible to arrange."

"Secret?" I say. "Then why do you know about it?"

He turns and fixes me with a hard glare. "Sonoman-Versailles is *my* kingdom. I know about the meeting because it's my business to know everything that's happening in Sonoman-Versailles."

I force myself not to twitch under his gaze, instead raising one shoulder in a nonchalant shrug.

"Duke Tremain has been rallying support to overthrow me. It's an age-old story: a kingdom is created, succession rolls forth for a few generations, the kingdom thrives, the people are happy, and some bastard says, well, can't have that. Need a good bloody war."

I remain silent. He has a point.

"Only, these days we fight with votes and numbers instead of swords and guns." The King flicks over a few pieces on a half-played chessboard. "He wants to replace me with that damned upstart Harrisford."

Sir Spencer. I wonder if Lord Aaron knows. Or for that matter, I wonder if Sir Spencer knows. But he must. "One young king for another? Where's his argument?"

But the King is already shaking his head. "A puppet. Tremain will rule through him for twenty years until he's no longer a young king. Essentially a seamless succession. If my father were still alive . . ." His voice chokes off, and I feel an uncomfortable tightness in my throat.

"And you just assume I'll support you with my shares?" I say, forcing a subject change. "I like Sir Spencer." I raise an eyebrow at him, trying to look both calm and intimidating, but his eyes flash with a fiery hatred, and before I can take a breath he's bearing down on me.

His hands go to my shoulders, shoving me backward so hard my head bounces off the wood paneling. Then—my nightmares made flesh—one large hand spans my throat and I struggle to breathe as his fingers tighten.

But they are not quite cutting off my air, I realize after a moment of blind panic. His fingers are higher, clenching at the sides of my jaw with aching strength, forcing my head up. "Your scheming mother left me with precious little choice but to marry you. In return, she promised to help me keep my kingdom."

"But—"

"Shut up and listen!" he hisses, giving me a teeth-rattling shake. "I am a good CEO. A good goddamn King. I've planned this all very carefully, to disrupt the board's *coup* while appearing to be an impulsive, lovesick fool. I've been planting seeds for weeks, and I will not let anyone—least of all *you*—get in my way."

His hand is still bruisingly tight on my jaw, but his face softens and he steps closer, his body aligning with mine. His other hand trails lightly down my neck, rippling over my collarbones to the swell of my breasts pushed above my *décolletage*. "We could work well together, you know. I know you're smart. Lord knows you're headstrong. This engagement got off to a rocky start, but if you'll give me a chance, I can be most accommodating."

I try my best to squirm away, but he's holding me fast and I'm afraid I'll damage some tender part of me if I struggle too hard.

His grip on my face is iron, and I don't know which would break first: my jaw, or his hand.

"That said, marital bliss is not my top priority." His fingers tighten suddenly, eliciting from me a squeal of pain. "You'll vote with me at that meeting or I'll transform your existence into a long and living hell. Don't imagine your mother will save you. She couldn't even if she wanted to."

The tip of his tongue darts out to make a small sticky-wet spot on my neck, and I close my eyes against the violation. Then, abruptly, he releases me. He steps back so swiftly it's almost as though there's a hole in the air where he used to be.

"You underestimate me," he says, and I'm so disoriented it takes me a moment to figure out where he is—back behind his desk, looking every centimeter the King he is. "You always have. Hell, everyone does. I'm nineteen, what could I know? But while you were reciting times tables, I was studying economics and statistics. You wrote stories about what you wanted to be when you grew up; I wrote analytical reports on administrative *coups* in multinational corporations. About the time you got your first crush, I took an entire corporation as my mistress." He's speaking quietly, scarce above a whisper, but every word strikes my ear-drums like a shout. "I will not give up my company without a fight, and, Danica, I've been trained in the deadliest of corporate combat. I don't take prisoners and I'm not particularly concerned about casualties. If you don't want to be one of them, you'll play the part your clueless mother has finagled for you and then you'll stay the hell out of my way."

I don't flee. Not quite. I can't bring myself to speak—I'm not certain I can open my mouth without breaking down.

But I don't run. I pause and drop a curtsy, slow and graceful. Then, feeling the King's eyes on my every movement, I turn and walk out of the room.

TWENTY-FOUR

I SUPPOSE I should have known that Saber would be waiting outside the office door—the last person I want to see in this state. The sight of him shoves me over the edge, and I'm suddenly gasping for breath and blinking back tears that have no intention of staying put.

I cover as best I can. Chin high, I pivot sharply and stride toward my rooms, taking the back way, hoping not to run into anyone who'll bother to look too closely. Those I do encounter simply incline their heads and return to a quiet glass of port by the fire. I finally reach the small hallway that will take me through Saber's bedroom to the back entrance of my own. I hear his feet behind me but don't stop to look.

I tap out a pass code on the petals of an inlaid wooden rose, then peer into a lion's eye for a retinal scan—sneaking *out* of the Queen's Rooms is far easier than sneaking in—but finally the system allows me entrance and I hold the door open for Saber to slip in with me; then I turn and stride away, assuming he'll get the message not to follow.

"M.A.R.I.E.," I order as I walk, "clear my private chambers, please. Close the doors and bar them. I don't wish to be disturbed again until morning. Not even by the King." *Especially* not by the King, but that isn't something one can explain to a machine. Not that anything I say to M.A.R.I.E. will actually stop him, I suppose, should he take it into his head to come calling.

As I work my way through the maze of small chambers behind my much-larger bedchamber, I ponder what sorts of hacks I might employ to escalate my credentials above those of the King, and how long I could prevent the IT department from locking me out again. For all her excellent AI, M.A.R.I.E. doesn't reason. But her passivity has limits, and there's an art to knowing how far those limits can be stretched. Want to hack into the King's private bedchamber? It might be possible, with an advanced degree in machine intelligence. Less interesting windows and doors are generally susceptible to simple key cracks and well-timed denials of service. But barring entrance to the King? I'm not that good. And since I was pulled from my programming classes the day I was betrothed to the King, now I never will be.

For now, at least, M.A.R.I.E. has obeyed my commands and the bedroom is empty, the main doors shut tight. I slump into the chair at my dressing table and say quietly, "Hair, please." A bot whizzes up and starts pulling pins from my high *coiffure*. My whole skull aches, and even though I think my hairstyle softened the blow against the wood paneling, the spot on the back of my head still feels bruised and tender.

Closing my eyes, I allow myself to slump over, the boning in my corset digging hard against my belly, leftover tears leaking from my eyes. After a few minutes, I hear a soft whir as the bots finish their task and back away, waiting to be summoned again. But I've no energy to stir.

I knew my encounters with the King were growing steadily more violent, but now I see it's much worse than that; he's getting comfortable. Comfortable with me as a person, yes, but also comfortable with our situation. To hear him talk, you'd almost think he *wanted* to marry me.

Three weeks. Just a little less than three weeks. I try to tell myself that if my funds and *clientèle* continue to grow, I can possibly pull it off. But it seems hopeless.

"Are you okay?"

At the sound of Saber's voice, I sit up ramrod straight. "What are you doing here?" I ask, trying to gather up what might remain of my dignity, meeting his gaze in the mirror instead of straight-on.

"You didn't send me away," he says. "And you seemed . . . in distress."

I shake my head at his words, wishing they meant anything. That he didn't despise me and merely tolerate my presence because I'm an assignment from his employer. I take up a linen cloth from the table and set to work repairing my streaked face as best I can, trying not to look like I'm merely covering up the evidence of tears.

"Did he hurt you?"

"His *existence* hurts me," I say dryly.

"Let me—" Saber takes a few steps forward, and I stiffen. He pauses, but when I don't rise he takes a few more steps, then drops to one knee beside me.

I don't look at him. But I can't ignore the gentle touch of his hand on the very tip of my chin.

"I can see his fingers on your neck."

The observation enrages me, and though I know it's irrational even as I do it, I push him away and rise, my skirts swinging about in a circle at my feet as I put distance between us. "I'm not your concern."

"Any person with finger marks around their neck concerns me."

"You despise me."

"I wish I did; maybe this whole thing would be easier."

I stand there, my breath too short, hair tumbling down my back, with nothing to say. Thoughts whiz through my head, but I can't slow them down enough to pluck a single coherent one out. He steps closer.

One step.

Two.

His fingers rest on my chin again, lifting it, and though my impulse is to turn away, step back, the tingling in my stomach tells me he's not simply looking for bruises along my neck this time.

And still the brush of his lips on that tender spot takes me by delicious surprise.

My hands reach out for something to steady them and meet only the warm chest in front of me. I'm drowning in the bone-melting pleasure of the moment and trying not to consider what will happen tomorrow. When he pulls back to look at me, my own shock mirrored in his eyes, it's the tremble of his thumb against my bottom lip that convinces me this isn't an act.

As though there were no other choice, his palm slides along my cheek, and no force in the world could have prevented the tiny lift of my chin to meet the feather-soft question that is his kiss. When he begins to pull away again, my hands rise to his face and bring him back. This is my answer.

But I'm not the only force pulling us together this time as he grasps at the back of my gown, snugging me hard against him, pushing my neck up, his mouth moving firmly against mine. I try to twine my arms around his neck, but I can't raise them much higher than his shoulders, trapped as they are by my tight silk sleeves.

Desperation crashes over me like a surge of claustrophobia and I command, "M.A.R.I.E., my dress," against his lips without breaking contact. I pull him backward several steps until my feet find my new dressing stool. Two bots whir forward, and as they unhook and unlace my gown, I'm pushing the embroidered jacket off Saber's shoulders, understanding for the first time the appeal of the loose, thin cotton shirts the tourists wear.

Saber's hands join mine in their task the instant they're freed from the sleeves of his jacket, peeling my bodice down and off my shoulders even as the bots loosen me from my confines, bit by bit. I've never thought of my gown as a cage until this moment; Saber has to give up his task when the bodice gets stuck on the cage of my *panniers,* but as the bots take over, he steals a moment to shed his waistcoat, then returns to me, his lips exploring the skin from my bare shoulder, where the strap of my chemise hangs uselessly, to that delicate spot behind my ears, kissing away my hurts, his lips ever so gently touching the reddened areas left by the Royal Asshole's hands.

As my dress falls to the ground with the clatter of at least a dozen pots of Glitter, I feel little mechanical fingers start to untie the satin ribbons of my stays. "Just loosen them. Four centimeters," I order breathlessly before delving into Saber's lips again. I can't take them all the way off. Between tonight's tight lacing and the feel of Saber's skin against me, I'm certain I'd only end up passed out on the floor.

Even standing there in my long chemise and corset—technically my underclothing—I'm still basically clothed, but the removal of my gown and underskirts allows me to feel. Without the thick cloth I can press myself against him, feel the warmth of his skin, raise my arms to tuck my face against his neck and cling there, feeling safe for the first time in days.

Months.

Weeks and weeks I've known Saber, and even from the first moment I saw him, this is what I wanted. The backs of my knees hit the bed, and I break our kiss long enough to sit down and scoot back, making room. My eyes invite him to join me, and for a moment I see a flicker of indecision, and something else—something deeper I don't want to analyze. For several long seconds, I think he won't.

Then he lets out a groan that sounds more like disappointment than desire, and he lifts a knee to hoist himself onto the bed, where he poises his body over mine. He doesn't hesitate to give me his mouth again.

THE RAIN ON the windowpanes isn't real; it's my favorite effect, and M.A.R.I.E. turns it on automatically now. But genuine or not, the harmony of rainfall and Saber's measured breathing is tremendously soothing. I don't know how long it's been since I left His Majesty's office, but long enough for our initial savage need to have slowly drained away, until we're content to lie in each other's arms, bodies flush, Saber's hand gently stroking my arm.

"I was certain you hated me," I finally say, breaking the silence. He says nothing for a long while as my heart pounds, as I wait for him to confirm that this was nothing but a moment of stupidity, pity maybe, toward the girl who just got roughly handled by her affianced.

"I don't hate you. I hate him."

"The King?"

Saber snorts. "Him, too. No, I meant Reginald. I hate him *so much*. And I hate that you work for him, and that you . . . that you do what you do," he says, a quick glance at the ceiling telling me he's remembering M.A.R.I.E.

Probably wise. Wiser than what we just did potentially in front of the cameras.

"Then why do you work for him? Why not walk away?"

"Why don't you leave the palace? Instead of doing what you're doing?" he asks, turning it right back around to me in that uncomfortable way he has.

"I can't," I answer defensively. "I'm still a minor; my mother won't let me, and since all I have is a Sonoman-Versailles passport, I can't go anywhere without her permission until I'm eighteen. And even if I were eighteen, where could I go? Do you think the Princess of England could just up and leave? Besides which, I have no—"

"Shhh," Saber says with a finger to my lips, cutting me off. "What you're saying is that you have no choice, *oui?*"

"Exactly," I say, still a little bristly.

"Neither do I."

"But—"

"No choice," Saber says, cutting me off again.

I lay my head on his shoulder and try to understand his words. To understand how he could be trapped. But I don't dare ask and risk disturbing the peace we've somehow found.

"Do you know what I thought the first time I saw you?" Saber asks.

I let out quite an unladylike snicker. "That I was desperate and insane?"

"I guess technically the first time I saw you was in the catacombs. But I meant in the car. In Paris. The first time we met."

"Oh, that time. Hmmm," I say, tapping my chin as though thinking quite hard. "You thought . . . that I was an evil, crazed witch?"

Saber laughs, and when I hear the sound roll around in his chest, nothing seems half as awful as it did a few hours ago. "No," he says. "You were incredible. I—I couldn't breathe. No lie," he adds when I make a sound of disbelief. "You were so beautiful and determined and—I was supposed to cajole you. Speak fancy to you and convince you I was Reginald, so you wouldn't have to see his face." He runs his fingers along my shoulder, and I have the urge to curl up and purr like a kitten. "But you made me speechless, and by the time I gathered myself together, you'd already figured out I wasn't who you wanted to see."

"It wasn't an insult," I say, burrowing closer.

"I know." He turns his head and kisses my brow. "I've wanted to be near you ever since, and I fought it so hard because . . ." His voice trails off, and for a while I think he won't finish. "Because I hate what you do."

"Does it help if I hate it too?" I ask, although a part of me wonders if that's entirely true. I've been nurturing a burgeoning sense of pride at having built such a profitable business from nothing. And though I'd perish before admitting it aloud, the gleam of addiction I saw in Duchess Darzi's eye the other night sent a thrill of success coursing through my veins.

"Some," Saber says, then yawns. "But you don't hate it enough."

TWENTY-FIVE

OPENING THIS NEW door with Saber has filled me with fresh resolve. I *will* meet Reginald's price. In three weeks' time, I *will* leave Sonoman-Versailles forever.

And I'm going to take Saber with me. Take him away from Reginald.

There's much to do. As I look over my coded report of Glitter orders from Lady Ebele, I realize that my suggestion to Duchess Darzi—that she pawn her unwanted jewels to fund her habit—resulted not only in a surge of new orders, but an increase in demand from my existing *clientèle*.

"They were probably being careful," Saber says when I ask him. "Scrimping, I guess. Tossing cash around, even going through the exchange process at the bank here in the palace, gets noticed."

"So they were buying as little as possible, and now that they've realized there's a black market for cash, they're . . . stocking up?"

"You've given them a way to buy greater quantities secretly." He glances my way and then averts his eyes. "They've got to realize they need more now."

I sober, my shoulders slumping a bit. I'm sitting atop my father's enormous desk, gown hiked up and wrapped around my hips like a silky nest. With the doors closed in case my mother wanders by, the hot plate Saber is using to mix product imparts a bit more warmth to the room than M.A.R.I.E. ordinarily permits.

I swallow hard and answer his query. "Yes, I assume some of them must be catching on. But I haven't heard any discussion on the matter."

"That's because they assume you're using as well," Saber says, gesturing vaguely toward my glittering eye shadow. "They think you're all sharing the secret."

"I'm not sure how any of them could consider this a secret." I indicate the rows and rows of gloss pots Saber has just finished pouring, sitting on the windowsill to set. "Hundreds. Every day. I'm pretty sure even the King knows I'm selling Glitter at this point. It's one of my biggest concerns. I'm trusting an awful lot of people. Rather less-than-sober people."

Saber finishes wiping his hands on a towel and tosses it onto the desk beside me. "There's a sense of . . . naughtiness," he says, standing between my crisscrossed knees and placing his hands on the skin just above my lacy garters, "an appeal in the forbidden." He dips his head closer to mine, and his hands slide smoothly upward. "There's also"—his lips brush mine, ever so softly—"an allure in the mysterious. People might know that there's a mystery, but they also know that solving it might force an end to the naughtiness." He grasps my bottom lip very gently between his teeth for a moment. "And what fun would that be?"

"Mmmm, no fun at all," I agree, kissing him fully, feeling his hands move higher still. This room has become our personal sanctuary in precisely the same way it's been my safe place for

Glitter. There's much work to be done, that's true, but it's possible we've spent more time here than is strictly necessary these last few days.

Saber raises his hand to my neck, tipping my head to deepen his kiss, and with his sleeves rolled up I see again the dark tattoo that spans his left forearm. "Someday I'm going to find out what that means," I say breathlessly.

"I certainly hope not," he replies, pulling one of my legs free to wrap about his waist.

I'm floating so high on the sensations of Saber's body against mine that I'm uncertain how I hear the warning rattle of the doorknob, but I do—and I push Saber from me with a gasp, tossing my skirts back over my legs as my mother walks in. I snap my spine straight but can't imagine she's fooled.

"I've been sent to retrieve you," she says testily. "The King's been trying to summon you for nearly half an hour. What, precisely, have you been doing?" She glares at me, and I can't tell if my heart is racing or has ceased to beat altogether. "Why are you not wearing your Lens?"

"I got something in my eye," I lie. Badly. "I took it out. It's in Father's bathroom."

"You are the Queen-to-be, Dani. You cannot frolic about off the grid. Beyond being exceptionally inconvenient for His Highness, it's not safe." The way her eyes studiously avoid flickering over to Saber tells me exactly what sort of "danger" she has in mind.

My mother has always had a talent for making me feel like a tiny, awkward child, and to be dressed down so thoroughly in front of Saber makes everything worse. Every nerve in my body begs me to scream at her even as my ability to form actual coherent sentences flees.

"I fear 'tis my fault, my lady," Saber says, dropping into a deep, flourishing bow. "I suggested that Her Highness rest her eye after her ordeal with the Lens. It was quite reddened." He reaches out and turns my chin, as though I were a poodle on display, and says cheerfully, "Ah! Observe. The eye looks quite well now."

I'm astounded. In ten seconds Saber has managed to change from himself into a subservient, fussing employee. Even his speech—though just a touch stilted—was convincing enough.

My mother, however, doesn't appear pacified in the least. "You," she says, turning to Saber as he slips back into his livery jacket. "Dani's new *secretary*. His Majesty doesn't like you, and neither do I. I've already set a meeting to discuss your termination with Human Resources. Until then, endeavor to stay out of my sight."

"Of course, my lady," he says with another bow. I'm ashamed at myself for not coming to his rescue the way he did for me.

Then Mother glances around the room, aware for the first time of something other than Saber and me. "What's going on here?"

At last, something I have a prepared answer for. "I'm handcrafting some cosmetics for a few intimate friends. I've been doing so for weeks."

My mother is staring at the two hundred pots, and her brow wrinkles in concentration. Before she can think about it too hard, I say, "You must be aware how much bribery it's going to take for the right people to accept me."

"Don't say *bribery*, Dani. It's vulgar."

"You know what I mean, though," I press. "In fact, I have a parcel of these being sent over to Duchess Darzi this afternoon. We spoke the other day, and she's expecting them." Entirely truth.

My mother stands still, her eyes glued to me. I've invoked the name of the highest-ranking woman in the entire court. It's not in my mother's nature to let such a remark pass without contemplating how it might be turned to her advantage.

I use her moment of indecision to reassert my authority. "I've taken great pains these last few months to become a favorite of the court. You can do all the arranging you like, but if the social hierarchy at the palace doesn't accept me, it won't much matter that I'm the King's wife, will it?"

"True," she replies after a long pause, then bristles and straightens, shaking a finger at me. "But you do have an appointment. Put in your Lens and let's be on our way."

"Certainly," I say, dropping her a very shallow curtsy before turning to slip my shoes back on so I can walk down the hallway to the washroom.

"Where's your father?" my mother asks, still staring too intently for my comfort at the Glitter on the sideboard.

"Napping." By which we both know I mean lying on his bed in a blissful stupor.

"As usual," she mutters.

I'm loath to leave Saber alone with her, but there isn't anything else I can do, so I hurry instead, coming back down the hallway less than a minute later with a linen cloth, still dabbing at the saline under my eye and trying not to smudge my eyeliner. "Where are we headed, Mother?" I ask as I burst into the room, heedless of whether or not I'm interrupting.

She looks away from the grid of lip gloss, and I can practically hear the cogs in her brain grinding out hypotheses concerning the true nature of my activities here. The best I can do is get her out of the vicinity before she manages to formulate anything too close to the truth. "Your chambers," she says after a long pause.

I ignore the com notifications blinking at the corner of my vision. I don't have time to sort through them now; I need to keep all of my attention on my mother. Muting the incoming messages with a blink, I raise my brows and stare haughtily at Saber, knowing that after our adventures Sunday night he'll understand it's naught but an act. "You can tidy up here, can't you?"

"Of course, Highness," he says with a bow, slipping easily into his role.

"Good. Meet me in my chambers when you've finished. We'll plan my ensemble for tonight. Oh, and see that these are delivered where they belong. You're a good chap." I tap his shoulder with my fan, hoping I haven't gone too far over the top. But my mother pivots and leads the way out of the study, giving me a chance to cast Saber a grateful look.

In the atrium, I reach for my valise on the table by the front door and stop my mother's forward movement with a light finger on her shoulder. "A moment, if you please," I say, pulling on my gloves. "I don't mind granting you precedence in your own home—you are my mother, after all—but that door," I say, pointing to the main entrance of our apartments, "is in full view of anyone who might happen to be passing by. I'm the future Queen of Sonoman-Versailles, and it would be disgraceful for anyone to witness you presuming to precede me out of a room."

It's a petty scrap of vengeance, but I savor it. My mother thinks herself the mistress of this elaborate scheme, but her own actions have put me in a position of power over her. I'm not the biddable, helpless daughter I was six months ago—I'm an international celebrity and soon to reign as Queen.

We glide in silence for a fair while, the whisper of our skirts on the marble floor our only accompaniment. "I know what's going on," my mother says in a soft voice.

"Do share," I reply, keeping my voice calm, though my stomach instantly feels sick. I have far too many secrets for a sentence such as that to sit well with me.

"You and that *secretary,*" she says, like the word tastes foul in her mouth.

"Everyone dallies with their staff." It's not the Glitter. I can fob off her other suspicions as long as she doesn't know about the Glitter.

"You can't afford to."

"I don't see why not. My affianced has made little secret of his own infidelity. You of all people should know that this isn't a love match, whatever the illusion His Royal Highness has decided to cast."

"But he is trying to cast it. You'd be unwise to disrupt his plans."

"I'm being cautious."

"So cautious I walked in on you with your legs wrapped around him."

I pause and turn to face her. "It wasn't nearly as salacious as you'd like to paint it," I hiss. "One knee touching a man's hip is hardly *in flagrante delicto.*"

"But it is something, and I caught you easily," she retorts, hands on hips.

I shake my head minutely. Anyone in the world could pass by and see that she's angry with me. I, however, refuse to play the little girl. I raise my chin, clasp my hands loosely in front of me, and look down on her as if she were a toddler throwing a tantrum rather than the woman who brought me into the world. Giovanni calls it creating a *tableau:* altering someone's perspective on any scene simply by changing how *you* are perceived.

Now anyone passing us will see an older woman making a big deal of nothing and a tall, regal figure indulging her.

"Mother, you're the only person who'd ever be in the position of walking in on Saber and me in that particular room. I'm hardly indulging in the royal suites in broad daylight—what sort of ninny do you take me for?"

"Dani. Danica." She reaches out and touches my arm, and it's all I can do not to recoil. "I know you're fighting this, but I wish you could see what it really means. I'm not even saying you can't have your . . . fling with that commoner. But wait."

I clamp my teeth together and avert my eyes, though I don't turn my head. Too obvious.

"Just until you're married and the King can't back out. Don't you understand? You have a lifetime of grandeur and freedom in front of you. As much as you refuse to believe it, this has never been about me. It's always been a gift for you."

"A gift?" I say, scoffing openly. "I don't suppose it comes with a return receipt?" Before she can answer, I spin with a flourish and stride toward the Queen's Apartments.

My mother is forced to scurry to keep up. More scraps of vengeance—comeuppance *hors d'oeuvres,* whetting my appetite for the day when I disappear forever and my scheming mother is left with nothing at all for her troubles.

"What's so important that you came to find me in person, anyway?" I say, adopting a tone of boredom.

"A team of specialized *modistes* is waiting for you in the *Salon des Nobles.* You need to be fitted for your wedding gown."

With that, my mother scratches out any victory, any control I thought I had wrenched away from her. In the end, I'm still her prisoner, still affianced of my nightmare, still dancing on her puppet strings.

And she knows it.

TWENTY-SIX

EVEN THE APPRECIATIVE look on Saber's face when he walks into the *Salon des Nobles* can't erase the painful pit in my chest at being decked out for a wedding that may as well be my funeral.

I'm sure I look resplendent. His Sneakiness must have had seamstresses secretly working on the elaborate gown for weeks—months. The voluminous garment of shimmering snow-white satin is covered in silver floss embroidery that twinkles and shines in the light from the chandelier, and I can see at a glance that it's one hundred percent hand-stitched—not a single thread or button applied with the assistance of fabricators or nanostitchers. The bodice had to be carefully pinned and basted into place, but by the time Saber enters, it hugs my form with lace edging around a *décolletage* that practically serves up my cleavage for offer on a scallop-edged platter.

Thanks to my corset-tightening, I know my waistline is far too extreme to be fashionable, but the *modiste*—or, I suppose, simply a designer, since she's from Paris, not Versailles—makes a hum of approval as she gives the waist another tuck in, and the hips an extra tuck *out*.

At least someone appreciates it.

Make that two people, I think as Saber takes me in from head to toe, his eyes brimming with approval. Even the fact that it's a white wedding dress doesn't seem to turn him off.

When I left my parents' apartments, I resented that I wasn't able to fill my *pannier* pockets with Glitter, but it turns out to have been a blessing, as I was stripped down to nearly nothing the instant I walked into the *Salon des Nobles.* Besides, the bulging roundness of Saber's messenger bag tells me he's brought plenty to get us through the assembly tonight, before we tackle yet another public Wednesday on the morrow.

Though perhaps Saber and I can hide away from the tourists in my nonpublic rooms and make up some excuse, like planning a prewedding *soirée,* to get some time alone.

"Oh!" I let out a little squeak of pain as a pin pricks at my hip.

"You must stand straight, Your Highness," the Parisian woman says as I realize I had crumpled into a languid half-slump at the thought of what I could do with—to!—Saber tomorrow. I can't let him steal my attention and focus, no matter how delightsome a thief he is.

Saber seems to regain control of himself about the same time I do, and he taps his messenger bag and tips his head toward my bedchamber in an unspoken message. He cranes his neck to keep his eyes on me as he traverses the room and stashes the bag just inside the golden double doors, then tucks himself out of the way against the wall where I can see him clearly.

I'm glad he's here. I was feeling desperately lonely. I'm not sure what Molli is doing today, but her Lens was set to Unavailable and

I didn't want to invite anyone else to the fitting who didn't understand what a nightmare this prospective marriage is. It's hard enough to maintain my own composure in front of the seamstresses; if I had to fake euphoria for an audience as well, it would be too much.

My knees are feeling weak and my head a little light when they finally pull the satin away from me, full of pins, stitches, and light blue markings, leaving me in nothing but undergarments that are both low-cut and near-transparent. The Parisians treat Saber as a genderless peon, not worth my modesty—apparently Paris and Versailles remain alike in their treatment of "inferiors." A week ago I'd have been humiliated, but today I stand with a smile barely concealed as the satin falls away, leaving me in rather stunning *déshabillé*. His eyes widen, and though I only hear his fast intake of breath because I was listening for it, it's definitely there.

As soon as all the pieces are removed from my body, I accept a silk robe from one of the Parisian designers and beckon for Saber to follow me into the bedchamber. "We've just enough time to pick an ensemble for tonight's assembly," I say without looking at him. "But we must hurry."

The doors close us in and Saber grabs me from behind, pulling me against him and kissing my neck. "Hurry indeed," he growls in my ear.

"Well," I say, turning in his arms to face him, to offer him my mouth, "we'll have to hurry a little."

I'm drowning in Saber's kisses and considering whether I can get away with crying off the assembly entirely when a knock sounds at my door. I want to ignore it, but M.A.R.I.E. Lenses me a feed of the person on the other side. Molli's oddly nervous expression entreats me, and I know I can't turn her away.

"It's Molli." I pull myself from Saber's arms and hurry through the gilded gate to perch at my dressing table. "Give me twenty seconds, then open the door. Hair, M.A.R.I.E.," I whisper. Saber waits just long enough for the bot to reach me before pulling open the double doors and bowing low.

I meet Molli's eyes in my mirror and then turn and smile. "Molli!"

She hesitates in the doorway. "I missed your com. I was worried."

"Don't be," I say, rising to take her by both hands and pulling her over the threshold. "I had a long and tiresome fitting and just wanted some company."

"You're not dressed yet," she says hesitantly. "I should—"

"The bots are fast," I say, cutting her off. This awkward, nervous Molli makes me uncomfortable, and I've seen a lot more of her in the last couple of months than ever before. "And certainly no one actually expects me to be punctual." I nod at Saber to close the doors, and after a moment of hesitation he does, shutting himself onto the opposite side.

Molli stares at the closed doors for several seconds before commenting, "He is so beautiful. I don't think I'd be able to resist."

I snort, which only makes me choke, and then we both start to laugh. It feels good to laugh with her. But all too soon Molli's laughter dies away and she avoids my eyes. I step forward and take both of her hands in mine again, pulling her to a settee and sitting her down beside me. "What's wrong, *petite*?"

She's silent for a long time, and I'm about to lean forward to make her look at me when she says in a small, choked voice, "I know I'm a nobody, Danica, but you were a nobody when I met you too."

"You're not a nobody. Not in my eyes."

"I am," she says simply. "In the eyes of the court that's precisely what I am. Untitled, unremarkable. And we both know it. We used to jest about it."

"Technically," I say sardonically, "I'm still a nobody; my title is a courtesy at best."

She lets out a bitter laugh. "No one in court gives a damn about that, and you know it. But when I met you, you were skinny and too tall, and you still had a crooked nose."

"I think His Majesty has classified that as a state secret," I say, pointing a commanding finger at her with a grin. But the humor is forced, and after a few seconds of taut silence, I wish I hadn't said it at all.

"The point is," Molli says, graciously pushing past the awkward moment, "I accepted you long before either of us had any clue you'd end up in this bedroom. And now that you have, you've left me behind."

I try to interrupt, but she continues spewing out words as though it's taken her weeks to build up the courage to say them and now that she's started, she can't stop.

"At first I thought for sure you'd offer me a position on your staff for the *lever,* especially since it was me you came to, to lament the day that it went so very badly. But two weeks later I had to find out from Lady Nuala that you'd already filled the positions. Lady

Nuala, who poured wine down your dress! Then you started selling your Glitter makeup, and when you started giving me a pot every week, at least I thought maybe you were taking pity on me because I have so little pin money, but no. It's become quite obvious that there's something special about the makeup you sell to the titled ladies, and you give me something *different*. A cheap imitation, I assume, but I don't . . . Danica, I thought we were friends."

I'm utterly horrified as she lays out my sins before me. But how do you tell someone that they're so good, so untouched, that you can't bear to let them be a part of your seedy underworld? "But . . . but you're a tour guide on Wednesdays," I say lamely.

"Please. Tour Guide is Level G employment. *Lever* staff? Level B. Who in their right mind would decline such a promotion? Triple the salary, and worlds more prestige. I thought for certain . . ." Her voice trails off, and she's silent for a few seconds. "Friends, *real* friends, bring each other along when they ascend. And it—it makes me question if we ever were. You're found more frequently in Lady Mei's company these days than mine."

I can't deny that's true; Lady Mei has proved a most enthusiastic Glitter consumer. "I'm sorry," I say to Molli, and I am. "I should have spoken to you about all of this at the very least. I made . . . assumptions that perhaps I had no right to make. But it was never malicious. I hope you know that."

She's sitting ramrod straight, but her eyes are closed like she regrets having said anything at all. She nods, and one tear escapes from beneath her eyelid.

I lay my head against hers, not only to comfort her, but also so I don't have to look her in the face while I lie. "I honestly didn't think you'd be interested. Being part of the *lever* staff? To be honest, it's rather degrading. They wash my cleavage, Molls."

She lets out a giggle that still sounds choked, but at least there's a ghost of a smile.

"It's incredibly intrusive, and I can only imagine it's uncomfortable for them as well. But," I say, taking a deep breath, "you're right. I should have asked you."

In truth, I selected everyone on my *lever* staff so they could help me run my business, and I reward them with a drug addiction. To involve Molli in the *lever* would entangle her in everything I've worked so hard to protect her from.

But, I realize, I only have to procrastinate a few weeks.

"Do you still want it?" I ask softly.

"Want what?"

"A position on my staff?"

She rolls her eyes. "I didn't come here to beg for a job." She rises from the settee and begins rearranging her skirts.

"I know," I say with a hand on her arm to stop her. "But whatever your purpose, you've given me an opportunity to right a wrong, and I'm not too proud to accept a second chance." The illusion of a second chance. "I mean, you can't start tomorrow or anything; you need to take M.A.R.I.E.'s special training course. And I'll have to take it up with the Human Resources bureaucrats, but . . ." I fake a quick laugh and shake my head. "His Royal Highness owes me a favor, and I can't imagine he would deny me seven ladies instead of six."

Her eyes brighten with tears, but I have my suspicions they're not sad tears this time. "I really didn't come here for this."

I link my arm through hers and smile. "I know."

"Are you certain?"

I place my hands on both her shoulders and wait until she looks up and meets my eyes. "Positive. You're absolutely right, and I'm glad you came here tonight. I think sometimes I become so focused on my troubles, I forget that everyone around me has their own." I take a deep breath and force a smile. "The next little while is going to be a veritable roller coaster, Molli, but there's no one I'd rather have on it with me than you."

Finally she appears convinced and leans forward to hug me. When she pulls back, she reaches out with a finger and touches my eyelid, where I'm wearing my glitter today. "What's so special about your cosmetics, Danica?"

I try to laugh away her question. "What drives any fad? If I knew that, I'd certainly take further advantage. My supplier is obsessed with the *avant-garde*—"

But she's already shaking her head. "No. It's more than that. Everyone who wears them—and continues to buy them in spite of the exorbitant cost, I might add—traipses around with an aura of smugness. Like they're all part of an exclusive club with an exciting secret. And, of course, they think I'm part of the club too. But I'm not. Everyone swears that your cosmetics are better than what the apothecary sells at a hundredth of the price, but I don't feel any difference at all. That's how I realized that whatever you've been giving me, it isn't real. Why isn't mine real?"

She's staring straight at me, and dread settles into my heart. "You're not wrong," I finally confess, and an expression of relief flitters across Molli's face. "Yours is different. Lord Aaron's as well," I add so she doesn't feel alone.

"I wondered, after your party."

"The cosmetics I sell . . . they make you feel good. Happy." That's as simple and close to the truth as I can get with M.A.R.I.E. listening.

"And you didn't want that for me?"

"I didn't want you to need it."

"Like an alcoholic? Like your father? Is this because I always used to get drunk on Saturday nights? Do you think I'm like him?"

"No, no, of course not." She's so protected by her parents, so sheltered in our society, that even when I've told her the truth, she doesn't quite understand. It breaks my heart all over. But I have to tell her something. "It's somewhat like that. But more . . . more, perhaps, like homeopathics." If I weren't already condemned to the deepest pits of hell, where all betrayers go, the circle reserved for liars would have quite a claim. "But stronger," I add at the acute stab of guilt. "I thought it would help the general atmosphere at court." My lie is nearly taking on a life of its own.

"But not me."

"Again," I say, desperate to leave this conversation aside, "I should have consulted with you. We should have talked. I was wrong."

"Can I have it now?"

Her words freeze my heart into ice. After all these months, can I give it to her? It's not as though I could stop her at this point. It's precisely as she said: everyone thinks she's in on it. No one would think twice of letting her "borrow" their makeup. "I'm out," I say desperately. Then, at her flash of skepticism, I blurt, "But I'll make sure you get some tomorrow. I dispense a lot of it on Wednesdays because security is so lax." That was probably one sentence too many, I realize as Molli gives me a puzzled look. "Do you want to sleep over tonight?" I ask, more to cover up my *faux pas* than because I've thought it through.

"Tomorrow's Wednesday."

I groan. "Can you imagine?"

"Forget the minor scandal your half-moon caused—can you imagine the heyday the gossip feeds would have if you woke for your *lever* with another girl in your bed?"

"I can see it now," I say dramatically as I walk her to the double doors. "Danica Grayson, having an illicit lesbian affair right under her affianced sovereign's nose!"

"His overlarge, pigheaded nose," she says. But she whispers it, because M.A.R.I.E. is listening. "Even you would have difficulty dispersing a scandal such as that."

I smile and open the door, and we exchange parting pleasantries before she walks away. When she's out of earshot, I lean heavily against the doorframe and whisper, "You have no idea."

TWENTY-SEVEN

"ARE YOU HIDING from my mother?"

Saber's head pops out from behind a tall potted plant beside the door to my parents' apartments. "Is she still trying to get me fired?"

"You have a point."

"What's that?" Saber asks, pointing at a small but elaborately wrapped little box complete with a red bow as I let us into the apartments.

"Payment. An overstuffed envelope of cash is evidently too *gauche*."

He lifts the top corner of the little box and peers in, eyes widening at the brick of bills. "Some party."

"Much needed. Duchess Sells paid for a private demonstration for twelve of her dearest friends."

"Congrats?" Saber asks, never willing to truly encourage.

I don't let it deter me. "Every woman in attendance was either a director, a major shareholder, or married to one. Together they control nearly a third of the disposable wealth in the entire palace, and at least that much prestige," I say as I glance at my reflection in the atrium mirror. "If I'm going to make my new deadline, this is exactly the kind of *clientèle* I need." What I don't say is that they're all older women than I would have originally felt comfortable selling to. My standards are unraveling.

"Thanks for letting me sleep in," Saber says, dropping a kiss on my forehead. "Are you going to need to rest before the assembly tonight? I could make the run out to Giovanni's myself."

"Tempting," I admit.

"You know you can trust me."

"Of that I'm certain." We both take a scant moment to remove our Lenses before I key in my father's code on the decorative inlay and bend for the facial scan. "I just don't want to get caught skipping my *dance lesson.*"

"You could sleep in the car," Saber suggests, stepping slightly in front of me to hold the door open. "I make a pretty soft pillow, I'm told."

"There's a possibility." I drop my reticule on the desktop, and at the moment I look to the side, my foot hits something soft and warm.

I look down in confusion and find my mother, sprawled on the floor. A trickle of blood has dried under her nose.

"Oh lord." I remember her snooping about on Tuesday and alarm clangs like a bell, reverberating through my entire body. Saber rushes to her side and drops to one knee. His fingers go to her throat, and when he looks up at me with fear-glazed eyes, I know.

"She's dead?"

Saber just nods.

"But I . . . I picked up product for the party an hour ago. She wasn't here!" A sob wrenches out of my mouth, and I slap my hand over it. My throat convulses, but I let no more noise escape. If you had asked me two minutes ago if I'd be pleased to see my mother dead, my answer would have been yes. But the reality is more devastating than I could possibly have imagined. There were days, years' worth of them, when I knew—or at least thought—my mother loved me. It's those days that come back now, threatening to bowl me over with remorse.

Remorse for her death? I ask myself when rational thought finally worms through my tangle of emotions. I'm not convinced that's what it is. For the waste. The potential. The could-have-beens.

Questions form and fizzle in my brain as I force myself to take deep breaths. Could the King be responsible for this? What does her death mean for me? What contingencies did my mother have in place for something like this?

Do I still have to marry Justin Wyndham?

"Danica, look." Saber's voice brings me back to the present. The top drawer of the desk is open.

"Oh no." The words are barely audible as they wisp from my lips.

With clenched teeth, Saber kneels to lift my mother's head, revealing a blood-caked cheek, shards of glass, and the unmistakable glimmer of Sonoman-Versailles's favorite cosmetic additive. The remains of a vial of raw Glitter.

Automatically, I estimate the loss in production and profit, and though I haven't loved this woman in a very long time, I'm ashamed at the reflex.

"Go get a washcloth. Damp, not wet. Hurry."

"What?" Saber's calm but firm words sound like a different language.

"We have to fix this—go get a washcloth. Please," he adds, and strangely, that's what gets me moving. I jog down the hall—cursing my clicking slippers—and wet a washcloth from my father's bathroom. At the last second, I poke my head into his *boudoir* but am relieved to see him sleeping. For a moment I panic and wonder if he's dead too, but I hear a light snuffling snore, so I hurry back to Saber.

"We'll clean up the Glitter and reposition her body," Saber says with a calm I can't even begin to feel. How have I become the person who covers up two deaths in six months?

"I don't understand, what happened?"

"I can only guess," Saber says as he dabs at the blood on her cheek, trying to remove the sparkling drug. "She probably got suspicious and came back to snoop when she saw you had that party on your schedule. She knew you'd be out of the way. Looks like she got into the desk somehow. If she tried to taste the Glitter, or sniff it, and got like ten doses at once, she'd have collapsed and—" He gestures at her fallen form.

Saber's doing everything, and I'm feeling so queasy, I just let him. Part of my brain reminds me that he's been working with Reginald for . . . I don't even know how long. This probably isn't the first death he's tidied up. For all I know, he's caused a few. I wouldn't presume to know just how dark Reginald's underworld gets.

"If she didn't overdose immediately, it's possible she just tripped and landed on the vial. Then when the glass cut into her cheek . . ." He shakes his head. "Who knows how much got into her bloodstream? With it delivered that way, her heart and lungs would have quit within seconds."

I close my eyes against the horror. This is my fault. "An overdose, then. Either way."

"Massive. But if we can make it look like an accident . . . here," he says, handing me the bloodied washcloth. "Put it into your *pannier* pockets. I'll get rid of it in Paris later."

I'm hiding evidence. Bloody evidence.

"Be careful," he adds. "Don't handle it without your gloves."

"What are you going to do?" I ask as he wrestles Mother's unwieldy form up against his chest.

"Better you don't even ask," he mutters. "All the cosmetics need to go in your *pannier* pockets. Clean out all those drawers, then make sure they're locked," he adds, dragging her around to the front of the desk.

I remove my supplies from the desk and place them in my *panniers* alongside the washcloth and makeup pots before locking the drawer. I've just shoved the key down the front of my dress when a sickening thud startles my attention back to Saber.

He's standing over my mother's body, having apparently let her fall, and I'm glad I didn't see her head crack against the corner of the desk. My stomach curdles at the eight- or nine-centimeter gash he's made in her forehead, which is oozing blood onto the carpet.

"What did . . . why . . . ?" But the urge to retch overwhelms me, and I have to hold my hand over my mouth while my stomach heaves.

"Actually, if you're going to puke, you should do it over here,"

Saber says, pulling me toward him. I'm forced to remove one hand from my mouth to lift my skirts and step over my mother's body.

I don't understand any of this.

Saber takes me by both shoulders and shakes me gently. "We found her on the floor," he says. His voice is quiet and gentle, and yet somehow steely, and all I can do is nod. "It looked like she tripped on the carpet and fell, hitting her head on the desk," he says very deliberately. "When you couldn't rouse her, you ran to get help. Do you understand?"

"She tripped," I repeat.

"Yes. You have a dozen high-ranking ladies of the court to verify that you were nowhere near this apartment."

I nod, the seriousness of needing an alibi making the situation crystallize in my mind.

"Can you rumple up the carpet near her foot so it looks plausible? I'm going . . . I'm going to use gravity to make her head bleed a bit more, to corroborate our story. Maybe don't look."

But I can't just look away, after a pronouncement such as that. I flip up the corner of the beautiful Indian rug in front of my father's desk while keeping Saber in my peripheral vision. Carefully working around my mother's bulky skirts, he lifts her lower body, and I have to turn away again at the unnatural angles her limbs fall into.

I cough and barely manage to keep down the contents of my stomach before asking, "Is it done?"

"Yes, and if you can manage, I'd like help arranging her dress so it looks right. Maybe even take one shoe off?"

I turn and see my mother again, now with a thick puddle of

blood beneath the gaping split in her head. Still holding my fingers over my mouth, I say, "It's actually in the King's best interest to assume this is an accident. He knows I could easily point a finger at him for a motive for murder."

"Really?" Saber looks a little skeptical, but I nod quickly, not entirely trusting myself to speak. "Then let's hope we can get him to take a personal interest in this. Does she look ready?"

I look down at my mother—at the dragon in my life. The villain, sometimes. I adjust her skirts to make it look like she stumbled on the crumpled corner of the rug.

The *tableau* looks surprisingly innocent, and I hate myself for the relief I feel.

"Right now, your M.A.R.I.E. is our best friend and worst enemy," Saber says, and I remember telling him something similar about Lenses not very long ago.

Lenses. "Her Lens!" I cry. "She always wears it."

Saber curses, and I drop to my knees beside her. "Can you take it out without it recording you?"

"I have to at least check," I whisper. I lift the corner of her left eyelid and find . . . nothing.

Emotions war within me. My mother always wore her Lens—ever ready to snatch up a few seconds of blackmail. Why wouldn't she . . . ? And then I understand. "She knew she was going to find something bad," I say softly. "She didn't want it to incriminate me."

"Well, that makes our cover story significantly less complicated," Saber says, all business, but he doesn't grasp the significance. Maybe he can't, having not grown up with her. Even in her convoluted way, she was protecting me. She didn't want anyone to be able to discover whatever she was sure she would find in my father's desk. A very childlike part of me wants to tear up at the fact that she had some sort of motherly consideration for me.

"Your security people will see that your mother came in alive," Saber continues in his calm tone. "M.A.R.I.E. will have seen her crossing the atrium less than an hour ago, which will match the time of death. Your father will be seen sleeping in his room—no chance of foul play there. All surveillance will point to an accident. Which it was, technically."

"Will that be good enough?" I ask. I don't feel anything anymore. I'm empty and numb.

"Hopefully. Any investigator worth his salt will realize something isn't right, and a competent autopsy—much less decent blood work—will raise even worse questions. But if we can get this all written up as a clear accident, none of those things will even come into play. With luck, the authorities will scratch their heads for a while and you'll be long gone before they solve too much of the puzzle. But if, at any point, someone tries to take you into custody," Saber says softly, "get to your dance man in Paris, take your money, and run."

I don't remind him that there's nowhere for me to run—that this has been the problem all along. Instead I nod, reaching out to grasp his hand in a gesture that's far more desperation than affection.

"Okay, when you're ready, we're going to burst out of the office and you're going to com your security people, or whatever it is you do to report problems around here. We keep our stories simple and identical." He puts both hands on my shoulders. "Good?"

"Good. I'm ready."

It's a performance worthy of the Parisian stage. I shout at M.A.R.I.E. for emergency response, and within two minutes security is there and I'm letting my pent-up emotions flow freely. Saber fawns over me like I'm a helpless female, and I let him—all the better for our new audience. He responds to nearly all of the questions on my behalf; hard to have differing answers when only one person speaks.

I expect things to be far more difficult, but within about ten minutes, medical aides in white scrubs have arrived with a stretcher. Less than an hour later, the security man who ran a quick digital scan of the room is handing me a tablet with a dictated statement. There's a place at the bottom for each of us to sign.

Clean, fast, efficient. Easy. It's baffling to watch the death of a human being swept to the side with so little fuss. Not even an elderly person who's reached her time—a woman in her early fifties. I have to wonder if the simplicity of it all is down to the fact that I'm soon to be Queen. Everyone in Sonoman-Versailles knows how much we as a country benefit from avoiding political scandal, and, well, I'm nearly the most famous person at court now. If I'm connected to a suspicious death, the entire country could well be shrouded in suspicion.

One of the aides turns to me with sad-looking eyes and asks if I'd like to accompany my mother's body down to the morgue. "It sometimes helps people achieve closure," she says.

I suppose this is what someone who doesn't hate her mother would do.

With a quick nod, I try to look serenely bereft, then tilt my head to Saber to indicate he should follow. We trail the stretcher down the hallway to the lift, where the aide presses a button and we descend into the rarely seen basement levels of Versailles Palace.

"It's not a morgue in the full sense of the word; we so rarely have need," the woman says, smiling patronizingly at me as we enter a rather bare room. "You said up in your apartments not to disturb your father at this time?" she queries.

"That's right," I say. "He's . . . not well."

"All right." She glances down at her tablet. "I'll give you a moment alone while I file my reports. Please request assistance from M.A.R.I.E. should you need any."

Then she leaves through a plain door with a little square window in it, and I watch until she disappears from view.

It really is a modern world down here. Modern and sparse. The walls are white, not a fresco or gilt buttress to be seen, and other than Saber and me, everyone is wearing maintenance jumpsuits or those shapeless so-called scrubs. I feel hopelessly out of place, even though my neo-Baroque life is situated just meters above my head. Will I ever feel at home once I'm out in the world?

"I can't believe she's gone," I whisper. "She's been the driving force in my life since . . . forever. And now—conquered. But not really. Maybe not ever."

"How do you mean?"

"She'll have planned for this, somehow." Assuming her death didn't trigger some sort of release, at minimum I'm going to have to track down the video of the King's confession in that dark hallway. There might be multiple copies, depending on how carefully she tried to inure herself against the possibility of dying in a mysterious accident. Well, the joke's on her; she truly did die in a mysterious accident, but the King had nothing to do with it. "Everything I'm wrapped up in can be laid at her feet, because she wasn't content simply controlling my father's shares. She always wanted more."

Saber crinkles his brow. "Family trait?"

I let out a snort. "Please. No. My father never even wanted what he got, much less more of it. Given half a chance, the King would probably . . ." My words trail off as the realization slams into me. "My father. The King. What have I done!"

TWENTY-EIGHT

I TEAR FROM the room as quickly as I can, my skirts raised high, ignoring the clattering of Glitter containers and sprinting for the lift. Hopefully the woman in the office will assume I was overwhelmed by my emotions. And she won't be wrong—they simply aren't emotions that have anything to do with mourning my mother. As soon as the lift doors close, I slump against the wall.

"I'm so foolish," I mutter.

"I don't understand," Saber says, breathing hard.

"My father. I left him completely vulnerable. I always think of my mother as the powerful one, but she was only powerful because she controlled my father. My father *is* the source of power. He's the one with the votes."

"Votes?"

"How soon could Justin have really heard?" I say, speaking more to myself than to Saber. "Maybe I'll be on time." But I'm not optimistic. A death in the palace—especially his future mother-in-law? His Highness would have been informed immediately.

And unlike me—a novice at the power game—he would have seen his opportunity instantly.

The doors to the Grayson apartments are closed and all is

quiet. I tap in my code tremulously, half anticipating that it will be denied. Were I the King and I arrived first, I'd lock me out. The fact that the doors respond to my code and open gives me a spark of hope.

The empty atrium gives me another.

A quick code entry and facial scan get me into my father's office, and my heart races when I see the room cordoned off with tape barriers but otherwise empty. I want to yell for him, but my heart feels as though it's blocking my throat. Without a word to Saber, I turn and hurry down the hallway, not bothering to muffle the clicking of my heels. I swing around into my father's bedroom, my shoes skidding beneath me as I take that final corner.

The King is standing behind my father, who's bleary-eyed and sitting in a small armchair. On his shoulders rest the King's many-ringed fingers, clasped almost protectively.

But I know who the predator is here.

I hate that he's caught me off guard, and I force myself to pause, to stand tall, chin lifted, shoulders rolled back.

"My love," the King says mockingly. "We were just discussing you. When I broke the unfortunate news of your mother's death, your poor father expressed a wish to make some rather long-due amends to you."

"Step away from him, Justin. He just lost his wife."

"You fear for his safety?" His Highness asks melodramatically. "I wouldn't dream of harming him."

"I should say not," I snap. "You need him."

"I do indeed," replies the King, almost jovially.

I feel rather than see Saber approach, slinking along the wall so he remains out of sight of the King but just within my own vision as I linger in the doorway. I remain silent. His Royal Highness has not yet made his play, and I'll not reveal anything that might assist him.

Or that might assist me.

"Your father seems quite convinced that you don't want to marry me at all. Could that be true, darling?"

"A fact you've always known, my *lord*. Let's cease these childish games."

"Games?" he asks, removing one hand from my father's stooped form and walking around to his right side. "It certainly is a game sometimes. I wish this one were more fun."

"You're not having fun?"

But he doesn't rise to my jab. He lets out a sigh that almost sounds like a growl. "Neither are you. Let's end this, Danica." He sounds oddly tired—appears more his age than usual—and I can't help but wonder if, for once, he's being honest. "Your father, I believe, would benefit from a change in scenery. I propose to send him into retirement. We won't call it that, of course. We'll call it medical leave. Wouldn't want anyone to question his ability to vote *in absentia*, would we?"

"Certainly not," I agree, waiting.

"There's a lovely town in the south of France—in Languedoc-Roussillon—temperate. Almost Mediterranean. Sonoma Inc. has a luxury retirement community there. I could get him in. My expense. No one would question it."

I've never seen the King this way. Calm. I might even describe him as gentle. The dissonance makes a strange sort of fear fill my chest.

"And I'm happy to have my secretaries manage the details. We could have him moved by the end of the week."

It sounds beyond reasonable. But the fact is, there's no way my father can go. I've seen him when he can't get his fix, and I fear the withdrawal might kill him. Damn Reginald and the ridiculously high doses he fed my father! Although my father has failed me many times, I can't send him to an agonizing death, no matter how luxurious his deathbed.

But neither can I confess any of this to His Highness.

I consider the possibility that I could send Father with fifty patches and tell him—but no. I'm deluding myself. I'd be lucky if he didn't overdose and kill himself the same way my mother did. Two deaths on my hands then. No, he has to be watched.

"In exchange," His Highness says, glaring pointedly at me, "in three weeks I'll send you to join him, under the excuse that you need time out of the public eye to mourn your mother properly. Same agreement: full financial support in exchange for your votes always—*always*—in my corner."

"Three weeks?" I echo, understanding now. "Our wedding is in fifteen days."

"I always said there was more to you than a pretty face," His Highness nearly coos, sounding much more himself now. "No, scratch that, I never said anything of the sort. You are, nonetheless, correct. We must still wed in order for you to gain control over the Queen's shares."

"Why not wed someone else? I happen to know someone who'd jump at the opportunity, with the added bonus that you're already sleeping with her."

His Highness leans almost languidly against the bedpost and shakes his head. "Lady Cyn? Might as well wed myself to a yapping dog."

Though I wholeheartedly agree, I say nothing.

"Imagine, if you will," he says at last, not losing an ounce of bravado, "my throwing you over on the very day of your mother's untimely death, choosing Lady Cyn, and going forward with a wedding prepared for another woman. The board would think me barking mad, and half of my supporters would abandon me to obvious insanity. No, the time for substitutions is long past; it's got to be you."

I open my mouth, but he silences me.

"This isn't the eighteenth century, Dani," he says, back to that unnervingly calm voice again. "Marriage doesn't last forever. I propose two years. Two years of a marriage that starts to crumble right from the beginning, when my distraught bride refuses to return from mourning and eventually wishes to abdicate her role as Queen entirely." He gives a slight nod in my direction. "And during those years, I'll enact a few exceptionally profitable policies I've been planning for years and win the board back. We divorce, and I continue with my original plan of marrying sometime in my late thirties for the sole purpose of reproducing."

"Lucky girl," I mutter.

"Indeed," His Royal Highness snaps. "One who'll undoubtedly recognize that fact in a way that you certainly never have."

I raise an eyebrow.

He clenches his teeth. "I am the King, Danica. Everyone in this palace seems to understand that but you. Maybe if you gave my position the tiniest bit of respect, I wouldn't have to shove my way about so much. In our relationship, I'm not your worst enemy; you are."

I give him my back, my arms crossed over my chest, adrenaline and rage surging through me.

"It's a generous offer, considering the turmoil you've brought into my life," the King says softly. "In addition, I swear to lie stunningly about a consummation that I promise will never actually occur—so long as you agree to do the same."

That addition catches me by surprise and makes his offer all the more tempting. If I got enough patches from Reginald to support my father for the rest of his probably short life, I'd be there to distribute them. Maybe wean him carefully off Reginald's dangerously high dosage.

I'd still have to wed Justin. But with the promise of a divorce in just two years! Assuming he was inclined to keep his word. Which he might not be. I can't forget that beneath all this corporate intrigue, I'm first and foremost a witness to murder—a loose end who hasn't quite outlived her usefulness. So what happens when I do?

Still . . . something to consider. Very *seriously* consider.

I turn to face him again. "Might I bring my manservant?" I hate that my voice trembles.

"The one skulking in the hallway?"

At that I hear a soft shifting, and Saber comes around the

corner. I don't look, but judging by the expression on His Majesty's face, a glaring war ensues.

"I suppose you'll need someone to unlace your damned corsets," His Highness accedes. "If it must be him, so be it." He looks down at my father, who's slumped even farther down in his chair, wearing the look of a guilty child as the King and I argue over his head. "Your father has already agreed. I was about to have paperwork drawn up when you interrupted us. *He* is going. The only question is whether you'll follow. You and this dandy here."

I feel Saber ruffle at being called a dandy, but his ego is hardly my first concern right now.

As the moment draws out, His Highness steps forward, looking, for the first time in months, entirely earnest. As though we were friends. Peers. "Come on, Dani," he says softly. "Agree. We can put this whole miserable chapter of both our lives behind us for good. Neither of us wanted any of this to begin with, and now we can be free. Say yes."

And for a fleeting heartbeat I think I can. I think I *will*.

But—

But in that moment I understand what's at stake. Not the votes. Or rather, *more* than the votes. If I say yes now, His Highness gains control of my father, which means he maintains control of me. But if I say no, the King loses his control over far more than just my father—he loses control over his future.

And *I* take it.

Which wouldn't be alluring in the least if it were simply control for the sake of control. But the King is a murderer! I could bring him down. If I decline his offer, finish raising the money I need, and leave the night before the wedding, everything His Majesty has worked for his entire life—most especially in the last two years—will be destroyed. But more than that, if he gets away with murder once, only to gain even more power, what's to stop him from doing it again and again? Who would question him? But if he loses my votes at the last moment, he'll lose the board, lose his throne, lose his power over me—over everyone. And I don't see any way for him to get it back, ever.

I would win.

He would lose.

Isn't that justice? For Sierra? For my mother? For future victims?

A surge of adrenaline pumps through my body, and it's all I can do to hold absolutely still. My lungs feel like they've shrunk to half their normal volume and are begging me to take soft, panting breaths. But I master myself. I breathe slowly, I raise my chin, and I look Justin in the eye.

"No."

It's as though he doesn't hear me for a few seconds. Or simply cannot comprehend my refusing him. Indeed, *I* can scarcely comprehend it.

"No? How is it even possible that you're refusing this?" He claps a hand on my father's shoulder, looking friendly enough, but I see my father grimace from the force His Majesty likely isn't even aware he's applying. "Your poor father wants to go to Languedoc-Roussillon and live out the rest of his life in luxurious peace. With you by his side. You'd deny him that?"

"My father has changed his mind," I say slowly, evenly. "My

father wants to stay here." I lower my head to glare at my father, his eyes cloudy and—I'm certain—his understanding hazy at best. "Because this is his home, where he can make himself *happy*." I stress the final word, and though I fear I'm being too blunt, anything less might not get the message through. His eyes widen a few seconds later, and I breathe an inward sigh of relief that he understands.

"Certainly not," His Highness argues. "He's going. Are you telling me you want to stay here and be my wife in every conceivable way?" His leer makes my stomach clench, but I only place one hand on my hip and stand straighter—Giovanni's training lending me the appearance of confidence from the tips of my toes to the top of my *pompadour*.

"You send him away, you lose his votes. The only way my father will vote with you is if you leave him here with me. Isn't that right, Father? You want to stay now, don't you?"

"Stay, yes. I'd like to stay. Danica knows best."

I couldn't have coached him into a more effective answer. "You think I've lost control of my father because my mother is dead? It's *she* who lost control of him. Months ago." I walk forward until we are literally toe to toe, my skirts pressing against the King's legs. "There's only one Grayson who's been running things for the last three months, and that's *me*. Nothing has changed about our deal, Justin, except your perception of it."

We stand there, still as statues, the air practically crackling with manic energy. And then the *coup de grâce*. Quietly, so Saber doesn't hear, I bluff, "I have the video."

That makes the King's jaw tremble, and his entire form seems to melt in front of me. "You're never going to believe it was an accident, are you?" His voice is small. And reminds me oddly of Sir Spencer's soft timbre at that moment.

"It wasn't."

"It *was*." He straightens again, but the honesty in his eyes stays, haunting me. "It was just like I said; we were trying something new, I was startled when the plate broke, I squeezed too hard. I regret it, too. But you'll never believe that," he says, moving to block my path when I try to turn away. "Because then you'd have to admit that maybe we *both* did something by accident that night. That we're both responsible." His face draws so near I wonder if he's going to try to kiss me. "You need to believe I'm a monster. Because if I'm not, guess who is."

The King steps away from me, spins on his jeweled heel—coattails flying—and stalks from the room, slamming the door behind him.

TWENTY-NINE

I LOOK OVER at Saber to find him glaring. His jaw is tight, and his eyes fairly sparkle with an anger I don't understand. But before I can open my mouth to ask, he shakes his head and leaves the room, heading down the hallway toward the office.

Taking a moment to be a good daughter after just denying my father a luxurious retirement, I use the framed screen on the wall to manually order breakfast sent up for him. It's nigh lunchtime, but in a court with as many workaholics as indolent hedonists, breakfast is served from four in the morning to four in the afternoon.

I help him back into bed and tuck the covers around him. He's already nodding off, and I wonder if he realizes his wife is dead. Perhaps not—his hold on reality is tenuous at best. But even if he's mourning, I know he'll just mask it with his drugs. There's nothing I can do about that. Father taken care of, I head down the hallway to the office. To Saber.

"I think we're going to have to carry the lab with us—for the next few days, at any rate," I say as I enter. "At the very least, it's going to be a busy night." When Saber doesn't respond, I ask, "Care for some assistance?"

"I can do it alone," he responds, not meeting my eyes. "I'll get the supplies I need from Reginald this afternoon and start work as soon as the ball's over. There's no need to put yourself out."

"Put myself out?" I ask, a mite offended.

He sighs. "That's not what I meant."

"Then what did you mean?"

His gaze flits down the hallway to my father's bedchamber before he turns to regard me with bright, angry eyes. "He gave you an out. A good one. I thought escape was your plan, and I could sympathize with that. But now? This?" He points a finger at me, though the way the gesture makes me feel, it might as well be a dagger. "I haven't asked. Haven't really wanted to know. But right now you tell me what's so damn important that you're willing to destroy people's lives for it. Why you're making me do it too."

And just like that, I'm angry at him all over again—we're back at the beginning, with him treating me like a gross bug on his shoe. I didn't like it then, but now? I've seen those eyes turn to me in adoration, in acceptance and desire. To lose that would be far worse than the look of scorn itself.

I should have told him sooner.

"Five months ago," I begin, but my voice is shaking so hard I have to clear my throat and try again. "Five months ago I watched the King put his hands around a young woman's throat and choke her to death."

If Saber's shocked, he certainly doesn't show it.

"My mother stumbled on the scene and, like the harpy she always is—was—sold me and our silence to the King in exchange for the power and prestige of being the mother of the Queen."

Saber flinches—a reaction I don't quite understand.

"A week later I stole the jewels you saw at the catacombs and ran away. When that didn't work . . ." I wave my hand about vaguely. "Well, you know the rest."

"Why not just speak up? Tell someone what you saw?"

"It's too late for that—my mother is gone. Unless I can figure out what she did with the video, it would be the King's word against mine. And who do you suppose they'll be more inclined to believe?"

"But why let yourself get dragged into this whole thing to begin with?"

I shrug, reliving the despair of that night. The regret. "I was frightened. I didn't think fast enough. I was afraid no one would believe me. I'd been raised to obey my mother in all things. Pick a reason." I run my finger along the edge of the desk. "I hate that I was so weak. I promised myself I'd never be so again. Looking back, I think of other things, though. They'd both have stood against me. My mother, in hopes that she could still patch things up and make me Queen, the King because . . . well, because he did it. I was seventeen—still am seventeen. I have so little power, Saber, and the power I've managed to accumulate still might not be enough to keep me alive."

"That should make you *more* inclined to take his offer, Danica. Not less." He's leaning forward, his hands splayed on the desktop, and I feel like a little girl for what must be the hundredth time today. But his eyes don't condemn . . . they plead. "Help me understand. It was a way to get everything you wanted. And, to be totally blunt, to leave that stupid little King to deal with the Glitter mess you created. *We* created," he amends. He sounds shockingly near tears as he looks at me and asks, "Why?"

At that terrible edge in his voice, I suddenly want so desperately to defend myself. For him to understand. "There are a lot of reasons," I retort, but I hear the bristle in my voice and force myself to calm down. "There's my father's life, for one. Do you think he would survive three weeks on his own? With no Glitter? Would he live, Saber? For three weeks, with no one understanding what's happening to him—would he survive it?"

Saber hesitates but shakes his head. "I don't know. I've never seen Reginald push such a high dosage on someone so fast."

"But you know me too well to believe me to be entirely altruistic." It hurts to even say those words—to admit that's the kind of person I've become. But it's true. "The King's solution seemed generous. I almost took it. But even if he followed through and divorced me in two years, he'd have no reason to leave me alive—much less continue supporting me. What would I do? Where would I go?"

"You'd have two years to figure that out," Saber points out in a growl. "And you could stop selling Glitter. Stop hurting people."

"I'm going to stop in two weeks anyway. I've been doing this for months, Saber. Months! The damage is done." *And you were right.* But I don't say it. He knows. We both know. The truth is that I should never have started this in the first place. But that choice is gone. And if I were to stop now, I'd accomplish nothing. What I've put everyone through, what they'll go through when I leave, it would all be for nothing. It shouldn't be for nothing!

"But—"

"The withdrawals are going to be a bitch even if I leave to-morrow. That ship has sailed. But if I just go, he gets away with everything."

Saber doesn't buy it. "Once you run, he gets away with every-thing anyway."

But I'm already shaking my head. "That's what I realized. Why I can't say yes. This isn't just about me anymore. The King is about this close to losing his position as CEO of Sonoma Inc.," I say, holding my fingers a few millimeters apart. "Something that hasn't happened to a Sonoman-Versailles Wyndham in four generations. He's depending on my father's votes and my votes as Queen to help him maintain it. But imagine this: the night be-fore my wedding, I leave. Then, despite the confusion and scandal, there will still be a meeting of the board. They've been secretly planning it for months. And at that meeting they will vote to overthrow the King. Without me, without my father, he will lose everything. Everything, Saber. I can make that happen."

"Judge, jury, and executioner, are you?"

"Are you forgetting that there's an innocent dead girl here?"

Saber is quiet for a long time. "And that's worth it to you?"

"What do you mean?"

"Vengeance? Your personal definition of justice? That's worth drugging your neighbors without their knowledge or consent? Worth sacrificing your father? Your mother is *dead*, Danica! As much as you don't seem to care, your bringing Glitter into the castle killed her. Excuse me for saying so, but I think your ven-geance is a little hollow."

His idealism is infuriating. "This is all quite rich coming from you. My mother started this nightmare. I've spent the last few months in perpetual fear for my life! I've had to allow that man to paw me and manipulate me and expose me to the ridicule of the press and—" I shut my mouth when my voice begins to quaver. "Five months ago I stood by and did nothing, Saber. There's no worse feeling in the world. I have a chance, one chance, to do something to make him pay for everything."

He tosses his hands in the air and turns his back on me, but I'm not finished.

"You think this is just about some sort of petty revenge, but you're wrong. I would rather accept the consequences of doing something wrong than continue to live with the soul-destroying agony of doing *nothing*." I take a few seconds to gather my composure. I need him to understand. "I have no choice."

But there's no softening of his expression. "You don't know the meaning of *no choice*, Dani. You had your choice. And you made it. Now you have to live with it. And so does everyone else."

WHEN OUR SILENT, awkward run to Paris is completed, I set my status to Unavailable and toss off my robe to ready myself for the ball tonight. Saber goes right to my father's office.

"M.A.R.I.E., my corset." I lean over slightly and brace my arms on the gilded settee at the foot of the bed, allowing the nimble dressing-bots to undo my stays. As my corset loosens, I have to regulate my breathing. My lungs ache to expand, to fill, but if I let them, my head spins. I've wound up crumpled on the floor more than once. Only when the urge to gasp in air has passed can

I stand. Slowly. I keep one arm on the bedpost as I straighten. My spine feels weak and soft without the support of the polyethylene boning, and my innards feel like they want to slip into the wrong places.

One dressing-bot unfastens the six hooks that latch the busk into place, and the entire corset falls, leaving the thin, wrinkled linen of my shift clinging to my skin. I peel it carefully away, then pull it over my head. Naked, I step through the doorway and into the bathroom, where a steaming bath, heaping with bubbles, is already waiting for me.

In my hidden washroom I have a modern, water-saving shower, but standing upright while I wash, with a jet of water pounding at my back, is more than I can generally bear without my stays. I've switched to baths almost exclusively. I still get that sickening feeling of my stomach sloshing out of its proper place as I lean forward to wash my feet, but at least I don't have to stand upright and keep my balance at the same time the way I would in a shower. In the end, despite the steamy water and sweet-smelling soaps, it's a relief to be back on my dressing stool, my torso heavily powdered with fine talc and draped in a fresh shift, ready to be relaced.

As the bots begin to tighten my corset, I impulsively call out to M.A.R.I.E. and stop them. I've gone too far, I think. I can barely stand on my own until my stays bear me up. I swallow hard and say, "Four centimeters looser, please." That measurement will only return me to how tight I was lacing when I moved into this room. It's a start. Once the measurement is reached, I don't feel comfort— but it's bearable.

I wish I could turn back time. Two days ago, everything was perfect. Being with Saber made me feel smart, strong, and infinitely worthy. Having lost that, I feel low and selfish. By the time I'm fully decked out, I can't decide if I'm hoping Saber will accompany me to the ball, or if I'd rather preserve what's left of my deflated pride and avoid him for a while.

As it happens, the choice is out of my hands—as are so many things lately. The moment I enter the ballroom and the damned crier announces me at the top of his lungs, Saber falls into place at my right shoulder. Every eye turns to me, whether outright or subtly. It makes me uneasy, but I can hardly have expected anything else. My mother was alive yesterday, and now she's dead.

I'm wearing a more somber dress, befitting my state of mourning, and a wide black silk ribbon is tied around my upper arm. Thankfully, I don't have to be a veritable chirping bird tonight; I can let a touch of my melancholy show. Is any of the melancholy for her? I'd like to think so. One would hope a girl would mourn her own mother. And I'd like to believe that in her own way, my mother did care for me.

But I couldn't actually tell.

I nod silently as wave after wave of nobles and nobodies surges in to offer condolences. No one cares that I'm moody and morose; they simply want to make sure they're seen paying their respects and getting that tick mark in the brownie points column. Molli steps up silently and places a gloved hand in the crook of my arm and simply stands there, a warm presence at my side. I twinge once more at the way she had to come find me, nigh begging for her due as my longtime friend. I've underappreciated her, and it's only now, when there's no chance of turning back, that I understand how much I'll miss her when I'm gone.

It takes not quite two hours before the veritable assembly line ends. "Finally," I mutter to Molli. "I'm utterly parched." I lift a flute from a passing bot and down the entire thing before turning to peek over my shoulder at Saber. Proof of their good breeding, not a single person asked me about cosmetics tonight, but I suspect that Saber's doing brisk business in my wake. Indeed, his messenger bag looks quite flat now. I'll have to find a way to restock him from my still exceptionally full *pannier* pockets.

Unexpected respite comes in the form of Lord Aaron, who sidles up next to me and laughs quietly. "Finally rid of the scheming hag, eh?"

Molli gasps at his words. Trust Lord Aaron to be so bluntly honest, even if his words do feel like a blade to my battered heart.

"You seem jovial," I say instead of actually answering. Because I don't know what the answer is.

"Indeed, I am, thanks to you. Well, perhaps more appropriately, thanks to Sir Spencer, who has been . . . sharing. Whatever is that shimmery rubbish you've been giving me for three months? The other is much better."

I turn to him with wide eyes, too shocked to speak. But as I observe him more closely, the signs are unmistakable. His eyes are wide, pupils dilated, and the flush in his cheeks tells me he's floating right now. I recall having had the thought that Sir Spencer was acquiring quite a lot of Glitter the last week or two. Now I know why. I grip Molli's hand, just to reassure myself that she's there.

"I tell you, I never had any use for sports," Lord Aaron says, eyes still sparkling, "but now? I've seen the light, Your Grace."

He must be high; he never uses my title.

"One-on-one wrestling, fencing, even horseback riding. So much potential for body contact, a good excuse for sweat and short breath, not to mention a masculine respect which I shall never comprehend. Why, Sir Spencer and I have both suddenly discovered we were born for sport. Who knew!"

Lord Aaron has always been prone to fits of mania interspersed with weeks of depression—but this is a whole new level of chipper, a mood so bright it seems to oversaturate even the vibrant emerald of his brocade waistcoat. Which very nearly clashes with his mauve velvet jacket. This is what Glitter does to him. I feel like I'm flailing in black water, with no light to show me which way I should swim. I don't care that his lack of inhibition has led to him finally dallying with Sir Spencer a bit. I hate that he's using, I hate that I can tell, I hate that he doesn't even know. I'm so trapped in indecision I can't move.

"I may find it in me to compete!" Lord Aaron says, flinging his hands in the air and, in doing so, splashing the front of Saber's embroidered livery with the entire contents of his glass.

Saber sputters as the champagne begins to soak into his clothing, and Lord Aaron makes a gasping sound, depositing his empty flute on the tray of a very conveniently passing bot. "So sorry, my good man. I suppose I've had a few too many, eh?" Lord Aaron says a bit too cheerily.

Saber is silent, but his eyes are shooting daggers at Lord Aaron that seem more personal than the offense should justify, and I can't help but feel that I've missed something.

"Come, come. The least I can do is assist you in getting an appropriate change of clothes. Molli, dear," he says, removing her hand from my arm and kissing it twice. "You'll make our excuses, won't you? Back in a trice. Come, both of you," he says, striding away before she can argue.

I turn and glance at Molli as Lord Aaron drags me along, and I cast her an apologetic look, but she's smirking.

"Finally," Lord Aaron says in a far less exuberant tone once we've cleared the main crush. "You can't tell me you didn't want to escape for a few minutes."

"I thought that was what the ladies' retiring room was for, and a best friend who'll take the blame for its need."

"Sometimes, yes," he answers evasively. "Now, you, good man, where are your quarters?"

Saber hesitates, and I feel a flush work its way up my neck to my cheeks. "Actually, he stays in one of my rooms."

"Oh, does he?" Lord Aaron says, the vibrancy back in his voice.

"It's temporary," I say sternly. Which is true. Because we're running away soon.

"Hmm" is the only response I get from Lord Aaron. He turns toward my bedchamber, and we walk silently through two rooms before he whispers, "I suppose you've figured out I have ulterior motives for spiriting the two of you away. Your friend here is out of the rouge that I want, and he informed me—rather brusquely, in point of fact—that he'd have to find a private moment with you

before he could satisfy my request. Thus," he says, gesturing between us, "a private moment."

And thus those daggers in Saber's eyes. He could tell the
champagne was no accident.

"Let's get into my dressing room," I mutter under my breath as
the double doors to the Queen's Apartments open for me. "Here,"
I say, reaching for Saber's messenger bag once we're closed into my
dressing room. "You go change, I'll stock your bag."

"You're an angel," Lord Aaron says, kissing me enthusiasti-
cally on both cheeks. "I'll help Saber. Those jackets are quite fitted
and deucedly difficult to get off by oneself."

Saber starts to argue, but Lord Aaron cuts him off with a
sharp wave of his hand. "Please, it'll be faster this way. Dressing
handsome young men is not only my area of expertise but my
favorite activity as well."

Saber shakes his head and strides off toward his small chamber.

I've just finished emptying my *panniers* into the now-bulging
messenger bag when a door closes hard and Lord Aaron emerges
from the hallway decidedly white-faced.

"Lord Aaron," I say, rushing forward. "Are you ill?"

"Perhaps," he says, no longer sounding high at all. "But it
would put my mind greatly at ease if you would tell me why you've
brought a slave into your rooms."

THIRTY

"WHAT ON EARTH are you talking about?" I ask. For surely his words are a jest, if one in exceptionally poor taste. As a rule, Lord Aaron's taste is impeccable and beyond reproach in every regard, but the Glitter on his cheeks gives me room to doubt.

"Saber is a slave, and it's only my rather prolonged trust and intimacy with you that prevents me from believing that he's *your* slave."

It's ridiculous! "I know he's not in the staff quarters, but that's not because he's a slave. He's being paid, just not by the government of Sonoman-Versailles." I force myself to stop babbling and fix him with a hard stare. "Lord Aaron, it is the twenty-second century. No one in the world practices slavery anymore. Certainly not me."

"Of course not you," Lord Aaron says, then points at the narrow corridor he emerged from only moments before. "But that boy is a black-market slave—for many years, by the look of his mark. And at the moment, he appears to be in servitude to you. You can, I hope, understand how that looks."

My stomach feels hollow. *Mark.* The tattoo—I've seen it many times. Asked about it, even. But Saber told me it was nothing, and

I . . . well, I was easily distracted. I sink down onto the settee when my legs refuse to bear me up.

"You didn't know." Lord Aaron exhales with obvious relief. "Thank God you didn't know. I would hate to have been forced to think ill of you for the rest of my life." He gives me a grin at the end, but it looks more like a grimace.

"I asked him," I say in a choked voice. "He said it was nothing."

"Would *you* have told the truth?"

"Certainly not," I whisper. The words Saber flung at me this afternoon echo in my skull. *You don't know the meaning of no choice.* "*Mon dieu*, he must hate me."

"He doesn't hate you," Lord Aaron says, joining me on the settee.

"No, no, you don't understand. The things I said to him today. I told him my mother sold me to the King. Metaphorically." I remember the way Saber flinched. "But someone actually did sell him once. I think I might faint."

"You never faint."

"I just might." I sit for several long seconds before the buzzing in my head stops. "How can he be a slave?" I whisper. But what I'm really asking is, how could I have worked with a slave? I'm a slavery enabler, and that feels worse than anything else I've ever done. The fact that I didn't know doesn't make it any better, and suddenly the parallel to the hundreds of people I've tricked into unknowingly doing something illegal stabs like a thousand knives in my belly.

"Maybe you should ask him," Lord Aaron says, his eyes darting to the still-empty hallway that Saber has yet to appear from.

"I'll make your excuses—the two of you can decide whether or not to return." He takes the fingertips of both my hands in his and rubs them gently. "You have every reason not to."

"Thank you," I say, and attempt to muster a smile. Attempt and fail.

"Oh," he says, reaching into a pocket. He removes a folded stack of bills and puts them on my dresser, then digs three pots of Glitter out of the messenger bag. "This is the reason I brought you here in the first place." He bends down and kisses my temple. "It will work out. Maybe with this come to light, the two of you can understand each other at last. I've seen how you look at him."

And before I can protest, or say anything at all, his back is turned and he's gone, the wardrobe door swinging shut behind him.

I get to my feet shakily. It's not so much that I'm nervous about approaching Saber as that I'm utterly stunned there's any kind of slave market at all. Not surprised in the least that Lord Aaron knows about it; he's always involved himself more in the world outside our own than I have. But this? Certainly I had a sheltered upbringing, even before moving to the palace. We're a wealthy and somewhat insular people. But we're not stupid. There's not a nation in the world that condones slavery—hasn't been for decades. There are places where people are overworked, underpaid, in some cases perhaps not much better off than slaves. But to mark a person like a piece of inventory?

In this respect, at least, Reginald is more truly Baroque than anyone at the court he despises.

The door of Saber's chamber is ajar, but only a few centimeters. I raise my hand, knuckles forward, to knock, but hesitate.

Knock? On the door to a room we've shared? Where my sense of hope in life was rekindled after I thought it had been extinguished for good? And now to knock as though I'm a stranger—no. I relax my hand and push softly instead.

He's sitting on the bed with the fingertips of each hand touching. The pose appears casual at first, until I see that his fingers are pressed so tightly that they're white.

"Saber?"

He startles. He didn't hear me come in. But at least his fingers separate. He jumps to his feet and looks everywhere but at me. "Is he gone?"

"Lord Aaron? Yes."

"We should go too."

"I don't think we should."

"Why not?"

"Saber, you—"

"Nothing has changed, Danica. I'm the same person, living the same life." He pauses, his face a *tableau* of sharp angles. "You still have a job to do, and, quite frankly, so do I."

"Why didn't you tell me?"

"What good would it have done?" he whispers.

"I don't understand. It can't be legal."

"Says the person selling drugs."

I step back like he's slapped me across the face, but he's not wrong. "I don't . . . how? What happened?"

He shrugs as though it doesn't matter. "My family lived in Eastern Mongolia until I was eight. When the East Asia Conflict got bad, we fled—us, and a million others. We did better than most, got as far as Paris before we ran out of money. Reginald found us sleeping in an alley and said he could get my family to North America—at a price."

"You were the price."

He nods. "Made sense, really. I have four younger siblings. Add in my parents and it was a choice between saving six people and letting seven people starve. We weren't here legally—no papers, no money. Altan wasn't even two yet. I don't . . ." He hesitates. "I don't fault them," he says, more emotion creeping into his recitation now. "They didn't have any good choices."

"Ten years." It's not really a question, simply me doing the math. "And you never tried to—"

"Run away?" Saber asks with a bitter edge that makes my chest hurt. "You ever studied slavery? In *any* culture? Running rarely works out very well."

"But you're here. Can't I . . . I don't know, put you on a plane to somewhere?" I rush forward when he starts to protest. "I'm sure Lord Aaron and I could arrange it. I can use some of my earnings. You'd be on a different continent before Reginald even knew you were gone."

"Stop!" Saber says, his hands on my upper arms. "You think I haven't considered it? You think I haven't thought about all of this before? I'm not stupid."

"Of course not," I say. Almost plead. I just want to get him out of this situation. It makes me sick!

He pushes his shoulders back and slips out of the tight livery jacket. I realize what he's doing when he starts unbuttoning the cuffs of his linen shirt, and my heart starts to pound. I know what's there. But now, comprehending the significance of it, I can hardly bear it.

He pushes the shirt up, and I look more closely at the black mark. It's ten years old, but the lines are still crisp and dark.

"It's code," he says softly. "People with the equipment to decrypt it can see my . . . status. My name, who owns me. There are markings that can be added to say something about my skills, indicate that I'm for sale, even list a price. People like Reginald have diverse interests—drugs, counterfeiting, smuggling, you name it. And every single one of them is careful to the point of paranoia. The slave markings are one way they've found to do business without saying a single, possibly incriminating word."

It doesn't sound paranoid to me at all—it sounds insanely brazen. Tattooing sensitive information onto a human being, even encrypted, sounds like a recipe for disaster. It's so open. So obvious.

"So we get the tattoo removed. I'll take you to the clinic right now. Move-ins are often asked to have visible tattoos removed for historical accuracy."

"You don't understand, Danica. The tattoo doesn't make me a slave; it keeps me alive. Look," he says, pushing his right ear forward with an index finger so I can see behind it. "Do you see that scar?"

"I . . ." At first I don't, but on closer inspection, I can see a wrinkle that might once have been an incision, just where his jawline and earlobe meet. "Maybe?"

"Well, Reginald's plastic surgeons *are* some of the best in the world." Saber grimaces. "There's a chip in there. If it doesn't pick up the right authorization codes at the right time, it cooks my brain. The tattoo is a part of that process; the slaveminder—"

"Slaveminder," I repeat, my world swirling into a sickening surrealism I can't escape.

"It's a bot, just nowhere near as fancy as the ones you've got here. It scans my tat and blasts whatever it is my chip wants to hear. Then I'm safe for a while, but I'm never told how long I have before my next check-in comes due. It's why I sometimes meet with Reginald alone on the weekends."

I remember thinking yesterday that I didn't know how dark Reginald's underground world was. But this? "The police..." But the look of amusement on Saber's face makes my words trail off.

"Oh, they know. Some, anyway. But as far as they're concerned, all this tattoo means is that if they take me into custody, I'll be dead before I can be of use to them. Doesn't matter if they're trying to liberate me, or arrest me, or use me to get to my... employer. The markings are a warning to leave me alone."

I'm aghast, but my brain automatically shifts into coder mode. "Can't you... hack the chip? Get it removed? Surely someone—"

"Surely," Saber interrupts with a bitter chuckle, "someone, somewhere, is working on some way to fight the gangs, and the mobs, and the cartels. To free the slaves, to stop the drugs, to tax the smugglers. That's always true. But the chip in my head is designed to fry me at the first hint of tampering. You can probably imagine that there aren't a lot of slaves out there volunteering to beta-test solution proposals."

I can't give up. If I give up, I'm accepting, and I cannot accept this. "But—there has to be some way—"

He shakes his head. "No. Don't get me wrong; I'm not telling you out of some misguided belief that you might be able to help. I didn't want to tell you at all. I'm stuck, Danica, and I'm not getting unstuck." He shrugs. "So I do what I'm told. Who knows? Maybe someday Reginald'll free me. It's been known to happen."

I feel empty inside. Like knowing the truth about Saber has ripped my soul out and there's nothing to replace it. "You must hate me. The things I make you do. I'm as bad as him."

"I don't hate you. I tried to hate you, don't get me wrong. But I couldn't." He places his hands on both sides of my face and leans in to kiss me so very lightly on the mouth. "But make no mistake," he says, his breath warm against my lips, "I hate what you do."

"I'm so sorry," I say, and the tears I've been holding back spill over the edge, trailing down both cheeks. "I wish . . . I wish I could stop. For you. But I—"

"I know, you can't." He scrubs one tear away with his thumb. "You are the best thing that's happened to me since I was sold to Reginald, and I only get to have you for fifteen more days. So you can bet your ass I'm going to make the most of it."

I try to smile through my tears, but it's too difficult. I can't accept this the way he so obviously has. I hate that he has. Because I know his spirit, and I can only imagine what it must have taken to break it. "I don't know if I can leave without you, Saber. You— you make me feel like I don't have to pull my laces so tight. And I know that doesn't mean anything to you, but you"—I clamp my teeth down on my trembling lip—"you make me wish I were a better person than I am."

"Neither of us is really in a position to be good people right now. Maybe that's just the way it's supposed to be." He kisses me once more—long and lingering this time—then grabs his livery jacket. "Come on, help me into this damned thing."

"We're going back?"

"To the party? Yes. I promised a hell of a lot of batting eyelashes that I'd return with more product. Plus, if we don't move this stock tonight, we'll be too backlogged to catch up."

I give the jacket a good yank and settle the starched collar into place. He turns and offers me his arm, but before I take it, I look into his eyes and whisper, "I'm so, so sorry."

He raises my satin-gloved fingertips to his lips and kisses them with all the gallantry of a Sonoman gentleman. "I'm not."

THIRTY-ONE

DESPITE OUR MUTUAL melancholy, we move our inventory quickly. Heart in my throat, I palm a container of rouge and walk over to Molli.

"The real stuff?" she whispers when I show it to her.

"Of course," I say, and I hate the bright, beaming smile she graces me with at my words. I worked so hard to keep both Lord Aaron and Molli out of it and failed miserably.

"Be careful," I warn, because I must say something, but Saber's warning is bitter in my mouth as I repeat it to Molli. "A little goes a long way."

I hold out my hand, but my fingers are trembling. Can I truly give it to her? To Molli, who feels like the only innocent thing left in my life? Lord Aaron is already using; Saber's very existence is a sad testament to mankind's selfishness; but Molli is so true and loyal and pure. I open my mouth—to say what, I don't even know—but my hands shake so badly I lose my grip on the container and it clatters to the floor.

We both freeze when it lands—facedown, if that's lucky—next to a shimmering, jeweled shoe. I somehow already know whose face I'm going to find when I raise my eyelids.

His Highness stoops and picks up the canister without so much as glancing at its label or contents, and proffers it to Molli. "Yours?" he asks, barely waiting for her silent nod before dropping it into her gloved palm. "Come dance with me," he orders, yanking me alongside him toward the dance floor before I can say a word.

I'm not sure how I manage the steps of the dance as horror fills me. Was I going to give it to her? Would I have changed my mind? I don't honestly know the answer. But I suspect in the end I'd have let her have it, and that kills me inside.

At the end of the party, Saber sees me to my chamber, and I wait while he slips out the back door to my father's office—there to mix a double batch of new cosmetics. I don't offer to help. If he wonders why, he doesn't say.

After checking the back door to my suites and counting to one hundred, I slip out and make my way through the snail-spiral of rooms that belong to the King. Unable to locate him via Lens—and unsure of the wisdom of arranging a meeting by com—I continue trawling his rooms until I find his private office door locked.

I raise my hand and knock, and butterflies take flight in my belly. I've not changed from my ball finery, and I try to remember how elegant I look. How Queen-like. I must use every weapon in my arsenal to make this happen.

Several seconds pass—did I wake him? Or fail to wake him? Is he consulting with M.A.R.I.E. as to the identity of his visitor, or dithering over whether to admit me or send me away? I suppose he could simply be ignoring me. Finally, weasel-faced

Mateus pokes his head out and glares before stepping back to let me through.

"Leave us," I say with a wave of my hand.

I'm certain Mateus looks to his sovereign before obeying, but I don't turn to check. The door clicks shut behind me and I approach the King's desk. There I stand, my hands loosely clasped in front of me.

His Highness is almost ready to retire. He's removed both his jacket and waistcoat, and his long hair is tied back and away from his face—but his tablet is still out, and he's scribbling at it furiously with a stylus. Drafting legislation, perhaps, or approving purchase orders. When it comes to profits, political influence, and power, you can use any one to buy another; the King, scarcely older than me, has all three. It's too much for any one person. Lets him get away with murder.

With a sigh, His Majesty taps his stylus a few more times, then leans back, unfastening one more button on his linen shirt. "Yes, my love?" His tone is so sharp it could almost erase the reasonable pseudo-friend of this morning.

I refuse to cringe. "I've reconsidered," I say flat out. "I've come here to accept the offer you made to me earlier today. I was"—I swallow hard as the dream of his ruination drains away—"I was emotional and irrational. Understandably so, I think. Your offer was exceedingly generous, and a few hours of contemplation have shown me the wisdom of accepting it."

An oily smile crosses His Majesty's face, and I hurry to continue lest I lose control of this situation entirely.

"I do have a few requirements. With my mother so very sadly

deceased, I feel it would be in exceedingly poor taste not to have my father in attendance at my wedding. Therefore, I propose he remain here until we both leave together, a few days after the wedding. Well, all three of us. I shall still require my secretary to continue to manage my affairs." I can't quite hold his gaze as I add that last bit.

It's the most important part.

I have to take him with me. I have to find a way. If I take the King's offer, I won't have to pay for my escape, so I'll have my Glitter profits. Much as the thought sickens me, if I have to *buy* Saber from Reginald to free him, I will. It's a temporary solution—I'll never know peace while the King knows my whereabouts, but Saber's freedom is more important.

His Highness leans back in his chair, looking thoroughly amused. It unnerves me and I continue talking, doing my best to keep my words from unraveling into rambling. But I have to get it all out while I still have the courage.

"For the sake of appearances, my father and I should both be present at the board meeting following the wedding—I'll make sure my father behaves himself—and then there'll be no question of tampering or undue influence. It's in both of our interests. We can leave for Languedoc-Roussillon directly following the vote. That very night, if it pleases you." My votes. My father's votes. I'm selling them to him. All hope of revenge—of justice for Sierra Jamison—gone. A deal with the devil seems more palatable.

But I'll be with Saber. Somehow. I'll free him. I'll find a way to free myself after that.

His Highness doesn't speak for a long time. He's getting what he wants—he should be gloating. But he merely sits, a smirk on his face, looking relaxed. Looking satisfied.

"Really?" he finally says.

"Indeed."

Then, like a snake springing from a coil, His Majesty lets his chair tilt forward and rises from his seat. "I don't think that's the way things are going to happen at all."

Icy fear freezes in my chest as His Highness makes his way around the desk and stalks behind me, running one fingertip along the skin just above my off-the-shoulder gown, producing an insuppressible shiver.

"You see, you're not the only one who's had a few hours to reconsider, love. I did a fair amount of ruminating on my hasty offering as well." He continues to circle and gestures casually with one hand as a sense of foreboding washes over me. "The offer itself wasn't a bad one, *per se*. But your reaction to it changed a lot of things in my mind."

"My reaction?" I say, my face as emotionless as a piece of white parchment.

"I offered you freedom—you instantly rebelled. Everything in my offer hinges upon your voting the way I ask. If I can't control you when you're standing right in front of me, how can I ever expect to maintain my influence over your votes from seven hundred kilometers away?"

"But I'm cooperating."

"You're cooperating now." He's standing at my left shoulder, and he lifts an errant lock of hair, leans down to bring it to his nose. "Your little rebellion was infuriating, yes, but also arousing."

"Don't forget about the video," I say casually, though terror is clawing at my self-control.

"That video never even reached M.A.R.I.E.," the King says in tones of mock condolence. "Your mother made several encrypted copies on storage devices she mailed to coconspirators with fairly explicit instructions. Sadly, none seem to have reached their intended destinations."

"You missed one," I snap, refusing to lose the upper hand. For all I know, he's bluffing too. "Don't underestimate—"

"Enough." The King grabs my arm, spins me around, and pushes me against his desk so quickly that I'm pinned before it even occurs to me to resist. And in that moment, I know I've lost. I've lost for me, I've lost for my father, I've lost for Saber. A squeak escapes my mouth, but His Highness covers it with one hand and places the other firmly behind my back. Planting himself between my knees, he pulls me tight against him, and I feel tears start to prick my eyes.

"I think I want you right here," he says, his lips brushing my neck with each word. "Where I can keep an eye on you. And perhaps a few other things on you as well."

I raise my hands to his chest to push against him, but he's holding me too tightly, and with my feet off the floor, I have no leverage.

"It occurred to me," he continues, his hand so hard against my mouth that my lips are pushing painfully against my teeth, "that your father is in such poor health he could drop dead any day. I shouldn't send him away in such a state. Besides"—his mouth drifts to my *décolletage,* and I try to wrench away but only succeed in pulling my neckline down farther. "When he dies, his only child will inherit his not-insignificant shares. Those plus the Queen's shares will make you one of the most influential women in the kingdom. A real *treasure*."

He's nuzzling my exposed cleavage, and I can't hold back my tears any longer. I've lost everything. I'm not sure I'm going to leave this meeting with my soul intact.

And then his mood seems to take an about-face. Anger clouds his features and he grabs my arms with both hands, sweeping me away from the desk and slamming me up against the wall. Both his hands are around my neck, squeezing, and I feel my airways pinch shut. I scrabble for his hands, claw at them, but I'm still wearing my satin gloves and my fingernails are useless. Darkness hovers at the edges of my vision, and I'm distantly aware of that same awful gagging sound from that long-ago night, this time coming from my own throat.

Then I'm crumpling onto the floor, gasping in cool, fresh air that burns as much as it soothes. It takes several seconds of rasping before my sight filters back in; once I can see again, His Majesty's face invades my vision and I wish I were still blind. He's crouched beside me, entirely too relaxed for a man who has almost killed.

Again.

"You will learn not to defy me, Dani."

"Danica," I rasp instinctively.

"I will call you whatever the hell I desire, and that's the last time you will *ever* correct me." He pauses, perhaps waiting for me to agree, but I'd rather perish on the spot. "We will be wed in fifteen days' time. Your father will vote with me, or I will take his life. You will vote with me or I will make your life a living hell."

He reaches out for my sleeve and yanks it down my arm, nearly exposing my breast, but I don't have the energy to cover myself, much less fight him.

"And I get to keep you," he says, caressing the bare patch of skin. "Maybe forever."

THIRTY-TWO

I DON'T GO to assist Saber when I leave His Majesty's office, even though I should. I can't. I can't face him. Not after the way I failed him—even if he doesn't know it.

Why didn't I accept the King's offer this afternoon? Why! Why did I decide vengeance was worth more than freedom? Why did I think I could have everything?

Knowing I defied him has made him worse than ever. He didn't do more than terrify me tonight. Terrify and disgust me. But he will. After he gets my votes. Fear is his weapon—it always has been. I was a fool to forget it.

When I get back to my room and the bots have removed my finery, instead of loosening my laces, I have M.A.R.I.E. tighten them. Only when I can't breathe without pain do I let the bots tie the strings. I take twice my regular dose of sleeping pills and lie gingerly across the bed, my ribs screaming. I can't do more than breathe shallowly, and just before drifting away I wonder if it's possible to suffocate in one's sleep via stays.

But six hours later I open cottony eyes and the world continues to turn. My head aches and my ribs are so sore I can't move without gritting my teeth, but I live.

I don't let the bots touch my ribbons, though. I deserve this. I destroyed everything. Worse, I had salvation in my hands, and I threw it away. I stand utterly still while the bots whirl around my dressing stool, tossing layers of silk and satin over my head. I see nothing. I try to be quiet—I imagine Saber was working until five or six this morning, and I at least attempt to let him sleep.

But I want . . . I want someone who knew me when I was still a good person. I'm quite certain that label doesn't fit me anymore. This isn't what I planned or expected when I started this journey. I knew I was skirting decency—that selling Glitter wasn't something I'd have done if I didn't feel my life was in peril. But somewhere between my mother's death and discovering the kind of morals I'm enabling via Saber, I've truly begun to wonder if this has all been a mistake.

I want Molli. As soon as I'm presentable, I leave my rooms. My vision feels like a tunnel as I turn down the long wing that houses the families of the lower nobility, and I'm desperate to reach her. A crowd is gathered at the end of the hallway, and I grumble under my breath. It's the last thing I need right now. But as I draw nearer, I realize that among the many, many doors in this section of the palace, the one they're surrounding is Molli's. My heart begins to pound as trepidation roars in my mind.

"Excuse me," I say softly, tapping one man on the shoulder. But I might as well be a gentle breeze for all the attention he shows me. Apprehension bubbles in my chest as the tension and chatter around me rise.

Then something, some pathos-drenched idiom from Giovanni's lessons or maybe even before, whispers, *Remember who you are.* Instantly, reflexively, I cease my gentle tapping of shoulders and stand ramrod straight instead. "Make way," I bark in as Queenly a manner as I can. "Royal business. Stand aside!"

Layers of people peel away as I stride forward, and I don't feel guilty in the least as I finally near the door. What good is power if one cannot use it? There are yet more people inside the tiny atrium of Molli's apartment, but at least the official guards in security livery are holding most of them at bay. One of them steps forward with his hands in front of him like he would stop me from going farther, but I shake my head, wave his hand away, and continue walking toward Molli's bedroom.

He doesn't try to stop me again.

The cramped interior manages to feel crowded even in the absence of a true crowd; I'd almost forgotten that her room is so small. Sometimes I wondered if the administration was trying to get her family to move out without actually evicting them. If there's such a thing as being poor within the Palace of Versailles, the Percy family qualifies.

There's water slopped all over the bathroom floor, and a white sheet has been draped over the form that lies there, sticking almost transparently in patches of wetness.

But the naturally golden hair spreading across the tiles in limp, damp waves is unmistakable. When I hear a guttural cry echo off the tiled walls, it takes several seconds for me to realize it's mine. I'm on my knees beside the body in moments, and I know neither how I got there nor how many people I shoved out of the way. I yank the sheet toward me, and in the moment when my fingers have grasped the wet cotton but haven't yet revealed her face, I indulge in the hope that I'm wrong.

Hands pull at my arms, my shoulders, but I push them away and reach for Molli's body; I cradle her wet hair against my shoulder and feel water trickle down my skin, seeping through my bodice. It might as well be blood.

"What happened?" I ask, once my throat stops convulsing enough for me to speak.

"She drowned," a medical aide says simply. She's not the one who came to clean up after my mother. I'm glad.

"In a bathtub?" I demand, my words dripping with scorn.

The woman visibly tightens her jaw, then shakes her head. "Your . . . Grace? Her father says she's been known to drink heavily. That can result . . . well . . ."

The aide seems to want to say more, but my eyes are fixed on Molli's face. At the top of one cheekbone, I spot a shimmery residue that tells me all I need to know. With her strict parents and the dearth of luxury in her life, Molli's always been one to overindulge when the opportunity presents itself. I should have remembered that. How much did she use? How much has the water already washed away?

"There was only one bot for the entire apartment," the aide goes on, oblivious to the tears that have started rolling down my face anew. "So no one to assist her with her bathing. If she passed out and slipped under—she wouldn't have felt any pain." As though *that* makes any difference.

Whether she overdosed or simply took enough to fly her so

high she couldn't save herself, Molli is dead because of me. I clutch her body until the bathroom is tidied and the gurney has arrived to take her. Reluctantly, I let them lift her up and away from me. The woman offers to allow me to accompany the body to the morgue, but I shake my head.

"Where are her parents?" I ask.

"They were both pretty distraught. Due to their age, we thought it best to sedate them for a few hours. A nurse is sitting in the room with them."

I nod numbly and follow the gurney out of the room. But when it reaches the lift, I hold back and simply watch as they take Molli down to the morgue, all alone.

Molli died because I gave her Glitter. And because she was too poor to afford extra bots. And because, in the end, I didn't do enough for her. Two deaths, and both on my head. Their blood on my hands. When did I lose control?

THIRTY-THREE

I FEEL NOTHING as I walk slowly back toward my chambers. The hem of my dress is soaked, as is the front of my bodice, and it drags and weighs me down like a millstone. I'm certain I look awful, and that the people I see in the halls turn and whisper into their hands the moment I pass, but I don't care.

My feet take me through the *Salle du Sacre,* the Guard Room, the Antechamber, the *Salon des Nobels:* four enormous rooms that lead to the Queen's Bedchamber, but that are all technically "the Queen's Rooms." *My* rooms. Molli's entire family apartment could have fit into any one of them.

As I approach the room that was once, and most famously, occupied by Marie-Antoinette, the double doors open automatically. At a word, they close behind me, and I stand alone in one of the finest rooms in the palace—no, one of the finest bedchambers in the entire world—and I hate myself.

When I start to shiver from the clammy damp of my clothes, I stumble toward the wardrobe, twisting my ankle when I misstep on my heels. My jeweled heels, each worth a fortune by itself. With a savage grunt I kick them off, and one hits the far wall, leaving a dark scuff. In sodden stockings I walk to my vanity, where the empty perfume diffuser sits. I take it in one cold hand, raise it close to my face, and study the angles of the cut glass that catch the light and sparkle, throwing off rainbows.

With a scream, I dash it against the wall.

The sound and sight of shattering glass make me feel better.

No, not better. I'm beginning to imagine that I might never feel better again. But *different,* momentarily. A canister of face cream follows the diffuser, globs of white smearing the walls and dripping down in thick stripes. Farther into the room, past the golden gate, a statue from the bureau. Then a decorative ceramic thimble that might actually be an antique. I don't hesitate. Expensive smashes as loudly as cheap.

A familiar whir sounds in my ears and I turn to see two small cleaning-bots busily collecting crystal shards and misting purple cleaning solution over the smear of lotion. They're far from the only bots in this room; I also have two dressing-bots devoted to me at any given time of the day. Does my schedule include a private visit from the royal *modiste*? Two more will be sent in to assist. Even when I lived with my parents, I usually had a bot to myself. I never thought of it as a safety precaution—in fact, I often found it exceedingly annoying.

But if Molli had had one . . .

I stop looking for porcelain or glass and just start throwing everything I can get my hands on. Shoes, jewelry, bedding, pillow after stupid, pointless pillow. Sealing wax and pens. My writing tablet, which makes five dents in the wall before the screen finally cracks, showing at last the rainbow shards that mean it'll never display an intelligible word again. When there's nothing else to throw, I grab the edge of my dressing table and lift with all my might. The spindly-legged table doesn't stand a chance. It tips precariously, then falls, its curlicue-edged mirror exploding against the golden rail with an earsplitting crash.

In the wake of that cacophony the room goes utterly silent. But then the sound of the whirring bots invades my ears again; time hasn't stopped.

Molli's still dead.

My knees crumple beneath me, and the boning in my corset jars against my already-bruised ribs as I fall to the ground. I welcome the sensation. Sobs shake my body; my mother would have been mortified by the sounds escaping from between my gritted teeth.

I don't know how much time passes before I feel warm arms steal around me. I thought I'd be ashamed to see Saber after failing him so completely last night, but I grasp at whatever comfort he's willing to offer. He holds me cradled against his chest, rocking back and forth like I'm a child. He's saying something, but it's neither English nor French, and in the end, it's not the words he's saying that matter nearly as much as the fact that he's saying them.

I close my eyes and press my face into his shirt and howl against him, liquid agony pouring from me. He smooths my hair from my face and continues to murmur, but he never shushes me, never tells me to stop. Never tells me it'll be all right. He knows life too well to believe such lies.

It feels like hours before my body gives up, too weary to sob any longer. My muscles feel like jelly, and I slump against the first slave to work in Versailles in centuries and somehow, impossibly, the least bitter human being I know. I feel a light tugging at the back of my dress and dimly realize that Saber is unhooking my sodden gown. Slowly, I straighten to give him better access. My arm muscles are sore; I wonder just how hard I've been clutching him.

Once the fastenings at my back are undone, Saber pulls me to my feet. His deft hands peel the soaked bodice down my arms and ribs to my waist, untie my *panniers,* then wrench the whole mess past my wet underskirt until it crumples to the floor. He strips away my damp layers, even though he knows he could ask for mechanical assistance. Soon I'm standing in a silk shift and my stays and stockings. Saber pivots to stand behind me, and I feel him start to untie my laces. "Don't," I say, turning to put my hand on his.

"You need to sleep."

"I sleep in my stays."

"I know, but they're too tight."

Tighter than ever. And still it doesn't help. I thought I was too weary to cry, but tears slide soundlessly down my face. "They have to be," I whisper. "Everything feels wrong when they aren't tight enough."

He gives me a probing look, but after the first few seconds I can't meet his eyes any longer and I close mine. "At least let me loosen them," he whispers.

I can't speak; I just hang my head in defeat.

His fingers are quick and nimble, and it occurs to me to wonder where he learned the intricacies of a woman's corset; then I decide I don't want to know. At first the loosening is a relief, but he keeps going, and soon the corset hangs and I fight the urge to vomit and faint. Gasping, I lean forward and reach for the edge of the bed.

"Are you okay?"

I shake my head, not ready to speak.

"Don't move."

I can't tell where he's gone; I don't have the strength to focus on anything beyond staying conscious. A few more breaths and I'm able to stand upright again, albeit with one hand on the edge of the bed to support me.

Saber emerges from my dressing room with a stack of dry white linen. But I also catch sight of one of my pastel-blue embroidered corsets. "Here," he says. He reaches for the busk in the front of the sodden one and unfastens the six pins. It drops to the ground with a weighty thud, and I know I'll never be able to bring myself to wear it again. "I'll be fast," Saber says, holding the clean, dry shift ready to cast over my head.

I'm not ashamed. I peel the wet cap sleeves off my arms and let the shift drop, the wide *décolletage* easily skimming past my hips. Saber's ready with the new slip, but as he works it over my head, his eyes drop and then widen.

"What happened?" he asks, one finger touching the dark bruising around my ribs, striped with indentations from the wet boning that has pressed against them for hours.

I reach for the dry shift and he seems to snap back into caretaker mode, settling the garment around my hips and covering me up again. He grabs for the blue stays but hesitates. "Can't you take a break?"

After the punishing tightness I subjected myself to last night,

I probably ought to. It's never hurt so badly to come out of my corset.

When I hesitate, Saber adds, "I'll hold you tight," and all I can do is nod.

Soon Saber and I are spooned in the bed, me under the comforter getting warm and him on top of it, his arm tight around my waist like he promised. I gave particular orders to M.A.R.I.E. not to let anyone in, but even these few stolen minutes in the middle of the day are risky. M.A.R.I.E. is always watching. After a fit like the one I just threw, I can imagine amused security workers paying particular attention to this room. But I can't bring myself to care. Slowly, haltingly, I tell Saber about Molli. I don't tell him about the King last night. Or that I chose him over revenge; tried to, anyway.

It can hardly matter now.

"Danica," Saber says hesitantly, "your mother died yesterday. The woman who raised you. I know you were close to Molli, but I'm worried that you're in denial about your mother."

I'm already shaking my head. "I ceased to be a person to my mother years ago. I was a thing. A tool. A road like that goes both ways. Eventually, I stopped thinking of her as a person too."

"But—"

"Saber, do you hate your parents?"

"No," he says instantly and with a vehemence that assures me his words are true.

"Why not?"

"They had no choice," Saber says, emotion making his voice husky, and if this conversation weren't so serious, I'd find it incredibly appealing. "They had to sacrifice one child to save four others. If I—" He takes a long breath. "If I'd been in their shoes I'd have made the same choice."

"That's the difference." I turn now so I can see his face—our lips only a few centimeters apart, though I don't lean closer. Not now. "My mother's been grooming me as a tool for years. Since I was about fourteen."

"Because she dressed you so pretty and made sure you had all of your . . . poise lessons?"

I smirk. "That as well. This isn't the nose I was born with, Saber."

His eyes widen. "Really?"

"At fifteen." My amusement fades and I meet his eyes. "I became a *thing*. A thing to help launch her into social and political success. Every aspect of my life was shaped for the sole purpose of luring the King. And then she put my life in danger for the prestige of being the Queen's mother. She didn't do it for me; she did it for her. And if I'd been in her place, I would never have made the same decision."

"But—"

"I tried, Saber. I tried to remember good things, to feel a spark of the love I know I used to have. What child wants to give up on her mother? But . . . all I can see is the way she looked that night as she bargained me away to the King." I clamp my jaw down as my throat begins to burn. "I hate that I stood by and didn't make a decision at all."

"You were powerless, though."

I shake my head. "I could have done something. I should have done something. If I had, Molli would still be alive."

"Maybe. But where would you be?"

"It doesn't matter. Molli was innocent. So innocent." The tears leak down my temple. "I'll never forgive myself."

"Never is a long time."

"I'll never deserve it."

Saber kisses my skin, right where the path of my tears runs. Tucking my head into the space just below his chin, I curl against his warmth and try to let it seep into me.

I doubt I'll ever feel warm again.

THIRTY-FOUR

IT DOESN'T TAKE warmth to sell Glitter. Which is fortunate, as I seem to have lost my ability to feel anything at all. I smile, I curtsy, and I peddle my illicit cosmetics as though my life depended on it—which was, of course, always the point. I approve wedding plans and have a final fitting for my amazing dress, which can no longer ignite within me even the smallest spark of pleasure. And when the day's whirl is over, I tuck myself into my rooms with Saber and imagine it all away.

It's the last Thursday before my wedding, and Saber and I climb into our carefully watched sedan for my final trip into Paris—my final "dancing lesson." His Highness tried to get me to fob it off, what with the wedding in two days, but I've scarcely spoken to him since that awful night in his private office, and have used clipped, careful tones whenever conversation has become unavoidable. The language I used to reply to this particular suggestion was probably more vulgar than I should have allowed myself. Still, it's the clearest way to decline a suggestion in two words.

Saber's messenger bag is round with just over half a million in euros, and each of my *pannier* pockets is similarly lined. Almost a million and a half between us—the biggest take I've ever delivered to Giovanni, and my nerves are clanging at the prospect of being caught. Of having it all taken away, when I'm so close.

Once we add this to the pile, I'll have four and a half million euros. With two more days until my wedding, though, sales have gotten . . . complicated. Cash is increasingly scarce in Sonoman-Versailles, and unwanted jewels are going out the doors with personal servants in a river of trade that has devolved quickly from gray market to black. Orders didn't drop off this week, but neither did they grow. It's a carefully balanced pile of stones waiting to collapse at the slightest provocation.

Two more days. I'll encourage larger orders with the false insinuation that I'll be leaving for a honeymoon a few days after the wedding. That should take me well over my goal, and I'll be gone before anyone knows it's a lie.

That my life is a lie.

The night before my wedding, I'll hack my way out—with Lord Aaron's help, if necessary. I'll escape via horseback if that's what it takes. One can never trust technology not to fail at the most crucial moment. That leaves me almost exactly forty-eight hours to collect five hundred thousand euros. Once I might have thought such a task impossible.

Saber and I sit silently, fingers entwined, as the car moves smoothly down the road. Saber squeezes gently, and I look up to see that soft affection brimming in his eyes. I don't call it love; it's too difficult to think of it that way. Considering the past six months, the last thing I need or desire is a fiery, adventurous romance. Saber's quiet steadiness has become more than a comfort— the way he reaches out to touch my hand at just the right moment is all the stability I have left. His simple presence, two steps behind my left shoulder as I go about my palace business, makes me stronger.

The car stops and Saber slides from the seat, reaching out a hand to assist me. The door of the dance studio opens, and for an instant we all don our masks—the haughty noblewoman, her scandalously handsome secretary, the subservient dance teacher. Closing the door behind us feels like closing out another world.

"Just pull it out. I'll take care of stacking it," Saber says as we kneel in front of Giovanni's closet, one floor up, a few minutes later. "You're obviously anxious—you head out, I'll finish here and then join you."

"Thank you," I say, rising to my feet. I was hoping for an opportunity like this. I hurry down the stairs and pause for just a moment to thank Giovanni again, then pull my black cloak over my rose-colored silk gown before slipping out the back door.

I'm not there first, but it doesn't appear Reginald's been waiting long. "I'll need ten vials this week," I say softly.

"This week?" he asks, clearly finding humor in my words. I find none. "I thought you were leaving in two days."

"Large orders in anticipation of my absence. For my supposed honeymoon."

"Desperate, eh?"

"Certainly not," I reply with a scoff. "But it can't hurt to have some additional capital on hand in whatever new life you've prepared for me. The goal of five million is essentially met."

"Essentially?"

I decline to dignify his taunt with a reaction. "I need you to be ready. My plan is to leave the palace on Friday night—well, technically early Saturday morning, say three a.m.-ish? I'll need a dependable way to contact you."

"Easy." He hands me a small cell phone. It's an archaic and clumsy device compared to the Lenses, and I wasn't entirely sure they still existed. But I suppose they have their uses. Especially if you're a criminal.

"My contact information's already programmed in there. I'll be ready."

"Good, good." I swallow hard, but I know this is the only chance I'm going to get. "Reginald, I want Saber."

"A blind man could see that," Reginald says, then guffaws at his own joke.

"I want to you to free him; send him with me."

His face freezes. "And why the hell would I do that?"

"We both know you never actually expected me to raise the five million. And saying my Glitter sales at the palace have been outstanding is a gross understatement." I raise an eyebrow. "My worth to you in the last few months more than justifies a small favor, in my opinion."

He hawks low in his throat and spits on the ground. "That's what I think of your opinion, missy. Saber belongs to me, and that's that."

"Be reasonable."

"I'm always reasonable."

I force myself to keep my voice calm. "I could attempt to offer you more money for him, but I've already given you something better. We both know how much you hate Sonoman-Versailles; I've handed you the power to make another five million off them with utter ease. Or contact the authorities and send them in on a raid. Do that and you might well topple the entire kingdom, dissolve the pocket sovereignty, and restore the palace to the people of France. I've handed you my entire *world* to do with as you will, and you know it—you almost certainly planned it. All I'm asking is one life. Just one." My voice cracks at the end, but I haven't the pride to feel ashamed.

Reginald's face is inexplicably stony as he leans forward, the acrid scent of stale tobacco filling my nostrils. "And if you want it, you're going to have to pay for it, just like the next sorry sod, and you ain't got enough money for two."

My eyes widen and my mouth is so dry I can't swallow.

I thought for sure . . .

I hear the slightest scuff behind me and spin to see Saber leaning against the wall. I feel the blood drain from my face as I realize that if he didn't hear the entire conversation, he heard enough.

"Here," Reginald says, holding out several vials of shimmering Glitter. We go through our regular routine of tucking them into the pockets that hang under my skirts as though nothing out of the ordinary has happened. The moment we're finished, I'm itching to get away, but Reginald halts us. "Almost forgot these," he says, handing an envelope to Saber, who wordlessly tucks it into his breast pocket and continues to Giovanni's back door.

That's right. My father's patches. The force that propelled me into this nightmare to begin with. I'm so disgusted with Reginald that all I want is to get out of his presence. I hate that I need him. I hate that he owns Saber.

The door from the alley closes, and Saber whirls on me. "What were you thinking?"

His anger feels like a blow. "I—how can it hurt to ask?"

"Hurt? You've destroyed everything!"

"I don't see how that's even possible."

"I fly under the radar, Danica. I do as I'm told, I never complain, I'm never punished. But now?" He runs his fingers through his hair with a low groan. "That was clumsy at best, but seriously, the worst possible way to go about it with Reginald. Insinuating that he owed you? What did you think would happen?"

I'm feeling my own temper rise as Giovanni comes around the corner, looking concerned.

"I thought he would see how much I've done for him. That he would be rational."

"He's not rational! He's the height of irrational. How the hell could anyone rational live the life he lives? Why didn't you tell me what you were going to do?"

"I thought it would work. I wanted to help you; to free you."

But Saber's already shaking his head. "You think you can just do things and mess with people's lives without consulting them. That's your problem—that's the problem with all of this!" he says, spreading his hands wide. "You think your little life is so important that you can change other people's futures and it doesn't matter what they want, or think. And somehow, you're sure you have the power to make everything all right."

"Power?" I shoot back, almost yelling. "I have no power, Saber. I've never felt so powerless in my life. But I thought that this one thing—this one tiny thing—maybe I could do it and . . . and . . ."

"And redeem yourself?" Saber asks. "One nearly useless life for the hundreds you've ruined?"

"I wanted to bring you with me," I shout back, and silence falls over the studio.

"Ah," Saber says after a long pause. "So even freeing me was self-serving in the end."

I want to argue with him, but the words catch in my throat in a surge of indignation. I feel falsely accused, and the hurt and anger war into a tight ball of emotions I can't speak past.

He's right, of course. I should have talked to him. Not only so that the person who knows Reginald best could advise my strategy, but simply because I should have asked if he even wanted to come. I took his future and tried to shape it to my own liking. The thought that makes the anger drain away and the shame take over is that I treated him like the slave he is.

Saber mentioned punishments; would Reginald hurt him for this? Kill him for this? The thought makes me ill.

"I'm sorry," I whisper through my tears. But it's too late. I've ruined any chance of his coming with me, and I'll leave him with a strained relationship with the man who controls every aspect of his life. It's possible I've destroyed any already-dim future Saber might have dreamed of, in one fell swoop.

Saber's shoulders crumple at my words, and he steps forward to enfold me in his arms. "I'll handle it," he says gruffly. "As long as I can convince him I didn't put you up to it, it should end up okay."

"Why would he think you had anything to do with it?"

Saber arches an eyebrow. "How else would you know about my situation at all?"

I hadn't even considered that. Of course Reginald would think Saber had told me a sob story and we'd hatched a plan—a plan for Saber to essentially run away.

Saber's right—I was stupid.

"Let's get back to that godforsaken palace one last time," Saber says with false cheeriness. "We have a job to do."

The ride back to Versailles somehow feels both longer and shorter than usual. In two days I'm expected to wed the King. In two days, to keep that from happening, I'll have to leave Saber behind, and my father as well. I'm too beaten to feel triumphant, too triumphant to feel beaten.

The car glides through the golden gates, around to the back of the palace, and into the underground garage. I wish I could hold Saber's hand as we walk from the car to the lift that will take us back into palace life. Even the lift ride feels too long. When we step out of it and back into the frescoed hallway, three guards are waiting, and after dropping quick bows, they gesture both Saber and me into a small alcove. "What on earth is going on?" I demand.

One of the guards holds up his tablet to show me a document with a few scrawled signatures at the bottom. "Warrant," he says. "My apologies, but I'll need to search you, Your Grace."

My heart seems to stop and then race almost simultaneously. "I don't understand," I say, but my voice is much quieter now.

"A tip that something might be brought in from Paris" is all the man says. "Don't worry; there's no need for this to be uncomfortable. If you would please turn around for me, Your Grace?"

Saber, however, is not shown nearly the courtesy I am. The

guard closest to him shoves him against the wall and yanks his arms behind him before applying magnetic cuffs.

"Is there a need for those?" I say, stepping forward, then halting when a thick arm snakes out in front of me.

"Just searching him, too, Your Grace. More likely to be him than you, if you get my meaning."

He laughs, but the sound dies away under my withering glare at his insulting assumption.

"If you both hold still, this'll be over before you know it."

"Somehow I doubt that," I say wryly. I glare at the man but hold stock-still as his hands range very tremulously over my form. I keep a careful eye on Saber, who's patted down roughly, his breeches nearly torn when they turn his pockets out. Even without a warning from me, however, he's not fighting. I hate that he knows better.

They dump his messenger bag on the floor but hardly look at the contents once they prove to be run-of-the-mill. Thank goodness I had the foresight to carry all of the illegal vials myself.

My valise is similarly emptied, though it's poured out gently onto a nearby table. I have to stifle a hysterical giggle when the three pots of Glitter are examined and set aside. The guard searching me apologizes before zipping open my *pannier* pockets and reaching carefully into them. I'm not worried. It was Saber's idea to line the seam of the pockets with Velcro, and unless this guard feels some odd need to press quite hard on the bottom of my shallow pockets, he'll never discover they lead to a much vaster space.

He doesn't push, and I let my breath out slowly, silently, tasting victory.

Until a voice sounds from my right. "Sir, I've got something."

I turn, my eyes wide with horror as I realize, immediately, what they've found. The torn-open envelope of patches is held aloft in the guard's hand, and I can see a hint of frustration etched across Saber's face. The guard holding the tablet takes the envelope, removes a patch, and lays it on his tablet, where a red line scans it. I hold my breath. After a few seconds it beeps, and the guard looks confused and does it again. When the tablet beeps a second time, the guard purses his lips, then looks up and says, "Arrest him. Take him downstairs."

Saber turns to look at me, and for just a moment, before he hides it, I see fear in his eyes. Damn that envelope! Damn my father for needing it! But there's nothing I can do as the guards pull him to the still-open lift, and, frozen in terror, I watch as the doors close between us.

A soft chuckle pulls me from my terrible thoughts, and I turn just in time to see Lady Cyn cover her Glittery lips with one gloved hand—as though to belatedly stifle the sound—then disappear around the corner.

THIRTY-FIVE

I FIGHT THE urge to run after her and slap her across her too-pretty face. Perhaps with the back of my hand, which bears two sharp rings. But Lady Cyn isn't the actual problem. She's simply desperate. She's about to lose the only dream she's ever truly held in her entire life; after that awful moment in the Hall of Mirrors, I should have expected one last, desperate act of malice from her.

Still . . .

A tip, the guard said. No one would search the future Queen on a simple suggestion from an adolescent lady of the court. No, even if Lady Cyn was the betrayer, the order would have to come from the King himself. I tipped my hand when I allowed him to see how much I needed Saber. When Lady Cyn ratted out her own supplier to her lover, she must have hoped the King would see me for what I really am—and throw me over, just days before the wedding.

Foolish whore. All she did was hand His Majesty a reason to separate me from the one person he thought I might sneak away with, leaving her path clear.

I spin from wherever Lady Cyn is headed and aim for the

King's public rooms instead. He'll be there, likely surrounded by a dozen cronies, forcing me to face him very much in the court's eye if I want to confront him at all. Sure enough, I find him in the *Salon d'Apollon* enjoying *apéritifs* with what looks like half the governing board. It's strange to see him there with a group of powerful men, each no less than fifteen years his senior. I see for the first time just how hard he must work to hide his youth from them. But there's no room in my heart for sympathy today.

"My liege," I say with a calm smile.

"My love," he replies, raising his glass jovially.

My insides explode, like the crystal diffuser I threw against Marie-Antoinette's wall, but I don't let myself betray so much as a flicker of my eyelashes. I simply stand, arms in careful ballerina arcs, fingertips touching in front of my skirts, with my head tilted slightly to the side in a pose of anticipation.

The men's eyes keep darting to me, and I can feel the tension around us rise as I stand, so obviously wanting His Highness' attention; His Highness so clearly ignoring me.

Finally he can avoid it no longer. "Do you require something, darling?"

That I don't lash out at his false show of affection in this crucial moment is possibly the greatest victory a dance instructor has ever won.

"A brief word, Justin?" I ask, lowering my eyelids and bobbing the shallowest of curtsies as I commit the grievous sin of addressing him by his first name in front of his much-older toadies.

"A word and a kiss, perhaps?" he says, challenge glimmering in his eyes alongside anger.

Silently, I offer him not my mouth, nor my cheek, but raise my gloved hand.

The men around him burst into laughter, and though he shoots me a swift glare, His Majesty joins them.

"Methinks my lady is displeased with me." The wry comment is made in Duke Darzi's ear and behind a gloved hand, but easily loud enough for everyone in the vicinity to hear. There are mutters of good-natured ribbing, and the King steps forward, makes me a deep, elaborate bow with multiple flourishes, then rises and offers me his arm.

"A turn about the *salon* would be lovely," I say, making it clear that we are not to adjourn to his private office.

"The better to be seen, my dear."

"My, what large teeth you have," I reply. The brandy on his breath makes my stomach simmer. As we depart the gentlemen, I tilt my head toward his as though I have secrets to share. "You've just deprived me of my personal secretary, two days before my wedding. I fail to see how you expect me to get anything done."

"Not to worry—I'm bringing in a dozen extra staff this evening. Any and all of them are at your disposal." He makes no attempt to deny that it was his doing.

"There's so much that will need to be redone without Saber's presence."

"I'm replacing him with twelve ladies," His Highness says, putting a clear emphasis on the new staff members' gender. "I'm confident you'll manage."

I quickly glance around us. "Abandon this pretense, Justin. Why?" I stop walking and turn to look him square in the face.

"I was informed that this outsider was bringing illicit substances into the palace. You know I can't turn a blind eye to that."

"You could have waited until after the wedding. Why now? And for God's sake, tell me the truth for once."

The King takes both my hands and raises my fingertips to his lips, not quite kissing them. "Danica, in our months together I've told you many truths. I only wish you'd believed them." He drops my hands abruptly and offers his arm again, starting to move forward without waiting to see if I'll accept. I almost have to lunge for his elbow to keep up. "It's not easy, but I am trying not to underestimate you. You'd be fighting every last wedding plan if you didn't think you could run away. In truth, you never would have spurned the offer I made two weeks ago if you didn't already have a plausible escape at the ready. And who's the one person most likely to assist you in carrying out such a plan?"

I don't answer. I don't have to.

"You understand, then, why I couldn't allow him to remain at your side. Oh, one more thing," he says, leaning down so his mouth is close to my ear. "You'll be pleased to know that, owing to the unfortunate circumstances surrounding your mother's death, safety protocols have been revised—no more unmonitored offices in the residential areas of the palace. A life could have been saved. Alternative arrangements will be made to ensure the business privacy of our noble board members, of course, but we'd hate to have a repeat incident."

What he doesn't say is that he knows Saber and I have been spending many hours alone in that unmonitored space. He assumes he knows what we were doing there.

That's not where we did that.

"We wouldn't want anything to happen to your surviving parent, would we?" His last words come out in a growl, and I understand that this is a threat. And not an empty one. If my father were to die, the King would lose nothing; my father's shares and votes would pass to me, and the King—already assigned as my guardian and taking it upon himself to authorize my otherwise illegal underage marriage—would wield them. "Consider yourself under lock and key," His Highness says in a whisper.

We've finished our circuit of the large room and are approaching the group of loud, tipsy men again. My entire body is numb, and it's only my hand tucked into the crook of His Highness' arm that keeps me moving forward at all.

"You must join us in a toast, my pet," His Majesty says, pushing me toward the center of the circle and effectively ending our private conversation. "They got in a case of Henri Jayer Cros-Parantoux—five thousand euros a bottle, and that a bargain, I'm assured."

The men around him chuckle.

"Here," he says, putting a tiny silver goblet into my gloved hand and closing my fingers around it, seeming to understand that I've grown too numb, too frazzled, to grip it without assistance. "To us."

I take the small glass of outrageously expensive wine without a word, and in one gulp, I toss back an ounce of liquid worth nearly six pots of drugged cosmetics. "Indeed," I say, whipping out my fan and fluttering it over my chest as my throat begins to burn. "This has been enlightening."

I leave without a backward glance.

THIRTY-SIX

TONIGHT IS THE last *fête* before selected press members descend upon us tomorrow, and the King has requested that we give an informal performance of the elaborate dance we've been practicing for three weeks. The one we're supposed to perform for all the cameras tomorrow night. The one that made him realize he truly does want me for his Queen.

The one I taught Molli.

I know my face must be going back and forth between being flushed with mortification and white from despair, but I can't seem to get hold of my emotions tonight.

As the music plays, I can feel the oily weight of His Highness' eyes on me—mostly the part of me below my shoulders—and it's all I can do not to flee the hall. Finally, we strike our last pose and His Majesty comes forward, clapping his hands. He grabs me tight and forces a kiss on me.

"My Queen in nearly every way," he declares to a smattering of applause. "How glorious it'll be when you're finally *fully* mine," he says, for my ears only. His fingers tighten on my bodice, a centimeter below my breasts, and a groan of want rumbles low in his throat.

The King finally lets me go and leads me to the high table, where course after course of delicacies is placed before me. I try to eat—I know I'm going to need my strength—but even the desserts can't tempt me.

The champagne, however, goes down fine.

"Of course I'm delighted," I say, beaming at yet another noble as I walk through the crowds once the meal is finally complete. I couldn't say which noble; they've all become a blur, and when this one moves on and a new one steps in front of me, I notice nothing until he shakes my arm hard.

"Danica, are you okay?"

My eyes must have been completely out of focus, and I'm uncertain for how long. "Lord Aaron," I say in a whoosh of a sigh. "Take me for a turn about the room? I fear I've had more to drink than I realized."

"Certainly." Instead of offering me his arm, Lord Aaron places a firm hand at my waist, steadies the nearly empty flute of champagne in my hand, and steers me rather defensively through the milling crowd toward the balcony doors on the far end of the Hall of Mirrors.

It's a small balcony, and I'm not sure coming here was a great idea, but Lord Aaron says something to the other two occupants *sotto voce,* and they drop quick bows and leave. Then Lord Aaron turns his back to the warm, overfilled hall and shields his hands as he pulls out a small wireless keypad and fiddles with it.

"That . . . should . . . do it!" he says, pocketing the keypad as the sliding double doors hiss shut and lock with a click. "M.A.R.I.E. will figure it out in about ten minutes, but—"

"Ten minutes is a godsend, Lord Aaron, thank you."

"You don't look well."

I laugh. "You certainly know how to ingratiate yourself with a lady."

"I know how to be honest with a friend."

That sobers me, and I nod. "You're right. Is it obvious?"

"Probably only to me."

"Or Molli, if she were here." I shouldn't have said her name. Instantly I'm blinking back tears.

"Or Molli," he whispers, raising his own glass, which has a splash of port in the bottom. "May she know how well she was loved." He tings his glass against mine and we both take a sip. "Where's Saber?" Lord Aaron asks, staring out at the cloudy evening sky.

"Arrested."

"Arrested?" Lord Aaron asks, his voice far louder than mine, and I have to shush him. "For what?"

"Carrying an illicit substance."

"Illicit? Not . . ." He gestures at the smear of Glittery rouge at the top of his own cheekbone. He's probably shut off M.A.R.I.E.'s microphones as well as hacking the door closed, but we should keep our voices low anyway.

"Not precisely, no," I say, choosing my words carefully. "But similar. The important part is that the charge might be *legitimate*."

"Who spilled?" Lord Aaron asks.

"Who else? Lady Cyn."

"Shall we ruin her?"

"I haven't the time." Though, sadly, this move of hers may mean I now have all the time in the world. His Majesty's plan has derailed my own more thoroughly than he can possibly know. I suspect he thought himself clever, cutting off the room he assumed Saber and I were trysting in. But despite Lady Cyn's malicious tip, I don't think the King actually knows the true nature of the Glitter. With the patches in his security staff's possession, it may only be a matter of time, but clearly what he's concerned about is my running off with a paramour—not escaping via a fortune in dirty money.

Still, since the King has reinstated the monitoring in my father's rooms, even if I had Saber to help me, I've no way to make more product. Nothing to sell. And still half a million shy. Besides which, the thought of leaving Saber is killing me.

"I'm short my fee," I confess to Lord Aaron with a quavering voice.

"Your fee?"

"To the man in the catacombs. And without Saber, I can't . . . make it up."

Lord Aaron nods; then his eyes widen as he puts the pieces together. His jaw drops open and he stares at me for long seconds. "You've been . . . this—" He points at his cheek again, then straightens and laughs. "You're brilliant."

But I shake my head. "Not brilliant enough. Not brilliant at all, really. Just desperate. And not without"—I choke on the word and have to clear my throat—"without consequences," I finish in a whisper.

"Oh, Dani," Lord Aaron says, softly, but with a terrible edge of understanding. "What have—"

"Please do not ask me," I interrupt, my voice so wobbly the

words barely get out. "There are secrets so dangerous one shouldn't even confess them to the dearest of friends."

He hesitates, then whispers, "Like, perhaps, that one is in love with a newlywed nobleman whose father-in-law intends to use him to usurp the King?" Lord Aaron's face is utterly devoid of amusement. "Only to be two days too late to save my dearest friend from a hellish marriage?"

So Lord Aaron knows. That means Sir Spencer knows.

"The King is aware," I whisper.

"Of course he is. That's why you're getting married in two days."

It's to be all-out corporate warfare, then. "It's possible my secrets are even worse," I say with a tight smile.

"Worse than the usurpation of an entire kingdom?"

"No. Worse because if I say the words aloud they might collapse my soul, which already rivals the Tower of Pisa in its skew."

"What can I do?" Lord Aaron asks after a very long silence.

"I don't know. My safe place is . . . no longer safe. The cosmetics are in one place, and the . . . special ingredient in another, and I can't get the two of them together. And I've only"—I glance through the glass doors to the enormous clock on the wall—"about thirty-six hours to think of something else."

"Why think of something else when what you're doing has been working?"

"I can't!" I protest. "I have no product."

Lord Aaron taps a finger against his lips. "If you did, could you make the money you need tonight?"

"I intended to convince several people to buy extra, with the excuse that I'll be headed off on my honeymoon next week. That would have taken me above what I need." I peer up at him from under my lashes. "The hope was to have something to . . . take with me."

"Understood." The LED on the double doors starts blinking, and Lord Aaron's gaze flits over to it. "M.A.R.I.E.'s initiating an override; Cinderella time."

I let out an exceptionally unladylike snort and lift the edge of my gown. "It's always Cinderella time here, Lord Aaron." I blink back tears; the champagne is making me downright morose. "And I suppose it always will be, now."

"Your Grace," Lord Aaron says sternly, "you're giving up too easily. Come," he adds, offering his arm as the double doors slide open. "I'm going to introduce you to the delightful world of preorders."

The idea strikes me as something I should have come up with myself, and I groan. "I'm an idiot."

"You'd have thought of it if you hadn't been drowning your sorrows in quite so much champagne," Lord Aaron says, sliding a sideways glance at me. He's likely right. "Come; follow my lead."

"You're going to help me?"

"Have I ever done anything else?"

His words are so true. I'll owe Lord Aaron favors until I'm cold and rotting in the ground. "Thank you," I say softly, because that's all the volume I can manage with the lump in my throat.

On Lord Aaron's arm, I flit through the ballroom, trying my best to act the part of delighted bride-to-be—a role I've been sadly remiss in the last two weeks. Lord Aaron gushes about a prolonged honeymoon at an Italian villa, a tale that grows more extravagant with each telling. "Two weeks!" he exclaims to Duchess Darzi. "So order accordingly, and Her Grace's supplier promises to deliver the day after the wedding."

"Splendid!" the duchess proclaims, and arranges to have her fee sent to my rooms in the morning.

Everyone is caught up in the whirl of the festivities, the splendor of the invented honeymoon, and the heart-racing promise of larger quantities of Glitter; tall stacks of money are handed over almost without thought. By the end of the night, my *pannier* pockets are weighted down with three hundred thousand euros, with nearly half a million promised on the morrow.

It's like accompanying a magician—Lord Aaron waves his wand of false promise and money appears. But like all magic, it's an illusion. There will be no delivery the day after the wedding. I'll be gone, the court will have been tricked, and though he says nothing about it, we both know I'm leaving Lord Aaron to pick up the pieces.

THIRTY-SEVEN

ON THE MORNING of the day before my wedding, I receive word that my father is severely ill. The physicians suspect food poisoning. I'd suspect the King's hand, if I didn't already know it was withdrawal.

The patches Saber was bringing for my father were confiscated by security, so he hasn't had a hit in more than twenty-four hours. I don't know what to do. I have one pot of real Glitter left in my reticule; I could go and ease his suffering some. But the best I can do is postpone the inevitable, because I'm leaving Versailles today, one way or another, and I haven't the power to bring him with me. Perhaps Father's being cut off is best for everyone.

My conscience is frayed nigh to pieces; months ago I asked myself if my life was worth what it would take to raise this money. At the time I said yes. Now that it's nearly done, I'm not so sure. Is it truly worth saving your life if you lose your soul in the process? But like a cart careening down a hill, I've set too many processes in motion. At this point they're being carried out with or without my cooperation.

I'm watched wherever I go, but so many wedding gifts and

cards are arriving in my chambers that no one notices the thick envelopes I sneak into my pockets.

At two in the afternoon, I hit my goal.

By five I have nearly a quarter of a million euros to keep for myself.

Using the phone he provided, I send a text to Reginald to let him know I have the money. He doesn't send a response. I'd feel inordinately better if I knew for sure there'd be someone ready to pick me up at Giovanni's.

There's someone around me at nearly every moment of the day, but at least the toilet is still a private event. I don't know what to bring, and finally I settle on the jeans and shirt I used the night I tried to escape in the catacombs. My half-boots will match well enough, and no one will think it too odd that I'm wearing them, even with my more formal gown. I'm beginning a new life—there's truly nothing else to bring that won't mark me as a former citizen of Sonoman-Versailles. I roll the clothes tightly and scrunch them into the cage of my *panniers* on the left side. The right is stacked with euros. I'm as prepared as I can be and am simply waiting for the ridiculous ball tonight to be over. It's an unfamiliar sensation, looking forward to something; for months I've been begging the clock to stop, to turn back. Two hours before the ball, I'm dressed and ready when Lord Aaron presents himself at my door, all smiles and low, flourishing bows.

"Your Grace," he says, bending to kiss my hand. "I have a present for you," he adds softly. "I think I can override the system to let you visit Saber in the prisons, and still make my way in after the *soirée*. If you're game to risk it."

My chin trembles, but I know my answer without having to think. "Of course."

"I'm taking Her Almost-Highness on a stroll," Lord Aaron informs a stern-looking woman—one of my new staff, who, knowing His Highness, must be trained much more thoroughly in security than in couturiery. "We shan't leave the palace," he assures her before she can protest.

She lets us depart, but about ten seconds after we leave the Queen's Bedchamber, I glance back and see one of the younger new maids—even younger than me, I think—stepping through the double doors with an armload of satin, looking for all the world like she's been sent on an errand.

"We have a tail," I murmur to Lord Aaron.

"As expected. Not to worry." He laughs brightly at something I haven't said, but I don't dare join him. My nerves are stretched tight, and any sound I made would be false and brittle.

He carries my hand in his, held formally high, and chatters and giggles all the way down one hallway and then another. The girl continues to follow us, her cheeks red as it becomes evident that she's on no errand for the dressmaker.

"A little faster now," Lord Aaron says as he approaches the end of a long wing.

We turn and he looks up at the ceiling. "Blackout spot."

"Really?" This is a new secret.

"Not always," Lord Aaron says, confirming my suspicions. "Just for the next five minutes. Here!" He nearly swings me around another corner and into a lift waiting with its doors open. "Press *B*, quick!"

I hear the young woman's footsteps, but the doors close fully before she makes it around the corner. "It's going to be obvious where we've gone," I say.

"A little faith, Dani, please." Lord Aaron pulls out the wireless keypad he used on the balcony yesterday evening. "We're not hiding—of course she'll know where we've gone. But now she can't follow us, can she? At least not without running to the emergency stairs on the other end of this wing, which she may or may not have clearance to enter." He pulls a length of optic fiber from his pocket and patches it into a small opening in the lift panel. "More likely she'll wait for the lift to return, and that'll be her mistake."

"Jam the lift; of course." An elementary bit of hacking.

"Done," Lord Aaron says, snatching the fiber back out and curling it into his fist as the doors open on the starkly modern—and thus barren-looking—basement. "This way," he says after glancing down at his tablet, fingers flying across the surface, inputting coordinates. I recognize this as an update to his location hack—he's telling M.A.R.I.E. that our Lenses aren't on the grid. I suppress a twinge of curiosity—or maybe jealousy. He's always been a better hacker than me. Ironically, I was always too worried about breaking rules.

We follow a veritable maze of hallways, and I'm once again struck by how massive this level is. Obviously it's a mirror of the palace layout above, but without the cavernous *salons* and ballrooms, it seems they can fit hundreds of tiny cubicles and storage rooms down here, and I can't help but wonder what secrets they hold.

"This one." Lord Aaron points at a door with a large window

in it, then opens it for me with a graceful swing of his arm—all smiles and tittering laughter.

The room that greets us is small and stark, with one heavy door and a single counter in front of a desk, where a man in a black uniform sits. My stomach quivers when I see a gun at his belt. I've rarely seen such a weapon, and never this close.

"Visiting pass," Lord Aaron says, holding up his tablet with a document on it that looks much like the one the security guard showed me yesterday when he searched us.

Forgery? Well, Lord Aaron's talents do astound.

I expect the man to be stern and demand . . . something more from us, but he merely shrugs, then rises and comes around the desk to the heavy door. He slides an ID card and holds still for a retinal scan before a loud clank sounds—presumably, the release of the internal locking mechanisms. My stomach writhes within me at the twin fears of being caught and seeing Saber again. We hardly parted on good terms.

The guard pauses with the door open a crack. "I'll be watching you on the monitor out here," he says, attempting to sound reassuring. "But if you need me to intervene at any point, you can just give a yell."

I raise my nose into the air. "I'm in no danger from that person. He's my former secretary, and I simply need some details regarding plans for my wedding."

The guard gives a shrug. He's not dressed in the manner of Sonoman-Versailles, and I find myself wondering if he has any idea what's happening in our glimmering world ten meters overhead. "I'll lock you in now, ma'am."

Ma'am? Definitely not court.

"Ten minutes. I open the door again, you're done."

I nod curtly, every nerve within me dancing.

When I step through the doorway, Saber's eyes widen when he sees me, and though he maintains a calm expression, he bounces on his toes in impatience. I swallow hard and tears sting my eyes at the sight of him behind bars, but I force myself to remain still until the door closes behind me. As soon as the locks clang back into place, I rush forward. "Saber!"

His arms reach for me through the bars, and I don't even care that I hit my cheekbone against the cold metal in my haste. His lips are warm and desperate on mine. Delving, then moving to my forehead, my cheeks, back to my mouth. Laughter bubbles up, and it seems impossible that it's only been a day since we last spoke.

"I'm so sorry I yelled," he whispers.

"I don't care."

"I love that you tried."

"I love *you.*" The words are out without preamble, and I smile at the rightness of them.

Saber doesn't answer in words, but his lips, hungry on mine, are response enough. Minutes fly by, and I know we should be speaking, but I can't break away.

"Why are you here?" he murmurs against my mouth, then covers it before I can answer.

"I had one chance to see you," I gasp when he lets me breathe. "I couldn't resist." My arms are through the bars now too, clinging to him. I should care that some random guard—not to mention Lord Aaron—is watching this entire exchange on the monitor, but

I can no longer afford pride. I can't even bring myself to care that M.A.R.I.E. is certainly monitoring. By tomorrow it won't matter. "What's going to happen to you?" I ask in the softest whisper I can manage, hoping any microphones down here will pick up only muffled words.

A grimace crosses his face. "Reginald will get me out. When he feels like it." He draws me close, his mouth brushing my ear. "Don't worry about me. Reginald's incredibly powerful."

"But if he doesn't—"

"Then I'm dead." Saber shrugs. "The chip is always counting down, and whether or not I get an extension has always been Reginald's decision, not mine."

A whimper escapes my mouth, and Saber sighs.

"Sorry if that sounds *macabre,* but when death lives on your shoulder, you get pretty used to it."

"Are you sure?"

"I've been in worse scrapes. Don't underestimate Reginald."

"So he could have had you out already?" I grumble.

"Yes. But that kind of interference might have put . . . the *other* in jeopardy. He'll wait until it's done." He kisses the rim of my ear, and shivers ripple down my spine. "But that power goes both ways. He can do what he said for you. You can be sure of that." He pulls back now to look me in the face. "I want you to promise me you'll do what you planned and won't worry about me. I'll be fine."

"I'm not certain I will be," I admit, tears spilling over.

He wipes them away with his thumbs, his hands cradling my face. "Promise me you'll be happy."

"I don't know if I can."

"Promise me you'll try."

More tears, but I can't speak. I simply nod and lean forward to kiss him again, knowing this will be the last time.

I start to panic when the door opens behind me. But when Saber takes my hands in his, pulls me to my feet through the bars, and raises my fingers to his lips, I manage a brave smile. Somehow I force my feet to turn, and somehow, somehow, I walk away and leave him behind.

"Here," Lord Aaron says, handing me a handkerchief. "I'm afraid we've got to be quick again. Getting in here undetected was only half the battle."

I dab at my face as we near-jog, trying to blot away the tears without smearing my makeup. I take deep breaths, but it feels like trying to blow back the ocean with a hand-fan.

"Splendid," Lord Aaron whispers as we come around the corner to find the lift still on the bottom floor, its doors open and waiting. "Still jammed."

The keypad is out of his pocket again, and soon we're on our way up.

"Let me help," Lord Aaron says, taking the handkerchief from me and swiping at a spot beneath my right eye.

"Thank you," I say, and even that tiny phrase makes my eyes mist again, and I pull out my fan and flutter it at my face. If I'm not entirely *ready* when the lift doors open on the top floor, at least I'm presentable.

Though His Majesty is the last person I expected to be waiting for me.

He stands there with one eyebrow raised, staring at us as if we're children with our hands in the cookie jar. "Couldn't resist, could you, darling?"

The blood in my cheeks is simmering and my feet feel nailed to the floor.

He takes me in from slippers to *pompadour*. "You're a bit mussed. That won't do for the gala. Much of the press is already here, and I want you looking perfect." He extends his gloved hand, and I know I have no choice but to take it. He pulls me from the lift and looks down his nose at Lord Aaron.

"Lord Aaron? Really? I wouldn't have suspected such a frivolous dandy had the know-how to pull this off. My compliments."

"Received," Lord Aaron says flatly.

"Nonetheless, you can't imagine I'm genuinely pleased. Off with you now. Your privileges are revoked." The King starts to turn and then stops, looking back over his shoulder at Lord Aaron. "*All* of them. Confined to quarters. M.A.R.I.E., see to it." He peers down at me, looking maddeningly unruffled. "Gads, love, your friends are all getting into such trouble."

THIRTY-EIGHT

I OPEN MY eyes on the morning of my wedding with the dismal thought that I might actually end this day a married woman.

After escorting me from the lift, His Highness wouldn't let me escape his grasp, and that phraseology is in no way metaphorical. My fingertips remain clamped in his gloved hand the entire night. He fairly flaunted me before the attending press, and there was nothing I could do but smile.

Afterward, I was escorted to my rooms, and the watchers placed at every exit made no effort to conceal themselves from me. Apparently His Majesty decided that M.A.R.I.E.'s eyes were insufficiently all-seeing.

This morning I was sent a com from the medical center informing me that my father is still ill and receiving both fluids and medication intravenously. There's mention of multiple seizures, and a declaration that the cause is still unknown despite tests. I'm relieved he survived the night. I've no idea how drastic withdrawal can be, and there certainly isn't anyone left for me to ask. Still, as long as he's alive and a patient in the Marie-Antoinette Medical Clinic, he's essentially a hostage.

Lord Aaron is out of reach to me. Though his house arrest gives him a damned good alibi, it cripples my ability to get away. It's possible I could hack my way out on my own, but not while being watched so closely.

Waking up this morning was like a Wednesday *lever*, except that all of the ladies were hired by the King and none of them was my friend. The wedding is in two hours, and I've yet to be permitted to leave the room. I'm fully decked out in my wedding gown of outrageous width and weight, and my hair is piled so high I feel a bit off-balance. I have no doubt I look exquisite, and take absolutely no pleasure in that fact.

I've seen what feels like thousands of one-line coms pop up on my Lens wishing me good fortune on my big day, but with Molli and Mother dead, Father indisposed, Lord Aaron under full lockdown, and Saber imprisoned, every well-wishing feels hollow. How have I come to this place where thousands of people are at my beck and call and yet I've not a true friend or family member left to hear from? Both Lady Mei and Lady Nuala sent rather long, rambling coms that looked both friendly and intimate, but my relationship with them is as much a lie as my romance with the King.

I managed to slip into my dressing room alone for all of two minutes and shoved the nearly one million euros into my *panniers* in a lingerie sack. I was forced to rip out the bottoms of the tiny pockets in this wedding gown, as I certainly couldn't have requested such a thing when it was being sewn. Even though I can't fathom a way in which I can escape, I need to stay prepared.

There's a light knock on my door, and an unfamiliar woman flanked by four security guards appears. "I've been asked to escort you to a small *salon* just off the Royal Chapel," she says dully. "We need you in place before the press are let in, a quarter of an hour hence."

The blood drains from my face. The moment has arrived.

"Your Grace," the woman prompts with more than a hint of impatience.

My fingers are shaking, and I fleetingly wish I'd made my dressers tighten my corset a bit more.

The woman gestures for me to follow her, and as I do, the guards fall into place: two just in front of me and two behind. I imagine Marie-Antoinette herself was led very much this way to the guillotine where she lost her life. Today feels no less dire to me. Though the press is still being kept out, the velvet ropes that we normally use on Wednesdays are up, and a few court members are rushing about, straightening flowers, checking displays, adjusting seating. As we pass through the chambers that overlook the Marble Courtyard, I shudder at the buzz of the crowd waiting there—I don't dare look. As it is, I'm barely keeping tears at bay.

The woman leads me to the north wing and past the still-closed entrance to the Royal Chapel. "You'll wait in here until Duke Florentine comes for you," she says, leaning over to input a code on the keypad at the door.

So I'm to be given away by the King's CFO. How fitting.

"There's a light luncheon inside, as well as a retiring room. I'm afraid you'll have to sit tight for a little over an hour. But it's for your safety," she adds with an encouraging smile.

My safety. Of course that's what His Highness would tell them.

After a quick retinal scan, the door opens and the woman walks into the room. I take a step forward to follow her, but one of the guards places a hand on my shoulder. Even as I look back to question him, I hear a thud from inside the room, and then the door clicks closed as a man with a huge bouquet of white lilies steps into view.

"Calm yourself," Reginald says from behind the flowers when I gasp, scarcely looking at me as he takes the place of the now-unconscious woman he just left lying on the floor behind that closed door. "We're walking calmly to the end of the wing, carrying flowers, that's all."

My heart jolts as despair is replaced by hope so quickly my brain struggles to adjust. My guards don't so much as twitch, and remembering the restraining hand on my shoulder, I realize they're not palace guards at all—or if they are, they take their pay from more than one employer. Saber told me Reginald had power.

We continue down the hallway at such a leisurely pace I want to scream. But when we approach a window at the end of the hall, I see Reginald's hand thrust forward with some kind of remote in it, and a green light flashes from the window sash. Still not slowing our steps, we all stride toward the window, and Reginald sets the huge mass of flowers down and tosses back the drapes.

The window is open and, if I'm lucky, just wide enough for my gown to fit through. Reginald steps over the sash as though it were nothing more than a crack in the floor, and the two guards in front of me do the same. When my turn comes, I hardly know where to start. I duck my tall hair under the window frame and lift my silk skirts to thrust one high-heeled shoe out and over the window ledge, where Reginald grasps me just above the knee and pulls at the front of my gown. Not my most graceful moment.

I feel utterly ridiculous as I practically dive through and fall into the waiting arms of one of the guards, but I defy anyone in meter-wide skirts to do better. Two seconds later the guards behind me step through the window, Reginald raises his remote again, the window closes, and I'm outside the palace!

I have little enough time to enjoy my escape, as Reginald immediately—and none too gently—shoves me into a waiting SUV. But escaping maidens in distress can hardly be choosy. Ten more seconds and the door of the vehicle closes, and we're gliding around the side of the palace and down a narrow lane. The cars and crowds of wedding traffic are all relegated to the other side, so there's no one here to see us or impede our progress.

"I can't believe that just happened," I say, turning in my seat to see the Palace of Versailles receding from view as we traverse the small, barely paved service road.

"I want my five million euros," Reginald replies in his typical *gauche* fashion. "Where is it?"

"At the dance studio where we usually meet."

"As I suspected," he grumbles, but he leans forward to whisper directions to his driver. When we arrive at Giovanni's ten minutes later, the car pulls right up to the stoop, so it's difficult for anyone to see me as I slide from the vehicle and through the front door.

"We'll have to hurry," Reginald warns as I stand next to Giovanni, grasping his hand and whispering. "I'll take you somewhere to change clothes after this, but right now I need to get as much distance between us and Sonoman-Versailles as possible."

"It's upstairs," Giovanni says, finding his voice after I've given him the barest of bare-bones explanations. "In duffels. Prepacked. Everything ready to go."

Once Reginald has headed upstairs with his cronies, I spin and say to Giovanni, "Help me." I lift my unwieldy skirts and gesture for him to hold them as I dig out the sack of euros from my *panniers* to make up what's missing from the closet. I don't want Reginald to see how much I have left over. Just in case. I also don't want him to know I have the ten vials of pure Glitter he gave me two days ago. I just can't bring myself to put them back into his hands.

In less than a minute the guards clomp down the stairs, each carrying a black duffel. "This is the rest," I say when Reginald descends with a sour look on his face. I proffer a large stack of euros and the expression disappears.

"We don't have a problem, then. Let's be on our way."

I spin to Giovanni, tears springing to my eyes. He looks pained—he wants to say something, to ask questions, to interfere. Loyal to the last, he refrains. "Thank you so much," I say, squeezing him tight. "You made this possible."

He smiles and wipes a tear from my cheek. "I hope you're making the right choice, *chouchou*," he says simply, and my heart seems to drop within my chest.

"It's a little late for that," I say, choking on a building sob.

"Be happy, then."

I can hardly bear hearing Saber's words in Giovanni's mouth, so I hide my face and hug him instead, and then Reginald is pulling me away.

"Hurry," he snaps. "We don't have time for this." I wave once more as he bodily sweeps me out the door.

I sit facing Reginald in the black SUV and finally breathe a sigh and let all of the muscles in my body relax. How long have they been clenched? Weeks?

"Did you know my father's in the clinic?" I ask softly, my eyes closed as I lean my head back against the seat.

"Withdrawal?" Reginald asks.

"Saber was carrying the patches when we were searched."

"My mistake," Reginald says genially. "I should have handed them to you. You were always safer."

"Perhaps." I open my eyes and meet his gaze. "But will you . . . will you watch out for him?"

Reginald waves his hand. "He'll be okay. Withdrawal is a bitch, but your father's in better physical shape than he appears."

"And . . ." I lower my lashes. "And Saber?"

"Don't you worry about him, either. I'm not going to let him languish in prison."

"I wish you'd recon—"

"Don't even start, Highness. You've paid your fee; don't push me." He sits a little straighter. "Speaking of your fee, there are a few specifics we haven't discussed yet."

"In my defense, you didn't believe I could do it."

"No, no, I didn't." He grins. "But as it's going to make me a hefty profit, I was rooting for you."

"I'm delighted," I say dryly.

"However. You promised me five million euros, and I promised to spirit you away where no one can find you." He glances down at his fingernails. "But I didn't say when."

I wrinkle my nose. *"Pardonnez?"*

He looks up, and I can see a smile of amusement blooming across his face. "I didn't say *when,*" he repeats slowly. He leans back now, spreading both arms over the seat backs beside him. "I mean, look at you. Dolled up like a freaking princess. Every little girl dreams of her wedding day—we wouldn't want you to miss yours."

"What the hell are you talking about?" I demand.

"I've spent eight years developing Glitter. Thought I was doing pretty good, too. But in you waltz with this crazy idea of using it as makeup. I have to tell you, I didn't let on at the time, but that was a revelation. Needed some tests, though, which you were so kind as to carry out for me." He leans forward, his eyes never leaving my face. "Now, you and me, we've got a good thing going here. I want your cosmetics to go global. I want to be able to let loose whispers into the world that the Queen of Sonoman-Versailles herself indulges now and again."

"But I don't!" I shoot back in a panic.

"Who said rumors have to be true to be effective? Point is, five million is nothing. All you've shown me is that there are billions to be made with your little idea." He grins now, and the cruelty shines through and turns my stomach. "And I need you right there in the middle of it."

"No, we had a deal," I shout. "We had a deal!"

"We still have a deal. The fact that you neglected to double-check the small print isn't my problem. I'll get you out," he says, his voice suddenly very serious. "When I'm done with you."

Something catches my eye out the window, and in a wave of horror, I realize it's the golden gates of Versailles Palace—the gates I rejoiced in leaving such a short time ago. At the sight, all my self-control drains away. "No," I plead. "You can't do this! The whole point was to escape this marriage. He could kill me, Reginald. Then what good am I to you?"

"I have faith in your coping abilities," Reginald says, his eyes fixed on something outside the window. "And his."

"You don't understand. I oversold; I have no product. I can't even make it anymore. You're throwing me to the lions!"

He pats my hand, gripping painfully when I try to pull away. "Now, now, Your Grace, how cruel do you think I am? I'll make sure you have everything you need."

I should have expected this, my mind screams. This is a man who deals in forged documents, illegal drugs, black-market slavery, and who knows what other despicable trades. Why was I so egocentric as to believe he'd deal fairly with me? Everything I've done, everyone who's suffered—dear God, Molli—all for nothing. What I feel goes beyond remorse, dismay, horror, to a kind of numbness. I am nothing now.

He's not even sneaking me back in—the car rolls slowly through the milling crowds in front of the palace. The instant it stops, Reginald's liveried guards slip from the backseat. My door opens, and rough hands grab my arms and drag me out. I'm set hard on my feet in the midst of a very surprised—very pleased—audience of tourists, and somehow my knees hold me. The guards have positioned themselves right in front of and behind me again.

I'm in exactly the same position I was half an hour ago. Exactly. Except that now I'm in the *Orangerie* just below the Hall of Mirrors, surrounded by camera flashes as the loitering press begins to realize just who has emerged from the SUV.

Reginald slips between the two guards on my right. "Be a good girl today, Dani. Smile for the press, say all the right words, and maybe—just maybe—you'll get your *secretary* back in one piece."

I hiss in a breath. *Saber.*

"Oh, one more thing," Reginald says, rather jovially. He ducks into the backseat and emerges with a large, elaborately wrapped white box. "For you." He gives it a shake, and I hear a very familiar rattle. "Since you've lost your workshop." He leans close and says conspiratorially, "I wouldn't open it in front of anyone else, though."

He hands the large box to one of the guards, gives me a wink as though he hasn't just utterly betrayed me, and slides back into the car, which rolls slowly away through the assembled throng.

My lungs ache. I can't remember how to breathe.

"This way, Your Grace," one of the guards says, beckoning me toward the grand double doors, already thrown wide as though in anticipation of my rearrival. And despite everything—despite the money and the deceptions and the deaths—here I am. In the last place in the world I ever wanted to be.

My own wedding.

ACKNOWLEDGMENTS

So many people had their hands in the creation of this book. Thanks to my agent, Mandy Hubbard, who scraped me off the pavement after I'd been kicked to the curb not once but twice and who believed in *Glitter* right from the beginning. To my editor, Caroline Abbey, who put so much time into the development of this story. Truly above and beyond. To Emi Haze for an incredible cover for a super-quirky book. To Mollie Glick, who gave me some crucial advice about the setting of *Glitter,* even though I didn't end up signing with her. Thank you, Mollie!

To Lauren DeStefano for an early read and critique, not to mention hundreds of whiny emails. Hundreds. To all of the Cave Creek ladies (+2 gents) who were so supportive when I didn't even know what to do with good news. To Sandy for all of those runs when I spaced out because I started plotting. To Kristin Harmel for amazing feedback and a wonderful listening ear. You are one of my favorite finds of the last few years. To Skyelyte, who gave me a super-early beta read, even though it meant she'll have to wait for*ever* for the sequel. Thank you for your time and DMs and RTs.

My family and family-in-law are always so very supportive. Especially when I'm under deadline and am useless for anything else. My kids, who are endlessly patient with their Writer Mom. And my husband. Oh man, Kenny. I would melt down into a puddle of mush without you and everything you do.

APRILYNNE PIKE

is the critically acclaimed, internationally and #1 *New York Times* bestselling author of the Wings series. She has been spinning stories since she was a child with a hyperactive imagination. She received a BA in Creative Writing from Lewis-Clark State College in Lewiston, Idaho. She lives in Arizona with her family. Visit her online at aprilynnepike.com and follow her on Twitter at @AprilynnePike.

DISCUSSION QUESTIONS

1. In the palace where Danica lives, everyone is monitored and cared for by a supercomputer. People have given up almost all of their privacy in exchange for a lot of comfort and convenience. Would you? Are there ways you already have?

2. There is a saying that "absolute power corrupts absolutely." How might being politically powerful cause someone to behave like King Justin? Is it possible to get and keep a large fortune without hurting other people in the process?

3. The palace is mostly run by machinery—almost everything once done by human employees is done by robots instead. What would you do with your time if all the work in your community were being done by robots?

4. To fulfill a contract with France, the people of Sonoman-Versailles dress in the style of the Baroque era. What other reasons might people have to dress in clothing styles from the past? Have you ever "dressed up" for a Renaissance fair, a Civil War reenactment, or a cosplay convention? How might that differ from "dressing up" for a dance, a funeral, or a job interview?

5. Glitter is a fictional drug, but real drugs are killing real people at an increasing rate. In the year 2000, about 18,000 Americans died from drug overdoses. In 2015, more than 50,000 Americans died from drug overdoses. Why do so many communities have a serious and growing drug problem? What might be done to reverse that trend?

6. When you put a lot of time or effort into something—such as a hobby, a television show, or a relationship—you may find it difficult to give up on that thing even when it stops being good, useful, or enjoyable. This is sometimes called the sunk cost fallacy. How does Danica fall prey to the sunk cost fallacy with regard to her escape plan? At what point, if any, should she have chosen differently?

7. Danica's mother, Angela, does everything she can to place her daughter in a position of wealth and power. Most parents want their children to succeed in life and will do whatever they can to make that happen, but parents and children don't always agree on the definition of success. Do your parents have ambitions or offer guidance for your future? How do you handle that?

8. Justin is physically and sexually aggressive with Danica, and though he seems to find her genuinely attractive, his behavior is aimed at establishing dominance and control. Do you ever see this kind of dominance attempted in your life? Is there a clear line between expressing interest in someone and forcing interest on someone? What line would you set for yourself, both as a potential aggressor and as a potential victim?

9. King Louis XIV created the *grand lever* as a way to exercise complete control over his subjects by making them do every little thing for him. It might be argued that having his nobles assist him in such simple tasks made him look weak. What do you think? Did the *lever* debase King Louis or his subjects? In *Glitter*, does the *lever* humiliate Danica or strengthen her position?

10. Addiction comes in many forms, and a company that can get you hooked on its products may have a customer for life. The original formula for a popular soft drink once included measurable amounts of the drug we now call cocaine. Caffeine, a legal, relatively mild drug that occurs naturally in things like coffee, is added to some brands of breakfast cereal and even bottled water. Though caffeine is listed as an ingredient on the packaging, many people, including children, consume caffeinated foods and beverages without knowing or understanding the nature of the drug or the possibility of addiction. Though rare, overdose is possible.

How is Danica's decision to "enhance" her product with a drug so new it's not even technically illegal different from the food industry's practice of adding legal but addictive substances to your food? What if she told her customers what was in her makeup without explaining its addictive properties?

The problem with a carefully crafted plan is
that it can be so delicate. One little misstep
and the whole thing could shatter.

The shocking and thought-provoking sequel to *Glitter*

SHATTER

ROYALTY. ROMANCE.
REBELLION.

APRILYNNE PIKE
#1 *NEW YORK TIMES* BESTSELLING AUTHOR OF *WINGS*

READ ON FOR A SNEAK PEEK.

INTERLUDE

I MARCH DOWN the aisle, my face shrouded beneath a veil of *tulle*, and if my eyes are empty or haunted, no one can possibly tell. I'm slow and ponderous in my lavish Baroque wedding gown but feel naked and vulnerable without Saber at my shoulder. Even the white corset reinforcing my posture seems insufficient to keep my innards in place; my heart is climbing my throat, and my stomach has become an aching pit.

I pause as the twinkling constellation of camera flashes momentarily blinds me. I shouldn't be here. I blink against the purple afterimage, waking the Lens in my right eye; the calendar it superimposes on my slowly returning vision shows an urgent notification, set weeks ago by Angela Grayson. My mother's digital ghost is reminding me not to miss my own wedding. A push from beyond the grave.

Just one more thing to do. I take three steps forward and hand off my bouquet to a waiting attendant. A last-minute substitution when the one I'd selected died.

His Majesty glances over his shoulder and looks almost surprised to see me. Perhaps he should; he's given me ample reason to develop cold feet. Atop the murder that launched this sordid affair, he's imprisoned the man I love and holds my ailing father hostage. I'd have left them both behind had things gone according to plan. What choice did I have? I couldn't marry the King.

I *still* can't marry the King.

But Reginald betrayed me. *Cheated* me. Took my money and agreed to spirit me away—but only when he has no more use for me. The anger that manages to cut through my despair is short-lived, but it propels me another step toward the altar. Another step toward the throne.

There are other ways out, of course. There have always been other ways out. But I refuse to retreat to the impoverished fringes of civilization. I refuse to trade one kind of misery for another. And having come within a breath of losing him forever, I refuse to leave Saber behind.

I can only help him if I stay. I can only stay if I become Queen. And I only become Queen if I continue down this aisle.

I never wanted to be Queen. But I was too desperate. I chose badly, and Molli died for it. She can't have died for nothing. This is my penance. This is the price I have to pay. I will sift through the shattered wreckage of my dreams in search of something sufficiently sharp to cut my way free. And this time, I *will* take Saber with me, though hell should bar the way.

MY FIRST *LEVER* as Queen. I suppose it ought to feel momentous, but since the King has had me doing this particular chore for months, it feels almost comfortingly normal. Lady Mei powders my shoulders with gardenia-scented talc, and I try not to sneeze. "The duke has been raging about, trying to find out who voted for the King because he was certain he had it in the bag," she whispers. "People lie in public, but when it comes to actually voting, they let their real selves show."

I swallow hard—she's only telling me this because she assumes I voted for my husband. Everyone does. They all thought the King would lose. But if I voted for Tremain, that means there are even more people than he suspects who turned coat. There must be; numbers don't lie.

"Tremain is blaming the young shareholders," Lady Mei continues, hiding her mouth from the eyes—and lip-reading Lens apps—of our audience, behind a fan, which she now hands me. "Fickle, he says. Several of us think some votes changed your way because we like your Glitter."

My face registers shock before I remember to mask it. "You think so?"

"Of course. Easier to buy Glitter from the Queen." She smirks and I'm clearly supposed to appreciate the news that my illegal dealings continue to have unexpected and far-reaching consequences.

The crowd of tourists jostles and applauds as the *lever* concludes and we exit the bedchamber, into my back rooms. Before I can open my mouth, the ladies are pulling paper euros from their *pannier* pockets and stacking them on my dresser. Between this and the half million from before my wedding, I'm pushing my first new million all over again. I stare at that stack of money and I hate it. Hate it with a red-hot fury that threatens to spill out of my tight control.

Until I have a thought. Perhaps there is yet some purpose for it.

I'm startled from my brainstorm by Lady Mei jabbing her elbow into my side. "Something sparkly, perhaps?" Oh yes. Their payment. I've saved exactly enough Glitter to give each lady a canister for her service in my *lever,* but I have nothing else. And several hundred thousand euros' worth of orders.

I don't know what to do. Reginald promised more, but I don't know how much, and I certainly couldn't say when it will arrive. All I can hope is that Reginald loves money and hates Sonoman-Versailles enough to keep supplying me. To keep his word. Because I've certainly discovered that honor doesn't compel him.

After letting my ladies out the small back entrance from my private rooms, I nearly bowl headlong into Saber—holding an enormous white box with a silver bow.

"It was waiting beside the rail in your bedchamber when the tourists exited," Saber says darkly. "I don't know how he managed. That man has tricks I can't begin to understand."

My mouth goes dry. For over twenty-four hours we've avoided even mentioning Glitter. We don't want to fight. But here it is, in Saber's very hands, and we can postpone it no longer.

Saber sets the box on the floor, and I crouch beside it and lift the lid to find the entire thing crammed full of canisters of Glitter, in more than the three colors I'd been mixing. Evidently, Reginald thinks the Sonoman ladies should have their choice of varied hues of drug-laced eye shadow, in addition to the foundation, lip gloss, and rouge. The thought of rouge makes my stomach lurch, remembering the glint of Glitter on Molli's face. I place a hand over my stomach and breathe deeply; every thought of Molli feels like a knife to the stomach. I keep expecting the knife's edge to dull, but it doesn't.

"What do I do?" I ask.

Saber stands there, peering steadily at me. "Quit?" he says dryly. "Just say no?"

"It's more complex than that and you know it."

"But is it really?"

"Yes!" This whole damnable situation is even worse than when I made the original decision. Thanks to Reginald's perfidy, I'm exactly where I would have been had I done nothing at all, minus one dear friend and one scheming mother. Plus one criminal nemesis and a clawing court of addicts.

And plus one Saber. That part I find difficult to resent.

"I don't know," Saber finally says. He kicks the box, not hard enough to do damage, but the inventory clatters loudly within. "Reginald doesn't care about people or their lives or their families—he just wants to make money. But I know you. You do care." He lifts an eyebrow. "At least you used to."

"I do!" I hurry to say. "But . . ." What can I say? I'm not sure there's ever going to be a good enough reason for Saber.

He meets my eyes for a moment, then looks away.

"Even if I wanted to continue selling long-term, which I don't," I add for Saber's benefit, but perhaps also to hear the words come out of my own mouth, "I can't. My business model isn't sustainable," I say. "It was never supposed to *be* sustainable. The whole operation is held together with resin and twine. Eventually customers are going to run out of jewelry, and the CFO will have to hike the credit exchange rate and . . . and—" I breathe deeply, pressing the back of my hand to my mouth. "The nurse at the clinic told me my father's brain has been damaged."

Saber stands straight, away from the wall. "Does she know about the patches?"

I shake my head. "She noted the residue, but I said they were nicotine patches." I close my eyes and give voice to my greatest fear. "Is that going to happen more, or . . . ?"

This time when I turn my face up to Saber, he's glaring at the wall over my shoulder, looking both angry and guilty. "It's probably more related to dosage," he says softly, and I remember that most of my father's drug habit was foisted on him not by me but by Saber. Against Saber's will, but by him nonetheless. I wish I hadn't said anything. "There were times when I wasn't convinced he'd be *alive* when I got here for a delivery."

It's odd to remember that Saber had a life before me, but he was involved with my father for almost two months before we met.

"I don't blame you," I say genially. "I don't blame you for anything Reginald ever makes you do."

"Doesn't make it feel any better when I'm doing it," he says tightly, and I clamp my mouth shut. He sighs. "Sorry, that's not the point. You have to decide what to do with this." He nudges the box with his foot.

"We," I correct.

"You," he sends right back. "In the end, I'm still Reginald's man."

He's right. He can't be caught discouraging me. He tried as best he could, in the beginning, and I mistook his warnings for contempt. Fleetingly I wonder what sort of punishment he might have faced, had I actually backed out then.

My feet start to lose feeling from the way I'm crouching, so I flop backward onto the ground, legs sticking straight out in front of me in possibly the least graceful pose I've adopted in years. Saber cuts off a bark of a laugh, and I smile up at him despite the feeling that my stays are cutting me in two.

"I'm tired," I protest. Then add, "I didn't get much sleep last night."

"No, no you didn't," he murmurs.

But the box won't be ignored, though staring at it silently yields no answers. "When I started, I was so afraid that Justin would kill me. And I was angry," I say, looking up as Saber joins me on the floor, sitting cross-legged. "I was so sure of what I'd seen. I wanted him to pay."

"You *were* so sure? The woman he strangled? Have you changed your mind?"

My shoulders slump and I shake my head in confusion. "I don't know. He's told me multiple times that it was an accident and, to be honest, it kind of grosses me out to even think about it. But I *did* surprise him when I dropped that platter."

Saber lets me sit in silence, contemplating this. Contemplating just how guilty I truly am, perhaps.

"Regardless, the danger is different now. I can't imagine myself safe from Justin," I add darkly. "But by making me his Queen, he's made me far more difficult to simply *remove*. I'm not even certain he realizes it. Before, I justified everything I did because I was afraid for my life, or the lives of other possible victims. Now?" I flutter my hand at the box. "Now I'm damned if I continue and damned if I quit." Reginald's words from so very long ago echo through my head: *If you* truly *think your pathetic life is worth five million euros* . . . I don't know what price tag I'd put on my life, but I've already cost Molli everything.

She can't have died for nothing.

"Would it be so awful to stop? You could look at this entirely differently. That your confirmed role as Queen means you can't dabble in this sort of stuff anymore." Saber looks at me, and his eyes are filled with desperation, begging me to make the right choice this time. "You don't need the money anymore."

"I can't simply stop," I say bleakly, the truth jarring right that. Just a warning." Saber's tone is sharp, and frustration pours from him like waves.

I hang my head. "I don't know what else to do. If I can't stop, at least I can keep it from growing. Maybe it'll help some of the users cut back." I add in a mumble, not really trying to disguise my wishful thinking.

"Maybe."

"And I can sell less and less product each week. Force people to use it more sparingly. I don't know that there's a better way."

Saber nods, acceptance rather than agreement. "Let's be off, then," he says, offering both hands to pull me up. "It is your day to be seen."

"It's funny," I say, looking down at the white box. "I got into this mess to take control of a fate that was galloping off without me. Now I'm less in charge than ever."

Saber reaches an arm around my shoulders and squeezes me as he places a kiss on my brow. "I know. But let's be honest; it's not funny at all."

down to my spine. "Going on a little longer feels somehow less awful than having done everything for nothing."

"That's rationalization and you know it."

"If I stop all at once, my customers will go into withdrawal and it'll be obvious what's been happening," I argue. "I can claim to have been duped by my supplier, but I'm not confident in the outcome."

"And what would they do? Dethrone you?"

I remain silent. There would be social consequences, certainly. But I can't tell Saber the real reason I can't stop yet: if I quit selling Glitter, Reginald will take Saber back.

A little longer. That's all I need.

"Come on, Dani," he whispers. "Be better than this."

I curl up, resting my arms and head on my popped-up knees.

"I used to think I was a decent person. I'm not sure I am anymore. No, don't," I rush to say before Saber can protest. Before I can find out if he was going to protest. "I thought that because I was doing this for good reason, I could do it without becoming . . . tainted. But I have. It's like blackest ink, and you can't touch it without getting stained. At this point, I'm mostly afraid of how much worse it will get before I can finally be through."

Saber says nothing, just reaches over to run his fingers along my neck, massaging gently.

"So I . . . keep going," I say, and his fingers tense on my neck. "But I try to limit my damage. I don't take new customers, and I start to spread the word that I've reached maximum production capacity. When it's gone, it's gone."

"You'll be stampeded every time you get a delivery if you say

Looking for another kingdom filled with romance
and intrigue? Don't miss *Poison's Kiss*!

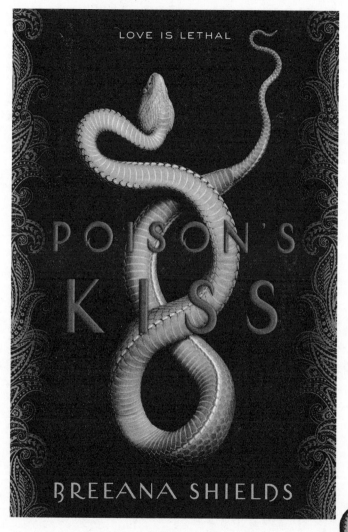

LOVE IS LETHAL

POISON'S KISS

BREEANA SHIELDS

A teenage assassin kills with a single kiss.
Until she is ordered to kill the one boy she loves . . .